Adventures of Huckleberry Finn

Mark Twain

THE EMC MASTERPIECE SERIES

Access Editions

EMC/Paradigm Publishing
St. Paul, Minnesota

Staff Credits:

For **EMC/Paradigm Publishing**, St. Paul, Minnesota

Laurie Skiba
Editor

Eileen Slater
Editorial Consultant

Shannon O'Donnell Taylor
Associate Editor

Jennifer J. Anderson
Assistant Editor

For **Penobscot School Publishing, Inc.**, Danvers, Massachusetts

Editorial	**Design and Production**
Robert D. Shepherd *President, Executive Editor*	Charles Q. Bent *Production Manager*
Christina E. Kolb *Managing Editor*	Sara Day *Art Director*
Kim Leahy Beaudet *Editor*	Diane Castro *Compositor*
Sara Hyry *Editor*	Janet Stebbings *Compositor*
Laurie A. Faria *Associate Editor*	
Sharon Salinger *Copyeditor*	
Marilyn Murphy Shepherd *Editorial Advisor*	

Cover:
Huckleberry Finn and Jim, 1936. Thomas Hart Benton. Missouri State Capitol © T.H. Benton and R.P. Benton Testamentary Trusts/Licensed by VAGA, New York

ISBN 0-8219-1639-4

Published by EMC/Paradigm Publishing
875 Montreal Way
St. Paul, Minnesota 55102

Printed in the United States of America.
10 9 8 7 6 5 4 3 2 xxx 08 07 06 05 04 03 02 01

Table of Contents

Mark Twain

Mark Twain

Mark Twain (1835–1910). Born Samuel Langhorne Clemens in Florida, Missouri, Mark Twain was a humorist, novelist, reporter, lecturer, travel writer, and licensed riverboat pilot who became one of the most important writers of American literature. While working as a riverboat pilot, Clemens encountered the phrase that later became his pseudonym, or pen name—Mark Twain. Workers on Mississippi riverboats called out "mark twain" to indicate that the water was two fathoms deep—just barely deep enough for a riverboat.

When Twain was four years old, his family moved from Florida, Missouri, to the nearby town of Hannibal. Hannibal lay on the banks of the Mississippi River and became an important riverboat port. The town not only inspired his dreams of becoming a riverboat pilot but also served as the setting for novels such as *The Adventures of Tom Sawyer* and *Adventures of Huckleberry Finn*. In these books Twain changed the name Hannibal to St. Petersburg, meaning "St. Peter's town," or heaven.

When Twain was twelve years old, his father died. Twain then had to worry about making a living, so he followed his older brother's footsteps and left school to learn the printing trade. He became an apprentice, a person who works for someone in order to learn a trade or skill, to a printer. At the age of eighteen, Twain left Hannibal to work as a printer, first in St. Louis and then in New York. By this time, Twain had already begun to write and submit pieces to newspapers and magazines. When he was twenty-one, he went to New Orleans to depart for a trip to the Amazon River in South America. The plan fell apart, but Twain was apprenticed by a Mississippi riverboat pilot, a prestigious job that fulfilled his childhood dream. Twain worked as a riverboat pilot until the start of the Civil War. Before the Civil War, the Mississippi River was a lucrative trading route. When the war interrupted that trade, Twain was forced to find other work. He volunteered as a Confederate soldier but soon deserted and went west, where he worked as a reporter in Virginia City, Nevada, and adopted the name Mark Twain. After traveling to San

Francisco and continuing his career in journalism, he met fellow frontier author Bret Harte, who encouraged Twain's literary sketches and stories. In 1865, Twain's short story "The Notorious Jumping Frog of Calaveras County" was published in the *Saturday Press*. This humorous story, a retelling of a popular nineteenth-century tall tale, won Twain national recognition as a writer. It focuses on a conversation between simple, uneducated men living in a frontier mining camp and is an excellent example of one of Twain's noted specialties— regional writing. Twain had a gift for capturing in his writing regional dialects, or versions of a language spoken by people of particular places and social groups.

In 1866, Twain took a job at the *Union* in Sacramento, California. The *Union* sent him to the Sandwich Islands, now Hawaii, as a roving reporter. His comic articles about his trip established his reputation as a humorist. When Twain returned, he was able to make a living giving lectures. In 1867, he traveled aboard the steamship *Quaker City* on a lecture tour of Europe, Egypt, and the Holy Land. He later compiled his lectures from this tour into *The Innocents Abroad*, a work which received considerable praise. Twain's unique background as a printer, writer, riverboat pilot, and wanderer provided him with plenty of interesting material on which to base a successful career as a writer and lecturer.

In 1870, Twain began a new stage of his life. He married Olivia Langdon, the daughter of a New York millionaire; invested in several unsuccessful business ventures; and moved to Hartford, Connecticut, where he would spend the rest of his life and write some of his most famous novels about his experiences on the Mississippi, including *The Adventures of Tom Sawyer* (1876), *Life on the Mississippi* (1883), and *Adventures of Huckleberry Finn* (1884). Today, *Huckleberry Finn* is considered Twain's masterpiece, and it is often called the great American novel. Twain's other well-known works from this period include *The Prince and the Pauper* (1882), *A Connecticut Yankee in King Arthur's Court* (1889), and *The Tragedy of Pudd'nhead Wilson* (1894).

In the 1890s, Twain suffered a series of misfortunes, including the deaths of his wife and two of his daughters, and monetary loss due to failed investments. Twain's later writings direct a great degree of bitterness at his fellow human beings. His most severe criticism, expressed in *The War Prayer* and *Letters from Earth*, was published after his death.

Time Line of Twain's Life

1835   Samuel Langhorne Clemens is born on November 30 in the town of Florida, Missouri. Halley's comet appears on the same day.

1839   The Clemens family moves to Hannibal, Missouri.

1846   By this time, the town of Hannibal has become a busy steamboat port on the Mississippi River. The area eventually serves as the setting for *The Adventures of Tom Sawyer* and *Adventures of Huckleberry Finn*.

1847   Clemens's father dies. Clemens is apprenticed to a printer.

1853   Clemens leaves Hannibal to work as a printer, first in St. Louis and later in New York. He begins to submit work to newspapers and magazines.

1854   Clemens travels to New Orleans, intending to sail to South America, but the plans fall through.

1856   Clemens pursues his childhood dream by becoming an apprentice to a steamboat pilot on the Mississippi River. He becomes a licensed pilot and holds this prestigious position for nearly three years.

1861   The Civil War breaks out and interrupts trade on the Mississippi River. Riverboats stop operating, and Clemens is forced to find another job. He decides to move west.

1863   Clemens adopts the pen name Mark Twain for a story published by the *Territorial Enterprise* of Virginia City, Nevada, where he works as a reporter.

1864   Twain moves to California and takes a job as a reporter in San Francisco.

1865   Twain publishes his story "The Celebrated Jumping Frog of Calaveras County" in the *Saturday Press*. This story brings him fame and launches his writing career.

1866   Twain takes a job at the *Union* in Sacramento, California. He is sent to the Sandwich Islands, now Hawaii, as a roving reporter. His comic articles about the trip establish his reputation as a humorist. When he returns, he makes his living giving lectures.

1867   Twain tours Europe, Egypt, and the Holy Land aboard the steamship *Quaker City*.

1869   Twain collects his lectures from his tour aboard the *Quaker City* in a book of sketches called *The Innocents Abroad*.

1870   Twain marries Olivia Langdon. He becomes joint owner and editor of a newspaper in Buffalo, New York, called the *Express*.

Twain sells his interest in the newspaper, having lost a great deal of money on the project. He moves to a comfortable home in Hartford, Connecticut. Twain becomes a skilled storyteller, turning out a new book every few years. **1872**

Twain publishes *The Gilded Age* about the years following the Civil War. **1873**

Twain publishes *The Adventures of Tom Sawyer*. With this book, Twain introduces something new to American fiction—a simple, natural writing style that resembles the speech of average Americans. **1876**

Twain publishes *A Tramp Abroad*. **1880**

Twain publishes *The Prince and the Pauper*. **1882**

Twain publishes *Life on the Mississippi*. This book is closely based on his experiences working on riverboats. **1883**

Twain publishes *Adventures of Huckleberry Finn*, long considered his masterpiece. Of this novel Ernest Hemingway would say, "All modern American literature comes from one book by Mark Twain called *Adventures of Huckleberry Finn*." **1884**

Twain publishes *A Connecticut Yankee in King Arthur's Court*. **1889**

Twain has lost a great deal of money in bad investments, and is forced to declare bankruptcy. He publishes *The Tragedy of Pudd'nhead Wilson* and *Tom Sawyer Abroad*. **1894**

Twain conducts a world lecture tour to pay his debts. One of his daughters dies while he is on tour. **1895**

Twain publishes *Tom Sawyer, Detective*. **1896**

Twain publishes *Following the Equator*, a book based on his lecture tour. **1897**

Twain is able to pay his debts. Nevertheless, his writing becomes increasingly dark and pessimistic. **1898**

The short story "The Man That Corrupted Hadleyburg," about greed in a small town, is published. It is the first of several pieces that show Twain's dark and angry side. **1900**

Twain's wife dies. **1904**

Twain's youngest daughter dies. **1909**

Mark Twain dies at the age of seventy-two in Redding, Connecticut. That same week, Halley's comet appears. Twain always believed that the appearance of the comet would mark his death as it did his birth. **1910**

Adventures of Huckleberry Finn

Adventures of Huckleberry Finn, published in 1885 at the peak of Twain's career, is considered a masterpiece of American literature. Writer Ernest Hemingway once noted that "All modern American literature comes from *Huckleberry Finn*." Indeed, the story of the adventures of runaway Huck and escaped slave Jim as they travel by raft down the Mississippi River contains themes and characters that are uniquely American—slavery, the treatment of African Americans, the frontier spirit, odd frontier characters, and the search for a personal destiny in a young, changing nation. The novel is a humorous satire of human nature and American culture. It provides an early example of the American "road story," a story that narrates the adventures of a pair of characters as they travel the American landscape.

Many of the details of the setting and of the activities that young Huck enjoys reflect Twain's nostalgia for his youth. In fact, many of the book's colorful characters are modeled on people the author encountered in his home town and when working as a riverboat pilot on the Mississippi River. For example, Huckleberry Finn is modeled after the village derelict's son whom Twain knew in Hannibal. Tom Sawyer, Huck's hometown friend, is a composite of Twain himself and some boyhood friends.

Despite the novel's popularity, *Adventures of Huckleberry Finn* has generated a lot of controversy because of its portrayal of African Americans and particularly Jim. Some readers see Jim's superstitions, gentleness, and gratitude to Huck as a condescending portrayal. Others recognize Jim's strict moral code, his brotherly and fatherly dedication to Huck, and his kindness as attributes that make him the most admirable character in the novel and the most positive role model in Huck's life.

Also controversial is Huck's attitude to slavery. Critics say that although Huck comes to realize Jim's worth, he fails to apply this insight to a critique of slavery. These issues have sparked debate and analysis since the novel first appeared before the public.

Before the novel begins Twain writes, "Persons attempting to find a motive in this narrative will be prosecuted; persons attempting to find a moral in it will be banished; persons attempting to find a plot in it will be shot." This statement is intended to be ironic, since the novel has a strong and definite social message. Although young readers can enjoy the humor and suspense in Huck's adventures, the book also can be appreciated on a much deeper level. Through the years, people have been moved by the work's psychological depth, moral message, skilled characterization, and honest insights into human nature.

Huckleberry Finn's Missouri

Adventures of Huckleberry Finn is set in the 1830s or 1840s, before the start of the Civil War in 1861, and forty to fifty years prior to the time in which Twain wrote it. The town of St. Petersburg, Missouri, home of Huck Finn and Tom Sawyer, is a fictional town modeled after Twain's boyhood home of Hannibal, located in northeastern Missouri, across the Mississippi River from Illinois. Jackson's Island, where Huck and Jim meet and begin their adventure, was an actual island, now gone, close to the Illinois shore.

Adventures of Huckleberry Finn is set within the "great era of steamboats" on the Mississippi and Missouri Rivers. Indeed, the Mississippi River played a prominent role in the development of the region and brought a variety of interesting and colorful characters via riverboat to such port towns as Hannibal. The riverboats that fascinated Twain and the young characters in his most famous novels were shallow, paddle-wheel-driven boats powered by steam. These boats, also known as packets, carried passengers and freight and were important to the economy of the United States in the nineteenth century. Steamboat traffic encouraged settlement along the Mississippi River. As the United States continued to expand to the west, Missouri sat on the edge of the nation's last frontier and adventurous settlers considered it the gateway to unknown territory. Readers might notice the influence of this exciting environment on Huckleberry Finn, whom Twain realistically portrays as fascinated by the river, by rafting, by steamboats, and by exploration.

Slavery in Huckleberry Finn's Missouri

The issue of slavery is central to *Adventures of Huckleberry Finn*. Many characters Huck and Jim encounter, including admirable ones, own slaves, and readers will experience Huck's personal struggle with the issue as he assists in Jim's escape. At the time of the story, slavery had been abolished in the northern states—which Huck and Jim refer to as "free states"—but was still an unfortunately integral part of the South's plantation system. When Missouri requested statehood in 1821, legislators decided after much controversy to admit it to the union as a slave state. Because of its location as a border state, however, the population of Missouri was not entirely unanimous in its stance on the issue. When the country entered the Civil War, bitterly divided on the issue of slavery, Missouri remained loyal to the cause of the northern states despite its status as a slave state.

Many readers throughout the years have objected to the way white characters treat and refer to black characters in both *Adventures of Huckleberry Finn* and *The Adventures of Tom Sawyer*. These references often reflect the racist attitudes of the era. Twain opposed slavery and racism. As a writer, however, he is known for his shamelessly realistic portrayals of characters and communities. In *Adventures of Huckleberry Finn*, Twain paints a realistic portrait of small villages in slave states during the Civil War era and wants his readers to confront the hypocrisy and cruelty of slavery. Far from condoning racism, Twain invites his readers to examine critically the ignorant attitudes held by some of his characters. Through the decisions Huck and Jim make, Twain also asks readers to consider that morality does not follow without question the rules of society if those rules are cruel and wrong.

Regionalism and the Emergence of Realism

The late nineteenth century, when Mark Twain wrote his most famous novels, was a period of tremendous westward expansion. Large numbers of settlers moved from the crowded cities of the East and from lands along the Mississippi River to the unexplored western frontier in search of better lives. Many of these settlers were Civil War veterans who, having traveled from home for the first time, developed a taste for adventure in unknown lands. Within a few decades, people of European descent had established homes across the American West, from the prairies of Nebraska to the coast of California. This era was also characterized by the Industrial

Revolution and the growth of cities. Industrialism created a class of wealthy business people, as well as a class of city laborers who struggled with poverty and terrible working conditions.

These changes in the character of the country also brought about changes in literature. The literature of the early nineteenth century in America was centered in New England and dominated by Romanticism. Romantic writers were, for the most part, scholarly and moralistic. Their writing was sentimental, nostalgic, idealistic, and designed to inspire lofty emotions. The expansion of the western frontier fostered the emergence of Midwestern, Southern, and Western writers. Many of these writers were women, such as Sarah Orne Jewett, Kate Chopin, and Mary Wilkins Freeman. Many were journalists and adventurers, such as Mark Twain, Bret Harte, and Stephen Crane. These authors added diversity to American literature, writing about ranchers, gunfighters, runaway slaves, Civil War soldiers, steamboat captains, riverboat gamblers, con artists, pioneer men and women, millionaire tycoons, and the urban poor. Twain's subjects include many such characters.

One development of the new literary diversity was Regionalism, or local color writing which focused on life in a particular region, or area. People in the East were eager to read stories about the American frontier, so journalists and humorists like Twain gave them descriptions of the odd characters who populated the new land. Bret Harte, a supporter of Twain's work, was one of the first of these local-color writers. Both Harte and Twain wrote humorously, incorporating local dialects and realistic descriptions of interesting characters in their stories. In turn, local-color writing gave rise to an important literary movement in American literature known as Realism. Realist writers, instead of creating romantic or overly idealistic portraits of people and places, presented realistic, often grim portraits of the world. Twain employed elements of Realism in his work, which featured humorous, often exaggerated descriptions of colorful characters. He was also skilled, as readers of *Adventures of Huckleberry Finn* will notice, in the use of dialect.

Characters in *Adventures of Huckleberry Finn*

Main Characters

Huckleberry Finn. The narrator of the story, Huck Finn, is a free-spirited boy who is one of literature's best-known characters. He has lived an unusual life, on his own, with his abusive father, and with the widow Douglas, who wants to "civilize" his wild ways. Huck is poorly educated, but he is inventive and practical. Throughout *Adventures of Huckleberry Finn*, Huck shows that he has common sense, ingenuity, and a great deal of sympathy for others. Because Huck is relatively free of the conventions of society, he often defines himself as "bad" or "wicked." It is this freedom from the conventional world, however, that allows him to think for himself and to help Jim, although society says it is wrong.

Jim. Jim is Miss Watson's slave who escapes when he learns that Miss Watson wants to sell him and thus separate him from his family. He hides on Jackson's Island and joins Huck on a journey on the Mississippi River. Jim is a gentle, honest, good-hearted man who serves as a friend, brother, and father to Huck. He teaches Huck, who reveres Jim's knowledge of the supernatural, about the natural world and about friendship.

Tom Sawyer. Tom is an active boy who is Huck's best friend. While Huck is practical by nature and relies on his own instincts, Tom relies on his knowledge of books to plan romantic, wildly impractical adventures. Tom is also more self-involved than Huck, taking charge of situations without thinking of the consequences of his actions. Like Huck, he is imaginative and is fascinated by the river, exploration, and adventure.

Pap. Pap is Huck's vicious and abusive father. Pap attempts to get control of Huck's money. Pap feels threatened when Huck goes to school, because he thinks Huck is trying to be better than his father. His violent anger and drinking make him destructive to himself and to Huck.

Widow Douglas. She is a generous and wealthy woman who takes Huck Finn into her home and attempts to civilize him. Although Huck appreciates her loving nature, she lives a quiet, strict life of prayer and schedules that Huck cannot tolerate.

Miss Watson. She is Widow Douglas's nasty, repressive, narrow-minded sister. She lives with Huck and Widow Douglas. Her harsh, cold treatment makes Huck feel lonely and bad about himself. Jim is Miss Watson's slave.

Judge Thatcher. Judge Thatcher is a respected and kind judge who invests money for Huck. When Huck's cruel and abusive father returns, Judge Thatcher agrees to hide Huck's money, and goes to court to fight Pap's suit for custody of Huck.

The Duke and the King. They are two con men who ride for a time on the raft with Huck and Jim. The younger man claims to be the exiled English Duke of Bridgewater and the older man claims to be Louis XVII, the rightful king of France. These two take over the raft and travel from village to village thinking of new ways to cheat people of their money. Their most complicated scam has them pretending to be the heirs to a fortune. They are willing to betray their companions for money.

Aunt Sally. She is Tom's aunt and the wife of Silas Phelps, the owner of the plantation on which Jim is imprisoned. She treats Huck and Tom well and tries to keep them out of trouble.

Silas Phelps. He owns the plantation on which Jim is imprisoned. He buys Jim from the king for the ransom money, and mistakenly believes that Jim has escaped from a plantation in New Orleans.

Other Characters

Mary Jane Wilks. Huck develops a crush on this young woman. She is conned by the duke and the king, believing them to be her uncles.

Aunt Polly. She is Tom's kind-hearted aunt—a simple, deeply religious woman who adores Tom. In *Adventures of Huckleberry Finn*, Aunt Polly does not make an appearance until the final pages.

Sidney. He is Tom Sawyer's half-brother, referred to as Sid. Although Sid does not make an actual appearance in *Adventures of Huckleberry Finn*, Tom takes on his identity at one point in the novel.

Joe Harper, Ben Rogers, and Little Tommy Barnes. They are friends of Tom and Huck and members of the "robber band" that Tom attempts to start.

Mrs. Loftus. She is a villager whom Huck visits dressed as a girl. From her, Huck learns that a reward is offered for the capture of Jim.

Jack Packard, Bill, and Jim Turner. They are robbers whom Huck and Jim find on a sinking steamboat. Huck goes to great lengths to try to save their lives.

The Grangerfords and the Shepherdsons. They are feuding families whom Huck meets. The Grangerfords take Huck into their care, and Huck enjoys the comforts of their home while he is there. He leaves in the middle of a violent battle between the two families.

Echoes:
Quotations from Mark Twain

On flattery: "I can live for two months on a good compliment."

On golf: "Golf is a good walk spoiled."

On grief and joy: "Grief can take care of itself, but to get the full value from joy you must have somebody to divide it with."

On his own writing: "You don't know about me without you have read a book by the name of *The Adventures of Tom Sawyer*; but that ain't no matter. That book was made by Mr. Mark Twain, and he told the truth, mainly."

On humans: "Man is the only animal that blushes. Or needs to."

On the desire to teach others to be good: "To be good is noble, but to teach others how to be good is nobler—and less trouble."

On obedience: "Of all God's creatures there is only one that cannot be made the slave of the lash. That one is the cat. If man could be crossed with the cat it would improve man, but it would deteriorate the cat."

On parents: "When I was a boy of fourteen, my father was so ignorant I could hardly stand to have the old man around. But when I got to be twenty-one, I was astonished at how much he had learned in seven years."

On politeness: "Good breeding consists in concealing how much we think of ourselves and how little we think of the other person."

On school: "I have never let my schooling interfere with my education."

On success: "All you need in this life is ignorance and confidence, and then success is sure."

Although John Fitch began experimenting with steamboats—shallow-draft, paddle wheel driven boats propelled by steam—as early as 1787, it wasn't until 1811 that Robert Fulton and Robert Livingstone developed a steamboat that could navigate the often treacherously shallow Mississippi River. The introduction of steamboats completely transformed life along the Mississippi River, including Twain's own Missouri (see map below). By the mid-1800s thousands of steamboats navigated the Mississippi, bearing the valuable cargo of the South— sugar and cotton—as well as passengers. The role of the Mississippi steamboats as the dominant method of transportation in the mid United States was increasingly threatened as railroads became more efficient in the 1870s. Gradually, steamboats were retired and the steamboat era on the Mississippi came to an end.

NOTICE

PERSONS attempting to find a motive in this narrative will be prosecuted; persons attempting to find a moral in it will be banished; persons attempting to find a plot in it will be shot.

BY ORDER OF THE AUTHOR,
Per G. G., Chief of Ordnance.

EXPLANATORY

In this book a number of dialects are used, to wit: the Missouri Negro dialect; the extremest form of the backwoods Southwestern dialect; the ordinary "Pike County" dialect; and four modified varieties of this last. The shadings have not been done in a haphazard fashion, or by guesswork; but painstakingly, and with the trustworthy guidance and support of personal familiarity with these several forms of speech.

I make this explanation for the reason that without it many readers would suppose that all these characters were trying to talk alike and not succeeding.

THE AUTHOR.

CHAPTER 1

I Discover Moses and the Bulrushers[1]

You don't know about me without you have read a book by the name of *The Adventures of Tom Sawyer;* but that ain't no matter. That book was made by Mr. Mark Twain, and he told the truth, mainly. There was things which he stretched, but mainly he told the truth. That is nothing. I never seen anybody but lied one time or another, without it was Aunt Polly, or the widow, or maybe Mary. Aunt Polly—Tom's Aunt Polly, she is—and Mary, and the Widow Douglas is all told about in that book, which is mostly a true book, with some stretchers, as I said before.

Now the way that the book winds up is this: Tom and me found the money that the robbers hid in the cave, and it made us rich. We got six thousand dollars apiece—all gold. It was an awful sight of money when it was piled up. Well, Judge Thatcher he took it and put it out at interest, and it fetched us a dollar a day apiece all the year round—more than a body could tell what to do with. The Widow Douglas she took me for her son, and allowed she would sivilize me; but it was rough living in the house all the time, considering how dismal regular and decent the widow was in all her ways; and so when I couldn't stand it no longer I lit out. I got into my old rags and my sugar-hogshead[2] again, and was free and satisfied. But Tom Sawyer he hunted me up and said he was going to start a band of robbers, and I might join if I would go back to the widow and be respectable. So I went back.

The widow she cried over me, and called me a poor lost lamb, and she called me a lot of other names, too, but she never meant no harm by it. She put me in them new clothes again, and I couldn't do nothing but sweat and sweat, and feel all cramped up. Well, then, the old thing commenced again. The widow rung a bell for supper, and you had to come to time. When you got to the table you couldn't go

◄ Why might some readers already be familiar with this story's narrator, Huckleberry Finn? What comment does Huck make about Mark Twain's style of writing?

◄ What happened to Huck and his friend Tom Sawyer at the end of The Adventures of Tom Sawyer?

◄ What does the Widow Douglas want to do to Huck? Why, at one time, did Huck leave the home of the Widow Douglas? What did Tom Sawyer say to convince Huck to return?

◄ What rules and rituals at Widow Douglas's home does Huck find most bothersome?

---

1. **Moses . . . Bulrushers.** From the Bible: Exodus 2:1-10. The infant Moses is discovered in a basket made of bulrushes (reeds) and adopted by the daughter of the Egyptian pharoah.
2. **sugar-hogshead.** Large barrel that once held sugar; Huck used to sleep in it.

Words For Everyday Use

com • mence (kə mens´) *vi.,* begin

right to eating, but you had to wait for the widow to tuck down her head and grumble a little over the <u>victuals</u>, though there warn't really anything the matter with them—that is, nothing only everything was cooked by itself. In a barrel of odds and ends it is different; things get mixed up, and the juice kind of swaps around, and the things go better.

After supper she got out her book and learned me about Moses and the Bulrushers, and I was in a sweat to find out all about him; but by and by she let it out that Moses had been dead a considerable long time; so then I didn't care no more about him, because I don't take no stock in dead people.

[handwritten: Huck lives in the moment]

Pretty soon I wanted to smoke, and asked the widow to let me. But she wouldn't. She said it was a mean practice and wasn't clean, and I must try to not do it any more. That is just the way with some people. They get down on a thing when they don't know nothing about it. Here she was a-bothering about Moses, which was no <u>kin</u> to her, and no use to anybody, being gone, you see, yet finding a power of fault with me for doing a thing that had some good in it. And she took snuff,[3] too; of course that was all right, because she done it herself.

Her sister, Miss Watson, a tolerable[4] slim old maid, with goggles on, had just come to live with her, and took a set at me now with a spelling book. She worked me middling hard for about an hour, and then the widow made her ease up. I couldn't stood it much longer. Then for an hour it was deadly dull, and I was fidgety. Miss Watson would say, "Don't put your feet up there, Huckleberry"; and "Don't scrunch up like that, Huckleberry—set up straight"; and pretty soon she would say, "Don't gap and stretch like that, Huckleberry—why don't you try to behave?" Then she told me all about the bad place, and I said I wished I was there. She got mad then, but I didn't mean no harm. All I wanted was to go somewheres; all I wanted was a change, I warn't particular. She said it was wicked to say what I said; said she wouldn't say it for the whole world; *she* was going to live so as to go to the good place. Well, I couldn't see no advantage in going where she was going, so I made up my mind I

▶ To what is Miss Watson referring as the "bad place"? Why might a character like Huck prefer the "bad place" over the "good place"?

---

3. **snuff.** Preparation of powered tobacco. At that time, it was not known that using snuff is a dangerous, addictive behavior.
4. **tolerable.** Fairly, somewhat

Words For Everyday Use	**vict • uals** (vit´′lz) *n.,* food **kin** (kin) *n.,* relatives, family

wouldn't try for it. But I never said so, because it would only make trouble, and wouldn't do no good.

Now she had got a start, and she went on and told me all about the good place. She said all a body would have to do there was to go around all day long with a harp and sing, forever and ever. So I didn't think much of it. But I never said so. I asked her if she <u>reckoned</u> Tom Sawyer would go there, and she said not by a considerable sight. I was glad about that, because I wanted him and me to be together.

Miss Watson she kept pecking at me, and it got tiresome and lonesome. By and by they fetched the niggers[5] in and had prayers, and then everybody was off to bed. I went up to my room with a piece of candle, and put it on the table. Then I set down in a chair by the window and tried to think of something cheerful, but it warn't no use. I felt so lonesome I most[6] wished I was dead. The stars were shining, and the leaves rustled in the woods ever so mournful; and I heard an owl, away off, who-whooing about somebody that was dead, and a whippowill[7] and a dog crying about somebody that was going to die; and the wind was trying to whisper something to me, and I couldn't make out what it was, and so it made the cold shivers run over me. Then away out in the woods I heard that kind of a sound that a ghost makes when it wants to tell about something that's on its mind and can't make itself understood, and so can't rest easy in its grave, and has to go about that way every night grieving. I got so downhearted and scared I did wish I had some company. Pretty soon a spider went crawling up my shoulder, and I flipped it off and it lit in the candle; and before I could budge it was all shriveled up. I didn't need anybody to tell me that that was an awful bad sign and would fetch me some bad luck, so I was scared and most shook the clothes off of me. I got up and turned around in my tracks three times and crossed my breast every time; and then I tied up a little lock of my hair with a thread to keep witches away. But I hadn't no confidence. You do that when you've lost a horseshoe

Irony

◄ *How is Huck feeling after his talk with Miss Watson? Why is he feeling this way?*

What does Huck believe will bring him bad luck?

---

5. **niggers.** Originally a dialect variant of *Negro;* now an unacceptable and hostile usage because of its use in a context of racial hatred
6. **most.** Almost
7. **whippowill.** Whippoorwill; bird with a haunting call

Words For Everyday Use	**reck • on** (rek´ən) *vt.,* figure, suppose

that you've found, instead of nailing it up over the door, but I hadn't ever heard anybody say it was any way to keep off bad luck when you'd killed a spider.

I set down again, a-shaking all over, and got out my pipe for a smoke; for the house was all as still as death now, and so the widow wouldn't know. Well, after a long time I heard the clock away off in the town go boom—boom—boom—twelve licks; and all still again—stiller than ever. Pretty soon I heard a twig snap down in the dark amongst the trees—something was a-stirring. I set still and listened. Directly I could just barely hear a "*me-yow! me-yow!*" down there. That was good! Says I, "*me-yow! me-yow!*" as soft as I could, and then I put out the light and scrambled out of the window on to the shed. Then I slipped down to the ground and crawled in among the trees, and, sure enough, there was Tom Sawyer waiting for me.

▶ At what time of night does Tom call Huck to come outside? How does Tom get Huck's attention?

CHAPTER 2

Our Gang's Dark Oath

We went tiptoeing along a path amongst the trees back towards the end of the widow's garden, stooping down so as the branches wouldn't scrape our heads. When we was passing by the kitchen I fell over a root and made a noise. We scrouched down and laid still. Miss Watson's big nigger, named Jim, was setting in the kitchen door; we could see him pretty clear, because there was a light behind him. He got up and stretched his neck out about a minute, listening. Then he says:

"Who dah?"

He listened some more; then he come tiptoeing down and stood right between us; we could a touched him, nearly. Well, likely it was minutes and minutes that there warn't a sound, and we all there so close together. There was a place on my ankle that got to itching, but I dasn't scratch it; and then my ear begun to itch; and next my back, right between my shoulders. Seemed like I'd die if I couldn't scratch. Well, I've noticed that thing plenty times since. If you are with the quality,[1] or at a funeral, or trying to go to sleep when you ain't sleepy—if you are anywheres where it won't do for you to scratch, why you will itch all over in upwards of a thousand places. Pretty soon Jim says:

"Say, who is you? Whar is you? Dog my cats ef I didn' hear sumf'n. Well, I know what I's gwyne to do: I's gwyne to set down here and listen tell I hears it agin."

So he set down on the ground <u>betwixt</u> me and Tom. He leaned his back up against a tree, and stretched his legs out till one of them most touched one of mine. My nose begun to itch. It itched till the tears come into my eyes. But I dasn't scratch. Then it begun to itch on the inside. Next I got to itching underneath. I didn't know how I was going to set still. This miserableness went on as much as six or seven minutes; but it seemed a sight longer than that. I was itching in eleven different places now. I reckoned I couldn't stand it more'n a minute longer, but I set my teeth hard and got ready to try. Just then Jim begun to breathe heavy; next he begun to snore—and then I was pretty soon comfortable again.

◄ *Why does Huck have trouble keeping still while the boys are waiting to sneak past Jim? What observation does Huck make about the urge to "scratch"?*

---

1. **quality.** People of high social position

Words For Everyday Use	**be • twixt** (bē twikst´) *adv.,* between

Tom he made a sign to me—kind of a little noise with his mouth—and we went creeping away on our hands and knees. When we was ten foot off Tom whispered to me, and wanted to tie Jim to the tree for fun. But I said no; he might wake and make a disturbance, and then they'd find out I warn't in. Then Tom said he hadn't got candles enough, and he would slip in the kitchen and get some more. I didn't want him to try. I said Jim might wake up and come. But Tom wanted to resk it; so we slid in there and got three candles, and Tom laid five cents on the table for pay. Then we got out, and I was in a sweat to get away; but nothing would do Tom but he must crawl to where Jim was, on his hands and knees, and play something on him. I waited, and it seemed a good while, everything was so still and lonesome.

As soon as Tom was back we cut along the path, around the garden fence, and by and by fetched up on the steep top of the hill the other side of the house. Tom said he slipped Jim's hat off of his head and hung it on a <u>limb</u> right over him, and Jim stirred a little, but he didn't wake. Afterwards Jim said the witches bewitched him and put him in a <u>trance</u>, and rode him all over the state, and then set him under the trees again, and hung his hat on a limb to show who done it. And next time Jim told it he said they rode him down to New Orleans; and, after that, every time he told it he spread it more and more, till by and by he said they rode him all over the world, and tired him most to death, and his back was all over saddle-boils. Jim was <u>monstrous</u> proud about it, and he got so he wouldn't hardly notice the other niggers. Niggers would come miles to hear Jim tell about it, and he was more looked up to than any nigger in that country. Strange niggers would stand with their mouths open and look him all over, same as if he was a wonder. Niggers is always talking about witches in the dark by the kitchen fire; but whenever one was talking and letting on to know all about such things, Jim would happen in and say, "Hm! What you know 'bout witches?" and that nigger was corked up and had to take a back seat. Jim always kept that five-center piece round his neck with a string, and said it was a charm the devil give to him with his own hands, and told him he could cure anybody with it and fetch witches whenever he wanted to just by saying something to it; but he never told what it

► *What prank does Tom play on Jim? Why does Jim become famous as a result of this prank?*

Words For Everyday Use	**limb** (lim) *n.,* branch of a tree
	trance (trans) *n.,* state resembling sleep during which voluntary action is lost
	mon • strous (män´strəs) *adv.,* extremely

was he said to it. Niggers would come from all around there and give Jim anything they had, just for a sight of that five-center piece; but they wouldn't touch it, because the devil had had his hands on it. Jim was most ruined for a servant, because he got stuck up on account of having seen the devil and been rode by witches.

Well, when Tom and me got to the edge of the hilltop we looked away down into the village and could see three or four lights twinkling, where there was sick folks, maybe; and the stars over us was sparkling ever so fine; and down by the village was the river, a whole mile broad, and awful still and grand. We went down the hill and found Joe Harper and Ben Rogers, and two or three more of the boys, hid in the old tanyard.[2] So we unhitched a skiff[3] and pulled down the river two mile and a half, to the big <u>scar</u> on the hillside, and went ashore.

◀ Whom do Huck and Tom meet? In what do the boys travel?

We went to a clump of bushes, and Tom made everybody swear to keep the secret, and then showed them a hole in the hill, right in the thickest part of the bushes. Then we lit the candles, and crawled in on our hands and knees. We went about two hundred yards, and then the cave opened up. Tom poked about amongst the passages, and pretty soon ducked under a wall where you wouldn't 'a' noticed that there was a hole. We went along a narrow place and got into a kind of room, all damp and sweaty and cold, and there we stopped. Tom says:

◀ Where do the boys settle for their meeting? What do they plan? Who seems to be in charge of the meeting?

"Now, we'll start this band of robbers and call it Tom Sawyer's Gang. Everybody that wants to join has got to take an <u>oath</u>, and write his name in blood."

Everybody was willing. So Tom got out a sheet of paper that he had wrote the oath on, and read it. It swore every boy to stick to the band, and never tell any of the secrets; and if anybody done anything to any boy in the band, whichever boy was ordered to kill that person and his family must do it, and he mustn't eat and he mustn't sleep till he had killed them and hacked a cross in their breasts, which was the sign of the band. And nobody that didn't belong to the band could use that mark, and if he did he must be sued; and if he done it again he must be killed. And if anybody that

---

2. **tanyard.** Tanning yard, where leather is made from animal hides
3. **skiff.** Flat-bottomed boat

| Words For Everyday Use | **scar** (scär) *n.,* disfiguring mark |
| | **oath** (ōth) *n.,* pledge, vow |

belonged to the band told the secrets, he must have his throat cut, and then have his <u>carcass</u> burnt up and the ashes scattered all around, and his name blotted off of the list with blood and never mentioned again by the gang, but have a curse put on it and be forgot forever.

Everybody said it was a real beautiful oath, and asked Tom if he got it out of his own head. He said some of it, but the rest was out of pirate books and robber books, and every gang that was high-toned had it.

Some thought it would be good to kill the families of boys that told the secrets. Tom said it was a good idea, so he took a pencil and wrote it in. Then Ben Rogers says:

"Here's Huck Finn, he hain't got no family; what you going to do 'bout him?"

"Well, hain't he got a father?" says Tom Sawyer.

"Yes, he's got a father, but you can't never find him these days. He used to lay drunk with the hogs in the tanyard, but he hain't been seen in these parts for a year or more."

They talked it over, and they was going to rule me out, because they said every boy must have a family or somebody to kill, or else it wouldn't be fair and square for the others. Well, nobody could think of anything to do—everybody was stumped, and set still. I was most ready to cry; but all at once I thought of a way, and so I offered them Miss Watson—they could kill her. Everybody said:

"Oh, she'll do. That's all right. Huck can come in."

Then they all stuck a pin in their fingers to get blood to sign with, and I made my mark[4] on the paper.

"Now," says Ben Rogers, "what's the line of business of this Gang?"

"Nothing only robbery and murder," Tom said.

"But who are we going to rob?—houses, or cattle, or—"

"Stuff! stealing cattle and such things ain't robbery; it's burglary," says Tom Sawyer. "We ain't burglars. That ain't no sort of style. We are highwaymen.[5] We stop stages and carriages on the road, with masks on, and kill the people and take their watches and money."

"Must we always kill the people?"

► From where does Tom get many of the ideas for his imaginative oath?

► Why is Huck told he can't be part of the "band of robbers"? What does he say to convince the others to include him?

► According to Tom, what must the boys do as "highwaymen"?

---

4. **made my mark.** Those who could not write could draw a symbol, typically an *X*, to stand for their name.

5. **highwaymen.** Robbers on horseback who stopped travelers on highways

---

"Oh, certainly. It's best. Some authorities think different, but mostly it's considered best to kill them—except some that you bring to the cave here, and keep them till they're <u>ransomed</u>."

"Ransomed? What's that?"

"I don't know. But that's what they do. I've seen it in books; and so of course that's what we've got to do."

"But how can we do it if we don't know what it is?"

"Why, blame it all, we've *got* to do it. Don't I tell you it's in the books? Do you want to go to doing different from what's in the books, and get things all muddled up?"

"Oh, that's all very fine to *say,* Tom Sawyer, but how in the nation are these fellows going to be ransomed if we don't know how to do it to them?—that's the thing I want to get at. Now, what do you *reckon* it is?"

"Well, I don't know. But per'aps if we keep them till they're ransomed, it means that we keep them till they're dead."

"Now, that's something *like.* That'll answer. Why couldn't you said that before? We'll keep them till they're ransomed to death; and a bothersome lot they'll be, too—eating up everything, and always trying to get loose."

"How you talk, Ben Rogers. How can they get loose when there's a guard over them, ready to shoot them down if they move a peg?"

"A guard! Well, that *is* good. So somebody's got to set up all night and never get any sleep, just so as to watch them. I think that's foolishness. Why can't a body take a club and ransom them as soon as they get here?"

"Because it ain't in the books so—that's why. Now, Ben Rogers, do you want to do things regular, or don't you?—that's the idea. Don't you reckon that the people that made the books knows what's the correct thing to do? Do you reckon *you* can learn 'em anything? Not by a good deal. No, sir, we'll just go on and ransom them in the regular way."

"All right. I don't mind; but I say it's a fool way, anyhow. Say, do we kill the women, too?"

"Well, Ben Rogers, if I was as <u>ignorant</u> as you I wouldn't let on. Kill the women? No; nobody ever saw anything in the books like that. You fetch them to the cave, and you're always as polite as pie to them; and by and by they fall in love with you, and never want to go home any more."

◀ *Why does Tom seem to know more than the other boys about outlaws and their adventures? In what activity does he probably spend a great deal of his time?*

irony

| Words For Everyday Use | **ran • som** (ran´səm) *vt.,* release from capture by paying a fee to the captors
ig • no • rant (ig´nə rənt) *adj.,* uninformed, inexperienced |

"Well, if that's the way I'm agreed, but I don't take no stock in it. Mighty soon we'll have the cave so cluttered up with women, and fellows waiting to be ransomed, that there won't be no place for the robbers. But go ahead, I ain't got nothing to say."

Little Tommy Barnes was asleep now, and when they waked him up he was scared, and cried, and said he wanted to go home to his ma, and didn't want to be a robber any more.

▶ Why do the boys make fun of Little Tommy Barnes? Why do they decide not to meet on Sunday?

So they all made fun of him, and called him crybaby, and that made him mad, and he said he would go straight and tell all the secrets. But Tom give him five cents to keep quiet, and said we would all go home and meet next week, and rob somebody and kill some people.

Ben Rogers said he couldn't get out much, only Sundays, and so he wanted to begin next Sunday; but all the boys said it would be wicked to do it on Sunday, and that settled the thing. They agreed to get together and fix a day as soon as they could, and then we elected Tom Sawyer first captain and Joe Harper second captain of the Gang, and so started home.

I clumb up the shed and crept into my window just before day was breaking. My new clothes was all greased up and clayey, and I was dog-tired.

CHAPTER 3

We Ambuscade the A-rabs

Well, I got a good going-over in the morning from old Miss Watson on account of my clothes; but the widow she didn't scold, but only cleaned off the grease and clay, and looked so sorry that I thought I would behave awhile if I could. Then Miss Watson she took me in the closet and prayed, but nothing come of it. She told me to pray every day, and whatever I asked for I would get it. But it warn't so. I tried it. Once I got a fish line, but no hooks. It warn't any good to me without hooks. I tried for the hooks three or four times, but somehow I couldn't make it work. By and by, one day, I asked Miss Watson to try for me, but she said I was a fool. She never told me why, and I couldn't make it out no way.

◄ In what way do Widow Douglas and Miss Watson differ in their reactions to Huck's mischief? Which of the two inspires Huck to try to "behave awhile"?

I set down one time back in the woods, and had a long think about it. I says to myself, if a body can get anything they pray for, why don't <u>Deacon</u> Winn get back the money he lost on pork? Why can't the widow get back her silver snuffbox that was stole? Why can't Miss Watson fat up? No, says I to myself, there ain't nothing in it. I went and told the widow about it, and she said the thing a body could get by praying for it was "spiritual gifts." This was too many for me, but she told me what she meant—I must help other people, and do everything I could for other people, and look out for them all the time, and never think about myself. This was including Miss Watson, as I took it. I went out in the woods and turned it over in my mind a long time, but I couldn't see no advantage about it—except for the other people; so at last I reckoned I wouldn't worry about it any more, but just let it go. Sometimes the widow would take me one side and talk about Providence[1] in a way to make a body's mouth water; but maybe next day Miss Watson would take hold and knock it all down again. I judged I could see that there was two Providences, and a poor chap would stand considerable show with the widow's Providence, but if Miss Watson's got him there warn't no help for him any more. I thought it all out,

◄ Why does Huck conclude that prayer is useless? What does the widow tell him he can get from praying? Does Huck seem to know what she means?

◄ What two "Providences" does Huck believe exist? Whose "Providence" does he feel might accept him, and whose does he feel might reject him?

---

1. **Providence.** God as the guiding power of the universe

Words For Everyday Use	**dea • con** (dē´kən) *n.*, officer of the church who helps the minister with duties not related to worship

and reckoned I would belong to the widow's if he wanted me, though I couldn't make out how he was a-going to be any better off then than what he was before, seeing I was so ignorant, and so kind of low-down and <u>ornery</u>.

▶ Why is Huck "comfortable" with not seeing his father?

Pap he hadn't been seen for more than a year, and that was comfortable for me; I didn't want to see him no more. He used to always whale[2] me when he was <u>sober</u> and could get his hands on me; though I used to take to the woods most of the time when he was around. Well, about this time he was found in the river drownded, about twelve mile above town, so people said. They judged it was him, anyway; said this drownded man was just his size, and was ragged, and had uncommon long hair, which was all like Pap; but they couldn't make nothing out of the face, because it had been in the water so long it warn't much like a face at all. They said he was floating on his back in the water. They took him and buried him on the bank. But I warn't comfortable long, because I happened to think of something. I knowed mighty well that a drownded man don't float on his back, but on his face. So I knowed, then, that this warn't Pap, but a woman dressed up in a man's clothes. So I was uncomfortable again. I judged the old man would turn up again by and by, though I wished he wouldn't.

▶ Why doesn't Huck believe that the drowned man found in the river is his father?

We played robber now and then about a month, and then I resigned. All the boys did. We hadn't robbed nobody, hadn't killed any people, but only just pretended. We used to hop out of the woods and go charging down on hog drivers and women in carts taking garden stuff to market, but we never hived[3] any of them. Tom Sawyer called the hogs "<u>ingots</u>," and he called the turnips and stuff "julery," and we would go to the cave and <u>powwow</u> over what we had done, and how many people we had killed and marked. But I couldn't see no profit in it. One time Tom sent a boy to run about town with a blazing stick, which he called a slogan (which was the sign for the Gang to get together), and then he said he had got secret news by his spies that next day a whole parcel of Spanish merchants and rich A-rabs[4] was going to camp in

---

2. **whale.** Whip
3. **hived.** Separated out any of a group for capture
4. **A-rab.** Dialect for the term *Arab*; its use reflects an intolerant view of any nonwhite or non-European people

Words For Everyday Use	
	or • ner • y (ôr´nər ē) *adj.,* mean, unpleasant
	so • ber (sō´bər) *adj.,* not drunk
	in • got (iŋ´gət) *n.,* bar of gold
	pow • wow (pou´wou´) *vi.,* hold a conference

Cave Hollow with two hundred elephants, and six hundred camels, and over a thousand "sumter" mules, all loaded down with di'monds, and they didn't have only a guard of four hundred soldiers, and so we would lay in ambuscade,[5] as he called it, and kill the lot and scoop the things. He said we must slick up our swords and guns, and get ready. He never could go after even a turnip cart but he must have the swords and guns all <u>scoured</u> up for it, though they was only lath and broomsticks, and you might scour at them till you rotted, and then they warn't worth a mouthful of ashes more than what they was before. I didn't believe we could lick such a crowd of Spaniards and A-rabs, but I wanted to see the camels and elephants, so I was on hand next day, Saturday, in the ambuscade; and when we got the word we rushed out of the woods and down the hill. But there warn't no Spaniards and A-rabs, and there warn't no camels nor no elephants. It warn't anything but a Sunday school picnic, and only a primer class at that. We busted it up, and chased the children up the hollow; but we never got anything but some dough-nuts and jam, though Ben Rogers got a rag doll, and Joe Harper got a hymn book and a tract; and then the teacher charged in, and made us drop everything and cut. I didn't see no di'monds, and I told Tom Sawyer so. He said there was loads of them there, anyway; and he said there was A-rabs there, too, and elephants and things. I said, why couldn't we see them, then? He said if I warn't so ignorant, but had read a book called *Don Quixote*,[6] I would know without asking. He said it was all done by enchantment. He said there was hundreds of soldiers there, and elephants and treasure, and so on, but we had enemies which he called magicians; and they had turned the whole thing into an infant Sunday school, just out of spite. I said, all right; then the thing for us to do was to go for the magicians. Tom Sawyer said I was a numskull.

"Why," said he, "a magician could call up a lot of <u>genies</u>, and they would hash you up like nothing before you could say Jack Robinson. They are as tall as a tree and as big around as a church."

◄ *What kind of adventure does Tom promise the boys?*

◄ *How does Tom explain the appearance of the Sunday school class where the boys expected a wild adventure? What does Tom call Huck?*

---

5. **ambuscade.** Ambush
6. **Don Quixote.** Hero of a seventeenth-century novel who attacks windmills believing them to be giants

Words
For
Everyday
Use

scoured (skour'd) *adj.*, polished

ge • nie (jē´nē) *n.*, magic spirit believed to take human form and serve the person who calls it

"Well," I says, "s'pose we got some genies to help *us*—can't we lick the other crowd then?"

"How you going to get them?"

"I don't know. How do *they* get them?"

"Why, they rub an old tin lamp or an iron ring, and then the genies come tearing in, with the thunder and lightning a-ripping around and the smoke a-rolling, and everything they're told to do they up and do it. They don't think nothing of pulling a shot-tower[7] up by the roots, and belting a Sunday school superintendent over the head with it—or any other man."

"Who makes them tear around so?"

▶ According to Tom, what is the job of "genies"?

"Why, whoever rubs the lamp or the ring. They belong to whoever rubs the lamp or the ring, and they've got to do whatever he says. If he tells them to build a palace forty miles long out of di'monds, and fill it full of chewing-gum, or whatever you want, and fetch an emperor's daughter from China for you to marry, they've got to do it—and they've got to do it before sunup next morning, too. And more: they've got to waltz that palace around over the country wherever you want it, you understand."

"Well," says I, "I think they are a pack of flatheads for not keeping the palace themselves 'stead of fooling them away like that. And what's more—if I was one of them I would see a man in Jericho before I would drop my business and come to him for the rubbing of an old tin lamp."

"How you talk, Huck Finn. Why, you'd have to come when he rubbed it, whether you wanted to or not."

"What! and I as high as a tree and as big as a church? All right, then; I would come; but I lay I'd make that man climb the highest tree there was in the country."

"Shucks, it ain't no use to talk to you, Huck Finn. You don't seem to know anything, somehow—perfect saphead."

I thought all this over for two or three days, and then I reckoned I would see if there was anything in it. I got an old tin lamp and an iron ring, and went out in the woods and rubbed and rubbed till I sweat like an Injun,[8] calculating to build a palace and sell it; but it warn't no use, none of the genies come. So then I judged that all that stuff was only just one of Tom Sawyer's lies. I reckoned he believed in the A-rabs and the elephants, but as for me I think different. It had all the marks of a Sunday school.

▶ What is Huck's final opinion of Tom's adventure tale?

---

7. **shot-tower.** Tall tower where shot (small pellets used in a shotgun) was made by dropping bits of molten metal from a great height into water

8. **Injun.** Indian; another dialect variant, here of the word used to indicate Native Americans, again unacceptable as a derogatory term

Responding to the Selection

What is your first impression of Huckleberry Finn, the narrator of the story? If you were living in Huck's village, whom would you prefer as a friend: Huck, Tom, or some of the other boys? Explain your response.

Reviewing the Selection

Recalling and Interpreting

1. **R:** In the opening lines of the novel, what important details does Huck give the reader about the end of *The Adventures of Tom Sawyer*? Where is Huck still living when he begins his own story?

2. **I:** In what way has the widow tried to change Huck? How does Huck seem to feel about her attempts to change him?

3. **R:** What specific rules and rituals in the home of the widow and Miss Watson are most difficult for Huck to accept?

4. **I:** Why is Huck's personality at odds with life in the widow's home? In what ways does the widow's treatment of Huck differ from Miss Watson's treatment of Huck? Who is most responsible for Huck's feelings of resentment toward being "civilized"?

5. **R:** At what time of night does Tom Sawyer call Huck out of his room? What does Tom "steal" from the widow's kitchen before they leave? What practical joke does Tom play on Jim? In what way does this joke make Jim "famous" when he later tells people about it?

6. **I:** What does the fact that Tom leaves money for candles that he is "stealing" say about his personality? Why does it seem appropriate that Miss Watson, rather than Widow Douglas, would own a slave? In what way is this fact in keeping with Miss Watson's narrow-minded, restrictive beliefs, as opposed to Widow Douglas's gentler, kinder nature?

7. **R:** When Huck and Tom meet with the other boys, where do they go? What kind of group does Tom want to organize? From where does he get most of his ideas for the group? Why is Huck almost excluded from the group?

8. **I:** Why do you think Tom is the group leader? Why do you think Huck offers Miss Watson, rather than Miss Douglas, as a person to be killed if he violates the group's

oath? Even though the boys want to be outlaws, they do not want to meet on Sunday, a church day, for their meetings. What does this fact say about the seriousness of their wishes to be outlaws?

Synthesizing

9. Huck tells readers, "The Widow Douglas, she took me for her son, and allowed she would sivilize me." Why do you think Huck finds being "civilized" so difficult?

10. In what ways do Huck and Tom seem to be similar? In what ways do they seem to be different?

Understanding Literature (QUESTIONS FOR DISCUSSION)

1. **Characterization. Characterization** is the use of literary techniques to create a character. Writers use three major literary techniques to create characters: direct description, portraying characters' behavior, and presenting the thoughts and emotions of characters. The main purpose of the first three chapters of *Adventures of Huckleberry Finn* is to begin to characterize Huck Finn. Which of the techniques described above does Twain use? Give one or two examples of each. What does each example show about Huck as a person?

2. **Narrator and Point of View.** A **narrator** is one who tells a story. **Point of view** is the vantage point from which a story is told. Huck's way of describing the events in his life contributes to the humor in *Adventures of Huckleberry Finn.* He is rather innocent in his dealings with people and reports things directly as he sees them. He is also often unaware when he has said something insightful. Give examples from the novel of Huck's style as a narrator. Name things that seem funny or strange when they are described from his point of view.

CHAPTER 4

The Hairball Oracle

Well, three or four months run along, and it was well into the winter now. I had been to school most all the time and could spell and read and write just a little, and could say the multiplication table up to six times seven is thirty-five, and I don't reckon I could ever get any further than that if I was to live forever. I don't take no stock in mathematics, anyway.

At first I hated the school, but by and by I got so I could stand it. Whenever I got uncommon tired I played hookey, and the hiding[1] I got next day done me good and cheered me up. So the longer I went to school the easier it got to be. I was getting sort of used to the widow's ways, too, and they warn't so raspy on me. Living in a house and sleeping in a bed pulled on me pretty tight mostly, but before the cold weather I used to slide out and sleep in the woods sometimes, and so that was a rest to me. I liked the old ways best, but I was getting so I liked the new ones, too, a little bit. The widow said I was coming along slow but sure, and doing very satisfactory. She said she warn't ashamed of me.

One morning I happened to turn over the saltcellar[2] at breakfast. I reached for some of it as quick as I could to throw over my left shoulder and keep off the bad luck, but Miss Watson was in ahead of me, and crossed me off. She says, "Take your hands away, Huckleberry; what a mess you are always making!" The widow put in a good word for me, but that warn't going to keep off the bad luck, I knowed that well enough. I started out, after breakfast, feeling worried and shaky, and wondering where it was going to fall on me, and what it was going to be. There is ways to keep off some kinds of bad luck, but this wasn't one of them kind; so I never tried to do anything, but just poked along low-spirited and on the watch-out.

I went down to the front garden and clumb over the stile[3] where you go through the high board fence. There was an inch of new snow on the ground, and I seen somebody's

◄ In what ways do Huck's feelings toward going to school and living according to the "widow's ways" begin to change? What does he do when he needs a "rest" from school and his new life?

---

1. **hiding.** Severe beating
2. **saltcellar.** Small container of salt placed on the dining table
3. **stile.** Double set of steps straddling a fence

Words For Everyday Use

rasp • y (ras´pē) adj., grating, irritating

▶ What does Huck notice in the snow? What seems to frighten him?

tracks. They had come up from the <u>quarry</u> and stood around the stile awhile, and then went on around the garden fence. It was funny they hadn't come in, after standing around so. I couldn't make it out. It was very curious, somehow. I was going to follow around, but I stooped down to look at the tracks first. I didn't notice anything at first, but next I did. There was a cross in the left boot-heel made with big nails, to keep off the devil.

I was up in a second and shinning down the hill. I looked over my shoulder every now and then, but I didn't see nobody. I was at Judge Thatcher's as quick as I could get there. He said:

"Why, my boy, you are all out of breath. Did you come for your interest?"

"No, sir," I says; "is there some for me?"

"Oh, yes, a half-yearly is in last night[4]—over a hundred and fifty dollars. Quite a fortune for you. You had better let me invest it along with your six thousand, because if you take it you'll spend it."

"No, sir," I says, "I don't want to spend it. I don't want it at all—nor the six thousand, nuther. I want you to take it; I want to give it to you—the six thousand and all."

He looked surprised. He couldn't seem to make it out. He says:

"Why, what can you mean, my boy?"

I says, "Don't you ask me no questions about it, please. You'll take it—won't you?"

He says:

"Well, I'm puzzled. Is something the matter?"

▶ What does Huck do with his money? Why do you think he does this?

"Please take it," says I, "and don't ask me nothing—then I won't have to tell no lies."

He studied awhile, and then he says:

"Oho-o! I think I see. You want to *sell* all your property to me—not give it. That's the correct idea."

Then he wrote something on a paper and read it over, and says:

"There; you see it says 'for a consideration.' That means I have bought it of you and paid you for it. Here's a dollar for you. Now you sign it."

4. **half-yearly . . . night.** Payment of six months' interest on Huck's invested money came in last night.

Words For Everyday Use

quar • ry (kwôr´ē) *n.*, excavation site for stones, rock

So I signed it, and left.

Miss Watson's nigger, Jim, had a hairball[5] as big as your fist, which had been took out of the fourth stomach of an ox, and he used to do magic with it. He said there was a spirit inside of it, and it knowed everything. So I went to him that night and told him Pap was here again, for I found his tracks in the snow. What I wanted to know was, what he was going to do, and was he going to stay? Jim got out his hairball and said something over it, and then he held it up and dropped it on the floor. It fell pretty solid, and only rolled about an inch. Jim tried it again, and then another time, and it acted just the same. Jim got down on his knees, and put his ear against it and listened. But it warn't no use; he said it wouldn't talk. He said sometimes it wouldn't talk without money. I told him I had an old slick <u>counterfeit</u> quarter that warn't no good because the brass showed through the silver a little, and it wouldn't pass nohow, even if the brass didn't show, because it was so slick it felt greasy, and so that would tell on it every time. (I reckoned I wouldn't say nothing about the dollar I got from the judge.) I said it was pretty bad money, but maybe the hairball would take it, because maybe it wouldn't know the difference. Jim smelt it and bit it and rubbed it, and said he would manage so the hairball would think it was good. He said he would split open a raw Irish potato and stick the quarter in between and keep it there all night, and next morning you couldn't see no brass, and it wouldn't feel greasy no more, and so anybody in town would take it in a minute, let alone a hairball. Well, I knowed a potato would do that before, but I had forgot it.

Jim put the quarter under the hairball, and got down and listened again. This time he said the hairball was all right. He said it would tell my whole fortune if I wanted it to. I says, go on. So the hairball talked to Jim, and Jim told it to me. He says:

"Yo' ole father doan' know yit what he's a-gwyne to do. Sometimes he spec he'll go 'way, en den agin he spec he'll stay. De bes' way is to res' easy en let de ole man take his own way. Dey's two angels hoverin' roun' 'bout him. One uv 'em is white en shiny, en t'other one is black. De white one gits

◄ What do Jim and Huck believe about the "hairball"? What upsetting news does Huck share with Jim and the "hairball"? What questions does Huck want to ask the "hairball"?

◄ What does the hairball "tell" Huck about his father?

---

5. **hairball.** Telling fortunes by means of a ball of hair from an ox's stomach was a practice with origins in Africa.

Words For Everyday Use

coun • ter • feit (kount´ ər fit´) *adj.*, imitation, fake

him to go right a little while, den de black one sail in en bust it all up. A body can't tell yit which one gwyne to fetch him at de las'. But you is all right. You gwyne to have considable trouble in yo' life, en considable joy. Sometimes you gwyne to git hurt, en sometimes you gwyne to git sick; but every time you's gwyne to git well agin. Dey's two gals flyin' 'bout you in yo' life. One uv 'em's light en t'other one is dark. One is rich en t'other is po'. You's gwyne to marry de po' one fust en de rich one by en by. You wants to keep 'way fum de water as much as you kin, en don't run no resk, 'kase it's down in de bills dat you's gwyne to git hung."

When I lit my candle and went up to my room that night there sat Pap—his own self!

CHAPTER 5

Pap Starts in on a New Life

I had shut the door to. Then I turned around, and there he was. I used to be scared of him all the time, he tanned me so much. I reckoned I was scared now, too; but in a minute I see I was mistaken—that is, after the first jolt, as you may say, when my breath sort of hitched, he being so unexpected; but right away after I see I warn't scared of him worth bothring about.

He was most fifty, and he looked it. His hair was long and tangled and greasy, and hung down, and you could see his eyes shining through like he was behind vines. It was all black, no gray; so was his long, mixed-up whiskers. There warn't no color in his face, where his face showed; it was white; not like another man's white, but a white to make a body sick, a white to make a body's flesh crawl—a tree-toad white, a fish-belly white. As for his clothes—just rags, that was all. He had one ankle resting on t'other knee; the boot on that foot was busted, and two of his toes stuck through, and he worked them now and then. His hat was laying on the floor—an old black slouch with the top caved in, like a lid.

◄ What does Pap look like? What is he wearing?

I stood a-looking at him; he set there a-looking at me, with his chair tilted back a little. I set the candle down. I noticed the window was up; so he had clumb in by the shed. He kept a-looking me all over. By and by he says:

"Starchy clothes—very. You think you're a good deal of a big-bug, *don't* you?"

"Maybe I am, maybe I ain't," I says.

"Don't you give me none o' your lip," says he. "You've put on considerable many frills since I been away. I'll take you down a peg before I get done with you. You're educated, too, they say—can read and write. You think you're better'n your father, now, don't you, because he can't? *I'll* take it out of you. Who told you you might meddle with such hifalut'n[1] foolishness, hey?—who told you you could?"

jealous

◄ Why do you think Pap is angry that Huck is in school, learning to read?

"The widow. She told me."

"The widow, hey?—and who told the widow she could put in her shovel about a thing that ain't none of her business?"

"Nobody never told her."

"Well, I'll learn her how to meddle. And looky here—you drop that school, you hear? I'll learn people to bring up a

---

1. **hifalut'n.** Highfalutin; ridiculously pretentious; pompous

boy to put on airs over his own father and let on to be better'n what *he* is. You lemme catch you fooling around that school again, you hear? Your mother couldn't read, and she couldn't write, nuther, before she died. None of the family couldn't before *they* died. I can't; and here you're a-swelling yourself up like this. I ain't the man to stand it—you hear? Say, lemme hear you read."

I took up a book and begun something about General Washington and the wars. When I'd read about a half a minute, he fetched the book a whack with his hand and knocked it across the house. He says:

"It's so. You can do it. I had my doubts when you told me. Now looky here; you stop that putting on frills. I won't have it. I'll lay for you, my smarty; and if I catch you about that school I'll tan you good. First you know you'll get religion, too. I never see such a son."

He took up a little blue and yaller picture of some cows and a boy, and says:

"What's this?"

"It's something they give me for learning my lessons good."

He tore it up, and says:

"I'll give you something better—I'll give you a cowhide."

He set there a-mumbling and a-growling a minute, and then he says:

► *What bothers Pap about Huck's new lifestyle? What does he demand from Huck?*

"*Ain't* you a sweet-scented <u>dandy</u>, though? A bed; and bedclothes; and a look'n'-glass; and a piece of carpet on the floor—and your own father got to sleep with the hogs in the tanyard. I never see such a son. I bet I'll take some o' these frills out o' you before I'm done with you. Why, there ain't no end to your <u>airs</u>—they say you're rich. Hey?—how's that?"

"They lie—that's how."

"Looky here—mind how you talk to me; I'm a-standing about all I can stand now—so don't gimme no sass. I've been in town two days, and I hain't heard nothing but about you bein' rich. I heard about it away down the river, too. That's why I come. You git me that money tomorrow—I want it."

"I hain't got no money."

"It's a lie. Judge Thatcher's got it. You git it. I want it."

"I hain't got no money, I tell you. You ask Judge Thatcher; he'll tell you the same."

Words For Everyday Use	**dan • dy** (dan´dē) *n.*, man who pays too much attention to his clothes and appearance
	airs (erz) *n.*, affected, superior manners

"All right. I'll ask him; and I'll make him pungle,[2] too, or I'll know the reason why. Say, how much you got in your pocket? I want it."

"I hain't got only a dollar, and I want that to—"

"It don't make no difference what you want it for—you just shell it out."[3]

He took it and bit it to see if it was good, and then he said he was going downtown to get some whisky; said he hadn't had a drink all day. When he had got out on the shed he put his head in again, and cussed me for putting on frills and trying to be better than him; and when I reckoned he was gone he come back and put his head in again, and told me to mind about that school, because he was going to lay for me and lick me if I didn't drop that.

Next day he was drunk, and he went to Judge Thatcher's and bullyragged[4] him, and tried to make him give up the money; but he couldn't, and then he swore he'd make the law force him.

The judge and the widow went to law to get the court to take me away from him and let one of them be my guardian; but it was a new judge that had just come, and he didn't know the old man; so he said courts mustn't interfere and separate families if they could help it; said he'd druther not take a child away from its father. So Judge Thatcher and the widow had to quit on the business.

◄ Whose side does the new judge take when Judge Thatcher and Widow Douglas try to take Huck from his father? What is the reasoning behind the new judge's decision?

That pleased the old man till he couldn't rest. He said he'd cowhide me till I was black and blue if I didn't raise some money for him. I borrowed three dollars from Judge Thatcher, and Pap took it and got drunk, and went a-blowing around and cussing and whooping and carrying on; and he kept it up all over town, with a tin pan, till most midnight; then they jailed him, and next day they had him before court, and jailed him again for a week. But he said he was satisfied; said he was boss of his son, and he'd make it warm for him.

When he got out the new judge said he was a-going to make a man of him. So he took him to his own house, and dressed him up clean and nice, and had him to breakfast and dinner and supper with the family, and was just old pie to him, so to speak. And after supper he talked to him about <u>temperance</u>

◄ In what way does the new judge try to help Huck's father? What does Huck's father promise to do?

2. **pungle.** Pay up
3. **Shell it out.** Pay it out
4. **bullyragged.** Bullied or browbeat; intimidated

Words For Everyday Use	**tem • per • ance** (tem´pər əns) *n.*, moderation or abstinence in the drinking of alcoholic beverages

and such things till the old man cried, and said he'd been a fool, and fooled away his life; but now he was a-going to turn over a new leaf and be a man nobody wouldn't be ashamed of, and he hoped the judge would help him and not look down on him. The judge said he could hug him for them words; so he cried, and his wife she cried again; Pap said he'd been a man that had always been misunderstood before, and the judge said he believed it. The old man said that what a man wanted that was down was sympathy, and the judge said it was so; so they cried again. And when it was bedtime the old man rose up and held out his hand, and says:

"Look at it, gentlemen and ladies all; take a-hold of it; shake it. There's a hand that was the hand of a hog; but it ain't so no more; it's the hand of a man that's started in on a new life, and'll die before he'll go back. You mark them words—don't forget I said them. It's a clean hand now; shake it—don't be afeard."

So they shook it, one after the other, all around, and cried. The judge's wife she kissed it. Then the old man he signed a pledge—made his mark. The judge said it was the holiest time on record, or something like that. Then they tucked the old man into a beautiful room, which was the spare room, and in the night some time he got powerful thirsty and clumb out on to the porch roof and slid down a stanchion and traded his new coat for a jug of forty-rod,[5] and clumb back again and had a good old time; and towards daylight he crawled out again, drunk as a fiddler, and rolled off the porch and broke his left arm in two places, and was most froze to death when somebody found him after sun-up. And when they come to look at that spare room they had to take soundings[6] before they could navigate it.

The judge he felt kind of sore. He said he reckoned a body could <u>reform</u> the old man with a shotgun, maybe, but he didn't know no other way.

► How does the new judge feel about Huck's father now?

---

5. **forty-rod.** Powerful whiskey
6. **take soundings.** Measure the depths of a body of water; here, meaning the room was deep in a chaotic mess

Words For Everyday Use

re • form (ri´fôrm) *vt.*, cause or persuade a person to give up misconduct and behave better

CHAPTER 6

Pap Struggles with the Death Angel

Well, pretty soon the old man was up and around again, and then he went for Judge Thatcher in the courts to make him give up that money, and he went for me, too, for not stopping school. He catched me a couple of times and <u>thrashed</u> me, but I went to school just the same, and dodged him or outrun him most of the time. I didn't want to go to school much before, but I reckoned I'd go now to spite Pap. That law trial was a slow business—appeared like they warn't ever going to get started on it; so every now and then I'd borrow two or three dollars off of the judge for him, to keep from getting a cowhiding. Every time he got money he got drunk; and every time he got drunk he raised Cain[1] around town; and every time he raised Cain he got jailed. He was just suited—this kind of thing was right in his line.

He got to hanging around the widow's too much and so she told him at last that if he didn't quit using around there she would make trouble for him. Well, wasn't he mad? He said he would show who was Huck Finn's boss. So he watched out for me one day in the spring, and catched me, and took me up the river about three mile in a skiff, and crossed over to the Illinois shore where it was woody and there warn't no houses but an old log hut in a place where the timber was so thick you couldn't find it if you didn't know where it was.

He kept me with him all the time, and I never got a chance to run off. We lived in that old cabin, and he always locked the door and put the key under his head nights. He had a gun which he had stole, I reckon, and we fished and hunted, and that was what we lived on. Every little while he locked me in and went down to the store, three miles, to the ferry, and traded fish and game for whisky, and fetched it home and got drunk and had a good time, and licked me. The widow she found out where I was by and by, and she sent a man over to try to get hold of me; but Pap drove him off

◄ Why does Huck's father continue to bother Judge Thatcher? Why does Huck continue to go to school, despite his father's punishments?

◄ What does Huck's father do to show that he is "Huck Finn's boss"?

---

1. **raised Cain.** Created a ruckus

Words For Everyday Use

thrash (thrash) *vt.,* give a severe beating

► What does Huck begin to like about living with his father? Why, however, does Huck eventually dislike being with his father? What does he decide to do?

with the gun, and it warn't long after that till I was used to being where I was, and liked it—all but the cowhide part.

It was kind of lazy and jolly, laying off comfortable all day, smoking and fishing, and no books nor study. Two months or more run along, and my clothes got to be all rags and dirt, and I didn't see how I'd ever got to like it so well at the widow's, where you had to wash, and eat on a plate, and comb up, and go to bed and get up regular, and be forever bothering over a book, and have old Miss Watson pecking at you all the time. I didn't want to go back no more. I had stopped cussing, because the widow didn't like it; but now I took to it again because Pap hadn't no objections. It was pretty good times up in the woods there, take it all around.

But by and by Pap got too handy with his hick'ry, and I couldn't stand it. I was all over <u>welts</u>. He got to going away so much, too, and locking me in. Once he locked me in and was gone three days. It was dreadful lonesome. I judged he had got drownded, and I wasn't ever going to get out any more. I was scared. I made up my mind I would fix up some way to leave there. I had tried to get out of that cabin many a time, but I couldn't find no way. There warn't a window to it big enough for a dog to get through. I couldn't get up the chimbly; it was too narrow. The door was thick, solid oak slabs. Pap was pretty careful not to leave a knife or anything in the cabin when he was away; I reckon I had hunted the place over as much as a hundred times; well, I was most all the time at it, because it was about the only way to put in the time. But this time I found something at last; I found an old rusty wood-saw without any handle; it was laid in between a rafter and the <u>clapboards</u> of the roof. I greased it up and went to work. There was an old horse-blanket nailed against the logs at the far end of the cabin behind the table, to keep the wind from blowing through the <u>chinks</u> and putting the candle out. I got under the table and raised the blanket, and went to work to saw a section of the big bottom log out—big enough to let me through. Well, it was a good long job, but I was getting towards the end of it when I heard pap's gun in the woods. I got rid of the signs of my work, and dropped the blanket and hid my saw, and pretty soon Pap come in.

Pap warn't in a good humor—so he was his natural self. He said he was downtown, and everything was going wrong. His

► Why isn't Pap in "good humor" when he returns from his trip to town? Why is Huck "shook up" to hear that the widow still wants to take him in?

Words For Everyday Use	**welt** (welt) *n.,* ridge raised on the skin by a blow
	clap • board (klab´ərd) *n.,* long, narrow board with one edge thicker than the other, used as siding on a building
	chink (chiŋk) *n.,* gap, narrow opening

lawyer said he reckoned he would win his lawsuit and get the money if they ever got started on the trial; but then there was ways to put it off a long time, and Judge Thatcher knowed how to do it. And he said people <u>allowed</u> there'd be another trial to get me away from him and give me to the widow for my guardian, and they guessed it would win this time. This shook me up considerable, because I didn't want to go back to the widow's any more and be so cramped up and sivilized, as they called it. Then the old man got to cussing, and cussed everything and everybody he could think of, and then cussed them all over again to make sure he hadn't skipped any, and after that he polished off with a kind of a general cuss all round, including a considerable parcel of people which he didn't know the names of, and so called them what's-his-name when he got to them, and went right along with his cussing.

He said he would like to see the widow get me. He said he would watch out, and if they tried to come any such game on him he knowed of a place six or seven mile off to <u>stow</u> me in, where they might hunt till they dropped and they couldn't find me. That made me pretty uneasy again, but only for a minute; I reckoned I wouldn't stay on hand till he got that chance.

◄ What does Pap say that makes Huck uneasy? What does Huck decide he must not do?

The old man made me go to the skiff and fetch the things he had got. There was a fifty-pound sack of corn meal, and a side of bacon, ammunition, and a four-gallon jug of whisky, and an old book and two newspapers for wadding,[2] besides some tow.[3] I toted up a load, and went back and set down on the <u>bow</u> of the skiff to rest. I thought it all over, and I reckoned I would walk off with the gun and some lines, and take to the woods when I run away. I guessed I wouldn't stay in one place, but just tramp right across the country, mostly night times, and hunt and fish to keep alive, and so get so far away that the old man nor the widow couldn't ever find me any more. I judged I would saw out and leave that night if pap got drunk enough, and I reckoned he would. I got so full of it I didn't notice how long I was staying till the old man hollered and asked me whether I was asleep or drownded.

◄ Where does Huck plan to go, and what will he take with him? When does he believe he will have the opportunity to go?

---

2. **wadding.** Matter stuffed into a gun's barrel to hold in the gunpowder
3. **tow.** Flax or hemp fibers

Words For Everyday Use	al • low (ə lou´) vt., give as one's opinion
	stow (stō) vt., store away
	bow (bou) n., front end of a boat

I got the things all up to the cabin, and then it was about dark. While I was cooking supper the old man took a swig or two and got sort of warmed up, and went to ripping again. He had been drunk over in town, and laid in the gutter all night, and he was a sight to look at. A body would 'a' thought he was Adam[4]—he was just all mud. Whenever his liquor begun to work he most always went for the govment. This time he says:

"Call this a govment! why, just look at it and see what it's like. Here's the law a-standing ready to take a man's son away from him—a man's own son, which he has had all the trouble and all the anxiety and all the expense of raising. Yes, just as that man has got that son raised at last, and ready to go to work and begin to do suthin' for *him* and give him a rest, the law up and goes for him. And they call *that* govment! That ain't all, nuther. The law backs that old Judge Thatcher up and helps him to keep me out o' my property. Here's what the law does: The law takes a man worth six thousand dollars and up'ards, and jams him into an old trap of a cabin like this, and lets him go round in clothes that ain't fitten for a hog. They call that govment! A man can't get his rights in a govment like this. Sometimes I've a mighty notion to just leave the country for good and all. Yes, and I *told* 'em so; I told old Thatcher so to his face. Lots of 'em heard me, and can tell what I said. Says I, for two cents I'd leave the blamed country and never come a-near it ag'in. Them's the very words. I says look at my hat—if you call it a hat—but the lid raises up and the rest of it goes down till it's below my chin, and then it ain't rightly a hat at all, but more like my head was shoved up through a jint o' stovepipe. Look at it, says I—such a hat for me to wear—one of the wealthiest men in this town if I could git my rights.

"Oh, yes, this is a wonderful govment, wonderful. Why, looky here. There was a free nigger there from Ohio—a mulatter,[5] most as white as a white man. He had the whitest shirt on you ever see, too, and the shiniest hat; and there ain't a man in that town that's got as fine clothes as what he had; and he had a gold watch and chain, and a silver-headed cane—the awfulest old gray-headed nabob[6] in the State. And what do you think? They said he was a p'fessor in a college, and could talk all kinds of languages, and knowed everything. And that ain't the wust. They said he could vote when

▶ How does Pap view himself and his situation? Is his description of his situation and his rights accurate? Why, or why not?

---

4. **Adam.** According to the Bible, the first man was created out of earth.

5. **mulatter.** Mulatto; person with one white parent and one black parent. Now considered an offensive term. At the time this novel takes place, race was so important that different terms were employed to specify the exact composition of a person's heritage. A person with one black ancestor could legally be held in slavery.

6. **nabob.** Rich or important person

he was at home. Well, that let me out. Thinks I, what is the country a-coming to? It was 'lection day, and I was just about to go and vote myself if I warn't too drunk to get there; but when they told me there was a state in this country where they'd let that nigger vote, I drawed out. I says I'll never vote ag'in. Them's the very words I said; they all heard me; and the country may rot for all me—I'll never vote ag'in as long as I live. And to see the cool way of that nigger—why, he wouldn't a give me the road if I hadn't shoved him out o' the way. I says to the people, why ain't this nigger put up at auction and sold?—that's what I want to know. And what do you reckon they said? Why, they said he couldn't be sold till he'd been in the state six months, and he hadn't been there that long yet. There, now—that's a <u>specimen</u>. They call that a govment that can't sell a free nigger till he's been in the state six months. Here's a govment that calls itself a govment, and lets on to be a govment, and thinks it is a govment, and yet's got to set stock-still for six whole months before it can take a-hold of a prowling, thieving, <u>infernal</u>, white-shirted free nigger, and—"

◀ In what way does Pap vent anger and hatred on the government and on innocent people?

Pap was a-going on so he never noticed where his old <u>limber</u> legs was taking him to, so he went head over heels over the tub of salt pork and barked both shins, and the rest of his speech was all the hottest kind of language—mostly hove at the nigger and the govment, though he give the tub some, too, all along, here and there. He hopped around the cabin considerable, first on one leg and then on the other, holding first one shin and then the other one, and at last he let out with his left foot all of a sudden and fetched the tub a rattling kick. But it warn't good judgment, because that was the boot that had a couple of his toes leaking out of the front end of it; so now he raised a howl that fairly made a body's hair raise, and down he went in the dirt, and rolled there, and held his toes; and the cussing he done then laid over anything he had ever done previous. He said so his own self afterwards. He had heard old Sowberry Hagan in his best days, and he said it laid over him, too; but I reckon that was sort of piling it on, maybe.

After supper Pap took the jug, and said he had enough whisky there for two drunks and one delirium tremens.[7] That

---

7. **delirium tremens.** Violent reaction, including hallucinations, to drinking excessive alcohol

Words For Everyday Use	spec • i • men (spes´ə mən) n., sample, example
	in • fer • nal (in fur´nəl) adj., hellish, inhuman
	lim • ber (lim´bər) adj., easily bent, flexible

was always his word. I judged he would be blind drunk in about an hour, and then I would steal the key, or saw myself out, one or t'other. He drank and drank, and tumbled down on his blankets by and by; but luck didn't run my way. He didn't go sound asleep, but was uneasy. He groaned and moaned and thrashed around this way and that for a long time. At last I got so sleepy I couldn't keep my eyes open all I could do, and so before I knowed what I was about I was sound asleep, and the candle burning.

▶ What strange behavior does Pap exhibit after drinking all night?

I don't know how long I was asleep, but all of a sudden there was an awful scream and I was up. There was Pap looking wild, and skipping around every which way and yelling about snakes. He said they was crawling up his legs; and then he would give a jump and scream, and say one had bit him on the cheek—but I couldn't see no snakes. He started and run round and round the cabin, hollering "Take him off! take him off! he's biting me on the neck!" I never see a man look so wild in the eyes. Pretty soon he was all fagged out,[8] and fell down panting; then he rolled over and over wonderful fast, kicking things every which way, and striking and grabbing at the air with his hands, and screaming and saying there was devils a-hold of him. He wore out by and by, and laid still a while, moaning. Then he laid stiller, and didn't make a sound. I could hear the owls and the wolves away off in the woods, and it seemed terrible still. He was laying over by the corner. By and by he raised up part way and listened, with his head to one side. He says, very low:

"Tramp—tramp—tramp; that's the dead; tramp—tramp—tramp; they're coming after me; but I won't go. Oh, they're here! don't touch me—don't! hands off—they're cold; let go. Oh, let a poor devil alone!"

Then he went down on all fours and crawled off, begging them to let him alone, and he rolled himself up in his blanket and wallowed in under the old pine table, still a-begging; and then he went to crying. I could hear him through the blanket.

By and by he rolled out and jumped up on his feet looking wild, and he see me and went for me. He chased me round and round the place with a clasp-knife, calling me the Angel of Death, and saying he would kill me, and then I couldn't come for him no more. I begged, and told him I was only Huck; but he laughed *such* a screechy laugh, and roared and cussed, and kept on chasing me up. Once when I turned short and dodged under his arm he made a grab and got me

---

8. **fagged out.** Tired

by the jacket between my shoulders, and I thought I was gone; but I slid out of the jacket quick as lightning, and saved myself. Pretty soon he was all tired out, and dropped down with his back against the door, and said he would rest a minute and then kill me. He put his knife under him, and said he would sleep and get strong, and then he would see who was who.

So he dozed off pretty soon. By and by I got the old split-bottom chair and clumb up as easy as I could, not to make any noise, and got down the gun. I slipped the ramrod[9] down it to make sure it was loaded, then I laid it across the turnip barrel, pointing towards Pap, and set down behind it to wait for him to stir. And how slow and still the time did drag along.

◄ *What does Huck do when he knows Pap is asleep?*

9. **ramrod.** Rod used to push ammunition into a gun

CHAPTER 7

I Fool Pap and Get Away

"Git up! What you 'bout?"

I opened my eyes and looked around, trying to make out where I was. It was after sunup, and I had been sound asleep. Pap was standing over me looking sour—and sick, too. He says:

"What you doin' with this gun?"

I judged he didn't know nothing about what he had been doing, so I says:

"Somebody tried to get in, so I was laying for him."

"Why didn't you roust me out?"

"Well, I tried to, but I couldn't; I couldn't budge you."

"Well, all right. Don't stand there <u>palavering</u> all day, but out with you and see if there's a fish on the lines for breakfast. I'll be along in a minute."

He unlocked the door, and I cleared out up the river-bank. I noticed some pieces of limbs and such things floating down, and a sprinkling of bark; so I knowed the river had begun to rise. I reckoned I would have great times now if I was over at the town. The June rise used to be always luck for me; because as soon as that rise begins here comes cordwood floating down, and pieces of log rafts—sometimes a dozen logs together; so all you have to do is to catch them and sell them to the woodyards and the sawmill.

I went along up the bank with one eye out for Pap and t'other one out for what the rise might fetch along. Well, all at once here comes a canoe; just a beauty, too, about thirteen or fourteen foot long, riding high like a duck. I shot head-first off of the bank like a frog, clothes and all on, and struck out for the canoe. I just expected there'd be somebody laying down in it, because people often done that to fool folks, and when a chap had pulled a skiff out most to it they'd raise up and laugh at him. But it warn't so this time. It was a drift canoe sure enough, and I clumb in and paddled her ashore. Thinks I, the old man will be glad when he sees this—she's worth ten dollars. But when I got to shore pap wasn't in sight yet, and as I was running her into a little creek like a gully,

▶ What story does Huck invent to explain why he has the gun?

▶ What does the rising of the river mean to Huck? What does Huck find in the river?

▶ What does Huck do with the canoe when he discovers that Pap is nowhere in sight? For what does he plan to use the canoe?

all hung over with vines and willows, I struck another idea: I judged I'd hide her good, and then, 'stead of taking to the woods when I run off, I'd go down the river about fifty mile and camp in one place for good, and not have such a rough time tramping on foot.

It was pretty close to the shanty, and I thought I heard the old man coming all the time; but I got her hid; and then I out and looked around a bunch of willows, and there was the old man down the path a piece just drawing a bead on a bird with his gun. So he hadn't seen anything.

When he got along I was hard at it taking up a "trot" line. He abused me a little for being so slow; but I told him I fell in the river, and that was what made me so long. I knowed he would see I was wet, and then he would be asking questions. We got five catfish off the lines and went home.

While we laid off after breakfast to sleep up, both of us being about wore out, I got to thinking that if I could fix up some way to keep Pap and the widow from trying to follow me, it would be a certainer thing than trusting to luck to get far enough off before they missed me; you see, all kinds of things might happen. Well, I didn't see no way for a while, but by and by pap raised up a minute to drink another barrel of water, and he says:

◄ What does Huck believe he must do to be successful in his escape from Pap and the widow?

"Another time a man comes a-prowling round here you roust me out, you hear? That man warn't here for no good. I'd 'a' shot him. Next time you roust me out, you hear?"

Then he dropped down and went to sleep again; what he had been saying give me the very idea I wanted. I says to myself, I can fix it now so nobody won't think of following me.

About twelve o'clock we turned out and went along up the bank. The river was coming up pretty fast, and lots of driftwood going by on the rise. By and by along comes part of a log raft—nine logs fast together. We went out with the skiff and towed it ashore. Then we had dinner. Anybody but Pap would 'a' waited and seen the day through, so as to catch more stuff; but that warn't Pap's style. Nine logs was enough for one time; he must shove right over to town and sell. So he locked me in and took the skiff, and started off towing the raft about half past three. I judged he wouldn't come back that night. I waited till I reckoned he had got a good start; then I out with my saw, and went to work on that log again. Before he was t'other side of the river I was out of the hole; him and his raft was just a speck on the water away off yonder.

◄ Why does Pap go into town? What does Huck do to escape the locked cabin?

I took the sack of cornmeal and took it to where the canoe was hid, and shoved the vines and branches apart and put it in; then I done the same with the side of bacon; then the whisky-jug. I took all the coffee and sugar there was, and all the ammunition; I took the wadding; I took the bucket and gourd; I took a dipper and a tin cup, and my old saw and two blankets, and the skillet and the coffeepot. I took fishlines and matches and other things—everything that was worth a cent. I cleaned out the place. I wanted an axe, but there wasn't any, only the one out at the woodpile, and I knowed why I was going to leave that. I fetched out the gun, and now I was done.

I had wore the ground a good deal crawling out of the hole and dragging out so many things. So I fixed that as good as I could from the outside by scattering dust on the place, which covered up the smoothness and the sawdust. Then I fixed the piece of log back into its place, and put two rocks under it and one against it to hold it there, for it was bent up at that place and didn't quite touch ground. If you stood four or five foot away and didn't know it was sawed, you wouldn't never notice it; and besides, this was the back of the cabin, and it warn't likely anybody would go around there.

It was all grass clear to the canoe, so I hadn't left a track. I followed around to see. I stood on the bank and looked out over the river. All safe. So I took the gun and went up a piece into the woods, and was hunting around for some birds when I see a wild pig; hogs soon went wild in them bottoms[1] after they had got away from the prairie farms. I shot this fellow and took him into camp.

I took the ax and smashed in the door. I beat it and hacked it considerable a-doing it. I fetched the pig in, and took him back nearly to the table and hacked into his throat with the ax, and laid him down on the ground to bleed; I say ground because it *was* ground—hard packed, and no boards. Well, next I took an old sack and put a lot of big rocks in it—all I could drag—and I started it from the pig, and dragged it to the door and through the woods down to the river and dumped it in, and down it sunk, out of sight. You could easy see that something had been dragged over the ground. I did wish Tom Sawyer was there; I knowed he would take an interest in this kind of business, and throw in the fancy touches. Nobody could spread himself like Tom Sawyer in such a thing as that.

Well, last I pulled out some of my hair, and blooded the ax good, and stuck it on the back side, and slung the ax in the corner. Then I took up the pig and held him to my breast with my jacket (so he couldn't drip) till I got a good piece below the house and then dumped him into the river. Now I thought of something else. So I went and got the bag of meal

► How does Huck hide the evidence of his escape from the cabin? Why does he believe that nobody will notice the hole he made?

► Why does Huck wish Tom Sawyer could be there? In what way would Tom add to the adventure?

► What scene is Huck trying to create? What does he want people to think?

---

1. **bottoms.** Lowlands through which a river flows

and my old saw out of the canoe, and fetched them to the house. I took the bag to where it used to stand, and ripped a hole in the bottom of it with the saw, for there warn't no knives and forks on the place—Pap done everything with his clasp-knife about the cooking. Then I carried the sack about a hundred yards across the grass and through the willows east of the house, to a shallow lake that was five mile wide and full of rushes—and ducks too, you might say, in the season. There was a slough[2] or a creek leading out of it on the other side that went miles away, I don't know where, but it didn't go to the river. The meal sifted out and made a little track all the way to the lake. I dropped Pap's whetstone[3] there too, so as to look like it had been done by accident. Then I tied up the rip in the meal sack with a string, so it wouldn't leak no more, and took it and my saw to the canoe again.

It was about dark now; so I dropped the canoe down the river under some willows that hung over the bank, and waited for the moon to rise. I made fast to a willow; then I took a bite to eat, and by and by laid down in the canoe to smoke a pipe and lay out a plan. I says to myself, they'll follow the track of that sackful of rocks to the shore and then drag the river for me. And they'll follow that meal track to the lake and go browsing down the creek that leads out of it to find the robbers that killed me and took the things. They won't ever hunt the river for anything but my dead carcass. They'll soon get tired of that, and won't bother no more about me. All right; I can stop anywhere I want to. Jackson's Island is good enough for me; I know that island pretty well, and nobody ever comes there. And then I can paddle over to town nights, and slink around and pick up things I want. Jackson's Island's the place.

I was pretty tired, and the first thing I knowed I was asleep. When I woke up I didn't know where I was for a minute. I set up and looked around, a little scared. Then I remembered. The river looked miles and miles across. The moon was so bright I could 'a' counted the drift logs that went a-slipping along, black and still, hundreds of yards out from shore. Everything was dead quiet, and it looked late, and *smelt* late. You know what I mean—I don't know the words to put it in.

I took a good gap and a stretch, and was just going to unhitch and start when I heard a sound away over the water. I listened. Pretty soon I made it out. It was that dull kind of a regular sound that comes from oars working in rowlocks

Why does Huck drag around the sack of rocks? the sack of cornmeal? Why does Huck decide to go to Jackson's Island?

2. **slough.** Swamp, bog, or marsh that is part of an inlet
3. **whetstone.** Abrasive stone for sharpening knives or other edged tools

when it's a still night. I peeped out through the willow branches, and there it was—a skiff, away across the water. I couldn't tell how many was in it. It kept a-coming, and when it was abreast of me I see there warn't but one man in it. Thinks I, maybe it's Pap, though I warn't expecting him. He dropped below me with the current, and by and by he came a-swinging up shore in the easy water, and he went by so close I could 'a' reached out the gun and touched him. Well, it *was* Pap, sure enough—and sober, too, by the way he laid his oars.

► Where does Huck go after spotting Pap in the skiff?

I didn't lose no time. The next minute I was a-spinning downstream soft, but quick, in the shade of the bank. I made two mile and a half, and then struck out a quarter of a mile or more toward the middle of the river, because pretty soon I would be passing the ferry landing, and people might see me and hail me. I got out amongst the driftwood, and then laid down in the bottom of the canoe and let her float. I laid there, and had a good rest and a smoke out of my pipe, looking away into the sky; not a cloud in it. The sky looks ever so deep when you lay down on your back in the moonshine; I never knowed it before. And how far a body can hear on the water such nights! I heard people talking at the ferry landing. I heard what they said, too—every word of it. One man said it was getting towards the long days and the short nights now. T'other one said *this* warn't one of the short ones, he reckoned—and then they laughed, and he said it over again, and they laughed again; then they waked up another fellow and told him, and laughed, but he didn't laugh; he ripped out something brisk, and said let him alone. The first fellow said he 'lowed to tell it to his old woman—she would think it was pretty good; but he said that warn't nothing to some things he had said in his time. I heard one man say it was nearly three o'clock, and he hoped daylight wouldn't wait more than about a week longer. After that the talk got further and further away, and I couldn't make out the words any more; but I could hear the mumble, and now and then a laugh, too, but it seemed a long ways off.

► To what does Huck compare Jackson's Island at night?

I was away below the ferry now. I rose up, and there was Jackson's Island, about two mile and a half downstream, heavy-timbered and standing up out of the middle of the river, big and dark and solid, like a steamboat without any lights. There warn't any signs of the bar at the head—it was all under water now.

It didn't take me long to get there. I shot past the head at a ripping rate, the current was so swift, and then I got into the dead water and landed on the side towards the Illinois shore. I run the canoe into a deep dent in the bank that I knowed about; I had to part the willow branches to get in; and when I made fast nobody could 'a' seen the canoe from the outside.

I went up and set down on a log at the head of the island, and looked out on the big river and the black driftwood and away over to the town, three mile away, where there was three or four lights twinkling. A monstrous big lumber raft was about a mile upstream, coming along down, with a lantern in the middle of it. I watched it come creeping down, and when it was most abreast of where I stood I heard a man say, "<u>Stern</u> oars, there! heave her head to stabboard!"[4] I heard that just as plain as if the man was by my side.

There was a little gray in the sky now; so I stepped into the woods, and laid down for a nap.

---

4. **stabboard.** Starboard, the right-hand side of a boat from the perspective of one who is facing the front, or bow, of the boat

Words For Everyday Use

stern (sturn) *n.*, rear end of a boat

Responding to the Selection

Huck's life changes when his father reappears. What are your feelings toward Huck's father and the way he treats Huck? What might you have done if you were in Huck's situation?

Reviewing the Selection

Recalling and Interpreting

1. **R:** What signs alert Huck to the fact that his father might be back in town? What does he decide to do with his money?

2. **I:** How does Huck seem to feel about his father? What does Huck's wish to hide his money reveal about what Pap might be like as a person? What does this action show about Huck's practical nature?

3. **R:** Where do Huck and Pap finally meet? What comments does Pap make about Huck's new lifestyle? For what, primarily, does Pap want money?

4. **I:** Why do you think Pap feels so threatened by the fact that Huck is going to school and living with such material refinements as clean clothes and a rug on his bedroom floor? Does Pap seem most concerned about Huck's welfare or is he most concerned about himself? How do you know this?

5. **R:** For what purpose does Huck's father go to court to retain custody of Huck? What does he want? Whose side does the new judge take when Judge Thatcher and Widow Douglas try to take custody of Huck?

6. **I:** Do you think Pap is truly concerned about being a father to his son? What, most likely, are his reasons for fighting so strongly to be with Huck? In what ways does he show that he resents losing power over Huck almost as much as he resents the loss of Huck's money?

7. **R:** What does Pap do to lose the support of the new judge? Why does Pap kidnap Huck and keep him locked in his cabin? What incident causes Huck to decide he must escape?

8. **I:** What does Huck like about living with Pap, rather than the Widow Douglas? What is the worst part of living with Pap?

Synthesizing

9. Why might Huck feel that his only option is escape from the only homes he has known—with the widow and with Pap? What does life with the widow represent to him? What does life with Pap represent to him?

10. What qualities does Huck show when he is held captive by his father? What kind of escape does he plan? Why, in his mind, is it necessary to plan the escape so that people will think he has been killed?

Understanding Literature (QUESTIONS FOR DISCUSSION)

1. Motivation. Motivation is a force that moves a character to think, feel, or behave in a certain way. After years of neglecting and abusing Huck, Pap returns to fight in court for custody of Huck. What is his motive? Do you think he has any motives besides Huck's money and a desire for control? What is Huck's motivation in planning his escape?

2. Motif. A **motif** is any element that recurs in one or more works of literature or art. Superstition is an important motif in *Adventures of Huckleberry Finn.* Throughout the novel, readers will see characters turning to superstitious beliefs. What are some superstitions that Huck and Jim believe?

CHAPTER 8

I Spare Miss Watson's Jim

The sun was up so high when I waked that I judged it was after eight o'clock. I laid there in the grass and the cool shade thinking about things, and feeling rested and ruther comfortable and satisfied. I could see the sun out at one or two holes, but mostly it was big trees all about, and gloomy in there amongst them. There was freckled places on the ground where the light sifted down through the leaves, and the freckled places swapped about a little, showing there was a little breeze up there. A couple of squirrels set on a limb and jabbered at me very friendly.

I was powerful lazy and comfortable—didn't want to get up and cook breakfast. Well, I was dozing off again when I thinks I hears a deep sound of "boom!" away up the river. I rouses up, and rests on my elbow and listens; pretty soon I hears it again. I hopped up, and went and looked out at a hole in the leaves, and I see a bunch of smoke laying on the water a long ways up—about abreast the ferry. And there was the ferryboat full of people floating along down. I knowed what was the matter now. "Boom!" I see the white smoke squirt out of the ferryboat's side. You see, they was firing cannon over the water, trying to make my carcass come to the top.[1]

I was pretty hungry, but it warn't going to do for me to start a fire, because they might see the smoke. So I set there and watched the cannon smoke and listened to the boom. The river was a mile wide there, and it always looks pretty on a summer morning—so I was having a good enough time seeing them hunt for my remainders if I only had a bite to eat. Well, then I happened to think how they always put quicksilver[2] in loaves of bread and float them off, because they always go right to the drownded carcass and stop there. So, says I, I'll keep a lookout, and if any of them's floating around after me I'll give them a show. I changed to the Illinois edge of the island to see what luck I could have, and I warn't disappointed. A big double loaf come along, and I most got it with a long stick, but my foot slipped and she floated out further. Of course I was where the current set in the closest to the shore—I knowed enough for that. But by and by along comes another one, and this time I won. I took

Margin notes:

► How does Huck feel as he awakens to his first morning on the island?

► Why are cannons being fired over the water?

► Why is bread floating in the water? What does Huck do with the bread?

---

1. **firing cannon . . . top.** Folk wisdom of the period thought cannon fire would raise a drowned corpse from the bottom of a body of water.

2. **quicksilver.** Mercury

out the plug and shook out the little dab of quicksilver, and set my teeth in. It was "baker's bread"—what the quality eat; none of your lowdown cornpone.[3]

I got a good place amongst the leaves, and set there on a log, munching the bread and watching the ferryboat, and very well satisfied. And then something struck me. I says, now I reckon the widow or the parson or somebody prayed that this bread would find me, and here it has gone and done it. So there ain't no doubt but there is something in that thing—that is, there's something in it when a body like the widow or the parson prays, but it don't work for me, and I reckon it don't work for only just the right kind.

◄ *What thoughts does Huck have about prayer as he eats his bread?*

I lit a pipe and had a good long smoke, and went on watching. The ferryboat was floating with the current, and I allowed I'd have a chance to see who was aboard when she come along, because she would come in close, where the bread did. When she'd got pretty well along down towards me, I put out my pipe and went to where I fished out the bread, and laid down behind a log on the bank in a little open place. Where the log forked I could peep through.

◄ *Why does Huck want to get a closer look at the ferryboat? Who does Huck see on board?*

By and by she come along, and she drifted in so close that they could 'a' run out a plank and walked ashore. Most everybody was on the boat. Pap, and Judge Thatcher, and Becky Thatcher, and Joe Harper, and Tom Sawyer, and his old Aunt Polly, and Sid and Mary, and plenty more. Everybody was talking about the murder, but the captain broke in and says:

brings everyone together

"Look sharp, now; the current sets in the closest here, and maybe he's washed ashore and got tangled amongst the brush at the water's edge. I hope so, anyway."

I didn't hope so. They all crowded up and leaned over the rails, nearly in my face, and kept still, watching with all their might. I could see them first-rate, but they couldn't see me. Then the captain sung out: "Stand away!" and the cannon let off such a blast right before me that it made me deef with the noise and pretty near blind with the smoke, and I judged I was gone. If they'd 'a' had some bullets in, I reckon they'd 'a' got the corpse they was after. Well, I see I warn't hurt, thanks to goodness. The boat floated on and went out of sight around the shoulder of the island. I could hear the booming now and then, further and further off, and by and by, after an hour, I didn't hear it no more. The island was three mile long. I judged they had got to the foot, and was giving it up. But they didn't yet awhile. They turned around the foot of the island and started up the channel on the Missouri side, under steam, and booming once in a while as they went. I

---

3. **cornpone.** Panfried bread made of cornmeal

▶ What does Huck do when he knows the ferryboat is gone and he will not be spotted?

▶ How is Huck feeling? What does he do to pass the time?

crossed over to that side and watched them. When they got abreast the head of the island they quit shooting and dropped over to the Missouri shore and went home to the town.

I knowed I was all right now. Nobody else would come a-hunting after me. I got my traps[4] out of the canoe and made me a nice camp in the thick woods. I made a kind of a tent out of my blankets to put my things under so the rain couldn't get at them. I catched a catfish and haggled him open with my saw, and towards sundown I started my camp-fire and had supper. Then I set out a line to catch some fish for breakfast.

When it was dark I set by my campfire smoking, and feel-ing pretty well satisfied; but by and by it got sort of lone-some, and so I went and set on the bank and listened to the current swashing along, and counted the stars and drift logs and rafts that come down, and then went to bed; there ain't no better way to put in time when you are lonesome.

And so for three days and nights. No difference—just the same thing. But the next day I went exploring around down through the island. I was boss of it; it all belonged to me, so to say, and I wanted to know all about it; but mainly I want-ed to put in the time. I found plenty strawberries, ripe and prime; and green summer grapes, and green razberries; and the green blackberries was just beginning to show. They would all come handy by and by, I judged.

Well, I went fooling along in the deep woods till I judged I warn't far from the foot of the island. I had my gun along, but I hadn't shot nothing; it was for protection; thought I would kill some game nigh[5] home. About this time I mighty near stepped on a good-sized snake, and it went sliding off through the grass and flowers, and I after it, try-ing to get a shot at it. I clipped along, and all of a sudden I bounded right on to the ashes of a campfire that was still smoking.

My heart jumped up amongst my lungs. I never waited for to look further, but uncocked my gun and went sneaking back on my tiptoes as fast as ever I could. Every now and then I stopped a second amongst the thick leaves and lis-tened, but my breath come so hard I couldn't hear nothing else. I slunk along another piece further, then listened again; and so on, and so on. If I see a stump, I took it for a man; if I trod on a stick and broke it, it made me feel like a person had cut one of my breaths in two and I only got half, and the short half, too.

---

4. **traps.** Trappings; gear, equipment
5. **nigh.** Near

When I got to camp I warn't feeling very <u>brash</u>, there warn't much sand in my craw; but I says, this ain't no time to be fooling around. So I got all my traps into my canoe again so as to have them out of sight, and I put out the fire and scattered the ashes around to look like an old last year's camp, and then clumb a tree.

I reckon I was up in the tree two hours; but I didn't see nothing, I didn't hear nothing—I only *thought* I heard and seen as much as a thousand things. Well, I couldn't stay up there forever; so at last I got down, but I kept in the thick woods and on the lookout all the time. All I could get to eat was berries and what was left over from breakfast.

By the time it was night I was pretty hungry. So when it was good and dark I slid out from shore before moonrise and paddled over to the Illinois bank—about a quarter of a mile. I went out in the woods and cooked a supper, and I had about made up my mind I would stay there all night when I hear a *plunkety-plunk, plunkety-plunk,* and says to myself, horses coming; and next I hear people's voices. I got every-thing into the canoe as quick as I could, and then went creeping through the woods to see what I could find out. I hadn't got far when I hear a man say:

◄ What does Huck hear? What does he decide he must do?

"We better camp here if we can find a good place; the horses is about beat out. Let's look around."

I didn't wait, but shoved out and paddled away easy. I tied up in the old place, and reckoned I would sleep in the canoe.

I didn't sleep much. I couldn't, somehow, for thinking. And every time I waked up I thought somebody had me by the neck. So the sleep didn't do me no good. By and by I says to myself, I can't live this way; I'm a-going to find out who it is that's here on the island with me; I'll find it out or bust. Well, I felt better right off.

So I took my paddle and slid out from shore just a step or two, and then let the canoe drop along down amongst the shadows. The moon was shining, and outside of the shadows it made it most as light as day. I poked along well on to an hour, everything still as rocks and sound asleep. Well, by this time I was most down to the foot of the island. A little ripply, cool breeze begun to blow, and that was as good as saying the night was about done. I give her a turn with the paddle and brung her nose to shore; then I got my gun and slipped out

Words For Everyday Use	**brash** (brash) *adj.,* bold

and into the edge of the woods. I sat down there on a log, and looked out through the leaves. I see the moon go off watch, and the darkness begin to blanket the river. But in a little while I see a pale streak over the treetops, and knowed the day was coming. So I took my gun and slipped off towards where I had run across that campfire, stopping every minute or two to listen. But I hadn't no luck somehow; I couldn't seem to find the place. But by and by, sure enough, I catched a glimpse of fire away through the trees. I went for it, cautious and slow. By and by I was close enough to have a look, and there laid a man on the ground. It most give me the fantods.[6] He had a blanket around his head, and his head was nearly in the fire. I set there behind a clump of bushes in about six foot of him, and kept my eyes on him steady. It was getting gray daylight now. Pretty soon he gapped and stretched himself and hove off the blanket, and it was Miss Watson's Jim! I bet I was glad to see him. I says:

"Hello, Jim!" and skipped out.

He bounced up and stared at me wild. Then he drops down on his knees, and puts his hands together and says:

"Doan' hurt me—don't! I hain't ever done no harm to a ghos'. I alwuz liked dead people, en done all I could for 'em. You go en git in de river ag'in, whah you b'longs, en doan' do nuffn to Ole Jim, 'at 'uz alwuz yo' fren'."

Well, I warn't long making him understand I warn't dead. I was ever so glad to see Jim. I warn't lonesome now. I told him I warn't afraid of *him* telling the people where I was. I talked along, but he only set there and looked at me; never said nothing. Then I says:

"It's good daylight. Le's get breakfast. Make up your campfire good."

"What's de use er makin' up de campfire to cook strawbries en sich truck? But you got a gun, hain't you? Den we kin git sumfn better den strawbries."

"Strawberries and such truck," I says. "Is that what you live on?"

"I couldn' git nuffn else," he says.

"Why, how long you been on the island, Jim?"

"I come heah de night arter you's killed."

"What, all that time?"

"Yes-indeedy."

"And ain't you had nothing but that kind of rubbage to eat?"

"No, sah—nuffn else."

"Well, you must be most starved, ain't you?"

▶ How does Huck feel about finding Jim on the island? What is Jim's first reaction to Huck? Why does he react this way?

▶ When did Jim come to the island?

---

6. **fantods.** Condition of nervous anxiety

"I reck'n I could eat a hoss. I think I could. How long you ben on de islan'?"

"Since the night I got killed."

"No! W'y, what has you lived on? But you got a gun. Oh, yes, you got a gun. Dat's good. Now you kill sumfn en I'll make up de fire."

So we went over to where the canoe was, and while he built a fire in a grassy open place amongst the trees, I fetched meal and bacon and coffee, and coffeepot and frying pan, and sugar and tin cups, and the nigger was set back considerable, because he reckoned it was all done with witchcraft. I catched a good big catfish, too, and Jim cleaned him with his knife, and fried him.

When breakfast was ready we lolled on the grass and eat it smoking hot. Jim laid it in with all his might, for he was most about starved. Then when we had got pretty well stuffed, we laid off and lazied.

By and by Jim says: "But looky here, Huck, who wuz it dat 'uz killed in dat shanty ef it warn't you?"

Then I told him the whole thing, and he said it was smart. He said Tom Sawyer couldn't get up no better plan than what I had. Then I says:

"How do you come to be here, Jim, and how'd you get here?"

He looked pretty uneasy, and didn't say nothing for a minute. Then he says:

"Maybe I better not tell."

"Why, Jim?"

"Well, dey's reasons. But you wouldn' tell on me ef I 'uz to tell you, would you, Huck?"

"Blamed if I would, Jim."

"Well, I b'lieve you, Huck. I—I *run off*."

"Jim!"

"But mind, you said you wouldn' tell—you know you said you wouldn' tell, Huck."

"Well, I did. I said I wouldn't, and I'll stick to it. Honest *Injun*, I will. People would call me a low-down Abolitionist[7] and despise me for keeping mum—but that don't make no difference. I ain't a-going to tell, and I ain't a-going back there, anyways. So, now, le's know all about it."

"Well, you see, it 'uz dis way. Ole missus—dat's Miss Watson—she pecks on me all de time, en treats me pooty rough, but she alwuz said she wouldn' sell me down to Orleans.[8] But I noticed dey wuz a nigger trader roun' de place

◄ What does Jim think of Huck's plan to escape Pap?

◄ What promise does Huck make to Jim? Why does he make this promise, even though he knows people would "despise" him for doing so?

◄ Why did Jim leave Miss Watson? What was she planning to do to him?

---

7. **Abolitionist.** One who favored ending slavery in the United States

8. **Orleans.** New Orleans. Slaves were treated far more harshly in the Deep South than in states such as Missouri which bordered free states.

considable lately, en I begin to git oneasy. Well, one night I creeps to de do' pooty late, en de do' warn't quite shet, en I hear old missus tell de widder she gwyne to sell me down to Orleans, but she didn' want to, but she could git eight hund'd dollars for me, en it 'uz sich a big stack o' money she couldn' resis'. De widder she try to git her to say she wouldn' do it, but I never waited to hear de res'. I lit out mighty quick, I tell you.

"I tuck out en shin down de hill, en 'spec to steal a skift 'long de sho' som'ers 'bove de town, but dey wuz people a-stirring yit, so I hid in de ole tumbledown cooper shop[9] on de bank to wait for everybody to go 'way. Well, I wuz dah all night. Dey wuz somebody roun' all de time. 'Long 'bout six in de mawnin' skifts begin to go by, en 'bout eight er nine every skift dat went 'long wuz talkin' 'bout how yo' pap come over to de town en say you's killed. Dese las' skifts wuz full o' ladies en genlmen a-goin' over for to see de place. Sometimes dey'd pull up at de sho' en take a res' b'fo' dey started acrost, so by de talk I got to know all 'bout de killin'. I 'uz powerful sorry you's killed, Huck, but I ain't no mo' now.

▶ On the day Jim began his escape, why was he able to hide all day without raising suspicion?

"I laid dah under de shavin's all day. I 'uz hungry, but I warn't afeard; bekase I knowed ole missus en de widder wuz goin' to start to de camp meet'n'[10] right arter breakfas' en be gone all day, en dey knows I goes off wid de cattle 'bout daylight, so dey wouldn' 'spec to see me roun' de place, en so dey wouldn' miss me tell arter dark in de evenin'. De yuther servants wouldn' miss me, kase dey'd shin out en take holiday soon as de ole folks 'uz out'n de way.

"Well, when it come dark I tuck out up de river road, en went 'bout two mile er more to whah dey warn't no houses. I'd made up my mine 'bout what I's agwyne to do. You see, ef I kep' on tryin' to git away afoot, de dogs 'ud track me; ef I stole a skift to cross over, dey'd miss dat skift, you see, en dey'd know 'bout whah I'd lan' on de yuther side, en whah to pick up my track. So I says, a raff is what I's arter; it doan' *make* no track.

"I see a light a-comin' roun' de p'int bymeby, so I wade' in en shove' a log ahead o' me en swum more'n halfway acrost de river, en got in 'mongst de driftwood, en kep' my head down low, en kinder swum agin de current tell de raff come along. Den I swum to de stern uv it en tuck a-holt. It clouded up en 'uz pooty dark for a little while. So I clumb up en laid down on de planks. De men 'uz all 'way yonder in de middle, whah de lantern wuz. De river wuz a-risin', en dey wuz

---

9. **cooper shop.** Store that made and sold barrels
10. **camp meet'n.** Camp meeting; religious revival held outdoors by a traveling preacher

a good current; so I reck'n'd 'at by fo' in de mawnin' I'd be twenty-five mile down de river, en den I'd slip in jis b'fo' daylight en swim asho', en take to de woods on de Illinois side.[11]

◀ How did Jim end up on the island?

"But I didn' have no luck. When we 'uz mos' down to de head er de islan' a man begin to come aft wid de lantern. I see it warn't no use fer to wait, so I slid overboard en struck out fer de islan'. Well, I had a notion I could lan' mos' anywhers, but I couldn't—bank too bluff. I 'uz mos' to de foot er de islan' b'fo' I foun' a good place. I went into de woods en jedged I wouldn' fool wid raffs no mo', long as dey move de lantern roun' so. I had my pipe en a plug er dog-leg, en some matches in my cap, en dey warn't wet, so I 'uz all right."

"And so you ain't had no meat nor bread to eat all this time? Why didn't you get mud turkles?"[12]

"How you gwyne to git 'm? You can't slip up on um en grab um; en how's a body gwyne to hit um wid a rock? How could a body do it in de night? En I warn't gwyne to show mysef on de bank in de daytime."

◀ In what ways have Huck and Jim had quite similar experiences?

"Well, that's so. You've had to keep in the woods all the time, of course. Did you hear 'em shooting the cannon?"

"Oh, yes. I knowed dey was arter you. I see um go by heah—watched um thoo de bushes."

Some young birds come along, flying a yard or two at a time and lighting. Jim said it was a sign it was going to rain. He said it was a sign when young chickens flew that way, and so he reckoned it was the same way when young birds done it. I was going to catch some of them, but Jim wouldn't let me. He said it was death. He said his father laid mighty sick once, and some of them catched a bird, and his old granny said his father would die, and he did.

And Jim said you mustn't count the things you are going to cook for dinner, because that would bring bad luck. The same if you shook the tablecloth after sundown. And he said if a man owned a beehive and that man died, the bees must be told about it before sunup next morning, or else the bees would all weaken down and quit work and die. Jim said bees wouldn't sting idiots; but I didn't believe that, because I had tried them lots of times myself, and they wouldn't sting me.

I had heard about some of these things before, but not all

---

11. **Illinois side.** Illinois was a free state, i.e., slavery was banned there
12. **turkles.** Turtles

| Words For Everyday Use | **light** (līt) *vi.,* come to rest after traveling through the air |

► *What does Huck notice about the signs Jim describes? What is Jim's response?*

of them. Jim knowed all kinds of signs. He said he knowed most everything. I said it looked to me like all the signs was about bad luck, and so I asked him if there warn't any good-luck signs. He says:

"Mighty few—an' *dey* ain't no use to a body. What you want to know when good luck's a-comin' for? Want to keep it off?" And he said: "Ef you's got hairy arms en a hairy breas', it's a sign dat you's a-gwyne to be rich. Well, dey's some use in a sign like dat, 'kase it's so fur ahead. You see, maybe you's got to be po' a long time fust, en so you might git discourage' en kill yo'sef 'f you didn' know by de sign dat you gwyne to be rich bymeby."

"Have you got hairy arms and a hairy breast, Jim?"

"What's de use to ax dat question? Don't you see I has?"

"Well, are you rich?"

"No, but I ben rich wunst, and gwyne to be rich ag'in. Wunst I had foteen dollars, but I tuck to specalat'n', en got busted out."

"What did you <u>speculate</u> in, Jim?"

"Well, fust I tackled stock."

"What kind of stock?"

"Why, livestock—cattle, you know. I put ten dollars in a cow. But I ain' gwyne to resk no mo' money in stock. De cow up 'n' died on my han's."

"So you lost the ten dollars."

"No, I didn't lose it all. I on'y los' 'bout nine of it. I sole de hide en taller for a dollar en ten cents."

"You had five dollars and ten cents left. Did you speculate any more?"

► *What activity caused Jim to lose his money?*

"Yes. You know that one-laigged nigger dat b'longs to old Misto Bradish? Well, he sot up a bank, en say anybody dat put in a dollar would git fo' dollars mo' at de en' er de year. Well, all de niggers went in, but dey didn't have much. I wuz de on'y one dat had much. So I stuck out for mo' dan fo' dollars, en I said 'f I didn' git it I'd start a bank mysef. Well, o' course dat nigger want' to keep me out er de business, bekase he says dey warn't business 'nough for two banks, so he say I could put in my five dollars en he pay me thirty-five at de en' er de year.

"So I done it. Den I reck'n'd I'd inves' de thirty-five dollars right off en keep things a-movin'. Dey wuz a nigger name'

Words For Everyday Use

spec • u • late (spek´yo͞o lāt´) *vi.*, invest in a risky business

Bob, dat had ketched a wood-flat,[13] en his marster didn' know it; en I bought it off'n him en told him to take de thirty-five dollars when de en' er de year come; but somebody stole de wood-flat dat night, en nex day de one-laigged nigger say de bank's busted. So dey didn' none uv us git no money."

"What did you do with the ten cents, Jim?"

"Well, I 'uz gwyne to spen' it, but I had a dream, en de dream tole me to give it to a nigger name' Balum—Balum's Ass[14] dey call him for short; he's one er dem chuckleheads, you know. But he's lucky, dey say, en I see I warn't lucky. De dream say let Balum inves' de ten cents en he'd make a raise for me. Well, Balum he tuck de money, en when he wuz in church he hear de preacher say dat whoever give to de po' len' to de Lord, en boun' to git his money back a hund'd times. So Balum he tuck en give de ten cents to de po', en laid low to see what wuz gwyne to come of it."

◄ What happened to Jim's ten cents?

"Well, what did come of it, Jim?"

"Nuffn never come of it. I couldn' manage to k'leck dat money no way; en Balum he couldn'. I ain' gwyne to len' no mo' money 'dout I see de <u>security</u>. Boun' to git yo' money back a hund'd times, de preacher says! Ef I could git de ten *cents* back, I'd call it squah, en be glad er de chanst."

"Well, it's all right anyway, Jim, long as you're going to be rich again some time or other."

"Yes; en I's rich now, come to look at it. I owns mysef, en I's wuth eight hund'd dollars. I wisht I had de money, I wouldn' want no mo'."

◄ Why does Jim consider himself rich now?

---

13. **wood-flat.** Flat-bottomed boat
14. **Balum's Ass.** Balaam, a Biblical character, rode an ass, or donkey, that spoke.

Words For Everyday Use	se • cu • ri • ty (si kyo͞or´ə tē) *n.*, something given as a pledge for repayment

CHAPTER 9

The House of Death Floats By

I wanted to go and look at a place right about the middle of the island that I'd found when I was exploring; so we started and soon got to it, because the island was only three miles long and a quarter of a mile wide.

This place was a tolerable long, steep hill or ridge about forty foot high. We had a rough time getting to the top, the sides was so steep and the bushes so thick. We tramped and clumb around all over it, and by and by found a good big cavern in the rock, most up to the top on the side towards Illinois. The cavern was as big as two or three rooms bunched together, and Jim could stand up straight in it. It was cool in there. Jim was for putting our traps in there right away, but I said we didn't want to be climbing up and down there all the time.

Jim said if we had the canoe hid in a good place, and had all the traps in the cavern, we could rush there if anybody was to come to the island, and they would never find us without dogs. And, besides, he said them little birds had said it was going to rain, and did I want the things to get wet?

So we went back and got the canoe, and paddled up abreast the cavern, and lugged all the traps up there. Then we hunted up a place close by to hide the canoe in, amongst the thick willows. We took some fish off of the lines and set them again, and begun to get ready for dinner.

The door of the cavern was big enough to roll a hogshead in, and on one side of the door the floor stuck out a little bit, and was flat and a good place to build a fire on. So we built it there and cooked dinner.

We spread the blankets inside for a carpet, and eat our dinner in there. We put all the other things handy at the back of the cavern. Pretty soon it darkened up, and begun to thunder and lighten; so the birds was right about it. Directly it begun to rain, and it rained like all fury, too, and I never see the wind blow so. It was one of these regular summer storms. It would get so dark that it looked all blue-black outside, and lovely; and the rain would thrash along by so thick that the

► Why does Jim suggest they bring their supplies to the cavern? What does he sense is about to happen?

a • breast (ə brest´) *adv.,* side by side with

trees off a little ways looked dim and spider-web[...] would come a blast of wind that would bend the[...] and turn up the pale underside of the leaves; and [...] fect ripper of a gust would follow along and set the[...] to tossing their arms as if they was just wild; and ne[...] it was just about the bluest and blackest—*fst!* it was a[...] as glory, and you'd have a little glimpse of treetops a-pl[...] about away off yonder in the storm, hundreds of yard[...] ther than you could see before; dark as sin again in a sec[...] and now you'd hear the thunder let go with an awful cra[...] and then go rumbling, grumbling, tumbling, down the s[...] towards the underside of the world, like rolling empty barre[...] downstairs—where it's long stairs and they bounce a good deal, you know.

"Jim, this is nice," I says. "I wouldn't want to be nowhere else but here. Pass me along another hunk of fish and some hot cornbread."

◄ How does Huck feel about being in the cavern eating dinner with Jim? For what does Jim take credit?

"Well, you wouldn't 'a' ben here 'f it hadn't 'a' ben for Jim. You'd 'a' ben down dah in de woods widout any dinner, en gittn' mos' drownded, too; dat you would, honey. Chickens knows when it's gwyne to rain, en so do de birds, chile."

The river went on raising and raising for ten or twelve days, till at last it was over the banks. The water was three or four foot deep on the island in the low places and on the Illinois bottom. On that side it was a good many miles wide, but on the Missouri side it was the same old distance across—a half a mile—because the Missouri shore was just a wall of high <u>bluffs</u>.

Daytimes we paddled all over the island in the canoe. It was mighty cool and shady in the deep woods, even if the sun was blazing outside. We went winding in and out amongst the trees, and sometimes the vines hung so thick we had to back away and go some other way. Well, on every old broken-down tree you could see rabbits and snakes and such things; and when the island had been overflowed a day or two they got so tame, on account of being hungry, that you could paddle right up and put your hand on them if you wanted to; but not the snakes and turtles—they would slide off in the water. The ridge our cavern was in was full of them. We could 'a' had pets enough if we'd wanted them.

◄ What do Jim and Huck spend their days doing?

One night we catched a little section of a lumber raft—nice

◄ What are Huck and Jim able to catch?

Words For Everyday Use

bluff (bluf) *n.,* steep bank or cliff

planks. It was twelve foot wide and about fifteen or sixteen foot long, and the top stood above water six or seven inches—a solid, level floor.

Another night when we was up at the head of the island, just before daylight, here comes a frame house down, on the west side. She was a two-story, and tilted over considerable. We paddled out and got aboard—clumb in at an upstairs window. But it was too dark to see yet, so we made the canoe fast and set in her to wait for daylight.

The light begun to come before we got to the foot of the island. Then we looked in at the window. We could make out a bed, and a table, and two old chairs, and lots of things around about on the floor, and there was clothes hanging against the wall. There was something laying on the floor in the far corner that looked like a man. So Jim says:

"Hello, you!"

But it didn't budge. So I hollered again, and then Jim says:

"De man ain't asleep—he's dead. You hold still—I'll go en see."

He went, and bent down and looked, and says:

"It's a dead man. Yes, indeedy; naked, too. He's ben shot in de back. I reck'n he's ben dead two er three days. Come in, Huck, but doan' look at his face—it's too gashly."[1]

I didn't look at him at all. Jim threw some old rags over him, but he needn't done it; I didn't want to see him. There was heaps of old greasy cards scattered around over the floor, and old whisky bottles, and a couple of masks made out of blackcloth; and all over the walls was the ignorantest kind of words and pictures made with charcoal. There was two old dirty calico dresses, and a sun-bonnet, and some women's underclothes hanging against the wall, and some men's clothing, too. We put the lot into the canoe—it might come good. There was a boy's old speckled straw hat on the floor; I took that, too. And there was a bottle that had had milk in it, and it had a rag stopper for a baby to suck. We would 'a' took the bottle, but it was broke. There was a seedy old chest, and an old hair trunk with the hinges broke. They stood open, but there warn't nothing left in them that was any account. The way things was scattered about we reckoned the people left in a hurry, and warn't fixed so as to carry off most of their stuff.

We got an old tin lantern, and a butcher knife without any handle, and a bran-new Barlow knife worth two bits in any store, and a lot of tallow candles, and a tin candlestick, and

---

1. **gashly.** Jim means ghastly; horrible, frightful.

came floating along the west side of the island?

▶ Who is in the house? What does Jim advise Huck not to do?

a gourd, and a tin cup, and a ratty old bedquilt off the bed, and a reticule[2] with needles and pins and beeswax and buttons and thread and all such truck in it, and a hatchet and some nails, and a fishline as thick as my little finger with some monstrous hooks on it, and a roll of buckskin, and a leather dog-collar, and a horseshoe, and some vials of medicine that didn't have no label on them; and just as we was leaving I found a tolerable good curry-comb, and Jim he found a ratty old fiddle-bow, and a wooden leg. The straps was broke off of it, but, barring that, it was a good enough leg, though it was too long for me and not long enough for Jim, and we couldn't find the other one.

And so, take it all around, we made a good haul. When we was ready to shove off we was a quarter of a mile below the island, and it was pretty broad day; so I made Jim lay down in the canoe and cover up with the quilt, because if he set up people could tell he was a nigger a good ways off. I paddled over to the Illinois shore, and drifted down most a half a mile doing it. I crept up the dead water under the bank, and hadn't no accidents and didn't see nobody. We got home all safe.

◄ *Because Jim is African American and an escaped slave, what must he do as they return to the island in broad daylight?*

---

2. **reticule.** Small handbag

What Comes of Handlin' Snakeskin

► What does Huck want to talk about when they return to the canoe? Why does Jim want to avoid the subject?

After breakfast I wanted to talk about the dead man and guess out how he come to be killed, but Jim didn't want to. He said it would fetch bad luck; and besides, he said, he might come and ha'nt us; he said a man that warn't buried was more likely to go a-ha'nting around than one that was planted and comfortable. That sounded pretty reasonable, so I didn't say no more; but I couldn't keep from studying over it and wishing I knowed who shot the man, and what they done it for.

► What do they find in an overcoat? What does Jim assume about the people who were in the house? What does Huck assume?

We rummaged the clothes we'd got, and found eight dollars in silver sewed up in the lining of an old blanket overcoat. Jim said he reckoned the people in that house stole the coat, because if they'd 'a' knowed the money was there they wouldn't 'a' left it. I said I reckoned they killed him, too; but Jim didn't want to talk about that. I says:

"Now you think it's bad luck; but what did you say when I fetched in the snakeskin that I found on the top of the ridge day before yesterday? You said it was the worst bad luck in the world to touch a snakeskin with my hands. Well, here's your bad luck! We've raked in all this truck and eight dollars besides. I wish we could have some bad luck like this every day, Jim."

"Never you mind, honey, never you mind. Don't you git too peart.[1] It's a-comin'. Mind I tell you, it's a-comin'."

It did come, too. It was a Tuesday that we had that talk. Well, after dinner Friday we was laying around in the grass at the upper end of the ridge, and got out of tobacco. I went to the cavern to get some, and found a rattlesnake in there. I killed him, and curled him up on the foot of Jim's blanket, ever so natural, thinking there'd be some fun when Jim found him there. Well, by night I forgot all about the snake, and when Jim flung himself down on the blanket while I struck a light the snake's mate was there, and bit him.

► What does Huck do with the snake he finds? What happens as a result of Huck's prank?

He jumped up yelling, and the first thing the light showed was the varmint[2] curled up and ready for another spring. I laid him out in a second with a stick, and Jim grabbed Pap's whisky-jug and begun to pour it down.

He was barefooted, and the snake bit him right on the heel. That all comes of my being such a fool as to not remember that wherever you leave a dead snake its mate

► Why does Huck call himself a fool?

---

1. **peart.** Pert; bold, saucy
2. **varmint.** Colloquial term for a person or animal regarded as troublesome

always comes there and curls around it. Jim told me to chop off the snake's head and throw it away, and then skin the body and roast a piece of it. I done it, and he eat it and said it would help cure him. He made me take off the rattles and tie them around his wrist, too. He said that that would help. Then I slid out quiet and throwed the snakes clear away amongst the bushes; for I warn't going to let Jim find out it was all my fault, not if I could help it.

Jim sucked and sucked at the jug, and now and then he got out of his head and pitched around and yelled; but every time he come to himself he went to sucking at the jug again. His foot swelled up pretty big, and so did his leg; but by and by the drunk begun to come, and so I judged he was all right; but I'd druther been bit with a snake than Pap's whisky.

Jim was laid up for four days and nights. Then the swelling was all gone and he was around again. I made up my mind I wouldn't ever take a-holt of a snakeskin again with my hands, now that I see what had come of it. Jim said he reckoned I would believe him next time. And he said that handling a snakeskin was such awful bad luck that maybe we hadn't got to the end of it yet. He said he druther see the new moon over his left shoulder as much as a thousand times than take up a snakeskin in his hand. Well, I was getting to feel that way myself, though I've always reckoned that looking at the new moon over your left shoulder is one of the carelessest and foolishest things a body can do. Old Hank Bunker done it once, and bragged about it; and in less than two years he got drunk and fell off of the shot-tower, and spread himself out so that he was just a kind of a layer, as you may say; and they slid him edgeways between two barn doors for a coffin, and buried him so, so they say, but I didn't see it. Pap told me. But anyway it all come of looking at the moon that way, like a fool.

Well, the days went along, and the river went down between its banks again; and about the first thing we done was to bait one of the big hooks with a skinned rabbit and set it and catch a catfish that was as big as a man, being six foot two inches long, and weighed over two hundred pounds. We couldn't handle him, of course; he would 'a' flung us into Illinois. We just set there and watched him rip and tear around till he drownded. We found a brass button in his stomach and a round ball, and lots of rubbage. We split the ball open with the hatchet, and there was a spool in it. Jim said he'd had it there a long time, to coat it over so and make a ball of it. It was as big a fish as was ever catched in the Mississippi, I reckon. Jim said he hadn't ever seen a bigger one. He would 'a' been worth a good deal over at the village.

◄ What does Huck make up his mind never to do again? Why?

◄ What do Huck and Jim do as soon as the river goes down?

They peddle out such a fish as that by the pound in the market-house there; everybody buys some of him; his meat's as white as snow and makes a good fry.

Next morning I said it was getting slow and dull, and I wanted to get a stirring-up some way. I said I reckoned I would slip over the river and find out what was going on. Jim liked that notion; but he said I must go in the dark and look sharp. Then he studied it over and said, couldn't I put on some of them old things and dress up like a girl? That was a good notion, too. So we shortened up one of the calico gowns, and I turned up my trouser legs to my knees and got into it. Jim hitched it behind with the hooks, and it was a fair fit. I put on the sunbonnet and tied it under my chin, and then for a body to look in and see my face was like looking down a joint of stovepipe. Jim said nobody would know me, even in the daytime, hardly. I practiced around all day to get the hang of the things, and by and by I could do pretty well in them, only Jim said I didn't walk like a girl; and he said I must quit pulling up my gown to get at my britches[3] pocket. I took notice, and done better.

I started up the Illinois shore in the canoe just after dark.

I started across to the town from a little below the ferry-landing, and the drift of the current fetched me in at the bottom of the town. I tied up and started along the bank. There was a light burning in a little <u>shanty</u> that hadn't been lived in for a long time, and I wondered who had took up quarters there. I slipped up and peeped in at the window. There was a woman about forty year old in there knitting by a candle that was on a pine table. I didn't know her face; she was a stranger, for you couldn't start a face in that town that I didn't know. Now this was lucky, because I was weakening; I was getting afraid I had come; people might know my voice and find me out. But if this woman had been in such a little town two days she could tell me all I wanted to know; so I knocked at the door, and made up my mind I wouldn't forget I was a girl.

► When Huck decides that he wants to go into town and find out what's going on, what does Jim suggest he do?

► Why is Huck drawn to the shanty? Why does he think that the woman might believe his act?

---

3. **britches.** Trousers

Words
For
Everyday
Use

shan • ty (shan´tē) *n.,* small, shabby dwelling; shack

CHAPTER 11

They're After Us!

"Come in," says the woman, and I did. She says: "Take a cheer."[1]

I done it. She looked me all over with her little shiny eyes, and says:

"What might your name be?"

"Sarah Williams."

"Where 'bouts do you live? In this neighborhood?'

"No'm. In Hookerville, seven mile below. I've walked all the way and I'm all tired out."

"Hungry, too, I reckon. I'll find you something."

"No'm, I ain't hungry. I was so hungry I had to stop two miles below here at a farm; so I ain't hungry no more. It's what makes me so late. My mother's down sick, and out of money and everything, and I come to tell my uncle Abner Moore. He lives at the upper end of the town, she says. I hain't ever been here before. Do you know him?"

"No; but I don't know everybody yet. I haven't lived here quite two weeks. It's a considerable ways to the upper end of the town. You better stay here all night. Take off your bonnet."

"No," I says; "I'll rest awhile, I reckon, and go on. I ain't afeared of the dark."

◀ What does Huck say his name is? What story does he invent to explain why he is there?

She said she wouldn't let me go by myself, but her husband would be in by and by, maybe in a hour and a half, and she'd send him along with me. Then she got to talking about her husband, and about her relations up the river, and her relations down the river, and about how much better off they used to was, and how they didn't know but they'd made a mistake coming to our town, instead of letting well alone—and so on and so on, till I was afeard I had made a mistake coming to her to find out what was going on in the town; but by and by she dropped on to pap and the murder, and then I was pretty willing to let her clatter right along. She told about me and Tom Sawyer finding the twelve thousand dollars (only she got it twenty) and all about pap and what a hard lot he was, and what a hard lot I was, and at last she got down to where I was murdered. I says:

"Who done it? We've heard considerable about these goings on down in Hookerville, but we don't know who 'twas that killed Huck Finn."

"Well, I reckon there's a right smart chance of people *here* that'd like to know who killed him. Some think old Finn done it himself."

◀ What important information about Huck's "murder" does the woman share? Who do people believe killed Huck? What rewards are being offered?

---

1. **cheer.** Chair

"No—is that so?"

"Most everybody thought it at first. He'll never know how nigh he come to getting <u>lynched</u>. But before night they changed around and judged it was done by a runaway nigger named Jim."

"Why *he*—"

I stopped. I reckoned I better keep still. She run on, and never noticed I had put in at all:

"The nigger run off the very night Huck Finn was killed. So there's a reward out for him—three hundred dollars. And there's a reward out for old Finn, too—two hundred dollars. You see, he come to town the morning after the murder, and told about it, and was out with 'em on the ferryboat hunt, and right away after he up and left. Before night they wanted to lynch him, but he was gone, you see. Well, next day they found out the nigger was gone; they found out he hadn't ben seen sence ten o'clock the night the murder was done. So then they put it on him, you see; and while they was full of it, next day, back comes old Finn, and went boo-hooing to Judge Thatcher to get money to hunt for the nigger all over Illinois with. The judge gave him some, and that evening he got drunk, and was around till after midnight with a couple of mighty hard-looking strangers, and then went off with them. Well, he hain't come back sence, and they ain't look-ing for him back till this thing blows over a little, for people thinks now that he killed his boy and fixed things so folks would think robbers done it, and then he'd get Huck's money without having to bother a long time with a lawsuit. People do say he warn't any too good to do it. Oh, he's sly, I reckon. If he don't come back for a year he'll be all right. You can't prove anything on him, you know; everything will be quieted down then, and he'll walk in Huck's money as easy as nothing."

"Yes, I reckon so, 'm. I don't see nothing in the way of it. Has everybody quit thinking the nigger done it?"

"Oh, no, not everybody. A good many thinks he done it. But they'll get the nigger pretty soon now, and maybe they can scare it out of him."

"Why, are they after him yet?"

"Well, you're innocent, ain't you! Does three hundred dol-lars lay around every day for people to pick up? Some folks

> ► Where has Pap gone? According to folks in town, why would Pap want to kill Huck?

Words For Everyday Use

lynch (linch) *vt.*, murder by mob action without trial

think the nigger ain't far from here. I'm one of them—but I hain't talked it around. A few days ago I was talking with an old couple that lives next door in the log shanty, and they happened to say hardly anybody ever goes to that island over yonder that they call Jackson's Island. Don't anybody live there? says I. No, nobody, says they. I didn't say any more, but I done some thinking. I was pretty near certain I'd seen smoke over there, about the head of the island, a day or two before that, so I says to myself, like as not that nigger's hiding over there; anyway, says I, it's worth the trouble to give the place a hunt. I hain't seen any smoke sence, so I reckon maybe he's gone, if it was him; but husband's going over to see—him and another man. He was gone up the river; but he got back today, and I told him as soon as he got here two hours ago."

◄ Why does the woman suspect that Jim is on Jackson Island? In what way does this information affect Huck? What does the woman watch Huck try to do?

I had got so uneasy I couldn't set still. I had to do something with my hands; so I took up a needle off of the table and went to threading it. My hands shook, and I was making a bad job of it. When the woman stopped talking I looked up, and she was looking at me pretty curious and smiling a little. I put down the needle and thread, and let on to be interested—and I was, too—and says:

"Three hundred dollars is a power of money. I wish my mother could get it. Is your husband going over there tonight?"

"Oh, yes. He went uptown with the man I was telling you of, to get a boat and see if they could borrow another gun. They'll go over after midnight."

◄ When will the woman's husband be going to Jackson's Island to look for Jim?

"Couldn't they see better if they was to wait till daytime?"

"Yes. And couldn't the nigger see better, too? After midnight he'll likely be asleep, and they can slip around through the woods and hunt up his campfire all the better for the dark, if he's got one."

"I didn't think of that."

The woman kept looking at me pretty curious, and I didn't feel a bit comfortable. Pretty soon she says:

◄ What mistake does Huck make?

"What did you say your name was, honey?"

"M—Mary Williams."

Somehow it didn't seem to me that I said it was Mary before, so I didn't look up—seemed to me I said it was Sarah; so I felt sort of cornered, and was afeared maybe I was looking it, too. I wished the woman would say something more; the longer she set still the uneasier I was. But now she says:

"Honey, I thought you said it was Sarah when you first come in?"

"Oh, yes'm, I did. Sarah Mary Williams. Sarah's my first name. Some calls me Sarah, some calls me Mary."

"Oh, that's the way of it?"

"Yes'm."

I was feeling better then, but I wished I was out of there, anyway. I couldn't look up yet.

Well, the woman fell to talking about how hard times was, and how poor they had to live, and how the rats was as free as if they owned the place, and so forth and so on, and then I got easy again. She was right about the rats. You'd see one stick his nose out of a hole in the corner every little while. She said she had to have things handy to throw at them when she was alone, or they wouldn't give her no peace. She showed me a bar of lead twisted up into a knot, and said she was a good shot with it generly, but she'd wrenched her arm a day or two ago, and didn't know whether she could throw true now. But she watched for a chance, and directly banged away at a rat; but she missed him wide, and said "Ouch!" it hurt her arm so. Then she told me to try for the next one. I wanted to be getting away before the old man got back, but of course I didn't let on. I got the thing, and the first rat that showed his nose I let drive, and if he'd 'a' stayed where he was he'd a been a tolerable sick rat. She said that was first-rate, and she reckoned I would hive the next one. She went and got the lump of lead and fetched it back, and brought along a hank of yarn which she wanted me to help her with. I held up my two hands and she put the hank over them, and went on talking about her and her husband's matters. But she broke off to say:

► What does the woman ask Huck to do?

"Keep your eye on the rats. You better have the lead in your lap, handy."

So she dropped the lump into my lap just at that moment, and I clapped my legs together on it and she went on talking. But only about a minute. Then she took off the hank and looked me straight in the face, and very pleasant, and says:

"Come, now, what's your real name?"

"Wh—what, mum?"

"What's your real name? Is it Bill, or Tom, or Bob?—or what is it?"

► What has the woman figured out? Why does she promise not to give away Huck's secret?

I reckon I shook like a leaf, and I didn't know hardly what to do. But I says:

"Please to don't poke fun at a poor girl like me, mum. If I'm in the way here, I'll—"

"No, you won't. Set down and stay where you are. I ain't going to hurt you, and I ain't going to tell on you, nuther. You just tell me your secret, and trust me. I'll keep it; and, what's more, I'll help you. So'll my old man if you want him to. You see, you're a runaway 'prentice, that's all. It ain't anything.

There ain't no harm in it. You've been treated bad, and you made up your mind to cut. Bless you, child, I wouldn't tell on you. Tell me all about it now, that's a good boy."

So I said it wouldn't be no use to try to play it any longer, and I would just make a clean breast and tell her everything, but she musn't go back on her promise. Then I told her my father and mother was dead, and the law had bound me out to a mean old farmer in the country thirty mile back from the river, and he treated me so bad I couldn't stand it no longer; he went away to be gone a couple of days, and so I took my chance and stole some of his daughter's old clothes and cleared out, and I had been three nights coming the thirty miles. I traveled nights, and hid daytimes and slept, and the bag of bread and meat I carried from home lasted me all the way, and I had a-plenty. I said I believed my uncle Abner Moore would take care of me, and so that was why I struck out for this town of Goshen.

"Goshen, child? This ain't Goshen. This is St. Petersburg. Goshen's ten mile further up the river. Who told you this was Goshen?"

"Why, a man I met at daybreak this morning, just as I was going to turn into the woods for my regular sleep. He told me when the roads forked I must take the right hand, and five mile would fetch me to Goshen."

"He was drunk, I reckon. He told you just exactly wrong."

"Well, he did act like he was drunk, but it ain't no matter now. I got to be moving along. I'll fetch Goshen before daylight."

"Hold on a minute. I'll put you up a snack to eat. You might want it."

So she put me up a snack, and says:

"Say, when a cow's laying down, which end of her gets up first? Answer up prompt now—don't stop to study over it. Which end gets up first?"

"The hind end, mum."

"Well, then, a horse?"

"The for'rard end, mum."

"Which side of a tree does the moss grow on?"

"North side."

"If fifteen cows is browsing on a hillside, how many of them eats with their heads pointed the same direction?"

"The whole fifteen, mum."

"Well, I reckon you *have* lived in the country. I thought maybe you was trying to hocus me again. What's your real name, now?"

"George Peters, mum."

◄ What new story does Huck invent about his situation?

◄ What questions does the woman ask Huck? What is she trying to figure out?

► According to the woman, how did Huck give himself away?

"Well, try to remember it, George. Don't forget and tell me it's Elexander before you go, and then get out by saying it's George Elexander when I catch you. And don't go about women in that old calico. You do a girl tolerable poor, but you might fool men, maybe. Bless you, child, when you set out to thread a needle don't hold the thread still and fetch the needle up to it; hold the needle still and poke the thread at it; that's the way a woman most always does, but a man always does t'other way. And when you throw at a rat or anything, hitch yourself up a-tiptoe and fetch your hand up over your head as awkward as you can, and miss your rat about six or seven foot. Throw stiff-armed from the shoulder, like there was a pivot there for it to turn on, like a girl; not from the wrist and elbow, with your arm out to one side, like a boy. And, mind you, when a girl tries to catch anything in her lap she throws her knees apart; she don't clap them together, the way you did when you catched the lump of lead. Why, I spotted you for a boy when you was threading the needle; and I contrived the other things just to make certain. Now trot along to your uncle, Sarah Mary Williams George Elexander Peters, and if you get into trouble you send word to Mrs. Judith Loftus, which is me, and I'll do what I can to get you out of it. Keep the river road all the way, and next time you tramp take shoes and socks with you. The river road's a rocky one, and your feet'll be in a condition when you get to Goshen, I reckon."

I went up the bank about fifty yards, and then I doubled on my tracks and slipped back to where my canoe was, a good piece below the house. I jumped in, and was off in a hurry. I went upstream far enough to make the head of the island, and then started across. I took off the sunbonnet, for I didn't want no blinders[2] on then. When I was about the middle I heard the clock begin to strike, so I stops and listens; the sound come faint over the water but clear—eleven. When I struck the head of the island I never waited to blow, though I was most winded, but I shoved right into the timber where my old camp used to be, and started a good fire there on a high and dry spot.

► What does Huck do before he reaches Jim?

Then I jumped in the canoe and dug out for our place, a mile and a half below, as hard as I could go. I landed, and slopped through the timber and up the ridge and into the cavern. There Jim laid, sound asleep on the ground. I roused him out and says:

---

2. **blinders.** Leather flaps attached to a harness that keep a horse from seeing to either side

"Git up and hump yourself, Jim! There ain't a minute to lose. They're after us!"

Jim never asked no questions, he never said a word; but the way he worked for the next half an hour showed about how he was scared. By that time everything we had in the world was on our raft, and she was ready to be shoved out from the willow cove where she was hid. We put out the campfire at the cavern the first thing, and didn't show a candle outside after that.

I took the canoe out from the shore a little piece, and took a look; but if there was a boat around I couldn't see it, for stars and shadows ain't good to see by. Then we got out the raft and slipped along down in the shade, past the foot of the island dead still—never saying a word.

Responding to the Selection

"There ain't a minute to lose. They're after us!" Do you think Huck and Jim make good traveling companions? What do the two have in common? Do you agree with what they are doing? Why, or why not?

Reviewing the Selection

Recalling and Interpreting

1. **R:** How does Huck know his plan to make people believe he has been killed is successful? What does he witness?

2. **I:** How does Huck feel during his first night on the island, after his successful escape? In what ways do his feelings change when the steamboat leaves and he realizes that "nobody else would come a-hunting" after him?

3. **R:** Why is Jim on Jackson's Island? When did he arrive? What circumstances prompted him to leave the village? What promise does Huck make to Jim?

4. **I:** How does Huck feel to have found a companion? How does Jim react to seeing Huck? Why does he react this way? What makes Huck uncomfortable about the promise he makes to Jim?

5. **R:** How do Huck and Jim spend their first few days together on the island? What are some of the items they find floating on the river? What do they find in the floating house?

6. **I:** In what way do Huck and Jim help each other to enjoy life on the island? How does Jim show protectiveness toward Huck when they are in the house with the dead body?

7. **R:** When Huck leaves the island, where does he go? What disguise does use? What does he learn that causes him to panic and rush back to Jim?

8. **I:** In what ways is Huck unsuccessful at fooling the woman he visits? In what ways is he successful? When Huck rushes back to Jim, he tells Jim, "They're after us!" Are people really after Huck? In what way does his reaction to news of a hunt for Jim show that Huck has begun to identify closely with Jim?

Synthesizing

9. Why do you think Huck agrees to keep Jim's secret even though he knows people in the village would "despise" him as a "low-down Abolitionist"? Why would people regard Huck's wish to hide Jim as a bad thing? Why does Huck make this decision despite what people may say? Why might Huck feel closer to Jim than to others in the village?

10. What traits do Jim and Huck share? How do they differ? What clues in the text show that their concern for each other and need of each other are growing?

Understanding Literature (QUESTIONS FOR DISCUSSION)

1. **Irony of Situation.** In **irony of situation,** an event occurs that violates the expectations of the characters, the reader, or the audience. Mark Twain's writing often depicts irony in human behavior. What is ironic about the fact that, although nobody went to Pap's cabin to rescue Huck, a crowd of people gathered on the steamboat to search for his remains? In another instance, what is ironic about the fact that there is a three hundred dollar reward being offered for the capture of Jim, but only a two hundred dollar reward being offered for the capture of Pap, a man believed to have murdered his son? What does this fact reveal about society's view of Jim, and the weight given to Jim's "crime"?

2. **Character.** A **character** is a person who figures in the action of a literary work. Many of Jim's actions are deeply rooted in seemingly odd superstitions. A careful reader, however, can see that many of Jim's superstitions are grounded in practical knowledge and a knowledge of the natural world. Describe some of Jim's superstitions concerning birds and stormy weather and about tampering with snakes. In what way is his advice, based on these beliefs, correct? When Huck asks Jim why only bad luck can be predicted in his "signs," what is logical about Jim's response?

3. **Theme. Theme** is the central idea of a literary work. In chapters 7–11, an important theme of the novel is raised—Huck's growing sense of compassion for other human beings, especially for Jim. Refer to the prank with the dead snake Huck plays on Jim in chapter 10. What is Huck's intent when he plays the prank? What is the unfortunate result of his prank? How does Huck feel when he realizes his mistake? What do his feelings reveal about his growing maturity and his feelings for Jim?

CHAPTER 12

"Better Let Blame Well Alone"

It must 'a' been close on to one o'clock when we got below the island at last, and the raft did seem to go mighty slow. If a boat was to come along we was going to take to the canoe and break for the Illinois shore; and it was well a boat didn't come, for we hadn't ever thought to put the gun in the canoe, or a fishing-line, or anything to eat. We was in ruther too much of a sweat to think of so many things. It warn't good judgment to put *everything* on the raft.

If the men went to the island I just expect they found the campfire I built, and watched it all night for Jim to come. Anyways, they stayed away from us, and if my building the fire never fooled them it warn't no fault of mine. I played it as low down on them as I could.

When the first streak of day began to show we tied up to a towhead in a big bend on the Illinois side, and hacked off cottonwood branches with the hatchet, and covered up the raft with them so she looked like there had been a cave-in in the bank there. A towhead is a sandbar that has cottonwoods on it as thick as harrow-teeth.[1]

We had mountains on the Missouri shore and heavy timber on the Illinois side, and the channel was down the Missouri shore at that place, so we warn't afraid of anybody running across us. We laid there all day, and watched the rafts and steamboats spin down the Missouri shore, and upbound steamboats fight the big river in the middle. I told Jim all about the time I had jabbering with that woman; and Jim said she was a smart one, and if she was to start after us herself *she* wouldn't set down and watch a campfire—no, sir, she'd fetch a dog. Well, then, I said, why couldn't she tell her husband to fetch a dog? Jim said he bet she did think of it by the time the men was ready to start, and he believed they must 'a' gone uptown to get a dog and so they lost all that time, or else we wouldn't be here on a towhead sixteen or seventeen mile below the village—no, indeedy, we would be in that same old town again. So I said I didn't care what was the reason they didn't get us as long as they didn't.

When it was beginning to come on dark we poked our

---

1. **harrow-teeth.** Discs on a harrow, a type of plow

Why do Huck and Jim bring the canoe and the raft? What do Huck and Jim plan to do if they come across a boat? Why is it a good thing that a boat never came?

Why did Huck build the campfire before they left the island? What was he hoping the men would do when they found it?

heads out of the cottonwood <u>thicket</u>, and looked up and down and across; nothing in sight; so Jim took up some of the top planks of the raft and built a snug wigwam[2] to get under in blazing weather and rainy, and to keep the things dry. Jim made a floor for the wigwam, and raised it a foot or more above the level of the raft, so now the blankets and all the traps was out of reach of steamboat waves. Right in the middle of the wigwam we made a layer of dirt about five or six inches deep with a frame around it for to hold it to its place; this was to build a fire on in sloppy weather or chilly; the wigwam would keep it from being seen. We made an extra steering-oar, too, because one of the others might get broke on a snag or something. We fixed up a short forked stick to hang the old lantern on, because we must always light the lantern whenever we see a steamboat coming downstream, to keep from getting run over; but we wouldn't have to light it for upstream boats unless we see we was in what they call a "crossing"; for the river was pretty high yet, very low banks being still a little under water; so upbound boats didn't always run the channel, but hunted easy water.

◀ What do Huck and Jim do to prepare their raft for comfortable travel?

This second night we run between seven and eight hours, with a current that was making over four mile an hour. We catched fish and talked, and we took a swim now and then to keep off sleepiness. It was kind of <u>solemn</u>, drifting down the big, still river, laying on our backs looking up at the stars, and we didn't even feel like talking loud, and it warn't often that we laughed—only a little kind of a low chuckle. We had mighty good weather as a general thing, and nothing ever happened to us at all—that night, nor the next, nor the next.

Every night we passed towns, some of them away up on black hillsides, nothing but just a shiny bed of lights; not a house could you see. The fifth night we passed St. Louis, and it was like the whole world lit up. In St. Petersburg they used to say there was twenty or thirty thousand people in St. Louis, but I never believed it till I see that wonderful spread of lights at two o'clock that still night. There warn't a sound there; everybody was asleep.

Every night now I used to slip ashore towards ten o'clock at some little village, and buy ten or fifteen cents' worth of

◀ What does Huck do each night? What bit of Pap's advice does he remember?

---

2. **wigwam.** Dome-shaped dwelling

| Words For Everyday Use | **thick • et** (thik´ət) n., thick growth of shrubs or small trees |
| | **sol • emn** (säl´əm) adj., serious, grave, impressive |

meal or bacon or other stuff to eat; and sometimes I lifted a chicken that warn't <u>roosting</u> comfortable, and took him along. Pap always said, take a chicken when you get a chance, because if you don't want him yourself you can easy find somebody that does, and a good deed ain't ever forgot, but I never see Pap when he didn't want the chicken himself.

Mornings before daylight I slipped into cornfields and borrowed a watermelon, or a mushmelon, or a punkin, or some new corn, or things of that kind. Pap always said it warn't no harm to borrow things if you was meaning to pay them back some time; but the widow said it warn't anything but a soft name for stealing, and no decent body would do it. Jim said he reckoned the widow was partly right and Pap was partly right; so the best way would be for us to pick out two or three things from the list and say we wouldn't borrow them any more— then he reckoned it wouldn't be no harm to borrow the others. So we talked it over all one night, drifting along down the river, trying to make up our minds whether to drop the watermelons, or the cantaloupes, or the mushmelons, or what. But towards daylight we got it all settled satisfactory, and concluded to drop crabapples and p'simmons.[3] We warn't feeling just right before that, but it was all comfortable now. I was glad the way it come out, too, because crabapples ain't ever good, and the p'simmons wouldn't be ripe for two or three months yet.

We shot a waterfowl now and then that got up too early in the morning or didn't go to bed early enough in the evening. Take it all round, we lived pretty high.

The fifth night below St. Louis we had a big storm after midnight, with a power of thunder and lightning, and the rain poured down in a solid sheet. We stayed in the wigwam and let the raft take care of itself. When the lightning glared out we could see a big straight river ahead, and high, rocky bluffs on both sides. By and by says I, "Hel-*lo*, Jim, looky <u>yonder</u>!" It was a steamboat that had killed herself on a rock. We was drifting straight down for her. The lightning showed her very distinct. She was leaning over, with part of her upper deck above water, and you could see every little chimbly-guy[4]

▶ What kind of weather do Huck and Tom experience on the fifth night after they pass St. Louis? What does Huck see in the water against a rock?

---

3. **crabapples and p'simmons.** Crabapples are wild, small, sour apples. Persimmons are a fruit that is sour and astringent until very ripe.
4. **chimbly-guy.** Rope attached to the smokestack by which things on deck could be secured

Words For Everyday Use	**roost • ing** (ro͞ost iŋ) *vi.,* resting on a perch **yon • der** (yän′dər) *adv.,* over there

clean and clear, and a chair by the big bell, with an old slouch hat hanging on the back of it, when the flashes come.

Well, it being away in the night and stormy, and all so mysterious-like, I felt just the way any other boy would 'a' felt when I see that wreck laying there so mournful and lonesome in the middle of the river. I wanted to get aboard of her and slink around a little, and see what there was there. So I says:

"Le's land on her, Jim."

But Jim was dead against it at first. He says:

"I doan' want to go fool'n 'long er no wrack. We's doin' blame' well, en we better let blame' well alone, as de good book says. Like as not dey's a watchman on dat wrack."

"Watchman your grandmother," I says; "there ain't nothing to watch but the texas and the pilot-house;[5] and do you reckon anybody's going to resk his life for a texas and a pilot-house such a night as this, when it's likely to break up and wash off down the river any minute?" Jim couldn't say nothing to that, so he didn't try. "And besides," I says, "we might borrow something worth having out of the captain's stateroom. Seegars, I bet you—and cost five cents apiece, solid cash. Steamboat captains is always rich, and get sixty dollars a month, and they don't care a cent what a thing costs, you know, long as they want it. Stick a candle in your pocket; I can't rest, Jim, till we give her a <u>rummaging</u>. Do you reckon Tom Sawyer would ever go by this thing? Not for pie, he wouldn't. He'd call it an adventure—that's what he'd call it; and he'd land on that wreck if it was his last act. And wouldn't he throw style into it?—wouldn't he spread himself, nor nothing?

Jim he grumbled a little, but give in. He said we mustn't talk any more than we could help, and then talk mighty low. The lightning showed us the wreck again just in time, and we fetched the stabboard derrick,[6] and made fast there.

The deck was high out here. We went sneaking down the slope of it to labboard,[7] in the dark, towards the texas, feeling our way slow with our feet, and spreading our hands out to fend off the guys, for it was so dark we couldn't see no sign

◄ *Why does Huck insist, against Jim's better judgment, that they board the steamboat?*

---

5. **texas and the pilot-house.** The texas was the chief officer's cabin, so called because it was the largest; the helmsman steered the boat inside the pilot-house, a small enclosed structure on deck.

6. **derrick.** Apparatus for lifting and moving heavy objects

7. **labboard.** Twain uses *labboard* for "port," or the left side of a boat.

Words For Everyday Use

rum • mag • ing (rum´ij ing) *n.,* thorough search

of them. Pretty soon we struck the forward end of the sky-light, and clumb on to it; and the next step fetched us in front of the captain's door, which was open, and by Jiminy,[8] away down through the texas-hall we see a light! and all in the same second we seem to hear low voices in yonder!

Jim whispered and said he was feeling powerful sick, and told me to come along. I says, all right, and was going to start for the raft; but just then I heard a voice wail out and say:

"Oh, please don't, boys; I swear I won't ever tell!"

Another voice said, pretty loud:

"It's a lie, Jim Turner. You've acted this way before. You always want more'n your share of the truck,[9] and you've always got it, too, because you've swore 't if you didn't you'd tell. But this time you've said it jest one time too many. You're the meanest, treacherousest hound in this country."

▶ When Huck and Jim discover that there are people on the steamboat, why does Huck remain on the steamboat instead of leaving for the raft with Jim? What frightening scene does he see?

By this time Jim was gone for the raft. I was just a-biling[10] with curiosity; and I says to myself, Tom Sawyer wouldn't back out now, and so I won't either; I'm a-going to see what's going on here. So I dropped on my hands and knees in the little passage, and crept aft[11] in the dark till there warn't but one stateroom[12] betwixt me and the cross-hall of the texas. Then in there I see a man stretched on the floor and tied hand and foot, and two men standing over him, and one of them had a dim lantern in his hand, and the other one had a pistol. This one kept pointing the pistol at the man's head on the floor, and saying:

"I'd *like* to! And I orter, too—a mean skunk!"

The man on the floor would shrivel up and say, "Oh, please don't, Bill; I hain't ever goin' to tell."

And every time he said that the man with the lantern would laugh and say:

"'Deed you *ain't!* You never said no truer thing 'n that, you bet you." And once he said: "Hear him beg! and yit if we hadn't got the best of him and tied him he'd 'a' killed us both. And what *for?* Jist for noth'n. Jist because we stood on our *rights*—that's what for. But I lay you ain't a-goin' to threaten nobody any more, Jim Turner. Put *up* that pistol, Bill."

▶ What has happened between the three robbers? Why have Bill and Jake tied Jim Turner?

Bill says:

"I don't want to, Jake Packard. I'm for killin' him—and didn't he kill old Hatfield jist the same way—and don't he deserve it?"

---

8. **by Jiminy.** Mild oath
9. **truck.** Goods; stuff
10. **a-biling.** Boiling
11. **aft.** Toward the stern or rear of a boat
12. **stateroom.** Private cabin

"But I don't *want* him killed, and I've got my reasons for it."

"Bless yo' heart for them words, Jake Packard! I'll never forgit you long's I live!" says the man on the floor, sort of blubbering.

Packard didn't take no notice of that, but hung up his lantern on a nail and started towards where I was there in the dark, and motioned Bill to come. I crawfished[13] as fast as I could about two yards, but the boat slanted so that I couldn't make very good time; so to keep from getting run over and catched I crawled into a stateroom on the upper side. The man came a-pawing along in the dark, and when Packard got to my stateroom, he says:

"Here—come in here."

And in he come, and Bill after him. But before they got in I was up in the upper berth,[14] cornered, and sorry I come. Then they stood there, with their hands on the ledge of the berth, and talked. I couldn't see them, but I could tell where they was by the whisky they'd been having. I was glad I didn't drink whisky; but it wouldn't made much difference anyway, because most of the time they couldn't 'a' treed me because I didn't breathe. I was too scared. And, besides, a body *couldn't* breathe and hear such talk. They talked low and earnest. Bill wanted to kill Turner. He says:

"He's said he'll tell, and he will. If we was to give both our shares to him *now* it wouldn't make no difference after the <u>row</u> and the way we've served him. Shore's you're born, he'll turn state's evidence;[15] now you hear me. I'm for putting him out of his troubles."

"So'm I," says Packard, very quiet.

"Blame it, I'd sorter begun to think you wasn't. Well, then, that's all right. Le's go and do it."

"Hold on a minute; I hain't had my say yit. You listen to me. Shooting's good, but there's quieter ways if the thing's got to be done. But what *I* say is this: it ain't good sense to go court'n around after a halter[16] if you can git at what you're up to in some way that's jist as good and at the same time don't bring you into no resks. Ain't that so?"

◄ *Why is Bill sure that they need to kill Jim Turner?*

---

13. **crawfished.** Crawled backward
14. **berth.** Built-in bed or bunk
15. **turn state's evidence.** Give evidence for the prosecution in a criminal case against one's criminal associates
16. **court'n . . . halter.** Seeking out the hangman's rope

Words For Everyday Use	**row** (rou) *n.*, noisy quarrel

► What is Jake's plan for killing Jim Turner? Why is this method better than shooting?

► What plan does Huck have to save the life of the one robber and get all three robbers into trouble? What bad news does Jim give him when he tries to return to the raft?

"You bet it is. But how you goin' to manage it this time?"

"Well, my idea is this: we'll rustle around and gather up whatever pickins we've overlooked in the staterooms, and shove for shore and hide the truck. Then we'll wait. Now I say it ain't a-goin' to be more'n two hours befo' this wrack breaks up and washes off down the river. See? He'll be drownded, and won't have nobody to blame for it but his own self. I reckon that's a considerble sight better 'n killin' of him. I'm unfavorable to killin' a man as long as you can git aroun' it; it ain't good sense, it ain't good morals. Ain't I right?"

"Yes, I reck'n you are. But s'pose she *don't* break up and wash off?"

"Well, we can wait the two hours anyway and see, can't we?"

"All right, then; come along."

So they started, and I lit out, all in a cold sweat, and scrambled forward. It was dark as pitch there; but I said, in a kind of a coarse whisper, "Jim!" and he answered up, right at my elbow, with a sort of a moan, and I says:

"Quick, Jim, it ain't no time for fooling around and moaning; there's a gang of murderers in yonder, and if we don't hunt up their boat and set her drifting down the river so these fellows can't get away from the wreck there's one of 'em going to be in a bad fix. But if we find their boat we can put *all* of 'em in a bad fix—for the sheriff'll get 'em. Quick—hurry! I'll hunt the labboard side, you hunt the stabboard. You start at the raft, and—"

"Oh, my lordy, lordy! *raf'*? Dey ain' no raf' no mo'; she done broke loose en gone!—en here we is!"

CHAPTER 13

Honest Loot from the *Walter Scott*

Well, I catched my breath and most fainted. Shut up on a wreck with such a gang as that! But it warn't no time to be sentimentering. We'd *got* to find that boat now—had to have it for ourselves. So we went a-quaking and shaking down the stabboard side, and slow work it was, too—seemed a week before we got to the stern. No sign of a boat. Jim said he didn't believe he could go any further—so scared he hadn't hardly any strength left, he said. But I said, come on, if we get left on this wreck we are in a fix, sure. So on we prowled again. We struck for the stern of the texas, and found it, and then <u>scrabbled</u> along forwards on the skylight, hanging on from shutter to shutter, for the edge of the skylight was in the water. When we got pretty close to the cross-hall door there was the skiff, sure enough! I could just barely see her. I felt ever so thankful. In another second I would 'a' been aboard of her, but just then the door opened. One of the men stuck his head out only about a couple of foot from me, and I thought I was gone; but he jerked it in again, and says:

"Heave that blame lantern out o' sight, Bill!"

He flung a bag of something into the boat, and then got in himself and set down. It was Packard. Then Bill *he* come out and got in. Packard says, in a low voice:

"All ready—shove off!"

I couldn't hardly hang on to the shutters, I was so weak. But Bill says:

"Hold on—'d you go through him?"

"No. Didn't you?"

"No. So he's got his share o' the cash yet."

"Well, then, come along; no use to take truck and leave money."

"Say, won't he suspicion what we're up to?"

"Maybe he won't. But we got to have it anyway. Come along."

So they got out and went in.

The door slammed to because it was on the <u>careened</u> side; and in a half second I was in the boat, and Jim come

◄ Why is finding the robbers' boat even more urgent now?

◄ What happens just as Huck finds the boat and is about to climb aboard?

◄ Why do the robbers go back inside the ferryboat? As soon as they are inside, what do Huck and Jim do?

Words For Everyday Use	**scrab • ble** (skrab´əl) *vi.,* paw or scratch as in looking for something **ca • reened** (kə rēnd´) *adj.,* tilted

tumbling after me. I out with my knife and cut the rope, and away we went!

We didn't touch an oar, and we didn't speak nor whisper, nor hardly even breathe. We went gliding swift along, dead silent, past the tip of the paddle-box, and past the stern; then in a second or two more we was a hundred yards below the wreck, and the darkness soaked her up, every last sign of her, and we was safe, and knowed it.

When we was three or four hundred yards downstream we see the lantern show like a little spark at the texas door for a second, and we knowed by that that the rascals had missed their boat, and was beginning to understand that they was in just as much trouble now as Jim Turner was.

Then Jim manned the oars, and we took out after our raft. Now was the first time that I begun to worry about the men—I reckon I hadn't had time to before. I begun to think how dreadful it was, even for murderers, to be in such a fix. I says to myself, there ain't no telling but I might come to be a murderer myself yet, and then how would I like it? So says I to Jim:

"The first light we see we'll land a hundred yards below it or above it, in a place where it's a good hiding place for you and the skiff, and then I'll go and fix up some kind of a yarn, and get somebody to go for that gang and get them out of their scrape, so they can be hung when their time comes."

But that idea was a failure; for pretty soon it begun to storm again, and this time worse than ever. The rain poured down, and never a light showed; everybody in bed, I reckon. We boomed along down the river, watching for lights and watching for our raft. After a long time the rain let up, but the clouds stayed, and the lightning kept whimpering, and by and by a flash showed us a black thing ahead, floating, and we made for it.

It was the raft, and mighty glad was we to get aboard of it again. We seen a light now away down to the right, on shore. So I said I would go for it. The skiff was half full of plunder which that gang had stole there on the wreck. We hustled it on to the raft in a pile, and I told Jim to float along down, and show a light when he judged he had gone about two mile, and keep it burning till I come; then I manned my oars and shoved for the light. As I got down towards it three or

▶ What begins to bother Huck? What does he want to try to do?

▶ What does Jim do as Huck goes ashore? Whom does Huck approach?

Words For Everyday Use

yarn (yärn) *n.*, tale or story

plun • der (plunʹdər) *n.*, loot, booty

four more showed—up on a hillside. It was a village. I
in above the shore light, and laid on my oars and floa
I went by I see it was a lantern hanging on the jacksi
double-hull ferryboat. I skimmed around for the wa
a-wondering whereabouts he slept; and by and b
him roosting on the bitts[2] forward, with his b
between his knees. I gave his shoulder two or
shoves, and begun to cry.

He stirred up in a kind of a startlish way; but when he see
it was only me he took a good gap and stretch, and then he
says:

"Hello, what's up? Don't cry, bub. What's the trouble?"

I says:

"Pap, and mam, and sis, and—"

Then I broke down. He says:

"Oh, dang it now, *don't* take on so; we all has to have our
troubles, and this 'n 'll come out all right. What's the matter
with 'em?"

"They're—they're—are you the watchman of the boat?"

"Yes," he says, kind of pretty-well-satisfied like. "I'm the
captain and the owner and the mate and the pilot and
watchman and head deckhand; and sometimes I'm the
freight and passengers. I ain't as rich as old Jim Hornback,
and I can't be so blame' generous and good to Tom, Dick,
and Harry as what he is, and slam around money the way he
does; but I've said many a time 't I wouldn't trade places with
him; for, says I, a sailor's life's the life for me, and I'm derned
if *I'd* live two mile out o' town, where there ain't nothing
ever goin' on, not for all his spondulicks[3] and as much more
on top of it. Says I—"

I broke in and says:

"They're in an awful peck of trouble, and—"

"*Who* is?"

"Why, Pap and Mam and Sis and Miss Hooker; and if you'd
take your ferryboat and go up there—"

"Up where? Where are they?"

"On the wreck."

"What wreck?"

"Why, there ain't but one."

"What, you don't mean the *Walter Scott*?"[4]

"Yes."

"Good land! what are they doin' *there*, for gracious sakes?"

"Well, they didn't go there a-purpose."

◄ How does the
man Huck approaches
describe himself?
According to the
watchman, why
would he never want
to trade places with
Hornback, the richest
man in town?

◄ What is Huck try-
ing to accomplish by
telling an elaborate
story to the watch-
man? Why would the
watchman probably
not go out of his way
to help the people on
the ferryboat if Huck
simply told the truth?

---

1. **jackstaff.** Mast
2. **bitts.** Posts on a steamboat
3. **spondulicks.** Money, cash
4. ***Walter Scott.*** Boat named for Sir Walter Scott, a Scottish novelist and poet

"I bet they didn't! Why, great goodness, there ain't no chance for 'em if they don't git off mighty quick! Why, how in the nation did they ever git into such a scrape?"

"Easy enough. Miss Hooker was a-visiting up there to the town—"

"Yes, Booth's Landing—go on."

"She was a-visiting there at Booth's Landing, and just in the edge of the evening she started over with her nigger woman in the horse-ferry to stay all night at her friend's house, Miss What-you-may-call-her—I disremember her name—and they lost their steering-oar, and swung around and went a-floating down, stern first, about two mile, and saddle-bagged[5] on the wreck, and the ferryman and the nigger woman and the horses was all lost, but Miss Hooker she made a grab and got aboard the wreck. Well, about an hour after dark we come along down in our trading-scow, and it was so dark we didn't notice the wreck till we was right on it; and so *we* saddle-bagged; but all of us was saved but Bill Whipple—and oh, he *was* the best cretur!—I most wish 't it had been me, I do."

"My George! It's the beatenest thing I ever struck. And *then* what did you all do?"

"Well, we hollered and took on, but it's so wide there we couldn't make nobody hear. So pap said somebody got to get ashore and get help somehow. I was the only one that could swim, so I made a dash for it, and Miss Hooker she said if I didn't strike help sooner, come here and hunt up her uncle, and he'd fix the thing. I made the land about a mile below, and been fooling along ever since, trying to get people to do something, but they said, 'What, in such a night and such a current? There ain't no sense in it; go for the steam ferry.' Now if you'll go and—"

"By Jackson, I'd *like* to, and, blame it, I don't know but I will; but who in the dingnation's a-going' to *pay* for it? Do you reckon your pap—"

"Why *that's* all right. Miss Hooker she tole me, *particular,* that her uncle Hornback—"

"Great guns! is *he* her uncle? Looky here, you break for that light over yonder-way, and turn out west when you git there, and about a quarter of a mile out you'll come to the tavern; tell 'em to dart you out to Jim Hornback's, and he'll foot the bill. And don't you fool around any, because he'll want to know the news. Tell him I'll have his niece all safe before he can get to town. Hump yourself, now; I'm a-going up around the corner here to roust out my engineer."

▶ Why does Huck tell the watchman that Hornback's niece is on the stranded ferryboat? In what way does Huck, with his clever story, accomplish what he set out to do?

---

5. **saddle-bagged.** Caught on the wreck

I struck for the light, but as soon as he turned the corner I went back and got into my skiff and bailed her out, and then pulled up shore in the easy water about six hundred yards, and tucked myself in among some woodboats; for I couldn't rest easy till I could see the ferryboat start. But take it all around, I was feeling ruther comfortable on accounts of taking all this trouble for that gang, for not many would 'a' done it. I wished the widow knowed about it. I judged she would be proud of me for helping these rapscallions, because rapscallions and deadbeats[6] is the kind the widow and good people takes the most interest in.

Well, before long here comes the wreck, dim and dusky, sliding along down! A kind of cold shiver went through me, and then I struck out for her. She was very deep, and I see in a minute there warn't much chance for anybody being alive in her. I pulled all around her and hollered a little, but there wasn't any answer; all dead still. I felt a little bit heavy-hearted about the gang, but not much, for I reckoned if they could stand it I could.

Then here comes the ferryboat; so I shoved for the middle of the river on a long downstream slant; and when I judged I was out of eye-reach I laid on my oars, and looked back and see her go and smell around the wreck for Miss Hooker's remainders, because the captain would know her uncle Hornback would want them; and then pretty soon the ferryboat give it up and went for the shore, and I laid into my work and went a-booming down the river.

It did seem a powerful long time before Jim's light showed up; and when it did show it looked like it was a thousand mile off. By the time I got there the sky was beginning to get a little gray in the east; so we struck for an island, and hid the raft, and sunk the skiff, and turned in and slept like dead people.

◀ How does Huck feel about the fact that he took the time to help the robbers on the ferryboat? According to Huck, why would the widow be proud of him?

◀ What does Huck notice about the sinking ferryboat as it floats by him? What appears to have happened to the gang on the ferryboat?

◀ What do Huck and Jim do as soon as Huck returns to the raft?

---

6. **rapscallions and deadbeats.** Scoundrels and lazy, idle people

CHAPTER **14**

Was Solomon Wise?

▶ *What items do Huck and Jim gather from the boat belonging to the robbers?*

By and by, when we got up, we turned over the truck the gang had stole off of the wreck, and found boots, and blankets, and clothes, and all sorts of other things, and a lot of books, and a spyglass, and three boxes of seegars. We hadn't ever been this rich before in neither of our lives. The seegars was prime. We laid off all the afternoon in the woods talking, and me reading the books, and having a general good time. I told Jim all about what happened inside the wreck and at the ferryboat, and I said these kinds of things was adventures; but he said he didn't want no more adventures. He said that when I went in the texas and he crawled back to get on the raft and found her gone he nearly died, because he judged it was all up with him anyway it could be fixed; for if he didn't get saved he would get drownded; and if he did get saved, whoever saved him would send him back home so as to get the reward, and then Miss Watson would sell him South, sure. Well, he was right; he was most always right; he had an uncommon level head for a nigger.

▶ *How does Huck feel about adventure? How does Jim feel about adventure? In what way did the loss of the raft and the possibility of being found on the sinking boat present a much more serious problem for Jim than it did for Huck?*

I read considerable to Jim about kings and dukes and earls and such, and how gaudy they dressed, and how much style they put on, and called each other your majesty, and your grace, and your lordship, and so on, 'stead of mister; and Jim's eyes bugged out, and he was interested. He says:

"I didn' know dey was so many un um. I hain't hearn 'bout none un um, skasely, but ole King Sollermun,[1] onless you counts dem kings dat's in a pack er k'yards. How much do a king git?"

"Get?" I says; "why, they get a thousand dollars a month if they want it; they can have just as much as they want; everything belongs to them."

"*Ain'* dat gay? En what dey got to do, Huck?"

"*They* don't do nothing! Why, how you talk! They just set around."

"No; is dat so?"

▶ *According to Huck, how do kings spend their time?*

"Of course it is. They just set around—except, maybe, when there's a war; then they go to the war. But other times they just lazy around; or go hawking[2]—just hawking and sp—Sh!—d'you hear a noise?"

---

1. **King Sollermun.** King Solomon was an ancient king of Israel noted for his wisdom.
2. **hawking.** Hunting small game with birds of prey

We skipped out and looked; but it warn't nothing but the flutter of a steamboat's wheel away down, coming around the point; so we come back.

"Yes," says I, "and other times, when things is dull, they fuss with the <u>parlyment</u>; and if everybody don't go just so he whacks their heads off. But mostly they hang round the harem."

"Roun' de which?"

"Harem."

"What's de harem?"

"The place where he keeps his wives. Don't you know about the harem? Solomon had one; he had about a million wives."

"Why, yes, dat's so; I—I'd done forgot it. A harem's a bo'd'n-house, I reck'n. Mos' likely dey has rackety times in de nussery. En I reck'n de wives quarrels considable; en dat 'crease de racket. Yit dey say Sollermun de wises' man dat ever live'. I doan' take no stock in dat. Bekase why would a wise man want to live in de mids' er sich a blim-blammin' all de time? No—'deed he wouldn't. A wise man 'ud take en buil' a biler-factry; en den he could shet down de biler-factry when he want to res'."

"Well, but he *was* the wisest man, anyway; because the widow she told me so, her own self."

Who taught Huck about King Solomon?

"I doan k'yer what de widder say, he *warn't* no wise man nuther. He had some er de dad-fetchedes' ways I ever see. Does you know 'bout dat chile dat he 'uz gwyne to chop in two?"[3]

"Yes, the widow told me all about it."

"*Well,* den! Warn' dat de beatenes' notion in de worl'? You jes' take en look at it a minute. Dah's de stump, dah—dat's one er de women; heah's you—dat's de yuther one; I's Sollermun; en dish yer dollar bill's de chile. Bofe un you claims it. What does I do? Does I shin aroun' mongs' de neighbors en fine out which un you de bill do b'long to, en han' it over to de right one, all safe en soun', de way dat anybody dat had any <u>gumption</u> would? No; I take en whack de bill in *two,* en give

---

3. **chile . . . two.** When two women came before King Solomon, each claiming to be the mother of the same child, Solomon announced that he would split the child in two, thus revealing the true mother to be the one who offered to give up the child rather than see it murdered.

Words For Everyday Use	**par • lia • ment** (pär´lə mənt) *n.,* lawmaking body of government
	gump • tion (gump´shən) *n.,* enterprise, common sense

▶ Why does Jim feel
that Solomon was
foolish and bad?
Why does Huck stop
talking about
Solomon?

half un it to you, en de yuther half to de yuther woman.
Dat's de way Sollermun was gwyne to do wid de chile. Now
I want to ast you: what's de use er dat half a bill?—can't buy
noth'n wid it. En what use is a half a chile? I wouldn' give a
dern for a million un um."

"But hang it, Jim, you've clean missed the point—blame it,
you've missed it a thousand mile."

"Who? Me? Go 'long. Doan' talk to me 'bout yo' pints. I
reck'n I knows sense when I sees it; en dey ain' no sense in
sich doin's as dat. De 'spute warn't 'bout a half a chile, de
'spute was 'bout a whole chile; en de man dat think he kin
settle a 'spute 'bout a whole chile wid a half a chile doan'
know enough to come in out'n de rain. Doan' talk to me
'bout Sollermun, Huck, I knows him by de back."

"But I tell you you don't get the point."

"Blame de point! I reck'n I knows what I knows. En mine
you, de *real* pint is down furder—it's down deeper. It lays in
de way Sollermun was raised. You take a man dat's got on'y
one or two chillen; is dat man gwyne to be waseful o'
chillen? No, he ain't; he can't 'ford it. *He* know how to value
'em. But you take a man dat's got 'bout five million chillen
runnin' roun' de house, en it's diffunt. *He* as soon chop a
chile in two as a cat. Dey's plenty mo'. A chile er two, mo'er
less, warn't no <u>consekens</u> to Sollermun, dad fetch him!"

I never see such a nigger. If he got a notion in his head
once, there warn't no getting it out again. He was the most
down on Solomon of any nigger I ever see. So I went to talking about other kings, and let Solomon slide. I told about
Louis Sixteenth that got his head cut off in France long time
ago; and about his little boy the dolphin,[4] that would 'a'
been a king, but they took and shut him up in jail, and some
say he died there.

"Po' little chap."

"But some says he got out and got away, and come to
America."

▶ Why does Jim feel
sorry for the French
king in America?
According to Huck,
what job options
does a king have in
America?

"Dat's good! But he'll be pooty lonesome—dey ain' no
kings here, is dey, Huck?"

---

4. **Louis Sixteenth . . . dolphin.** Louis XVI was beheaded in the French
Revolution of 1793. His son, the dauphin, was falsely believed to have survived.
Though he had not, many imposters claimed to be him, and thus, heir to the
throne.

**Words
For
Everyday
Use**   con • se • quence (kän´si kwens´) *n.,* importance

"No."

"Den he cain't git no <u>situation</u>. What he gwyne to do?"

"Well, I don't know. Some of them gets on the police, and some of them learns people how to talk French."

"Why, Huck, doan' de French people talk de same way we does?"

"No, Jim; you couldn't understand a word they said—not a single word."

"Well, now, I be ding-busted! How do dat come?"

"I don't know; but it's so. I got some of their jabber out of a book. S'pose a man was to come to you and say Polly-voo-franzy⁵—what would you think?"

"I wouldn' think nuff'n; I'd take en bust him over de head —dat is, if he warn't white. I wouldn't 'low no nigger to call me dat."

"Shucks, it ain't calling you anything. It's only saying, do you know how to talk French?"

"Well, den, why couldn't he *say* it?"

"Why, he *is* a-saying it. That's a Frenchman's *way* of saying it."

"Well, it's a blame ridicklous way, en I doan' want to hear no mo' 'bout it. Dey ain' no sense in it."

"Looky here, Jim; does a cat talk like we do?"

"No, a cat don't."

"Well, does a cow?"

"No, a cow don't, nuther."

"Does a cat talk like a cow, or a cow talk like a cat?"

"No, dey don't."

"It's natural and right for 'em to talk different from each other, ain't it?"

"Course."

"And ain't it natural and right for a cat and a cow to talk different from us?"

"Why, mos' sholy it is."

"Well, then, why ain't it natural and right for a *Frenchman* to talk different from us? You answer me that."

"Is a cat a man, Huck?"

"No."

"Well, den, dey ain't no sense in a cat talkin' like a man. Is

◀ *About what do Huck and Jim disagree next? In what ways are Huck and Jim good company for each other on the long raft trip?*

---

5. **Polly-voo-franzy.** *Parlez-vous Francais?* French for "Do you speak French?"

Words For Everyday Use	sit • u • a • tion (sichˊo͞o āˊshən) *n.*, position of employment

a cow a man?—er is a cow a cat?"

"No, she ain't either of them."

"Well, den, she ain't got no business to talk like either one er the yuther of 'em. Is a Frenchman a man?"

"Yes."

"*Well,* den! Dad blame it, why doan' he *talk* like a man? You answer me *dat!*"

I see it warn't no use wasting words—you can't learn a nigger to argue. So I quit.

CHAPTER 15

Fooling Poor Old Jim

We judged that three nights more would fetch us to Cairo,[1] at the bottom of Illinois, where the Ohio River comes in, and that was what we was after. We would sell the raft and get on a steamboat and go way up the Ohio amongst the free states, and then be out of trouble.

◄ What do Huck and Jim plan to do when they reach Cairo? When will they be out of trouble?

Well, the second night a fog begun to come on, and we made for a towhead to tie to, for it wouldn't do to try to run in a fog; but when I paddled ahead in the canoe, with the line to make fast, there warn't anything but little saplings to tie to. I passed the line around one of them right on the edge of the cut bank, but there was a stiff current, and the raft come booming down so lively she tore it out by the roots and away she went. I see the fog closing down, and it made me so sick and scared I couldn't budge for most a half a minute it seemed to me—and then there warn't no raft in sight; you couldn't see twenty yards. I jumped into the canoe and run back to the stern, and grabbed the paddle and set her back a stroke. But she didn't come. I was in such a hurry I hadn't untied her. I got up and tried to untie her, but I was so excited my hands shook so I couldn't hardly do anything with them.

◄ Why does Huck need to tie the raft? What happens to the raft when Huck tries to tie it?

As soon as I got started I took out after the raft, hot and heavy, right down the towhead. That was all right as far as it went, but the towhead warn't sixty yards long, and the minute I flew by the foot of it I shot out into the solid white fog, and hadn't no more idea which way I was going than a dead man.

Thinks I, it won't do to paddle; first I know I'll run into the bank or a towhead or something; I got to set still and float, and yet it's mighty fidgety business to have to hold your hands still at such a time. I whooped and listened. Away down there somewheres I hears a small whoop, and up comes my spirits. I went tearing after it, listening sharp to hear it again. The next time it come I see I warn't heading for it, but heading away to the right of it. And the next time I was heading away to the left of it—and not gaining on it much either, for I was flying around, this way and that and t'other, but it was going straight ahead all the time.

◄ What does Huck know he must not do, since he can't see anything?

◄ What do Huck and Jim do to keep track of each other in the fog?

I did wish the fool would think to beat a tin pan, and beat it all the time, but he never did, and it was the still places between the whoops that was making the trouble for me.

---

1. **Cairo.** The Mississippi and Ohio Rivers intersect here.

Well, I fought along, and directly I hears the whoop *behind* me. I was tangled good now. That was somebody else's whoop, or else I was turned around.

I throwed the paddle down. I heard the whoop again; it was behind me yet, but in a different place; it kept coming, and kept changing its place, and I kept answering, till by and by it was in front of me again, and I knowed the current had swung the canoe's head downstream, and I was all right if that was Jim and not some other raftsman hollering. I couldn't tell nothing about voices in a fog, for nothing don't look natural nor sound natural in a fog.

The whooping went on, and in about a minute I come a-booming down on a cut bank with smoky ghosts of big trees on it, and the current throwed me off to the left and shot by, amongst a lot of snags that fairly roared, the current was tearing by them so swift.

In another second or two it was solid white and still again. I set perfectly still then, listening to my heart thump, and I reckon I didn't draw a breath while it thumped a hundred.

I just give up then. I knowed what the matter was. That cut bank was an island, and Jim had gone down t'other side of it. It warn't no towhead that you could float by in ten minutes. It had the big timber of a regular island; it might be five or six miles long and more than half a mile wide.

I kept quiet, with my ears cocked, about fifteen minutes, I reckon. I was floating along, of course, four or five miles an hour; but you don't ever think of that. No, you *feel* like you are laying dead still on the water; and if a little glimpse of a snag slips by you don't think to yourself how fast you're going, but you catch your breath and think, my! how that snag's tearing along. If you think it ain't <u>dismal</u> and lonesome out in a fog that way by yourself in the night, you try it once—you'll see.

Next, for about a half an hour, I whoops now and then; at last I hears the answer a long ways off, and tries to follow it, but I couldn't do it, and directly I judged I'd got into a nest of towheads, for I had little dim glimpses of them on both sides of me—sometimes just a narrow channel between, and some that I couldn't see I knowed was there because I'd hear the wash of the current against the old dead brush and trash that hung over the banks. Well, I warn't long loosing the

► What does Huck realize about the cut bank? Where is Jim?

► How does Huck feel being out in the fog by himself?

Words For Everyday Use	**dis • mal** (diz´məl) *adj.*, causing gloom or misery; depressing

whoops down amongst the towheads; and I only tried to chase them a little while, anyway, because it was worse than chasing a Jack-o'-lantern.[2] You never knowed a sound dodge around so, and swap places so quick and so much.

I had to claw away from the bank pretty lively four or five times, to keep from knocking the islands out of the river; and so I judged the raft must be butting into the bank every now and then, or else it would get further ahead and clear out of hearing—it was floating a little faster than what I was.

Well, I seemed to be in the open river again by and by, but I couldn't hear no sign of a whoop nowheres. I reckoned Jim had fetched up on a snag, maybe, and it was all up with him. I was good and tired, so I laid down in the canoe and said I wouldn't bother no more. I didn't want to go to sleep, of course; but I was so sleepy I couldn't help it; so I thought I would take jest one little catnap.

◄ What does Huck fear might have happened to Jim?

But I reckon it was more than a catnap, for when I waked up the stars was shining bright, the fog was all gone, and I was spinning down a big bend stern first. First I didn't know where I was; I thought I was dreaming; and when things began to come back to me they seemed to come up dim out of last week.

It was a monstrous big river here, with the tallest and the thickest kind of timber on both banks; just a solid wall, as well as I could see by the stars. I looked away downstream, and seen a black speck on the water. I took after it; but when I got to it it warn't nothing but a couple of saw-logs made fast together. Then I see another speck, and chased that; then another, and this time I was right. It was the raft.

When I got to it Jim was setting there with his head down between his knees, asleep, with his right arm hanging over the steering-oar. The other oar was smashed off, and the raft was littered up with leaves and branches and dirt. So she'd had a rough time.

◄ When Huck catches up with the raft, what is Jim doing? How does Huck know that Jim and the raft had a "rough time"? How does Jim react to Huck's reappearance?

I made fast and laid down under Jim's nose on the raft, and began to gap, and stretch my fists out against Jim, and says:

"Hello, Jim, have I been asleep? Why didn't you stir me up?"

"Goodness gracious, is dat you, Huck? En you ain' dead—you ain' drownded—you's back ag'in? It's too good for true, honey, it's too good for true. Lemme look at you chile, lemme feel o' you. No, you ain' dead! you's back ag'in, 'live en soun', jis de same ole Huck—de same ole Huck, thanks to goodness!"

"What's the matter with you, Jim? You been a-drinking?"

---

2. **Jack-o'-lantern.** Phosphorescent light, appearing over marshland, caused by decaying plant life

"Drinkin'? Has I ben a-drinkin'? Has I had a chance to be a-drinkin'?"

"Well, then, what makes you talk so wild?"

"How does I talk wild?"

"*How?* Why, hain't you been talking about my coming back, and all that stuff, as if I'd been gone away?"

"Huck—Huck Finn, you look me in de eye; look me in de eye. *Hain't* you ben gone away?"

"Gone away? Why, what in the nation do you mean? I hain't been gone anywheres. Where would I go to?"

"Well, looky here, boss, dey's sumf'n wrong, dey is. Is I *me,* or who *is* I? Is I heah, or whah *is* I? Now dat's what I wants to know."

"Well, I think you're here, plain enough, but I think you're a tangle-headed old fool, Jim."

"I is, is I? Well, you answer me dis: Didn't you tote out de line in de canoe fer to make fas' to de towhead?"

"No, I didn't. What towhead? I hain't see no towhead."

"You hain't seen no towhead? Looky here, didn't de line pull loose en de raf' go a-hummin' down de river, en leave you en de canoe behine in de fog?"

"What fog?"

"Why, *de* fog!—de fog dat's been aroun' all night. En did-n't you whoop, en didn't I whoop, tell we got mix' up in de islands en one un us got los' en t'other one was jis' as good as los', 'kase he didn' know whah he wuz? En didn't I bust up agin a lot er dem islands en have a turrible time en mos' git drownded? Now ain' dat so, boss—ain't it so? You answer me dat."

"Well, this is too many for me, Jim. I hain't seen no fog, nor no islands, nor no troubles, nor nothing. I been setting here talking with you all night till you went to sleep about ten minutes ago, and I reckon I done the same. You couldn't 'a' got drunk in that time, so of course you've been dreaming."

"Dad fetch it, how is I gwyne to dream all dat in ten minutes?"

"Well, hang it all, you did dream it, because there didn't any of it happen."

"But, Huck, it's all jis' as plain to me as—"

"It don't make no difference how plain it is; there ain't nothing in it. I know, because I've been here all the time."

Jim didn't say nothing for about five minutes, but set there studying over it. Then he says:

"Well, den, I reck'n I did dream it, Huck; but dog my cats ef it ain't de powerfulest dream I ever see. En I hain't ever had no dream b'fo' dat's tired me like dis one."

▶ What lie does Huck tell Jim?

▶ What does Huck make Jim believe about the situation?

"Oh, well, that's all right, because a dream does tire a body like everything sometimes. But this one was a staving³ dream; tell me all about it, Jim."

So Jim went to work and told me the whole thing right through, just as it happened, only he painted it up considerable. Then he said he must start in and "'terpret" it, because it was sent for a warning. He said the first towhead stood for a man that would try to do us some good, but the current was another man that would get us away from him. The whoops was warnings that would come to us every now and then, and if we didn't try hard to make out to understand them they'd just take us into bad luck, 'stead of keeping us out of it. The lot of towheads was troubles we was going to get into with quarrelsome people and all kinds of mean folks, but if we minded our business and didn't talk back and aggravate them, we would pull through and get out of the fog and into the big clear river, which was the free states, and wouldn't have no more trouble.

It had clouded up pretty dark just after I got on to the raft, but it was clearing up again now.

"Oh, well, that's all interpreted well enough as far as it goes, Jim," I says; "but what does *these* things stand for?"

It was the leaves and rubbish on the raft and the smashed oar. You could see them first-rate now.

Jim looked at the trash, and then looked at me, and back at the trash again. He had got the dream fixed so strong in his head that he couldn't seem to shake it loose and get the facts back into its place again right away. But when he did get the thing straightened around he looked at me steady without ever smiling, and says:

"What do dey stan' for? I'se gwyne to tell you. When I got all wore out wid work, en wid de callin' for you, en went to sleep, my heart wuz mos' broke bekase you wuz los', en I didn' k'yer no' mo' what become er me en de raf'. En when I wake up en fine you back agin, all safe en soun', de tears come, en I could 'a' got down on my knees en kiss yo' foot, I's so thankful. En all you wuz thinkin' 'bout wuz how you could make a fool uv ole Jim wid a lie. Dat truck dah is trash; en trash is what people is dat puts dirt on de head er dey fren's en makes 'em ashamed."

◄ *Why is Jim disappointed in Huck? How does Huck feel after Jim scolds him? What does Huck vow never to do again?*

---

3. **staving.** Powerful

Then he got up slow and walked to the wigwam, and went in there without saying anything but that. But that was enough. It made me feel so mean I could almost kissed *his* foot to get him to take it back.

It was fifteen minutes before I could work myself up to go and humble myself to a nigger; but I done it, and I warn't ever sorry for it afterwards, neither. I didn't do him no more mean tricks, and I wouldn't done that one if I'd 'a' knowed it would make him feel that way.

CHAPTER 16

The Rattlesnake Skin Does Its Work

We slept most all day, and started out at night, a little ways behind a monstrous long raft that was as long going by as a procession. She had four long sweeps[1] at each end, so we judged she carried as many as thirty men, likely. She had five big wigwams aboard, wide apart, and an open campfire in the middle, and a tall flagpole at each end. There was a power of style about her. It *amounted* to something being a raftsman on such a craft as that.

◀ In what way does Huck describe the large raft? How would he feel being a raftsman on such a raft?

We went drifting down into a big bend, and the night clouded up and got hot. The river was very wide, and was walled with solid timber on both sides; you couldn't see a break in it hardly ever, or a light. We talked about Cairo, and wondered whether we would know it when we got to it. I said likely we wouldn't, because I had heard say there warn't but about a dozen houses there, and if they didn't happen to have them lit up, how was we going to know we was passing a town? Jim said if the two big rivers joined together there, that would show. But I said maybe we might think we was passing the foot of an island and coming into the same old river again. That disturbed Jim—and me too. So the question was, what to do? I said, paddle ashore the first time a light showed, and tell them Pap was behind, coming along with a trading-scow, and was a greenhand[2] at the business, and wanted to know how far it was to Cairo. Jim thought it was a good idea, so we took a smoke on it and waited.

◀ What thought concerns Huck and Jim as they approach Cairo? What plan does Huck create to solve the problem?

There warn't nothing to do now but to look out sharp for the town, and not pass it without seeing it. He said he'd be mighty sure to see it, because he'd be a free man the minute he seen it, but if he missed it he'd be in a slave country again and no more show for freedom. Every little while he jumps up and says:

"Dah she is?"

But it warn't. It was Jack-o'-lanterns, or lightning bugs; so he set down again, and went to watching, same as before.

---

1. **sweeps.** Oars used with a sweeping motion to propel or steer
2. **greenhand.** Inexperienced person; beginner

Words For Everyday Use

pro • ces • sion (prō sesh´ən) *n.*, parade or other formal movement of a group

▶ When Jim begins to talk about his freedom, why does Huck's conscience begin to bother him?

Jim said it made him all over trembly and feverish to be so close to freedom. Well, I can tell you it made me all over trembly and feverish, too, to hear him, because I began to get it through my head that he *was* most free—and who was to blame for it? Why, *me.* I couldn't get that out of my conscience, no how nor no way. It got to troubling me so I couldn't rest; I couldn't stay still in one place. It hadn't ever come home to me before, what this thing was that I was doing. But now it did; and it stayed with me, and <u>scorched</u> me more and more. I tried to make out to myself that *I* warn't to blame, because *I* didn't run Jim off from his rightful owner; but it warn't no use, conscience up and says, every time, "But you knowed he was running for his freedom, and you could 'a' paddled ashore and told somebody." That was so—I couldn't get around that no way. That was where it pinched. Conscience says to me, "What had poor Miss Watson done to you that you could see her nigger go off right under your eyes and never say one single word? What did

▶ What does Huck begin to remember about Miss Watson?

that poor old woman do to you that you could treat her so mean? Why, she tried to learn you your book, she tried to learn you your manners, she tried to be good to you every way she knowed how. *That's* what she done."

I got to feeling so mean and so miserable I most wished I was dead. I fidgeted up and down the raft, abusing myself to myself, and Jim was fidgeting up and down past me. We neither of us could keep still. Every time he danced around and says, "Dah's Cairo!" it went through me like a shot, and I thought if it *was* Cairo I reckoned I would die of miserableness.

▶ What does Jim plan to do once he gets to a free state?

Jim talked out loud all the time while I was talking to myself. He was saying how the first thing he would do when he got to a free state he would go to saving up money and never spend a single cent, and when he got enough he would buy his wife, which was owned on a farm close to where Miss Watson lived; and then they would both work to buy the two children, and if their master wouldn't sell them, they'd get an Ab'litionist to go and steal them.

It most froze me to hear such talk. He wouldn't ever dared to talk such talk in his life before. Just see what a difference it made in him the minute he judged he was about free. It was according to the old saying, "Give a nigger an inch and

Words For Everyday Use	**scorch** (skôrch) *vt.,* damage, burn

he'll take an ell."[3] Thinks I, this is what comes of my not thinking. Here was this nigger, which I had as good as helped to run away, coming right out flat-footed and saying he would steal his children—children that belonged to a man I didn't even know; a man that hadn't ever done me no harm.

I was sorry to hear Jim say that, it was such a lowering of him. My conscience got to stirring me up hotter than ever, until at last I says to it, "Let up on me—it ain't too late yet—I'll paddle ashore at the first light and tell." I felt easy and happy and light as a feather right off. All my troubles was gone. I went to looking out sharp for a light, and sort of singing to myself. By and by one showed. Jim sings out:

◄ What thought makes Huck feel better about himself?

"We's safe, Huck, we's safe! Jump up and crack yo' heels! Dat's de good ole Cairo at las', I jis knows it!"

I says:

"I'll take the canoe and go and see, Jim. It mightn't be, you know."

He jumped and got the canoe ready, and put his old coat in the bottom for me to set on, and give me the paddle; and as I shoved off, he says:

"Pooty soon I'll be a-shout'n' for joy, en I'll say, it's all on accounts o' Huck; I's a free man, en I couldn't ever ben free ef it hadn' ben for Huck; Huck done it. Jim won't ever forgit you, Huck; you's de bes' fren' Jim's ever had; en you's de *only* fren' ole Jim's got now."

◄ What does Jim say to Huck as Huck leaves in the canoe? How do Jim's words make Huck feel? Why do you think Huck has such mixed feelings?

I was paddling off, all in a sweat to tell on him; but when he says this, it seemed to kind of take the tuck all out of me. I went along slow then, and I warn't right down certain whether I was glad I started or whether I warn't. When I was fifty yards off, Jim says:

"Dah you goes, de ole true Huck; de on'y white genlman dat ever kep' his promise to ole Jim."

Well, I just felt sick. But I says, I got to do it—I can't get *out* of it. Right then along comes a skiff with two men in it with guns, and they stopped and I stopped. One of them says:

"What's that yonder?"

"A piece of a raft," I says.

"Do you belong on it?"

"Yes, sir."

"Any men on it?"

"Only one, sir."

"Well, there's five niggers run off tonight up yonder, above the head of the bend. Is your man white or black?"

◄ What do the men ask Huck? What is Huck's response? What do the men say they want to do?

I didn't answer up prompt. I tried to, but the words wouldn't

---

3. **ell.** Unit of measure equal to 45 inches

come. I tried for a second or two to brace up and out with it, but I warn't man enough—hadn't the spunk of a rabbit. I see I was weakening; so I just give up trying, and up and says:

"He's white."

"I reckon we'll go and see for ourselves."

"I wish you would," says I, "because it's Pap that's there, and maybe you'd help me tow the raft ashore where the light is. He's sick—and so is mam and Mary Ann."

"Oh, the devil! we're in a hurry, boy. But I s'pose we've got to. Come, buckle to your paddle, and let's get along."

I buckled to my paddle and they laid to their oars. When we had made a stroke or two, I says:

"Pap'll be mighty much obleeged to you, I can tell you. Everybody goes away when I want them to help me tow the raft ashore, and I can't do it by myself."

"Well, that's infernal mean. Odd, too. Say, boy, what's the matter with your father?"

"It's the—a—the—well, it ain't anything much."

They stopped pulling. It warn't but a mighty little ways to the raft now. One says:

"Boy, that's a lie. What is the matter with your pap? Answer up square now, and it'll be the better for you."

"I will, sir, I will, honest—but don't leave us, please. It's the—the—Gentlemen, if you'll only pull ahead, and let me heave you the headline, you won't have to come a-near the raft—please do."

"Set her back, John, set her back!" says one. They backed water. "Keep away, boy—keep to looard. Confound it, I just expect the wind has blowed it to us. Your pap's got the small-pox, and you know it precious well. Why didn't you come out and say so? Do you want to spread it all over?"

"Well," says I, a-blubbering, "I've told everybody before, and they just went away and left us."

"Poor devil, there's something in that. We are right down sorry for you, but we—well, hang it, we don't want the smallpox, you see. Look here, I'll tell you what to do. Don't you try to land by yourself, or you'll smash everything to pieces. You float along down about twenty miles, and you'll come to a town on the left-hand side of the river. It will be long after sunup then, and when you ask for help you tell them your folks are all down with chills and fever. Don't be

▶ What lie does Huck allow the men to believe so that they won't come near the raft? How do the men react?

▶ What advice do the men give Huck? How do the men feel about leaving Huck? What do they give him?

Words For Everyday Use	**spunk** (spuŋk) n., courage

a fool again, and let people guess what is the matter. Now we're trying to do you a kindness; so you just put twenty miles between us, that's a good boy. It wouldn't do any good to land yonder where the light is—it's only a wood-yard. Say, I reckon your father's poor, and I'm bound to say he's in pretty hard luck. Here, I'll put a twenty-dollar gold piece on this board, and you get it when it floats by. I feel mighty mean to leave you; but my kingdom! it won't do to fool with small-pox, don't you see?"

"Hold on, Parker," says the other man, "here's a twenty to put on the board for me. Good-bye, boy; you do as Mr. Parker told you, and you'll be all right."

"That's so, my boy—good-bye, good-bye. If you see any runaway niggers you get help and nab them, and you can make some money by it."

"Good-bye, sir," says I; "I won't let no runaway niggers get by me if I can help it."

They went off and I got aboard the raft, feeling bad and low, because I knowed very well I had done wrong, and I see it warn't no use for me to try to learn to do right; a body that don't get *started* right when he's little ain't got no show—when the pinch comes there ain't nothing to back him up and keep him to his work, and so he gets beat. Then I thought a minute, and says to myself, hold on; s'pose you'd 'a' done right and give Jim up, would you felt better than what you do now? No, says I, I'd feel bad—I'd feel just the same way I do now. Well, then, says I, what's the use you learning to do right when it's troublesome to do right and ain't no trouble to do wrong, and the wages is just the same? I was stuck. I couldn't answer that. So I reckoned I wouldn't bother no more about it, but after this always do whichever come handiest at the time.

I went into the wigwam; Jim warn't there. I looked all around; he warn't anywhere. I says:

"Jim!"

"Here I is, Huck. Is dey out o' sight yit? Don't talk loud."

He was in the river under the stern oar, with just his nose out. I told him they were out of sight, so he come aboard. He says:

"I was a-listenin' to all de talk, en I slips into de river en was gwyne to shove for sho' if dey come aboard. Den I was gwyne to swim to de raf' agin when dey was gone. But lawsy, how you did fool 'em, Huck! Dat *wuz* de smartes' <u>dodge</u>! I tell

◄ How does Huck feel about having lied to the men? Even though he knows he is breaking the law by helping Jim, how does he guess he would have felt if he had told them about Jim? What does he decide about "doing right"?

◄ What would Jim have done if the men had boarded the raft? How does Jim feel about what Huck did to help him?

Words For Everyday Use

dodge (däj) *n.*, trick or strategy of evasion

you, chile, I 'spec it save' ole Jim—ole Jim ain't going to forgit you for dat, honey."

Then we talked about the money. It was a pretty good raise—twenty dollars apiece. Jim said we could take deck passage on a steamboat now, and the money would last us as far as we wanted to go in the free states. He said twenty mile more warn't far for the raft to go, but he wished we was already there.

Towards daybreak we tied up, and Jim was mighty particular about hiding the raft good. Then he worked all day fixing things in bundles, and getting all ready to quit rafting.

That night about ten we hove in sight of the lights of a town away down in a left-hand bend.

I went off in the canoe to ask about it. Pretty soon I found a man out in the river with a skiff, setting a trot-line. I ranged up and says:

"Mister, is that town Cairo?"

"Cairo? no. You must be a blame' fool."

"What town is it, mister?"

"If you want to know, go and find out. If you stay here botherin' around me for about a half a minute longer you'll get something you won't want."

I paddled to the raft. Jim was awful disappointed, but I said never mind, Cairo would be the next place, I reckoned.

We passed another town before daylight, and I was going out again; but it was high ground, so I didn't go. No high ground about Cairo, Jim said. I had forgot it. We laid up for the day on a towhead tolerable close to the left-hand bank. I begun to suspicion something. So did Jim. I says:

"Maybe we went by Cairo in the fog that night."

He says:

"Doan' le's talk about it, Huck. Po' niggers can't have no luck. I awluz 'spected dat rattlesnake skin warn't done wid its work."

"I wish I'd never seen that snakeskin, Jim—I do wish I'd never laid eyes on it."

"It ain't yo' fault, Huck; you didn' know. Don't you blame yo'self 'bout it."

When it was daylight, here was the clear Ohio water inshore, sure enough, and outside was the old regular Muddy! So it was all up with Cairo.[4]

We talked it all over. It wouldn't do to take to the shore; we couldn't take the raft up the stream, of course. There warn't

▶ What thought starts to bother both Huck and Jim? On what do the two continue to blame their misfortunes?

▶ When Huck and Jim decide that they really did miss Cairo, what do they decide they must do? When they return to the raft after dark, what terrible discovery do they make?

---

4. **all up with Cairo.** Huck knows from the clear water mixed with the muddy that they have passed the point where the Ohio and Mississippi join; Cairo lies just above the intersection—they have floated too far downstream.

no way but to wait for dark, and start back in the canoe and take the chances. So we slept all day amongst the cotton-wood thicket, so as to be fresh for the work, and when we went back to the raft about dark the canoe was gone!

We didn't say a word for a good while. There warn't any-thing to say. We both knowed well enough it was some more work of the rattlesnake skin; so what was the use to talk about it? It would only look like we was finding fault, and that would be bound to fetch more bad luck—and keep on fetching it, too, till we knowed enough to keep still.

By and by we talked about what we better do, and found there warn't no way but just to go along down with the raft till we got a chance to buy a canoe to go back in. We warn't going to borrow it when there warn't anybody around, the way Pap would do, for that might set people after us.

So we shoved out after dark on the raft.

Anybody that don't believe yet that it's foolishness to handle a snakeskin, after all that that snakeskin done for us, will believe it now if they read on and see what more it done for us.

The place to buy canoes is off of rafts laying up at shore. But we didn't see no rafts laying up; so we went along dur-ing three hours and more. Well, the night got gray and ruther thick, which is the next meanest thing to fog. You can't tell the shape of the river, and you can't see no dis-tance. It got to be very late and still, and then along comes a steamboat up the river. We lit the lantern, and judged she would see it. Upstream boats didn't generly come close to us; they go out and follow the bars and hunt for easy water under the reefs; but nights like this they bull right up the channel against the whole river.

We could hear her pounding along, but we didn't see her good till she was close. She aimed right for us. Often they do that and try to see how close they can come without touch-ing; sometimes the wheel bites off a sweep, and then the pilot sticks his head out and laughs, and thinks he's mighty smart. Well, here she comes, and we said she was going to try and shave us; but she didn't seem to be sheering off a bit. She was a big one, and she was coming in a hurry, too, looking like a black cloud with rows of glowworms around it; but all of a sudden she bulged out, big and scary, with a long row of wide-open furnace doors shining like red-hot teeth, and her monstrous bows and guards hanging right over us. There was a yell at us, and a jingling of bells to stop the engines, a pow-wow of cussing, and whistling of steam—and as Jim went overboard on one side and I on the other, she come smash-ing straight through the raft.

◀ Why do Huck and Jim need a canoe to go back and then up the Ohio River? What do Huck and Jim decide is their only option?

◀ What happens when Huck and Jim encounter the steam-boat in their path?

I dived—and I aimed to find the bottom, too, for a thirty-foot wheel had got to go over me, and I wanted it to have plenty of room. I could always stay under water a minute; this time I reckon I stayed under a minute and a half. Then I bounced for the top in a hurry, for I was nearly busting. I popped out to my armpits and blowed the water out of my nose, and puffed a bit. Of course there was a booming current; and of course that boat started her engines again ten seconds after she stopped them, for they never cared much for raftsmen; so now she was churning along up the river, out of sight in the thick weather, though I could hear her.

▶ What does Huck do after he calls for Jim and gets no response?

I sung out for Jim about a dozen times, but I didn't get any answer; so I grabbed a plank that touched me while I was "treading water," and struck out for shore, shoving it ahead of me. But I made out to see that the drift of the current was towards the left-hand shore, which meant that I was in a crossing; so I changed off and went that way.

It was one of these long, slanting, two-mile crossings; so I was a good long time in getting over. I made a safe landing, and clumb up the bank. I couldn't see but a little ways, but I went poking along over rough ground for a quarter of a mile or more, and then I run across a big old-fashioned double log house before I noticed it. I was going to rush by and get away, but a lot of dogs jumped out and went to howling and barking at me, and I knowed better than to move another peg.

▶ What does Huck come across on land? What happens when he tries to get away?

Responding to the Selection

"Take it all round, we lived pretty high." This is how Huck describes their first days floating down the river on the raft. Do you agree or disagree? Would you like to set out on this kind of adventure?

Reviewing the Selection

Recalling and Interpreting

1. **R:** What do Huck and Jim do to prepare the raft for travel? What is unusual about the steamboat they encounter? Who takes the lead in deciding to explore the steamboat?

2. **I:** How are Jim and Huck feeling during their first few nights of rafting? When they find the steamboat, why do you think Jim wants to keep Huck from boarding it? In what way does he have the most to lose?

3: **R:** What almost hinders Huck's and Jim's escape from the steamboat? How do they finally get away?

4: **I:** Why doesn't Huck simply leave the men on the boat to their fate? Why does he fabricate an elaborate story in an attempt to help them? What does this reveal about Huck's character?

5. **R:** On a particularly foggy night, what causes Huck to lose sight of the raft and Jim? Where is the raft when he finally finds it, and what condition is it in? What prank does he try to play on Jim? When Jim catches on to the prank, what vow does Huck make?

6: **I:** What is Jim's reaction to seeing Huck? How does Jim feel about the joke Huck played on him? How does Huck feel after being scolded by Jim? How do you know, based on this incident, that Huck takes Jim's feelings and Jim's friendship seriously?

7. **R:** What does Jim plan to do when he gets his freedom? What does Huck plan to do when he takes the canoe ashore? What does Jim tell Huck as he is leaving in the canoe? What lies does Huck tell the men who are looking for runaway slaves?

8. **I:** Why does Huck begin to feel uncomfortable as Jim talks about his plans for the future? When Huck leaves the raft to go ashore, how do Jim's parting words affect him? Why does Huck decide that it's "troublesome to do right"?

Synthesizing

9. In what way has the rafting trip taken a much more serious turn for Huck? What issue related to himself and Jim is he forced to confront? By trying to help the robbers aboard the sinking steamboat and by making the decision to lie to the men searching for slaves, what is he revealing about his individuality and his personal sense of right and wrong?

10. In this section, when does Huck show himself to be both clever and practical? When does he show himself to be compassionate and mature?

Understanding Literature (QUESTIONS FOR DISCUSSION)

1. **Symbol.** A **symbol** is a thing that stands for or represents both itself and something else. What does the river represent to Huck and Jim? Of what might the fog be symbolic?

2. **Conflict.** A **conflict** is a struggle between two forces in a literary work. A struggle that takes place between a character and some outside force is called an **external conflict**. A struggle that takes place within a character is called an **internal conflict**. What internal conflicts does Huck face? How does he resolve this conflict, at least temporarily?

CHAPTER 17

The Grangerfords Take Me In

In about a minute somebody spoke out of a window without putting his head out, and says:

"Be done, boys! Who's there?"

I says:

"It's me."

"Who's me?"

"George Jackson, sir."

"What do you want?"

"I don't want nothing, sir. I only want to go along by, but the dogs won't let me."

"What are you prowling around here this time of night for—hey?"

"I warn't prowling around, sir; I fell overboard off of the steamboat."

"Oh, you did, did you? Strike a light there, somebody. What did you say your name was?"

"George Jackson, sir. I'm only a boy."

"Look here, if you're telling the truth you needn't be afraid —nobody'll hurt you. But don't try to budge; stand right where you are. Rouse out Bob and Tom, some of you, and fetch the guns. George Jackson, is there anybody with you?"

"No, sir, nobody."

I heard the people stirring around in the house now, and see a light. The man sung out:

"Snatch that light away, Betsy, you old fool—ain't you got any sense? Put it on the floor behind the front door. Bob, if you and Tom are ready, take your places."

"All ready."

"Now, George Jackson, do you know the Shepherdsons?"

"No, sir; I never heard of them."

"Well, that may be so, and it mayn't. Now, all ready. Step forward, George Jackson. And mind, don't you hurry—come mighty slow. If there's anybody with you, let him keep back—if he shows himself he'll be shot. Come along now. Come slow; push the door open yourself—just enough to squeeze in, d' you hear?"

I didn't hurry; I couldn't if I'd a-wanted to. I took one slow step at a time and there warn't a sound, only I thought I could hear my heart. The dogs were as still as the humans, but they followed a little behind me. When I got to the three log doorsteps I heard them unlocking and unbarring and

◄ When Huck is forced to identify himself, what does he say? What does he claim happened to him?

◄ How do the owners of the home react to Huck's appearance on the property? What do they ask Huck? Do they seem to trust his response?

unbolting. I put my hand on the door and pushed it a little and a little more till somebody said, "There, that's enough—put your head in." I done it, but I judged they would take it off.

The candle was on the floor, and there they all was, looking at me, and me at them, for about a quarter of a minute: Three big men with guns pointed at me, which made me wince, I tell you; the oldest, gray and about sixty, the other two thirty or more—all of them fine and handsome—and the sweetest old gray-headed lady, and back of her two young women which I couldn't see right well. The old gentleman says:

"There; I reckon it's all right. Come in."

As soon as I was in the old gentleman he locked the door and barred it and bolted it, and told the young men to come in with their guns, and they all went in a big parlor that had a new rag carpet on the floor, and got together in a corner that was out of the range of the front windows—there warn't none on the side. They held the candle, and took a good look at me, and all said, "Why, *he* ain't a Shepherdson—no, there ain't any Shepherdson about him." Then the old man said he hoped I wouldn't mind being searched for arms, because he didn't mean no harm by it—it was only to make sure. So he didn't pry into my pockets, but only felt outside with his hands, and said it was all right. He told me to make myself easy and at home, and tell all about myself; but the old lady says:

"Why, bless you, Saul, the poor thing's as wet as he can be; and don't you reckon it may be he's hungry?"

"True for you, Rachel—I forgot."

So the old lady says:

"Betsy" (this was a nigger woman), "you fly around and get him something to eat as quick as you can, poor thing; and one of you girls go and wake up Buck and tell him—oh, here he is himself. Buck, take this little stranger and get the wet clothes off from him and dress him up in some of yours that's dry."

Buck looked about as old as me—thirteen or fourteen or along there, though he was a little bigger than me. He hadn't on anything but a shirt, and he was very frowzy-headed.[1] He came in gaping and digging one fist into his eyes, and he was dragging a gun along with the other one. He says:

---

1. **frowzy-headed.** Messy-haired

Words
For
Everyday
Use

gape (gāp) *vi.*, stare, gawk

"Ain't they no Shepherdsons around?"

They said, no, 'twas a false alarm.

"Well," he says, "if they'd 'a' ben some, I reckon I'd 'a' got one."

They all laughed, and Bob says:

"Why, Buck, they might have scalped us all, you've been so slow in coming."

"Well, nobody come after me, and it ain't right. I'm always kept down; I don't get no show."

"Never mind, Buck, my boy," says the old man, "you'll have show enough, all in good time, don't you fret about that. Go 'long with you now, and do as your mother told you."

When we got upstairs to his room he got me a coarse shirt and a roundabout[2] and pants of his, and I put them on. While I was at it he asked me what my name was, but before I could tell him he started to tell me about a bluejay and a young rabbit he had catched in the woods day before yesterday, and he asked me where Moses was when the candle went out. I said I didn't know; I hadn't heard about it before, no way.

"Well, guess," he says.

"How'm I going to guess," says I, "when I never heard tell of it before?"

"But you can guess, can't you? It's just as easy."

"*Which* candle?" I says.

"Why, any candle," he says.

"I don't know where he was," says I; "where was he?"

"Why, he was in the *dark!* That's where he was!"

"Well, if you knowed where he was, what did you ask me for?"

"Why, blame it, it's a riddle, don't you see? Say, how long are you going to stay here? You got to stay always. We can just have booming times—they don't have no school now. Do you own a dog? I've got a dog—and he'll go in the river and bring out chips that you throw in. Do you like to comb up Sundays, and all that kind of foolishness? You bet I don't, but ma she makes me. Confound these ole britches! I reckon I'd better put 'em on, but I'd ruther not, it's so warm. Are you all ready? All right. Come along, old hoss."

Cold corn pone, cold corn beef, butter and buttermilk— that is what they had for me down there, and there ain't nothing better that ever I've come across yet. Buck and his ma and all of them smoked cob pipes, except the nigger woman, which was gone, and the two young women. They all smoked and talked, and I eat and talked. The young

---

2. **roundabout.** Short jacket

► What story does Huck tell the family about his background?

women had quilts around them, and their hair down their backs. They all asked me questions, and I told them how Pap and me and all the family was living on a little farm down at the bottom of Arkansaw, and my sister Mary Ann run off and got married and never was heard of no more, and Bill went to hunt them and he warn't heard of no more, and Tom and Mort died, and then there warn't nobody but just me and Pap left, and he was just trimmed down to nothing, on account of his troubles; so when he died I took what there was left, because the farm didn't belong to us, and started up the river, deck passage,[3] and fell overboard; and that was how I come to be here. So they said I could have a home there as long as I wanted it. Then it was most daylight and everybody went to bed, and I went to bed with Buck, and when I waked up in the morning, drat it all, I had forgot what my name was. So I laid there about an hour trying to think, and when Buck waked up I says:

"Can you spell, Buck?"

"Yes," he says.

"I bet you can't spell my name," says I.

"I bet you what you dare I can," says he.

"All right," says I, "go ahead."

"G-e-o-r-g-e J-a-x-o-n—there now," he says.

"Well," says I, "you done it, but I didn't think you could. It ain't no slouch of a name to spell—right off without studying."

► In the morning, what does Huck do when he realizes he cannot remember the false name he gave himself the night before?

I set it down, private, because somebody might want *me* to spell it next, and so I wanted to be handy with it and rattle it off like I was used to it.

It was a mighty nice family, and a mighty nice house, too. I hadn't seen no house out in the country before that was so nice and had so much style. It didn't have an iron latch on the front door, nor a wooden one with a buckskin string, but a brass knob to turn, the same as houses in town. There warn't no bed in the parlor, nor a sign of a bed; but heaps of parlors in towns has beds in them. There was a big fireplace that was bricked on the bottom, and the bricks was kept clean and red by pouring water on them and scrubbing them with another brick; sometimes they wash them over with red waterpaint that they call Spanish-brown, same as they do in town. They had big brass dogirons that could hold up a saw-log. There was a clock on the middle of the mantelpiece, with a picture of a town painted on the bottom half of the glass front, and a round place in the middle of it for the sun, and you could see the pendulum swinging behind it. It was

---

3. **deck passage.** Least expensive kind of riverboat travel; passengers slept on the deck.

beautiful to hear that clock tick; and sometimes when one of these peddlers had been along and scoured her up and got her in good shape, she would start in and strike a hundred and fifty before she got tuckered out. They wouldn't took any money for her.

Well, there was a big <u>outlandish</u> parrot on each side of the clock, made out of something like chalk, and painted up gaudy. By one of the parrots was a cat made of crockery, and a crockery dog by the other; and when you pressed down on them they squeaked, but didn't open their mouths nor look different nor interested. They squeaked through underneath. There was a couple of big wild-turkey-wing fans spread out behind those things. On the table in the middle of the room was a kind of a lovely <u>crockery</u> basket that had apples and oranges and peaches and grapes piled up in it, which was much redder and yellower and prettier than real ones is, but they warn't real because you could see where pieces had got chipped off and showed the white chalk, or whatever it was, underneath.

This table had a cover made out of beautiful oilcloth, with a red and blue spread-eagle painted on it, and a painted border all around. It come all the way from Philadelphia, they said. There was some books, too, piled up perfectly exact, on each corner of the table. One was a big family Bible full of pictures. One was *Pilgrim's Progress*,[4] about a man that left his family, it didn't say why. I read considerable in it now and then. The statements was interesting, but tough. Another was *Friendship's Offering*,[5] full of beautiful stuff and poetry; but I didn't read the poetry. Another was Henry Clay's Speeches,[6] and another was Dr. Gunn's *Family Medicine*,[7] which told you all about what to do if a body was sick or dead. There was a hymnbook, and a lot of other books. And there was nice split-bottom chairs, and perfectly sound, too—not bagged down in the middle and busted, like an old basket.

They had pictures hung on the walls—mainly Washingtons

---

4. *Pilgrim's Progress.* Popular religious allegory by John Bunyan
5. *Friendship's Offering.* Sentimental collection of poetry and prose
6. **Henry Clay's Speeches.** Collected speeches of famous member of Congress from Kentucky
7. **Dr. Gunn's *Family Medicine*.** Early household medical encyclopedia

Words For Everyday Use	
out • land • ish (out´lan´dish) *adj.,* very odd, strange	
crock • er • y (kräk´ər ē) *adj.,* made of baked clay	

and Lafayettes, and battles, and Highland Marys,[8] and one called "Signing the Declaration." There was some that they called crayons, which one of the daughters which was dead made her own self when she was only fifteen years old. They was different from any pictures I ever see before—blacker, mostly, than is common. One was a woman in a slim black dress, belted small under the armpits, with bulges like a cabbage in the middle of the sleeves, and a large black scoop-shovel bonnet with a black veil, and white slim ankles crossed about with black tape, and very wee black slippers, like a chisel, and she was leaning pensive on a tombstone on her right elbow, under a weeping willow, and her other hand hanging down her side holding a white handkerchief and a reticule, and underneath the picture it said "Shall I Never See Thee More Alas." Another one was a young lady with her hair all combed up straight to the top of her head, and knotted there in front of a comb like a chair-back, and she was crying into a handkerchief and had a dead bird laying on its back in her other hand with its heels up, and underneath the picture it said "I Shall Never Hear Thy Sweet Chirrup More Alas." There was one where a young lady was at a window looking up at the moon, and tears running down her cheeks; and she had an open letter in one hand with black sealing wax showing on one edge of it, and she was mashing a locket with a chain to it against her mouth, and underneath the picture it said "And Art Thou Gone Yes Thou Art Gone Alas." These was all nice pictures, I reckon, but I didn't somehow seem to take to them, because if ever I was down a little they always give me the fantods. Everybody was sorry she died, because she had laid out a lot more of these pictures to do, and a body could see by what she had done what they had lost. But I reckoned that with her <u>disposition</u> she was having a better time in the graveyard. She was at work on what they said was her greatest picture when she took sick, and every day and every night it was her prayer to be allowed to live till she got it done, but she never got the chance. It was a picture of a young woman in a long white gown, standing on

▶ *What do all of the dead daughter's crayon pictures seem to have in common?*

▶ *After looking at the daughter's pictures, what does Huck conclude about the daughter's disposition?*

---

8. **Washingtons . . . Highland Marys.** Portrayals of George Washington; the Marquis de Lafayette, a French general who served in the Continental Army in the American Revolution; and Mary Campbell, a woman who died young and was sentimentalized in poems by Scottish poet Robert Burns

| Words For Everyday Use | **dis • po • si • tion** (dis′pə zish′ən) *n.*, frame of mind, temperament |

the rail of a bridge all ready to jump off, with her hair all down her back, and looking up to the moon, with the tears running down her face, and she had two arms folded across her breast, and two arms stretched out in front, and two more reaching up towards the moon—and the idea was to see which pair would look best, and then scratch out all the other arms; but, as I was saying, she died before she got her mind made up, and now they kept this picture over the head of the bed in her room, and every time her birthday come they hung flowers on it. Other times it was hid with a little curtain. The young woman in the picture had a kind of a nice sweet face, but there was so many arms it made her look too spidery, seemed to me.

This young girl kept a scrapbook when she was alive, and used to paste <u>obituaries</u> and accidents and cases of patient suffering in it out of the *Presbyterian Observer,* and write poetry after them out of her own head. It was very good poetry. This is what she wrote about a boy by the name of Stephen Dowling Bots that fell down a well and was drownded:

◄ *What did the daughter keep in her "scrapbook"?*

ODE TO STEPHEN DOWLING BOTS, DEC'D[9]

> And did young Stephen sicken,
>   And did young Stephen die?
> And did the sad hearts thicken,
>   And did the mourners cry?
>
> No; such was not the fate of
>   Young Stephen Dowling Bots;
> Though sad hearts round him thickened,
>   'Twas not from sickness' shots.
>
> No whooping cough did rack his frame,
>   Nor measles <u>drear</u> with spots;
> Not these <u>impaired</u> the sacred name
>   Of Stephen Dowling Bots.
>
> Despised love struck not with woe
>   That head of curly knots,
> Nor stomach troubles laid him low,
>   Young Stephen Dowling Bots.

---

9. DEC'D. Deceased

Words For Everyday Use

o • bit • u • ar • y (ō bich´o͞o er´ē) *n.,* published death notice

drear (drir) *adj.,* gloomy

im • pair (im per´) *vt.,* spoil, injure

O no. Then list[10] with tearful eye,
   Whilst I his fate do tell.
His soul did from this cold world fly
   By falling down a well.
They got him out and emptied him;
   Alas it was too late;
His spirit was gone for to sport <u>aloft</u>
   In the <u>realms</u> of the good and great.

► What is the name of the Grangerford's dead daughter? What kind of poetry did she like to write?

If Emmeline Grangerford could make poetry like that before she was fourteen, there ain't no telling what she could 'a' done by and by. Buck said she could rattle off poetry like nothing. She didn't ever have to stop to think. He said she would slap down a line, and if she couldn't find anything to rhyme with it would just scratch it out and slap down another one, and go ahead. She warn't <u>particular</u>; she could write about anything you choose to give her to write about just so it was sadful. Every time a man died, or a woman died, or a child died, she would be on hand with her "<u>tribute</u>" before he was cold. She called them tributes. The neighbors said it was the doctor first, then Emmeline, then the undertaker—the undertaker never got in ahead of Emmeline but once, and then she hung fire on a rhyme for the dead person's name, which was Whistler. She warn't ever the same after that; she never complained, but she kinder <u>pined</u> away and did not live long. Poor thing, many's the time I made myself go up to the little room that used to be hers and get out her poor old scrapbook and read in it when her pictures had been <u>aggravating</u> me and I had soured on her a little. I

► How does Huck feel about the Grangerfords, "dead ones and all"? What does he try to do for Emmeline?

liked all that family, dead ones and all, and warn't going to let anything come between us. Poor Emmeline made poetry about all the dead people when she was alive, and it didn't seem right that there warn't nobody to make some about her now she was gone; so I tried to sweat out a verse or two myself, but I couldn't seem to make it go somehow. They kept Emmeline's room trim and nice, and all the things fixed in it just the way she liked to have them when she was alive, and nobody ever slept there. The old lady took care of the room herself, though there was plenty of niggers, and she

---

10. **list.** Listen

<table>
<tr><td rowspan="4">Words For Everyday Use</td><td>a • loft (ə lôft´) adv., far above the ground</td><td>trib • ute (trib´yo͞ot) n., something done in gratitude or to give honor</td></tr>
<tr><td>realm (relm) n., region</td><td rowspan="2">pine (pīn) vi., waste away through grief</td></tr>
<tr><td>par • tic • u • lar (pər tik´yə lər) adj., difficult to satisfy, choosy</td></tr>
<tr><td></td><td>ag • gra • vate (ag´rə vāt´) vt., annoy</td></tr>
</table>

sewed there a good deal and read her Bible there mostly.

Well, as I was saying about the parlor, there was beautiful curtains on the windows: white, with pictures painted on them of castles with vines all down the walls, and cattle coming down to drink. There was a little old piano, too, that had tin pans in it, I reckon, and nothing was ever so lovely as to hear the young ladies sing "The Last Link is Broken" and play "The Battle of Prague" on it. The walls of all the rooms was plastered, and most had carpets on the floors, and the whole house was whitewashed on the outside.

It was a double house, and the big open place betwixt them was roofed and floored, and sometimes the table was set there in the middle of the day, and it was a cool, comfortable place. Nothing couldn't be better. And warn't the cooking good, and just bushels of it too!

◄ *What does Huck enjoy about staying in the Grangerford home?*

CHAPTER 18

Why Harney Rode Away for His Hat

▶ According to Huck, what kind of man is Col. Grangerford?

Col.[1] Grangerford was a gentleman, you see. He was a gentleman all over; and so was his family. He was well born, as the saying is, and that's worth as much in a man as it is in a horse, so the Widow Douglas said, and nobody ever denied that she was of the first <u>aristocracy</u> in our town; and Pap he always said it, too, though he warn't no more quality than a mudcat[2] himself. Col. Grangerford was very tall and very slim, and had a darkish-paly complexion, not a sign of red in it anywheres; he was clean shaved every morning all over his thin face, and he had the thinnest kind of lips, and the thinnest kind of nostrils, and a high nose, and heavy eyebrows, and the blackest kind of eyes, sunk so deep back that they seemed like they was looking out of caverns at you, as you may say. His forehead was high, and his hair was gray and straight and hung to his shoulders. His hands was long and thin, and every day of his life he put on a clean shirt and a full suit from head to foot made out of linen[3] so white it hurt your eyes to look at it; and on Sundays he wore a blue tailcoat with brass buttons on it. He carried a mahogany[4] cane with a silver head to it. There warn't no frivolishness[5] about him, not a bit, and he warn't ever loud. He was as kind as he could be—you could feel that, you know, and so you had confidence. Sometimes he smiled, and it was good to see; but when he straightened himself up like a liberty-pole, and the lightning begun to flicker out from under his eyebrows, you wanted to climb a tree first, and find out what the matter was afterwards. He didn't ever have to tell anybody to mind their manners—everybody was always good-mannered where he was. Everybody loved to have him around, too; he was sunshine most always—I mean he made it seem like good weather. When he turned into a cloud-bank

---

1. **Col.** Colonel; honorary, nonmilitary title in some Southern states
2. **mudcat.** Type of catfish
3. **linen.** Fine cloth spun of flax; white linen would have been difficult to care for as it would soil and crease easily.
4. **mahogany.** Dark, heavy wood
5. **frivolishness.** Frivolity; silliness, lightmindedness

Words For Everyday Use	**ar • is • toc • ra • cy** (arˊi stäˊkrə sē) *n.,* privileged ruling class; nobility

it was awful dark for half a minute, and that was enough; there wouldn't nothing go wrong again for a week.

When him and the old lady come down in the morning all the family got up out of their chairs and give them good day, and didn't set down again till they had set down. Then Tom and Bob went to the sideboard[6] where the decanter[7] was, and mixed a glass of bitters[8] and handed it to him, and he held it in his hand and waited till Tom's and Bob's was mixed, and then they bowed and said, "Our duty to you, sir, and madam"; and they bowed the least bit in the world and said thank you, and so they drank, all three, and Bob and Tom poured a spoonful of water on the sugar and the <u>mite</u> of whisky or apple brandy in the bottom of their tumblers, and give it to me and Buck, and we drank to the old people too.

Bob was the oldest and Tom next—tall, beautiful men with very broad shoulders and brown faces, and long black hair and black eyes. They dressed in white linen from head to foot, like the old gentleman, and wore broad Panama hats.[9]

◄ *Who is in the Grangerford family?*

Then there was Miss Charlotte; she was twenty-five, and tall and proud and grand, but as good as she could be when she warn't stirred up; but when she was she had a look that would make you <u>wilt</u> in your tracks, like her father. She was beautiful.

So was her sister, Miss Sophia, but it was a different kind. She was gentle and sweet like a dove, and she was only twenty.

Each person had their own nigger to wait on them—Buck too. My nigger had a monstrous easy time, because I warn't used to having anybody do anything for me, but Buck's was on the jump most of the time.

This was all there was of the family now, but there used to be more—three sons; they got killed; and Emmeline that died.

The old gentleman owned a lot of farms and over a hundred niggers. Sometimes a stack of people would come there, horseback, from ten or fifteen mile around, and stay five or six days, and have such junketings[10] round about and on the river, and dances and picnics in the woods daytimes, and

---

6. **sideboard.** Piece of dining-room furniture for holding dishes and silverware
7. **decanter.** Decorative glass bottle for holding wine after it has been poured out of its bottle
8. **bitters.** Liquor containing herbs or roots
9. **Panama hats.** Broad-brimmed, light straw hats
10. **junketings.** Junkets; pleasure trips

Words For Everyday Use

mite (mīt) *n.,* small bit
wilt (wilt) *vi.,* shrivel up, like a plant without water

balls at the house nights. These people was mostly <u>kinfolks</u> of the family. The men brought their guns with them. It was a handsome lot of quality, I tell you.

▶ What is the name of the other "clan of aristocracy" in the area?

There was another clan of aristocracy around there—five or six families—mostly of the name of Shepherdson. They was as high-toned and well born and rich and grand as the tribe of Grangerfords. The Shepherdsons and Grangerfords used the same steamboat landing, which was about two mile above our house; so sometimes when I went up there with a lot of our folks I used to see a lot of the Shepherdsons there on their fine horses.

▶ What does Buck do when he spots a member of the Shepherdson family?

One day Buck and me was away out in the woods hunting, and heard a horse coming. We was crossing the road. Buck says:

"Quick! Jump for the woods!"

We done it, and then peeped down the woods through the leaves. Pretty soon a splendid young man come galloping down the road, setting his horse easy and looking like a soldier. He had his gun across his pommel.[11] I had seen him before. It was young Harney Shepherdson. I heard Buck's gun go off at my ear, and Harney's hat tumbled off from his head. He grabbed his gun and rode straight to the place where we was hid. But we didn't wait. We started through the woods on a run. The woods warn't thick, so I looked over my shoulder to dodge the bullet, and twice I seen Harney cover Buck with his gun; and then he rode away the way he come—to get his hat, I reckon, but I couldn't see. We never stopped running till we got home. The old gentleman's eyes blazed a minute—'twas pleasure, mainly, I judged—then his face sort of smoothed down, and he says, kind of gentle:

▶ What does Col. Grangerford tell his son when he hears about the shooting? What does Huck notice about Miss Sophia?

"I don't like that shooting from behind a bush. Why didn't you step into the road, my boy?"

"The Shepherdsons don't, father. They always take advantage."

Miss Charlotte she held her head up like a queen while Buck was telling his tale, and her nostrils spread and her eyes snapped. The two young men looked dark, but never said nothing. Miss Sophia she turned pale, but the color come back when she found the man warn't hurt.

---

11. **pommel.** Rounded front part of a saddle

Words For Everyday Use	**kin • folk** (kin´ fōk) *n.*, family, relatives

Soon as I could get Buck down by the corncribs under the trees by ourselves, I says:

"Did you want to kill him, Buck?"

"Well, I bet I did."

"What did he do to you?"

"Him? He never done nothing to me."

"Well, then, what did you want to kill him for?"

"Why, nothing—only it's on account of the feud."

"What's a feud?"

"Why, where was you raised? Don't you know what a feud is?"

"Never heard of it before—tell me about it."

"Well," says Buck, "a feud is this way: A man has a quarrel with another man, and kills him; then that other man's brother kills *him*; then the other brothers, on both sides, goes for one another; then the *cousins* chip in—and by and by everybody's killed off, and there ain't no more feud. But it's kind of slow, and takes a long time."

"Has this one been going on long, Buck?"

"Well, I should *reckon*! It started thirty year ago, or som'ers along there. There was trouble 'bout something, and then a lawsuit to settle it; and the suit went agin one of the men, and so he up and shot the man that won the suit—which he would naturally do, of course. Anybody would."

"What was the trouble about, Buck?—land?"

"I reckon maybe—I don't know."

"Well, who done the shooting? Was it a Grangerford or a Shepherdson?"

"Laws, how do *I* know? It was so long ago."

"Don't anybody know?"

"Oh, yes, pa knows, I reckon, and some of the other old people; but they don't know now what the row was about in the first place."

"Has there been many killed, Buck?"

"Yes; right smart chance of funerals. But they don't always kill. Pa's got a few buckshot in him; but he don't mind it 'cuz he don't weigh much, anyway. Bob's been carved up some with a bowie,[12] and Tom's been hurt once or twice."

"Has anybody been killed this year, Buck?"

◄ When did the feud between the Grangerfords and the Shepherdsons begin? When Huck asks why the feud started, what is Buck's response?

---

12. **bowie.** Kind of knife

Words For Everyday Use

feud (fyood) *n.*, long-lasting quarrel, sometimes between two families

"Yes; we got one and they got one. 'Bout three months ago my cousin Bud, fourteen year old, was riding through the woods on t'other side of the river, and didn't have no weapon with him, which was blame' foolishness, and in a lonesome place he hears a horse a-coming behind him, and sees old Baldy Shepherdson a-linkin' after him with his gun in his hand and his white hair a-flying in the wind; and 'stead of jumping off and taking to the brush, Bud 'lowed he could out run him; so they had it, nip and tuck, for five mile or more, the old man a-gaining all the time; so at last Bud seen it warn't any use, so he stopped and faced around so as to have the bullet holes in front, you know, and the old man he rode up and shot him down. But he didn't git much chance to enjoy his luck, for inside of a week our folks laid *him* out."

"I reckon that old man was a coward, Buck."

"I reckon he *warn't* a coward. Not by a blame' sight. There ain't a coward amongst them Shepherdsons—not a one. And there ain't no cowards amongst the Grangerfords either. Why, that old man kep' up his end in a fight one day for half an hour against three Grangerfords, and come out winner. They was all a-horseback; he lit off of his horse and got behind a little woodpile, and kep' his horse before him to stop the bullets; but the Grangerfords stayed on their horses and capered around the old man, and peppered away at him, and he peppered away at them. Him and his horse both went home pretty leaky and crippled, but the Grangerfords had to be *fetched* home—and one of 'em was dead, and another died the next day. No, sir; if a body's out hunting for cowards he don't want to fool away any time amongst them Shepherdsons, becuz they don't breed any of that *kind*."

Next Sunday we all went to church, about three mile, everybody a-horseback. The men took their guns along, so did Buck, and kept them between their knees or stood them handy against the wall. The Shepherdsons done the same. It was pretty ornery preaching—all about brotherly love, and such-like tiresomeness; but everybody said it was a good sermon, and they all talked it over going home, and had such a powerful lot to say about faith and good works and free grace and preforeordestination,[13] and I don't know what all, that

---

13. **preforeordestination.** Huck combines two doctrines of the Presbyterian Church, predestination and foreordination, to create this word.

Words
For
Everyday
Use

ca • per (kā´pər) *vi.,* skip or jump about

it did seem to me to be one of the roughest Sundays I had run across yet.

About an hour after dinner everybody was dozing around, some in their chairs and some in their rooms, and it got to be pretty dull. Buck and a dog was stretched out on the grass in the sun sound asleep. I went up to our room, and judged I would take a nap myself. I found that sweet Miss Sophia standing in her door, which was next to ours, and she took me in her room and shut the door very soft, and asked me if I liked her, and I said I did; and she asked me if I would do something for her and not tell anybody, and I said I would. Then she said she'd forgot her Testament,[14] and left it in the seat at church between two other books, and would I slip out quiet and go there and fetch it to her, and not say nothing to nobody. I said I would. So I slid out and slipped off up the road, and there warn't anybody at the church, except maybe a hog or two, for there warn't any lock on the door, and hogs likes a puncheon floor in summertime because it's cool. If you notice, most folks don't go to church only when they've got to; but a hog is different.

◄ What does Miss Sophia ask Huck to do? Why is Huck suspicious?

Says I to myself, something's up; it ain't natural for a girl to be in such a sweat about a Testament. So I give it a shake, and out drops a little piece of paper with "*half-past two*" wrote on it with a pencil. I <u>ransacked</u> it, but couldn't find anything else. I couldn't make anything out of that, so I put the paper in the book again, and when I got home and upstairs there was Miss Sophia in her door waiting for me. She pulled me in and shut the door; then she looked in the Testament till she found the paper, and as soon as she read it she looked glad; and before a body could think she grabbed me and give me a squeeze, and said I was the best boy in the world, and not to tell anybody. She was mighty red in the face for a minute, and her eyes lighted up, and it made her powerful pretty. I was a good deal astonished, but when I got my breath I asked her what the paper was about, and she asked me if I had read it, and I said no, and she asked me if I could read writing, and I told her "no, only coarse-hand,"[15] and then she said the paper warn't anything but a bookmark to keep her place, and I might go and play now.

---

14. **Testament.** Bible
15. **coarse-hand.** Printing

Words For Everyday Use	ran • sack (ran´sak´) vt., search through

I went off down to the river, studying over this thing, and pretty soon I noticed that my nigger was following along behind. When we was out of sight of the house he looked back and around a second, and then comes a-running, and says:

"Mars[16] Jawge, if you'll come down into de swamp I'll show you a whole stack o' water moccasins."[17]

Thinks I, that's mighty curious; he said that yesterday. He oughter know a body don't love water moccasins enough to go around hunting for them. What is he up to, anyway? So I says:

"All right; trot ahead."

I followed a half a mile; then he struck out over the swamp, and waded ankle deep as much as another half-mile. We come to a little flat piece of land which was dry and very thick with trees and bushes, and he says:

"You shove right in dah jist a few steps, Mars Jawge; dah's whah dey is. I's seed 'm befo'; I don't k'yer to see 'em no mo'."

► Where does Huck find Jim? Why is Jim not surprised to see Huck?

Then he slopped right along and went away, and pretty soon the trees hid him. I poked into the place aways and come to a little open patch as big as a bedroom all hung around with vines, and found a man laying there asleep—and, by jings, it was my old Jim!

I waked him up, and I reckoned it was going to be a grand surprise to him to see me again, but it warn't. He nearly cried he was so glad, but he warn't surprised. Said he swum along behind me that night, and heard me yell every time, but dasn't[18] answer, because he didn't want nobody to pick *him* up and take him into slavery again. Says he:

"I got hurt a little, en couldn't swim fas', so I wuz a considable ways behine you towards de las'; when you landed I reck'ned I could ketch up wid you on de lan' 'dout havin' to shout at you, but when I see dat house I begin to go slow. I 'uz off too fur to hear what dey say to you—I wuz 'fraid o' de dogs; but when it 'uz all quiet ag'in I knowed you's in de house, so I struck out for de woods to wait for day. Early in de mawnin' some er de niggers come along, gwyne to de fields, en dey tuk me en showed me dis place, whah de dogs can't track me on account o' de water, en dey brings me truck to eat every night, en tells me how you's a-gittin' along."

"Why didn't you tell my Jack to fetch me here sooner, Jim?"

► What has Jim been spending his time doing?

"Well, 'twarn't no use to 'sturb you, Huck, tell we could do sumfn—but we's all right now. I ben a-buyin' pots en pans en vittles, as I got a chanst, en a-patchin' up de raf' nights when—"

"*What* raft, Jim?"

---

16. **Mars.** Master
17. **water moccasins.** Poisonous water snakes
18. **dasn't.** Dare not

"Our ole raf'."

"You mean to say our old raft warn't smashed all to flinders?"

"No, she warn't. She was tore up a good deal—one en' of her was; but dey warn't no great harm done, on'y our traps was mos' all los'. Ef we hadn' dive' so deep en swum so fur under water, en de night hadn' ben so dark, en we warn't so sk'yerd, en ben sich punkin-heads, as de sayin' is, we'd 'a' seed de raf'. But it's jis' as well we didn't, 'kase now she's all fixed up ag'in mos' as good as new, en we's got a new lot o' stuff, in de place o' what 'uz los'."

"Why, how did you get hold of the raft again, Jim—did you catch her?"

"How I gwyne to ketch her en I out in de woods? No; some er de niggers foun' her ketched on a snag along heah in de ben', en dey hid her in a crick 'mongst de willows, en dey wuz so much jawin' 'bout which un 'um she b'long to de mos' dat I come to heah 'bout it pooty soon, so I ups en settles de trouble by tellin' 'um she don't b'long to none uv um, but to you en me; en I ast 'm if dey gwyne to grab a young white genlman's propaty, en git a hid'n for it? Den I gin 'm ten cents apiece, en dey 'uz mighty well satisfied, en wisht some mo' raf's 'ud come along en make 'm rich ag'in. Dey's mighty good to me, dese niggers is, en whatever I wants 'm to do fur me I doan' have to ast 'm twice, honey. Dat Jack's a good nigger, en pooty smart."

"Yes, he is. He ain't ever told me you was here; told me to come, and he'd show me a lot of water moccasins. If anything happens he ain't mixed up in it. He can say he never seen us together, and it'll be the truth."

I don't want to talk much about the next day. I reckon I'll cut it pretty short. I waked up about dawn, and was a-going to turn over and go to sleep again when I noticed how still it was—didn't seem to be anybody stirring. That warn't usual. Next I noticed that Buck was up and gone. Well, I gets up, a-wondering, and goes downstairs—nobody around; everything as still as a mouse. Just the same outside. Thinks I, what does it mean? Down by the woodpile I comes across my Jack, and says:

"What's it all about?"

Says he:

"Don't you know, Mars Jawge?"

"No," says I, "I don't."

"Well, den, Miss Sophia's run off! 'deed she has. She run off in de night some time—nobody don't know jis' when; run off to get married to dat young Harney Shepherdson, you

What has Miss Sophia done? What are the Grangerfords planning to do in retaliation?

know—leastways, so dey 'spec. De fambly foun' it out 'bout half an hour ago—maybe a little mo'—en' I tell you dey warn't no time los'. Sich another hurryin' up guns en hosses you never see! De women folks has gone for to stir up de relations, en ole Mars Saul en de boys tuck dey guns en rode up de river road for to try to ketch dat young man en kill him 'fo' he kin git acrost de river wid Miss Sophia. I reck'n dey's gwyne to be mighty rough times."

"Buck went off 'thout waking me up."

"Well, I reck'n he *did!* Dey warn't gwyne to mix you up in it. Mars Buck he loaded up his gun en 'lowed he's gwyne to fetch home a Shepherdson or bust. Well, dey'll be plenty un 'm dah, I reck'n, en you bet you he'll fetch one ef he gits a chanst."

I took up the river road as hard as I could put. By and by I begin to hear guns a good ways off. When I came in sight of the log store and the woodpile where the steamboats lands I worked along under the trees and brush till I got to a good place, and then I clumb up into the forks of a cottonwood that was out of reach, and watched. There was a wood-rank four foot high a little ways in front of the tree, and first I was going to hide behind that; but maybe it was luckier I didn't.

There was four or five men <u>cavorting</u> around on their horses in the open place before the log store, cussing and yelling, and trying to get at a couple of young chaps that was behind the wood-rank alongside of the steamboat landing; but they couldn't come it. Every time one of them showed himself on the river side of the woodpile he got shot at. The two boys was squatting back to back behind the pile, so they could watch both ways.

By and by the men stopped cavorting around and yelling. They started riding towards the store; then up gets one of the boys, draws a steady bead[19] over the wood-rank, and drops one of them out of his saddle. All the men jumped off of their horses and grabbed the hurt one and started to carry him to the store; and that minute the two boys started on the run. They got halfway to the tree I was in before the men noticed. Then the men see them, and jumped on their horses and took out after them. They gained on the boys, but it

▶ *From where does Huck watch the fight between the Grangerfords and the Shepherdsons?*

---

19. **draws a steady bead.** Aims

Words
For
Everyday
Use

ca • vort (kə vôrt′) *vi.,* prance about, frolic

didn't do no good, the boys had too good a start; they got to the woodpile that was in front of my tree, and slipped in behind it, and so they had the bulge on the men again. One of the boys was Buck, and the other was a slim young chap about nineteen years old.

The men ripped around awhile, and then rode away. As soon as they was out of sight I sung out to Buck and told him. He didn't know what to make of my voice coming out of the tree at first. He was awful surprised. He told me to watch out sharp and let him know when the men come in sight again; said they was up to some devilment[20] or other—wouldn't be gone long. I wished I was out of that tree, but I dasn't come down. Buck begun to cry and rip, and 'lowed that him and his cousin Joe (that was the other young chap) would make up for this day yet. He said his father and his two brothers was killed, and two or three of the enemy. Said the Shepherdsons laid for them in ambush. Buck said his father and brothers ought to waited for their relations—the Shepherdsons was too strong for them. I asked him what was become of young Harney and Miss Sophia. He said they'd got across the river and was safe. I was glad of that; but the way Buck did take on because he didn't manage to kill Harney that day he shot at him—I hain't ever heard anything like it.

All of a sudden, bang! bang! bang! goes three or four guns—the men had slipped around through the woods and come in from behind without their horses! The boys jumped for the river—both of them hurt—and as they swum down the current the men run along the bank shooting at them and singing out, "Kill them, kill them!" It made me so sick I most fell out of the tree. I ain't a-going to tell *all* that happened—it would make me sick again if I was to do that. I wished I hadn't ever come ashore that night to see such things. I ain't ever going to get shut of them—lots of times I dream about them.

I stayed in the tree till it begun to get dark, afraid to come down. Sometimes I heard guns away off in the woods; and twice I seen little gangs of men gallop past the log store with guns; so I reckoned the trouble was still a-going on. I was mighty downhearted; so I made up my mind I wouldn't ever go a-near that house again, because I reckoned I was to blame, somehow. I judged that that piece of paper meant that Miss Sophia was to meet Harney somewheres at half past two and run off; and I judged I ought to told her father about that paper and the curious way she acted, and then maybe he would 'a' locked her up, and this awful mess wouldn't ever happened.

◀ Where is Buck hiding? What does he tell Huck to do?

◀ Who has been killed so far in the fight? What disturbs Huck about Buck's attitude toward Harney?

◀ Why does Huck believe he is to blame for the feud? What does he feel he should have done?

---

20. **devilment.** Mischief

▶ What happened
to Buck?

When I got down out of the tree I crept along down the riverbank a piece, and found the two bodies laying in the edge of the water, and tugged at them till I got them ashore; then I covered up their faces, and got away as quick as I could. I cried a little when I was covering up Buck's face, for he was mighty good to me.

It was just dark now. I never went near the house, but struck through the woods and made for the swamp. Jim warn't on his island, so I tramped off in a hurry for the crick,[21] and crowded through the willows, red-hot to jump aboard and get out of that awful country. The raft was gone! My souls, but I was scared! I couldn't get my breath for most a minute. Then I raised a yell. A voice not twenty-five foot from me says:

"Good lan'! is dat you, honey? Doan' make no noise."

It was Jim's voice—nothing ever sounded so good before. I run along the bank a piece and got aboard, and Jim he grabbed me and hugged me, he was so glad to see me. He says:

"Laws bless you, chile, I 'uz right down sho' you's dead ag'in. Jack's been heah; he say he reck'n you's ben shot, kase you didn' come home no mo'; so I's jes' dis minute a startin' de raf' down towards de mouf er de crick, so's to be all ready for to shove out en leave soon as Jack comes agin en tells me for certain you *is* dead. Lawsy, I's mighty glad to git you back ag'in, honey."

I says:

"All right—that's mighty good; they won't find me, and they'll think I've been killed, and floated down the river—there's something up there that'll help them think so—so don't you lose no time, Jim, but just shove off for the big water as fast as ever you can."

I never felt easy till the raft was two mile below there and out in the middle of the Mississippi. Then we hung up our signal lantern, and judged that we was free and safe once more. I hadn't had a bite to eat since yesterday, so Jim he got out some corndodgers[22] and buttermilk, and pork and cabbage and greens—there ain't nothing in the world so good when it's cooked right—and whilst I eat my supper we talked and had a good time. I was powerful glad to get away from the feuds, and so was Jim to get away from the swamp. We said there warn't no home like a raft, after all. Other places do seem so cramped up and smothery, but a raft don't. You feel mighty free and easy and comfortable on a raft.

▶ How does Huck
feel when he's on a
raft?

---

21 **crick.** Creek
22. **corndodgers.** Small cornmeal cakes baked or fried hard

Responding to the Selection

If you were in Huck's place, how might you feel about the Grangerfords? What is unusual and disturbing about their lifestyle? Would you prefer the luxuries of their home or a more peaceful but less comfortable existence on the raft?

Reviewing the Selection

Recalling and Interpreting

1. **R:** How does Huck respond when he is asked his name by the strangers onto whose land he has wandered?

2. **I:** What might make Huck feel he is in danger? Is he really?

3. **R:** What kind of place is the Grangerfords' house? Why is the Grangerford home different from homes to which Huck is accustomed?

4. **I:** Does Huck appear to be impressed by the Grangerfords' way of life? Do you think he could live comfortably with them for long? Why, or why not?

5. **R:** Which character in the Grangerford family especially fascinates Huck? How does he learn more about her?

6. **I:** Why does Huck spends so much time studying the work and life of the dead sister Emmeline? How does he pass judgment on the somewhat peculiar inhabitants, dead or alive, of the Grangerford household?

7. **R:** What touches off the new fighting between the Grangerfords and the Shepherdsons?

8. **I:** Does anyone except Huck question the violence that ensues when Sophia runs away with Harney Shepherdson? How does Huck feel about it?

Synthesizing

9: How does the Shepherdson–Grangerford feud compare with the games that Tom Sawyer and his gang of robbers have played? In what way do the two scenarios differ?

10. Why is Huck so relieved to be back on the river with Jim? What does Huck learn about home as he considers life with the Grangerfords and living on the raft?

Understanding Literature (questions for discussion)

Satire. **Satire** is humorous writing or speech intended to point out errors, falsehoods, foibles, or failings. It is written for the purpose of reforming human behavior or human institutions. What instances of satire can you find in chapters 17 and 18? What could be the author's intention in satirizing feuding families or the poetic Emmeline?

CHAPTER 19

The Duke and the Dauphin Come Aboard

Two or three days and nights went by; I reckon I might say they swum by, they slid along so quiet and smooth and lovely. Here is the way we put in the time. It was a monstrous big river down there—sometimes a mile and a half wide; we run nights, and laid up and hid daytimes; soon as night was most gone we stopped navigating and tied up—nearly always in the dead water under a towhead; and then cut young cottonwoods and willows, and hid the raft with them. Then we set out the lines. Next we slid into the river and had a swim, so as to freshen up and cool off; then we set down on the sandy bottom where the water was about knee deep, and watched the daylight come. Not a sound anywheres—perfectly still—just like the whole world was asleep, only sometimes the bullfrogs a-cluttering, maybe. The first thing to see, looking away over the water, was a kind of dull line—that was the woods on t'other side; you couldn't make nothing else out; then a pale place in the sky; then more paleness spreading around; then the river softened up away off, and warn't black any more, but gray; you could see little dark spots drifting along ever so far away—trading scows, and such things; and long black streaks—rafts; sometimes you could hear a sweep screaking; or jumbled-up voices, it was so still, and sounds come so far; and by and by you could see a streak on the water which you know by the look of the streak that there's a snag there in a swift current which breaks on it and makes that streak look that way; and you see the mist curl up off of the water, and the east reddens up, and the river, and you make out a log cabin in the edge of the woods, away on the bank on t'other side of the river, being a woodyard, likely, and piled by them cheats so you can throw a dog through it anywheres; then the nice breeze springs up, and comes fanning you from over there, so cool and fresh and sweet to smell on account of the woods and the flowers; but sometimes not that way, because they've left dead fish laying around, gars and such, and they do get pretty <u>rank</u>; and next you've got the full day, and everything smiling in the sun, and the song-birds just going it!

◄ What routine do Huck and Jim follow over the next few days? Why does Huck say that the days and nights "swum by"?

Words For Everyday Use

rank (rank) *adj.,* foul smelling

▶ *What is life like for Huck and Jim during their first few days back on the raft? What word does Huck use to describe the river?*

A little smoke couldn't be noticed now, so we would take some fish off of the lines and cook up a hot breakfast. And afterwards we would watch the lonesomeness of the river, and kind of lazy along, and by and by lazy off to sleep. Wake up by and by, and look to see what done it, and maybe see a steamboat coughing along upstream, so far off towards the other side you couldn't tell nothing about her only whether she was a stern-wheel or side-wheel; then for about an hour there wouldn't be nothing to hear nor nothing to see—just solid lonesomeness. Next you'd see a raft sliding by, away off yonder, and maybe a galoot[1] on it chopping, because they're most always doing it on a raft; you'd see the ax flash and come down—you don't hear nothing; you see that ax go up again, and by the time it's above the man's head then you hear the *k'chunck!*—it had took all that time to come over the water. So we would put in the day, lazying around, listening to the stillness. Once there was a thick fog, and the rafts and things that went by was beating tin pans so the steamboats wouldn't run over them. A scow or a raft went by so close we could hear them talking and cussing and laughing—heard them plain; but we couldn't see no sign of them; it made you feel crawly; it was like spirits carrying on that way in the air. Jim said he believed it was spirits; but I says:

▶ *What does Jim call the other rafters whom they can see but not hear in the dense fog? Why does Huck disagree?*

"No; spirits wouldn't say, 'Dern the dern fog.'"

Soon as it was night out we shoved; when we got her out to about the middle we let her alone, and let her float wherever the current wanted her to; then we lit the pipes, and dangled our legs in the water, and talked about all kinds of things—we was always naked, day and night, whenever the mosquitoes would let us—the new clothes Buck's folks made for me was too good to be comfortable, and besides I didn't go much on clothes, nohow.

Sometimes we'd have that whole river all to ourselves for the longest time. Yonder was the banks and the islands, across the water; and maybe a spark—which was a candle in a cabin window; and sometimes on the water you could see a spark or two—on a raft or a scow, you know; and maybe you could hear a fiddle or a song coming over from one of them crafts. It's lovely to live on a raft. We had the sky up there, all speckled with stars, and we used to lay on our backs and look up at them, and discuss about whether they was made or only just happened. Jim he allowed they was made, but I allowed they happened; I judged it would have took too long to *make* so many. Jim said the moon could 'a' *laid* them; well, that looked kind of reasonable, so I didn't say nothing

▶ *What do Jim and Huck discuss as they lay on their backs at night?*

---

1. **galoot.** Clumsy or coarse person

against it, because I've seen a frog lay most as many, so of course it could be done. We used to watch the stars that fell, too, and see them streak down. Jim allowed they'd got spoiled and was hove out of the nest.

Once or twice of a night we would see a steamboat slipping along in the dark, and now and then she would belch a whole world of sparks up out of her chimbleys, and they would rain down in the river and look awful pretty; then she would turn a corner and her lights would wink out and her powwow[2] shut off and leave the river still again; and by and by her waves would get to us, a long time after she was gone, and joggle the raft a bit, and after that you wouldn't hear nothing for you couldn't tell how long, except maybe frogs or something.

◀ *What do the steamboats do that Huck calls "awful pretty"?*

After midnight the people on shore went to bed, and then for two or three hours the shores was black—no more sparks in the cabin windows. These sparks was our clock—the first one that showed again meant morning was coming, so we hunted a place to hide and tie up right away.

One morning about daybreak I found a canoe and crossed over a chute[3] to the main shore—it was only two hundred yards—and paddled about a mile up a crick amongst the cypress woods, to see if I couldn't get some berries. Just as I was passing a place where a kind of a cowpath crossed the crick, here comes a couple of men tearing up the path as tight as they could foot it. I thought I was a goner, for whenever anybody was after anybody I judged it was *me*—or maybe Jim. I was about to dig out from there in a hurry, but they was pretty close to me then, and sung out and begged me to save their lives—said they hadn't been doing nothing, and was being chased for it—said there was men and dogs a-coming. They wanted to jump right in, but I says:

◀ *Why do the men frighten Huck at first? What do they ask of Huck? What advice does Huck give them?*

"Don't you do it. I don't hear the dogs and horses yet; you've got time to crowd through the brush and get up the crick a little ways; then you take to the water and wade down to me and get in—that'll throw the dogs off the scent."

They done it, and soon as they was aboard I lit out for our towhead, and in about five or ten minutes we heard the dogs and the men away off, shouting. We heard them come along towards the crick, but couldn't see them; they seemed to stop and fool around awhile; then, as we got further and further away all the time, we couldn't hardly hear them at all; by the time we had left a mile of woods behind us and struck the river, everything was quiet, and we paddled over to the towhead and hid in the cottonwoods and was safe.

◀ *Why do you think Huck takes the men aboard?*

2. **powwow.** Noise made by the boat's mechanism
3. **chute.** Swift, narrow channel to the mainland

▶ What are the ages of the men? How are they dressed?

One of these fellows was about seventy or upwards, and had a bald head and very gray whiskers. He had an old battered-up slouch hat on, and a greasy blue woolen shirt, and ragged old blue jeans britches stuffed into his boot-tops, and home-knit galluses[4]—no, he only had one. He had an old long-tailed blue jeans coat with slick brass buttons flung over his arm, and both of them had big, fat, ratty-looking carpetbags.[5]

The other fellow was about thirty and dressed about as ornery. After breakfast we all laid off and talked, and the first thing that come out was that these chaps didn't know one another.

"What got you into trouble?" says the baldhead to t'other chap.

▶ Why were the two men being run out of their respective towns?

"Well, I'd been selling an article to take the tartar off the teeth—and it does take it off, too, and generly the enamel along with it—but I stayed about one night longer than I ought to, and was just in the act of sliding out when I ran across you on the trail this side of town, and you told me they were coming, and begged me to help you to get off. So I told you I was expecting trouble myself, and would scatter out *with* you. That's the whole yarn—what's yourn?"

"Well, I'd ben a-running' a little temperance revival[6] thar 'bout a week, and was the pet of the women folks, big and little, for I was makin' it mighty warm for the rummies, I tell you, and takin' as much as five or six dollars a night—ten cents a head, children and niggers free—and business a-growin' all the time, when somehow or another a little report got around last night that I had a way of puttin' in my time with a private jug on the sly. A nigger rousted me out this mornin', and told me the people was getherin' on the quiet with their dogs and horses, and they'd be along pretty soon and give me 'bout half an hour's start, and then run me down if they could; and if they got me they'd tar and feather me and ride me on a rail,[7] sure. I didn't wait for no breakfast—I warn't hungry."

"Old man," said the young one, "I reckon we might double-team it together; what do you think?"

"I ain't <u>undisposed</u>. What's your line—mainly?"

---

4. **galluses.** Suspenders
5. **carpetbag.** Old-fashioned traveling bag
6. **revival.** Public religious meetings characterized by confessions and professions of faith. A temperance revival focused on abstention from alcohol.
7. **tar and feather . . . ride me on a rail.** Punishment by mob action that consisted of covering a person with melted tar and feathers. Afterward the offender was placed on a long bar of wood and carried out of the community.

| Words For Everyday Use | **un • dis • posed** (un dis pōzd´) *adj.*, unwilling |

"Jour printer[8] by trade; do a little in patent medicines;[9] theater-actor—tragedy, you know; take a turn to mesmerism and phrenology[10] when there's a chance; teach singing-geography school for a change; sling a lecture sometimes—oh, I do lots of things—most anything that comes handy, so it ain't work. What's your lay?"

"I've done considerble in the doctoring way in my time. Layin' on o' hands[11] is my best holt—for cancer and paralysis, and sich things; and I k'n tell a fortune pretty good when I've got somebody along to find out the facts for me. Preachin's my line, too, and workin' camp meetin's, and missionaryin' around."

Nobody never said anything for a while; then the young man hove a sigh and says:

"Alas!"

"What're you alassin' about?" says the baldhead.

"To think I should have lived to be leading such a life, and be <u>degraded</u> down into such company." And he begun to wipe the corner of his eye with a rag.

"Dern your skin, ain't the company good enough for you?" says the baldhead, pretty pert and uppish.

"Yes, it *is* good enough for me; it's as good as I deserve; for who fetched me so low when I was so high? *I* did myself. I don't blame *you,* gentlemen—far from it; I don't blame anybody. I deserve it all. Let the cold world do its worst; one thing I know—there's a grave somewhere for me. The world may go on just as it's always done, and take everything from me—loved ones, property, everything; but it can't take that. Some day I'll lie down in it and forget it all, and my poor broken heart will be at rest." He went on a-wiping.

"Drot your pore broken heart," says the baldhead; "what are you heaving your pore broken heart at *us* f'r? *We* hain't done nothing."

"No, I know you haven't. I ain't blaming you, gentlemen. I brought myself down—yes, I did it myself. It's right I should

◀ *At what jobs have the men worked?*

---

8. **Jour printer.** Printers who worked day by day; they were known for moving from town to town.

9. **patent medicines.** Medicines that could be sold without prescriptions; often sold by traveling con artists

10. **mesmerism and phrenology.** Hypnotism and the pseudoscience of reading a person's character from bumps on his or her skull

11. **layin' on o' hands.** Faith healing through touching the ailing person

Words For Everyday Use	**de • grad • ed** (dē grād id) *adj.,* brought down in disgrace

suffer—perfectly right—I don't make any moan."

"Brought you down from whar? Whar was you brought down from?"

"Ah, you would not believe me; the world never believes—let it pass—'tis no matter. The secret of my birth—"

"The secret of your birth! Do you mean to say—"

▶ What does the younger man reveal about his background?

"Gentlemen," says the young man, very solemn, "I will reveal it to you, for I feel I may have confidence in you. By rights I am a duke!"

Jim's eyes bugged out when he heard that; and I reckon mine did, too. Then the baldhead says: "No! you can't mean it?"

"Yes. My great-grandfather, eldest son of the Duke of Bridgewater, fled to this country about the end of the last century, to breathe the pure air of freedom; married here, and died, leaving a son, his own father dying about the same time. The second son of the late duke seized the titles and estates—the infant real duke was ignored. I am the lineal descendant[12] of that infant—I am the rightful Duke of Bridgewater; and here am I, <u>forlorn</u>, torn from my high <u>estate</u>, hunted of men, despised by the cold world, ragged, worn, heart-broken, and degraded to the companionship of <u>felons</u> on a raft!"

Jim pitied him ever so much, and so did I. We tried to comfort him, but he said it warn't much use, he couldn't be much comforted; said if we was a mind to <u>acknowledge</u> him, that would do him more good than most anything else; so we said we would, if he would tell us how. He said we ought to bow when we spoke to him, and say "Your Grace," or "My Lord," or "Your Lordship"—and he wouldn't mind it if we called him plain "Bridgewater," which, he said, was a title anyway, and not a name; and one of us ought to wait on him at dinner, and do any little thing for him he wanted done.

Well, that was all easy, so we done it. All through dinner Jim stood around and waited on him, and says, "Will yo' Grace have some o' dis or some o' dat?" and so on, and a body could see it was mighty pleasing to him.

▶ With what does the older man seem uncomfortable?

But the old man got pretty silent by and by—didn't have much to say, and didn't look pretty comfortable over all that petting that was going on around that duke. He seemed to

---

12. **lineal descendant.** Person who is in direct line for inheritance of an ancestor's goods or title

Words For Everyday Use	
for • lorn (fôr lôrn´) *adj.*, wretched; without hope	
es • tate (e stāt´) *n.*, condition	
fel • on (fel´ən) *n.*, criminal	
ac • know • ledge (ak näl´ij) *vt.*, recognize the claims of	

have something on his mind. So, along in the afternoon, he says:

"Looky here, Bilgewater,"[13] he says, "I'm nation[14] sorry for you, but you ain't the only person that's had troubles like that."

"No?"

"No you ain't. You ain't the only person that's ben snaked down wrongfully out'n a high place."

"Alas!"

"No, you ain't the only person that's had a secret of his birth." And, by jings, *he* begins to cry.

"Hold! What do you mean?"

"Bilgewater, kin I trust you?" says the old man, still sort of sobbing.

"To the bitter death!" He took the old man by the hand and squeezed it, and says, "That secret of your being: speak!"

"Bilgewater, I am the late Dauphin!"

You bet you, Jim and me stared this time. Then the duke says:

"You are what?"

"Yes, my friend, it is too true—your eyes is lookin' at this very moment on the pore disappeared Dauphin, Looy the Seventeen, son of Looy the Sixteen and Marry Antonette."

"You! At your age! No! You mean you're the late Charlemagne;[15] you must be six hundred years old, at the very least."

"Trouble has done it, Bilgewater, trouble has done it; trouble has brung these gray hairs and this premature balditude. Yes, gentlemen, you see before you, in blue jeans and misery, the wanderin', <u>exiled</u>, trampled-on, and sufferin' rightful King of France."

Well, he cried and took on so that me and Jim didn't know hardly what to do, we was so sorry—and so glad and proud we'd got him with us, too. So we set in, like we done before with the duke, and tried to comfort him. But he said it warn't no use, nothing but to be dead and done with it all could do him any good; though he said it often made him feel easier and better for a while if people treated him according to his

◀ *Who does the older man claim to be?*

---

13. **Bilgewater.** Water that seeps into the lowest interior space of a boat, becoming stagnant and dirty
14. **nation.** Very
15. **Charlemagne.** Emperor of the Holy Roman Empire who died in AD 814

Words
For
Everyday
Use   **ex • iled** (eks´īld) *adj.*, cast out of one's birthplace

► How do Huck and Jim treat the king to make him feel better? How does the duke feel about this treatment?

rights, and got down on one knee to speak to him, and always called him "Your Majesty," and waited on him first at meals, and didn't set down in his presence till he asked them. So Jim and me set to majestying him, and doing this and that and t'other for him, and standing up till he told us we might set down. This done him heaps of good, and so he got cheerful and comfortable. But the duke kind of soured on him, and didn't look a bit satisfied with the way things was going; still, the king acted real friendly towards him, and said the duke's great-grandfather and all the other Dukes of Bilgewater was a good deal thought of by *his* father, and was allowed to come to the palace considerable; but the duke stayed <u>huffy</u> a good while, till by and by the king says:

"Like as not we got to be together a blamed long time on this h-yer raft, Bilgewater, and so what's the use o' your bein' sour? It'll only make things oncomfortable. It ain't my fault I warn't born a duke, it ain't your fault you warn't born a king—so what's the use to worry? Make the best o' things the way you find 'em, says I—that's my motto. This ain't no bad thing that we've struck here—plenty grub and an easy life— come, give us your hand, duke, and le's all be friends."

The duke done it, and Jim and me was pretty glad to see it. It took away all the uncomfortableness and we felt mighty good over it, because it would 'a' been a miserable business to have any unfriendliness on the raft; for what you want, above all things, on a raft, is for everybody to be satisfied, and feel right and kind towards the others.

► About what does Huck make up his mind? Why does he decide not to say anything to the men? What has Huck learned about the "best way to get along with his kind of people"? With whom does Huck associate the duke and the king?

It didn't take me long to make up my mind that these liars warn't no kings nor dukes at all, but just low-down humbugs[16] and <u>frauds</u>. But I never said nothing, never let on; kept it to myself; it's the best way; then you don't have no quarrels, and don't get into no trouble. If they wanted us to call them kings and dukes, I hadn't no objections, 'long as it would keep peace in the family; and it warn't no use to tell Jim, so I didn't tell him. If I never learnt nothing else out of Pap, I learnt that the best way to get along with his kind of people is to let them have their own way.

---

16. **humbugs.** Imposters

| Words For Everyday Use | **huf • fy** (huf´ē) *adj.*, easily offended |
| | **fraud** (frôd) *n.*, person who deceives |

CHAPTER 20

What Royalty Did to Parkville

They asked us considerable many questions; wanted to know what we covered up the raft that way for, and laid by in the daytime instead of running—was Jim a runaway nigger? Says I:

"Goodness sakes! would a runaway nigger run south?"

No, they allowed he wouldn't. I had to account for things some way, so I says:

"My folks was living in Pike County, in Missouri, where I was born, and they all died off but me and Pa and my brother Ike. Pa, he 'lowed he'd break up and go down and live with Uncle Ben, who's got a little one-horse place on the river, forty-four mile below Orleans. Pa was pretty poor, and had some debts; so when he'd squared up there warn't nothing left but sixteen dollars and our nigger, Jim. That warn't enough to take us fourteen hundred mile, deck passage nor no other way. Well, when the river rose Pa had a streak of luck one day; he ketched this piece of a raft; so we reckoned we'd go down to Orleans on it. Pa's luck didn't hold out; a steamboat run over the forrard corner of the raft one night, and we all went overboard and dove under the wheel; Jim and me come up all right, but Pa was drunk, and Ike was only four years old, so they never come up no more. Well, for the next day or two we had considerable trouble, because people was always coming out in skiffs and trying to take Jim away from me, saying they believed he was a runaway nigger. We don't run daytimes no more now; nights they don't bother us."

The duke says:

"Leave me alone to cipher[1] out a way so we can run in the daytime if we want to. I'll think the thing over—I'll invent a plan that'll fix it. We'll let it alone for today, because of course we don't want to go by that town yonder in daylight—it mightn't be healthy."

Towards night it begun to darken up and look like rain; the heat lightning was squirting around low down in the sky, and the leaves was beginning to shiver—it was going to be pretty ugly, it was easy to see that. So the duke and the king went to overhauling our wigwam, to see what the beds was like. My bed was a straw tick—better than Jim's, which was a corn-shuck tick;[2] there's always cobs around about in a shuck tick, and they poke into you and hurt; and when you roll

◄ Why does Huck have to make up another story about his background? What do the king and the duke suspect?

◄ What does the duke promise to do?

---

1. **cipher.** Decipher; figure
2. **straw tick . . . corn-shuck tick.** Cloths filled with straw or corn husks for use as mattresses

over the dry shucks sound like you was rolling over in a pile of dead leaves; it makes such a rustling that you wake up. Well, the duke allowed he would take my bed; but the king allowed he wouldn't. He says:

"I should 'a' reckoned the difference in rank would 'a' sejested to you that a corn-shuck bed warn't just fitten for me to sleep on. Your Grace 'll take the shuck bed yourself."

Jim and me was in a sweat again for a minute, being afraid there was going to be some more trouble amongst them; so we was pretty glad when the duke says:

"'Tis my fate to be always ground into the <u>mire</u> under the iron heel of <u>oppression</u>. Misfortune has broken my once <u>haughty</u> spirit; I yield, I <u>submit</u>; 'tis my fate. I am alone in the world—let me suffer; I can bear it."

We got away as soon as it was good and dark. The king told us to stand well out towards the middle of the river, and not show a light till we got a long ways below the town. We come in sight of the little bunch of lights by and by—that was the town, you know—and slid by, about a half a mile out, all right. When we was three-quarters of a mile below we <u>hoisted</u> up our signal lantern; and about ten o'clock it come on to rain and blow and thunder and lighten like everything; so the king told us to both stay on watch till the weather got better; then him and the duke crawled into the wigwam and turned in for the night. It was my watch below till twelve, but I wouldn't 'a' turned in anyway if I'd had a bed, because a body don't see such a storm as that every day in the week, not by a long sight. My souls, how the wind did scream along! And every second or two there'd come a glare that lit up the whitecaps[3] for a half a mile around, and you'd see the islands looking dusty through the rain, and the trees thrashing around in the wind; then comes a *h-whack!*—bum! bum! bumble-umble-um-bum-bum-bum-bum—and the thunder would go rumbling and grumbling away, and quit—and then *rip* comes another flash and another sockdolager.[4] The waves most washed me off the raft sometimes, but I hadn't any clothes on, and didn't mind. We didn't have no trouble about snags; the lightning was glaring and flittering around so constant that we could see them plenty soon enough to throw her head this way or that and miss them.

I had the middle watch, you know, but I was pretty sleepy

About what do the king and duke disagree?

What does the king direct Huck and Jim to do during the storm? What is Huck's response?

3. **whitecaps.** Waves of water with their crests turned to white foam
4. **sockdolager.** Extreme form of anything; here, loud thunder

Words For Everyday Use

mire (mīr) n., mud
op • pres • sion (ə presh´ən) n., tyranny, domination
haugh • ty (hôt´ē) adj., proud

sub • mit (sub mit´) vi., give in to the power of another person
hoist (hoist) vt., raise

by that time, so Jim he said he would stand the first half of it for me; he was always mighty good that way, Jim was. I crawled into the wigwam, but the king and the duke had their legs sprawled around so there warn't no show for me; so I laid outside—I didn't mind the rain, because it was warm, and the waves warn't running so high now. About two they come up again, though, and Jim was going to call me; but he changed his mind, because he reckoned they warn't high enough yet to do any harm; but he was mistaken about that, for pretty soon all of a sudden along comes a regular ripper and washed me overboard. It most killed Jim a-laughing. He was the easiest nigger to laugh that ever was, anyway.

I took the watch, and Jim he laid down and snored away; and by and by the storm let up for good and all; and the first cabin-light that showed I rousted him out, and we slid the raft into hiding quarters for the day.

The king got out an old ratty deck of cards after breakfast, and him and the duke played seven-up awhile, five cents a game. Then they got tired of it, and allowed they would "lay out a campaign," as they called it. The duke went down into his carpetbag, and fetched up a lot of little printed bills and read them out loud. One bill said, "The celebrated Dr. Armand de Montalban, of Paris," would "lecture on the Science of Phrenology" at such and such a place, on the blank day of blank, at ten cents admission, and "furnish charts of character at twenty-five cents apiece." The duke said that was *him*. In another bill he was the "world-<u>renowned</u> Shakespearian tragedian, Garrick the Younger, of Drury Lane, London."[5] In other bills he had a lot of other names and done other wonderful things, like finding water and gold with a "divining-rod,"[6] "<u>dissipating</u> witch spells," and so on. By and by he says:

"But the <u>histrionic muse</u> is the darling. Have you ever trod the boards,[7] Royalty?"

"No," says the king.

"You shall, then, before you're three days older, Fallen Grandeur,"[8] says the duke. "The first good town we come

◄ *What does the duke suggest they do next time they are in town?*

---

5. **tragedian . . . London.** Actor of tragedies; David Garrick was a famous actor and director of the Drury Lane Theatre in London. There was no Garrick the Younger.
6. **divining rod.** Forked branch that was purported to reveal underground water
7. **trod the boards.** Been on stage
8. **Fallen Grandeur.** The duke refers to the king by references to his supposed status, here as greatness that has come down in the world.

Words For Everyday Use	re • nowned (ri nound´) *adj.,* famous	muse (myooz) *n.,* mythical spirit that inspires artists—here, actors
	dis • si • pate (dis´ə pāt) *vt.,* break up	
	his • tri • on • ic (his´trē än´ik) *adj.,* having to do with acting	

to we'll hire a hall and do the sword fight in 'Richard III' and the balcony scene in 'Romeo and Juliet.' How does that strike you?"

"I'm in, up to the hub, for anything that will pay, Bilgewater; but, you see, I don't know nothing about play-actin', and hain't ever seen much of it. I was too small when Pap used to have 'em at the palace. Do you reckon you can learn me?"

"Easy!"

"All right. I'm jist a-freezin' for something fresh, anyway. Le's commence right away."

So the duke he told him all about who Romeo was and who Juliet was, and said he was used to being Romeo, so the king could be Juliet.

"But if Juliet's such a young gal, duke, my peeled head and my white whiskers is goin' to look oncommon odd on her, maybe."

"No, don't you worry; these country jakes won't ever think of that. Besides, you know, you'll be in costume, and that makes all the difference in the world; Juliet's in a balcony, enjoying the moonlight before she goes to bed, and she's got on her nightgown and her ruffled nightcap. Here are the costumes for the parts."

He got out two or three curtain-calico[9] suits, which he said was meedyevil[10] armor for Richard III and t'other chap, and a long white cotton nightshirt and a ruffled nightcap to match. The king was satisfied; so the duke got out his book and read the parts over in the most splendid spread-eagle[11] way, prancing around and acting at the same time, to show how it had got to be done; then he give the book to the king and told him to get his part by heart.

▶ *Why are the king, the duke, and Huck going to go into town?*

There was a little one-horse town about three mile down the bend, and after dinner the duke said he had ciphered out his idea about how to run in daylight without it being dangersome for Jim; so he allowed he would go down to the town and fix that thing. The king allowed he would go, too, and see if he couldn't strike something. We was out of coffee, so Jim said I better go along with them in the canoe and get some.

When we got there there warn't nobody stirring; streets empty, and perfectly dead and still, like Sunday. We found a sick nigger sunning himself in a back yard, and he said everybody that warn't too young or too sick or too old was gone to camp meeting, about two mile back in the woods. The king got the directions, and allowed he'd go and work that camp meeting for all it was worth, and I might go, too.

---

9. **curtain-calico.** Printed cotton curtain material
10. **meedyevil.** Medieval
11. **spread-eagle.** With large gestures of arms and legs

The duke said what he was after was a printing office. We found it; a little bit of a concern, up over a carpenter shop— carpenters and printers all gone to the meeting, and no doors locked. It was a dirty, littered-up place, and had ink marks, and handbills[12] with pictures of horses and runaway niggers on them, all over the walls. The duke shed his coat and said he was all right now. So me and the king lit out for the camp meeting.

We got there in about a half an hour fairly dripping, for it was a most awful hot day. There was as much as a thousand people there from twenty mile around. The woods was full of teams and wagons, hitched everywheres, feeding out of the wagon-troughs and stomping to keep off the flies. There was sheds made out of poles and roofed over with branches, where they had lemonade and gingerbread to sell, and piles of watermelons and green corn and such-like truck.

The preaching was going on under the same kinds of sheds, only they was bigger and held crowds of people. The benches was made out of outside slabs of logs, with holes bored in the round side to drive sticks into for legs. They didn't have no backs. The preachers had high platforms to stand on at one end of the sheds. The women had on sunbonnets; and some had linsey-woolsey frocks,[13] some gingham ones, and a few of the young ones had on calico. Some of the young men was barefooted, and some of the children didn't have on any clothes but just a tow-linen shirt. Some of the old women was knitting, and some of the young folks was courting on the sly.

The first shed we come to the preacher was lining out[14] a hymn. He lined out two lines, everybody sung it, and it was kind of grand to hear it, there was so many of them and they done it in such a rousing way; then he lined out two more for them to sing—and so on. The people woke up more and more, and sung louder and louder; and towards the end some begun to groan, and some begun to shout. Then the preacher begun to preach, and begun in earnest, too; and went weaving first to one side of the platform and then the other, and then a-leaning down over the front of it, with his arms and his body going all the time, and shouting his words out with all his might; and every now and then he would hold up his Bible and spread it open, and kind of pass it around this way and that, shouting, "It's the brazen serpent in the wilderness![15] Look upon it and live!" And people would shout out, "Glory!—A-a-men!" And so he went on, and the people groaning and crying and saying amen:

◀ *What is going on in the town?*

---

12. **handbills.** Posters
13. **linsey-woolsey frocks.** Dresses made of coarse wool and linen fabric
14. **lining out.** Teaching, line by line
15. **brazen serpent . . . wilderness.** Moses made a serpent of brass to heal the people of Israel of poisonous snakebites as related in the Bible (Numbers 21:9).

"Oh, come to the mourners' bench![16] come, black with sin! (*amen!*) come, sick and sore! (*amen!*) come, lame and halt and blind! (*amen!*) come, pore and needy, sunk in shame! (*a-a-men!*) come, all that's worn and soiled and suffering!—come with a broken spirit! come with a <u>contrite</u> heart! come in your rags and sin and dirt! the waters that cleanse is free, the door of heaven stands open—oh, enter in and be at rest!" (*a-a-men! glory, glory, hallelujah!*)

And so on. You couldn't make out what the preacher said any more, on account of the shouting and crying. Folks got up everywheres in the crowd, and worked their way just by main strength to the mourners' bench, with the tears running down their faces; and when all the mourners had got up there to the front benches in a crowd, they sung and shouted and flung themselves down on the straw, just crazy and wild.

► *What does the king do when he catches sight of the preacher? What lie does he tell the crowd?*

Well, the first I knowed the king got a-going, and you could hear him over everybody; and next he went a-charging up on to the platform, and the preacher he begged him to speak to the people, and he done it. He told them he was a pirate—been a pirate for thirty years out in the Indian Ocean—and his crew was thinned out considerable last spring in a fight, and he was home now to take out some fresh men, and thanks to goodness he'd been robbed last night and put ashore off of a steamboat without a cent, and he was glad of it; it was the blessedest thing that ever happened to him, because he was a changed man now, and happy for the first time in his life; and, poor as he was, he was going to start right off and work his way back to the Indian Ocean, and put in the rest of his life trying to turn the pirates into the true path; for he could do it better than anybody else, being acquainted with all pirate crews in that ocean; and though it would take him a long time to get there without money, he would get there anyway, and every time he convinced a pirate he would say to him, "Don't you thank me, don't you give me no credit; it all belongs to them dear people in Pokeville camp meeting, natural brothers and <u>benefactors</u> of the race, and that dear preacher there, the truest friend a pirate ever had!"

And then he busted into tears, and so did everybody. Then somebody sings out, "Take up a collection for him, take up a

---

16. **mourners' bench.** Front row of seats at a revival, for those who want to express remorse for their sins

---

Words For Everyday Use

con • trite (kən trīt´) *adj.,* remorseful, sorry, penitent

ben • e • fac • tor (ben ə fak´tər) *n.,* person who gives help, especially financial help

collection!" Well, a half a dozen made a jump to do it, but somebody sings out, "Let *him* pass the hat around!" Then everybody said it, the preacher too.

So the king went all through the crowd with his hat swabbing his eyes, and blessing the people and praising them and thanking them for being so good to the poor pirates away off there; and every little while the prettiest kind of girls, with the tears running down their cheeks, would up and ask him would he let them kiss him for to remember him by; and he always done it; and some of them he hugged and kissed as many as five or six times—and he was invited to stay a week; and everybody wanted him to live in their houses, and said they'd think it was an honor; but he said as this was the last day of the camp meeting he couldn't do no good, and besides he was in a sweat to get to the Indian Ocean right off and go to work on the pirates.

◄ What has the king tricked the crowd into allowing him to do?

When we got back to the raft and he come to count up he found he had collected eighty-seven dollars and seventy-five cents. And then he had fetched away a three-gallon jug of whisky, too, that he found under a wagon when he was starting home through the woods. The king said, take it all around, it laid over any day he'd ever put in in the missionarying line.[17] He said it warn't no use talking, heathens[18] don't amount to shucks alongside of pirates to work a camp meeting with.

The duke was thinking he'd been doing pretty well till the king come to show up, but after that he didn't think so so much. He had set up and printed off two little jobs for farmers in that printing office—horse bills—and took the money, four dollars. And he had got in ten dollars' worth of advertisements for the paper, which he said he would put in for four dollars if they would pay in advance—so they done it. The price of the paper was two dollars a year, but he took in three subscriptions for half a dollar apiece on condition of them paying him in advance; they were going to pay in cordwood and onions as usual, but he said he had just bought the concern and knocked down the price as low as he could afford it, and was going to run it for cash. He set up a little piece of poetry, which he made, himself, out of his own head—three verses—kind of sweet and saddish—the name of it was, "Yes, crush, cold world, this breaking heart"—and he left that all set up and ready to print in the paper, and didn't charge nothing for it. Well, he took in nine dollars and a half, and said he'd done a pretty square day's work for it.

---

17. **missionarying line.** "Business" of converting non-Christians to Christianity
18. **heathens.** Derogatory term used by people who hold certain religious beliefs to disparage those who hold different beliefs.

Then he showed us another little job he'd printed and hadn't charged for, because it was for us. It had a picture of a runaway nigger with a bundle on a stick over his shoulder, and "$200 reward" under it. The reading was all about Jim, and just described him to a dot. It said he run away from St. Jacques' plantation, forty mile below New Orleans, last winter, and likely went north, and whoever would catch him and send him back he could have the reward and expenses.

▶ Why does the duke have a sign made about an escaped slave? In what way will this sign enable them to raft in the daylight?

"Now," says the duke, "after tonight we can run in the daytime if we want to. Whenever we see anybody coming we can tie Jim hand and foot with a rope, and lay him in the wigwam and show this handbill and say we captured him up the river, and were too poor to travel on a steamboat, so we got this little raft on credit from our friends and are going down to get the reward. Handcuffs and chains would look still better on Jim, but it wouldn't go well with the story of us being so poor. Too much like jewelry. Ropes are the correct thing— we must preserve the unities,[19] as we say on the boards."

We all said the duke was pretty smart, and there couldn't be no trouble about running daytimes. We judged we could make miles enough that night to get out of the reach of the powwow we reckoned the duke's work in the printing office was going to make in that little town; then we could boom right along if we wanted to.

We laid low and kept still, and never shoved out till nearly ten o'clock; then we slid by, pretty wide away from the town, and didn't hoist our lantern till we was clear out of sight of it.

When Jim called me to take the watch at four in the morning, he says:

▶ What question does Jim ask Huck? How does Jim now seem to feel about the men?

"Huck, does you reck'n we gwyne to run acrost any mo' kings on dis trip?"

"No," I says, "I reckon not."

"Well," says he, "dat's all right, den. I doan' mine one er two kings, but dat's enough. Dis one's powerful drunk, en de duke ain' much better."

I found Jim had been trying to get him to talk French, so he could hear what it was like; but he said he had been in this country so long, and had so much trouble, he'd forgot it.

---

19. **Preserve the unities.** The ancient Greek philosopher Aristotle theorized that a playwright should preserve three unities in constructing a drama: all action should concern one theme, take place in one day, and be set in one locale.

CHAPTER 21

An Arkansaw Difficulty

It was after sunup now, but we went right on and didn't tie up. The king and the duke turned out by and by looking pretty rusty; but after they'd jumped overboard and took a swim it chippered them up a good deal. After breakfast the king he took a seat on the corner of the raft, and pulled off his boots and rolled up his britches, and let his legs dangle in the water, so as to be comfortable, and lit his pipe, and went to getting his "Romeo and Juliet" by heart. When he had got it pretty good him and the duke begun to practice it together. The duke had to learn him over and over again how to say every speech; and he made him sigh, and put his hand on his heart, and after a while he said he done it pretty well; "only," he says, "you mustn't <u>bellow</u> out *Romeo!* that way, like a bull—you must say it soft and sick and languishy,[1] so—R-o-o-meo! that is the idea; for Juliet's a dear sweet <u>mere</u> child of a girl, you know, and she doesn't <u>bray</u> like a jackass."

Well, next they got out a couple of long swords that the duke made out of oak laths, and begun to practice the sword fight—the duke called himself Richard III; and the way they laid on and pranced around the raft was grand to see. But by and by the king tripped and fell overboard, and after that they took a rest, and had a talk about all kinds of adventures they'd had in other times along the river.

After dinner the duke says:

"Well, Capet,[2] we'll want to make this a first-class show, you know, so I guess we'll add a little more to it. We want a little something to answer <u>encores</u> with, anyway."

"What's onkores, Bilgewater?"

The duke told him, and then says:

"I'll answer by doing the Highland fling or the sailor's hornpipe; and you—well, let me see—oh, I've got it—you can do Hamlet's <u>soliloquy</u>."

"Hamlet's which?"

◀ *What does the king do after breakfast?*

◀ *What will the men be doing for encores after their show?*

---

1. **languishy.** Languidly; in a weak, drooping manner
2. **Capet.** Family name of Louis XVI of France

Words For Everyday Use

bel • low (bel´ō) *vi.,* roar
mere (mir) *adj.,* nothing more than; only a
bray (brā) *vi.,* make a loud, harsh cry like a donkey
en • core (än´kôr´) *n.,* demand for further performance, shown by continued applause by the audience
so • lil • o • quy (sə lil´ə kwē) *n.,* lines in a drama that a character speaks as if to him- or herself

"Hamlet's soliloquy, you know; the most celebrated thing in Shakespeare. Ah, it's sublime, sublime! Always fetches the house. I haven't got it in the book—I've only got one volume—but I reckon I can piece it out from memory. I'll just walk up and down a minute, and see if I can call it back from recollection's vaults."

So he went to marching up and down, thinking, and frowning horrible every now and then; then he would hoist up his eyebrows; next he would squeeze his hand on his forehead and stagger back and kind of moan; next he would sigh, and next he'd let on to drop a tear. It was beautiful to see him. By and by he got it. He told us to give attention. Then he strikes a most noble attitude, with one leg shoved forwards, and his arms stretched away up, and his head tilted back, looking up at the sky; and then he begins to rip and rave and grit his teeth; and after that, all through his speech, he howled, and spread around, and swelled up his chest, and just knocked the spots out of any acting ever *I* see before. This is the speech—I learned it, easy enough, while he was learning it to the king:

> To be, or not to be; that is the bare bodkin
> That makes calamity of so long life;
> For who would fardels bear, till Birnam Wood do come to
>   Dunsinane,
> But that the fear of something after death
> Murders the innocent sleep,
> Great nature's second course,
> And makes us rather sling the arrows of outrageous fortune
> Than fly to others that we know not of.
> There's the respect must give us pause:
> Wake Duncan with thy knocking! I would thou couldst;
> For who would bear the whips and scorns of time,
> The oppressor's wrong, the proud man's contumely,
> The law's delay, and the quietus which his pangs might
>   take,
> In the dead waste and middle of the night, when church-
>   yards yawn
> In customary suits of solemn black,
> But that the undiscovered country from whose bourne no
>   traveler returns,
> Breathes forth contagion on the world,

Words For Everyday Use

sub • lime (sə blīm´) *adj.*, noble, exalted, grand

rec • ol • lec • tion (rek´ə lek´shən) *n.*, memory

vault (vôlt) *n.*, secure storage place

And thus the native hue of resolution, like the poor cat i'
   the adage,
Is sicklied o'er with care,
And all the clouds that lowered o'er our housetops,
With this regard their currents turn awry,
And lose the name of action.
'Tis a consummation devoutly to be wished.
But soft you, the fair Ophelia:
Ope not thy ponderous and marble jaws,
But get thee to a nunnery—go![3]

Well, the old man he liked that speech, and he mighty soon got it so he could do it first-rate. It seemed like he was just born for it; and when he had his hand in and was excited, it was perfectly lovely the way he would rip and tear and rair up behind when he was getting it off.

The first chance we got the duke he had some showbills printed; and after that, for two or three days as we floated along, the raft was a most uncommon lively place, for there warn't nothing but sword-fighting and rehearsing—as the duke called it—going on all the time. One morning, when we was pretty well down the state of Arkansaw, we come in sight of a little one-horse town in a big bend; so we tied up about three-quarters of a mile above it, in the mouth of a crick which was shut in like a tunnel by the cypress trees, and all of us but Jim took the canoe and went down there to see if there was any chance in that place for our show.

◄ *In what way does the raft become a "lively place"?*

We struck it mighty lucky; there was going to be a circus there that afternoon, and the country people was already beginning to come in, in all kinds of old shackly wagons, and on horses. The circus would leave before night, so our show would have a pretty good chance. The duke he hired the courthouse, and we went around and stuck up our bills. They read like this:

Shaksperean Revival ! ! !
Wonderful Attraction!
For One Night Only!
The world renowned tragedians,
David Garrick the younger, of Drury Lane Theatre,
London,
and
Edmund Kean[4] the elder, of the Royal Haymarket Theatre,
Whitechapel, Pudding Lane, Piccadilly, London,

---

3. **To be . . . go!** These lines are a fractured combination of *Hamlet*, *Macbeth*, and *Richard the Third*.
4. **Edmund Kean.** Great English actor who died in 1833

and the Royal Continental Theatres,
in their sublime Shaksperean Spectacle entitled
The Balcony Scene
in
Romeo and Juliet ! ! !

Romeo . . . . .Mr. Garrick
Juliet . . . . .Mr. Kean

Assisted by the whole strength of the company!
New costumes, new scenes, new appointments!
Also:
The thrilling, masterly, and blood-curdling
Broad-sword conflict
In Richard III ! ! !

Richard III . . . . .Mr. Garrick
Richmond .Mr. Kean

Also:
(by special request)
Hamlet's Immortal Soliloquy ! !
By the Illustrious Kean!
Done by him 300 <u>consecutive</u> nights in Paris!
For One Night Only,
On account of <u>imperative</u> European engagements!
Admission 25 cents; children and servants, 10 cents.

▶ *What details does Huck notice about the buildings in this town?*

Then we went loafing around town. The stores and houses was most all old, shackly, dried up frame concerns that hadn't ever been painted; they was set up three or four foot above ground on stilts, so as to be out of reach of the water when the river was overflowed. The houses had little gardens around them, but they didn't seem to raise hardly anything in them but jimpson-weeds, and sunflowers, and ash piles, and old curled-up boots and shoes, and pieces of bottles, and rags, and played-out tinware. The fences was made of different kinds of boards, nailed on at different times; and they leaned every which way, and had gates that didn't generly have but one hinge—a leather one. Some of the fences had been whitewashed some time or another, but the duke said it was in Clumbus's time, like enough. There was generly hogs in the garden, and people driving them out.

All the stores was along one street. They had white domestic awnings in front, and the country people hitched their

| Words For Everyday Use | con • sec • u • tive (kən sek´yo͞o tiv) *adj.,* continuous, one after the other |
| | im • per • a • tive (im per´ə tiv) *adj.,* command |

horses to the awning posts. There was empty drygoods boxes under the awnings, and loafers roosting on them all day long, whittling[5] them with their Barlow knives; and chawing tobacco, and gaping and yawning and stretching—a mighty ornery lot. They generly had on yellow straw hats most as wide as an umbrella, but didn't wear no coats nor waistcoats,[6] they called one another Bill, and Buck, and Hank, and Joe, and Andy, and talked lazy and drawly, and used considerable many cuss words. There was as many as one loafer leaning up against every awning post, and he most always had his hands in his britches pockets, except when he fetched them out to lend a chaw of tobacco or scratch. What a body was hearing amongst them all the time was:

"Gimme a chaw 'v tobacker, Hank."

"Cain't; I hain't got but one chaw left. Ask Bill."

Maybe Bill he gives him a chaw; maybe he lies and says he ain't got none. Some of them kinds of loafers never has a cent in the world, nor a chaw of tobacco of their own. They get all their chawing by borrowing; they say to a fellow, "I wisht you'd len' me a chaw, Jack, I jist this minute give Ben Thompson the last chaw I had"—which is a lie pretty much every time; it don't fool nobody but a stranger; but Jack ain't no stranger, so he says:

"*You* give him a chaw, did you? So did your sister's cat's grandmother. You pay me back the chaws you've awready borry'd off'n me, Lafe Buckner, then I'll loan you one or two ton of it, and won't charge you no back intrust, nuther."

"Well, I *did* pay you back some of it wunst."

"Yes, you did—'bout six chaws. You borry'd store tobacker and paid back nigger-head."

Store tobacco is flat black plug, but these fellows mostly chaws the natural leaf twisted. When they borrow a chaw they don't generly cut it off with a knife, but set the plug in between their teeth, and gnaw with their teeth and tug at the plug with their hands till they get it in two; then sometimes the one that owns the tobacco looks mournful at it when it's handed back, and says, <u>sarcastic</u>:

"Here, gimme the *chaw*, and you take the *plug*."

---

5. **whittling.** Cutting thin shavings from a piece of wood
6. **waistcoats.** Vests

◀ What kinds of people does Huck see in the streets of this town?

Words
For
Everyday
Use

sar • cas • tic (sär kas´tik) *adj.,* taunting, mocking, scornful

▶ What does Huck notice about the streets and roads? What seems to be the chief occupation of the town's inhabitants?

All the streets and lanes was just mud; they warn't nothing else *but* mud—mud as black as tar and nigh about a foot deep in some places, and two or three inches deep in *all* the places. The hogs loafed and grunted around everywheres. You'd see a muddy sow and a litter of pigs come lazying along the street and whollop herself right down in the way, where folks had to walk around her, and she'd stretch out and shut her eyes and wave her ears whilst the pigs was milking her, and look as happy as if she was on salary. And pretty soon you'd hear a loafer sing out, "Hi! *so* boy! sick him, Tige!" and away the sow would go, squealing most horrible, with a dog or two swinging to each ear, and three or four dozen more a-coming; and then you would see all the loafers get up and watch the thing out of sight, and laugh at the fun and look grateful for the noise. Then they'd settle back again till there was a dog fight. There couldn't anything wake them up all over, and make them happy all over, like a dog fight—unless it might be putting turpentine on a stray dog and setting fire to him, or tying a tin pan to his tail and see him run himself to death.

On the riverfront some of the houses was sticking out over the bank, and they was bowed and bent, and about ready to tumble in. The people had moved out of them. The bank was caved away under one corner of some others, and that corner was hanging over. People lived in them yet, but it was dangersome, because sometimes a strip of land as wide as a house caves in at a time. Sometimes a belt of land a quarter of a mile deep will start in and cave along and cave along till it all caves into the river in one summer. Such a town as that has to be always moving back, and back, and back, because the river's always gnawing at it.

The nearer it got to noon that day the thicker and thicker was the wagons and horses in the streets, and more coming all the time. Families fetched their dinners with them from the country, and eat them in the wagons. There was considerable whisky drinking going on, and I seen three fights. By and by somebody sings out:

"Here comes old Boggs!—in from the country for his little old monthly drunk; here he comes, boys!"

All the loafers looked glad; I reckoned they was used to having fun out of Boggs. One of them says:

"Wonder who he's a-gwyne to chaw up this time. If he'd a-chawed up all the men he's ben a-gwyne to chaw up in the last twenty year he'd have considerable ruputation now."

Another one says, "I wisht old Boggs 'd threaten me, 'cuz then I'd know I warn't gwyne to die for a thousan' year."

Boggs comes a-tearing along on his horse, whooping and yelling like an Injun, and singing out:

"Cler the track, thar. I'm on the waw-path, and the price uv coffins is a-gwyne to raise."

He was drunk, and weaving about in his saddle; he was over fifty year old, and had a very red face. Everybody yelled at him and laughed at him and sassed him, and he sassed back, and said he'd attend to them and lay them out in their regular turns, but he couldn't wait now because he'd come to town to kill old Colonel Sherburn, and his motto was, "Meat first, and spoon vittles to top off on."

He see me, and rode up and says:

"Whar'd you come f'm, boy? You prepared to die?"

Then he rode on. I was scared, but a man says:

"He don't mean nothing; he's always a-carryin' on like that when he's drunk. He's the best-naturedest old fool in Arkansaw—never hurt nobody, drunk nor sober."

Boggs rode up before the biggest store in town, and bent his head down so he could see under the curtain of the awning and yells:

"Come out here, Sherburn! Come out and meet the man you've swindled. You're the houn' I'm after, and I'm-a-gwyne to have you, too!"

And so he went on, calling Sherburn everything he could lay his tongue to, and the whole street packed with people listening and laughing and going on. By and by a proud-looking man about fifty-five—and he was a heap the best-dressed man in that town, too—steps out of the store, and the crowd drops back on each side to let him come. He says to Boggs, mighty ca'm and slow—he says:

"I'm tired of this, but I'll <u>endure</u> it till one o'clock. Till one o'clock, mind—no longer. If you open your mouth against me only once after that time you can't travel so far but I will find you."

Then he turns and goes in. The crowd looked mighty sober; nobody stirred, and there warn't no more laughing. Boggs rode off blackguarding[7] Sherburn as loud as he could yell, all down the street; and pretty soon back he comes and stops before the store, still keeping it up. Some men crowded

◄ How do people react to the man called old Boggs? Do they take him seriously? What does Boggs claim he is in town to do? What does he say to Huck?

◄ How does the mood of the crowd change when Sherburn appears? What does Sherburn tell Boggs? How does Boggs react? What do people in the town tell him?

---

7. **blackguarding.** Abusing with words

Words For Everyday Use

en • dure (en door´) vt., hold up under, bear

around him and tried to get him to shut up, but he wouldn't; they told him it would be one o'clock in about fifteen minutes, and so he *must* go home—he must go right away. But it didn't do no good. He cussed away with all his might, and throwed his hat down in the mud and rode over it, and pretty soon away he went a-raging down the street again, with his gray hair a-flying. Everybody that could get a chance at him tried their best to coax him off of his horse so they could lock him up and get him sober; but it warn't no use—up the street he would tear again, and give Sherburn another cussing. By and by somebody says:

"Go for his daughter!—quick, go for his daughter; sometimes he'll listen to her. If anybody can persuade him, she can."

So somebody started on a run. I walked down street a ways and stopped. In about five or ten minutes here comes Boggs again, but not on his horse. He was a-reeling across the street towards me, bareheaded, with a friend on both sides of him a-holt of his arms and hurrying him along. He was quiet, and looked uneasy; and he warn't hanging back any, but was doing some of the hurrying himself. Somebody sings out:

"Boggs!"

I looked over there to see who said it, and it was that Colonel Sherburn. He was standing perfectly still in the street, and had a pistol raised in his right hand—not aiming it, but holding it out with the barrel tilted up towards the sky. The same second I see a young girl coming on the run, and two men with her. Boggs and the men turned round to see who called him, and when they see the pistol the men jumped to one side, and the pistol-barrel come down slow and steady to a level—both barrels cocked. Boggs throws up both of his hands and says, "O Lord, don't shoot!" Bang! goes the first shot, and he staggers back, clawing at the air— bang! goes the second one, and he tumbles backwards onto the ground, heavy and solid, with his arms spread out. That young girl screamed out and comes rushing, and down she throws herself on her father, crying, and saying, "Oh, he's killed him, he's killed him!" The crowd closed up around them, and shouldered and jammed one another, with their necks stretched, trying to see, and people on the inside trying to shove them back and shouting, "Back, back! give him air, give him air!"

Colonel Sherburn he tossed his pistol on to the ground, and turned around on his heels and walked off.

They took Boggs to a little drug store, the crowd pressing around just the same, and the whole town following, and I

▶ What does Sherburn do to Boggs?

rushed and got a good place at the window, where I was close to him and could see in. They laid him on the floor and put one large Bible under his head, and opened another one and spread it on his breast; but they tore open his shirt first, and I seen where one of the bullets went in. He made about a dozen long gasps, his breast lifting the Bible up when he drawed in his breath, and letting it down again when he breathed it out—and after that he laid still; he was dead. Then they pulled his daughter away from him, screaming and crying, and took her off. She was about sixteen, and very sweet and gentle looking, but awful pale and scared.

Well, pretty soon the whole town was there, squirming and scrouging and pushing and shoving to get at the window and have a look, but people that had the places wouldn't give them up, and folks behind them was saying all the time, "Say, now, you've looked enough, you fellows; 'tain't right and 'tain't fair for you to stay thar all the time, and never give nobody a chance; other folks has their rights as well as you."

There was considerable jawing back,[8] so I slid out, thinking maybe there was going to be trouble. The streets was full, and everybody was excited. Everybody that seen the shooting was telling how it happened, and there was a big crowd packed around each one of these fellows, stretching their necks and listening. One long, <u>lanky</u> man, with long hair and a big white fur stovepipe hat on the back of his head, and a crooked-handled cane, marked out the places on the ground where Boggs stood and where Sherburn stood, and the people following him around from one place to t'other and watching everything he done, and bobbing their heads to show they understood, and stooping a little and resting their hands on their thighs to watch him mark the places on the ground with his cane; and then he stood up straight and stiff where Sherburn had stood, frowning and having his hat-brim down over his eyes, and sung out, "Boggs!" and then fetched his cane down slow to a level, and says "Bang!" staggered backwards, says "Bang!" again, and fell down flat on his back. The people that had seen the thing said he done it perfect; said it was just exactly the way it all happened.

◄ *Why does Huck sense that there is going to be trouble?*

---

8. **jawing back.** Talking back

Words For Everyday Use

lank • y (laŋk´ē) *adj.*, tall and thin

Then as much as a dozen people got out their bottles and treated him.

Well, by and by somebody said Sherburn ought to be lynched. In about a minute everybody was saying it; so away they went, mad and yelling, and snatching down every clothesline they come to to do the hanging with.

► *How do people in the town feel about what Sherburn did to Boggs? What do they want to do to Sherburn?*

CHAPTER 22

Why the Lynching Bee Failed

They swarmed up towards Sherburn's house, a-whooping and raging like Injuns, and everything had to clear the way or get run over and tromped to mush, and it was awful to see. Children was heeling it ahead of the mob, screaming and trying to get out of the way; and every window along the road was full of women's heads, and there was nigger boys in every tree, and bucks and wenches looking over every fence; and as soon as the mob would get nearly to them they would break and skaddle back out of reach. Lots of the women and girls was crying and taking on, scared most to death.

They swarmed up in front of Sherburn's palings[1] as thick as they could jam together, and you couldn't hear yourself think for the noise. It was a little twenty-foot yard. Some sung out "Tear down the fence! tear down the fence!" Then there was a racket of ripping and tearing and smashing, and down she goes, and the front wall of the crowd begins to roll in like a wave.

◄ What do people do when they get to Sherburn's house? What happens when Sherburn steps out of his house?

Just then Sherburn steps out on to the roof of his little front porch, with a double-barrel gun in his hand, and takes his stand, perfectly ca'm and <u>deliberate</u>, not saying a word. The racket stopped, and the wave sucked back.

Sherburn never said a word—just stood there, looking down. The stillness was awful creepy and uncomfortable. Sherburn run his eye slow along the crowd; and wherever it struck the people tried a little to outgaze him, but they couldn't; they dropped their eyes and looked sneaky. Then pretty soon Sherburn sort of laughed; not the pleasant kind, but the kind that makes you feel like when you are eating bread that's got sand in it.

Then he says, slow and scornful:

"The idea of *you* lynching anybody! It's amusing. The idea of you thinking you had pluck enough to lynch a *man!* Because you're brave enough to tar and feather poor friendless cast-out

---

1. **palings.** Fence

Words For Everyday Use

de • lib • er • ate (di lib´ə rit) *adj.,* unhurried and methodical

women that come along here, did that make you think you had grit enough to lay your hands on a *man*? Why, a *man*'s safe in the hands of ten thousand of your kind—as long as it's daytime and you're not behind him.

"Do I know you? I know you clear through. I was born and raised in the South, and I've lived in the North; so I know the average all around. The average man's a coward. In the North he lets anybody walk over him that wants to, and goes home and prays for a humble spirit to bear it. In the South one man all by himself, has stopped a stage full of men in the daytime, and robbed the lot. Your newspapers call you a brave people so much that you think you *are* braver than any other people—whereas you're just *as* brave, and no braver. Why don't your juries hang murderers? Because they're afraid the man's friends will shoot them in the back, in the dark—and it's just what they *would* do.

"So they always <u>acquit</u>; and then a *man* goes in the night, with a hundred masked cowards at his back and lynches the rascal. Your mistake is, that you didn't bring a man with you; that's one mistake, and the other is that you didn't come in the dark and fetch your masks. You brought *part* of a man— Buck Harkness, there—and if you hadn't had him to start you, you'd 'a' taken it out in blowing.

► What does Sherburn call the people in the crowd?

"You didn't want to come. The average man don't like trouble and danger. *You* don't like trouble and danger. But if only *half* a man—like Buck Harkness, there—shouts 'Lynch him! lynch him!' you're afraid to back down—afraid you'll be found out to be what you are—*cowards*—and so you raise a yell, and hang yourselves on to that half-a-man's coattail, and come raging up here, swearing what big things you're going to do. The pitifulest thing out is a mob; that's what an army is—a mob; they don't fight with courage that's born in them, but with courage that's borrowed from their mass, and from their officers. But a mob without any *man* at the head of it is *beneath* pitifulness. Now the thing for you to do is to droop your tails and go home and crawl in a hole. If any real lynching's going to be done it will be done in the dark, Southern fashion; and when they come they'll bring their masks, and fetch a *man* along. Now *leave*—and take your half-a-man with you"—tossing his gun up across his left arm and cocking it when he says this.

Words
For
Everyday
Use

ac • quit (ə kwit´) *vt.,* clear of guilt

The crowd washed back sudden, and then broke all apart, and went tearing off every which way, and Buck Harkness he heeled it after them, looking tolerable cheap. I could 'a' stayed if I wanted to, but I didn't want to.

I went to the circus and loafed around the back side till the watchman went by, and then dived in under the tent. I had my twenty-dollar gold piece and some other money, but I reckoned I better save it, because there ain't no telling how soon you are going to need it, away from home and amongst strangers that way. You can't be too careful. I ain't opposed to spending money on circuses when there ain't no other way, but there ain't no use in *wasting* it on them.

It was a real bully[2] circus. It was the splendidest sight that ever was when they all come riding in, two and two, a gentleman and lady, side by side, the men just in their drawers and undershirts, and no shoes nor stirrups, and resting their hands on their thighs easy and comfortable—there must 'a' been twenty of them—and every lady with a lovely complexion, and perfectly beautiful, and looking just like a gang of real sure-enough queens, and dressed in clothes that cost millions of dollars, and just littered with diamonds. It was a powerful fine sight; I never see anything so lovely. And then one by one they got up and stood, and went a-weaving around the ring so gentle and wavy and graceful, the men looking ever so tall and airy and straight, with their heads bobbing and skimming along, away up there under the tent-roof, and every lady's rose-leafy dress flapping soft and silky around her hips, and she looking like the most loveliest parasol.[3]

And then faster and faster they went, all of them dancing, first one foot out in the air and then the other, the horses leaning more and more, and the ringmaster going round and round the center pole, cracking his whip and shouting "Hi!—hi!" and the clown cracking jokes behind him; and by and by all hands dropped the reins, and every lady put her knuckles on her hips and every gentleman folded his arms, and then how the horses did lean over and hump themselves! And so one after the other they all skipped off into the ring, and made the sweetest bow I ever see, and then scampered out, and everybody clapped their hands and went just about wild.

Well, all through the circus they done the most astonishing things; and all the time that clown carried on so it most killed the people. The ringmaster couldn't ever say a word to him but he was back at him quick as a wink with the funniest

◀ What does the crowd do immediately after Sherburn's speech?

◀ What does Huck like about the circus clown?

---

2. **bully.** Great, terrific
3. **parasol.** Dainty umbrella, used for protection from the sun

things a body ever said; and how he ever *could* think of so many of them, and so sudden and so <u>pat</u>, was what I couldn't no way understand. Why, I couldn't 'a' thought of them in a year. And by and by a drunk man tried to get into the ring— said he wanted to ride; said he could ride as well as anybody that ever was. They argued and tried to keep him out, but he wouldn't listen, and the whole show come to a standstill. Then the people begun to holler at him and make fun of him, and that made him mad, and he begun to rip and tear; so that stirred up the people, and a lot of men begun to pile down off of the benches and swarm towards the ring, saying, "Knock him down! throw him out!" and one or two women begun to scream. So, then, the ringmaster he made a little speech, and said he hoped there wouldn't be no disturbance, and if the man would promise he wouldn't make no more trouble he would let him ride if he thought he could stay on the horse. So everybody laughed and said all right, and the man got on. The minute he was on, the horse begun to rip and tear and jump and cavort around, with two circus men hanging on to his bridle[4] trying to hold him, and the drunken man hanging on to his neck, and his heels flying in the air every jump, and the whole crowd of people standing up shouting and laughing till tears rolled down. And at last, sure enough, all the circus men could do, the horse broke loose, and away he went like the very nation, round and round the ring, with that sot laying down on him and hanging to his neck, with first one leg hanging most to the ground on one side, and then t'other one on t'other side, and the people just crazy. It warn't funny to me, though; I was all of a tremble to see his danger. But pretty soon he struggled up astraddle[5] and grabbed the bridle, a-reeling this way and that; and the next minute he sprung up and dropped the bridle and stood! and the horse a-going like a house afire too. He just stood up there, a-sailing around as easy and comfortable as if he warn't ever drunk in his life— and then he begun to pull off his clothes and sling them. He shed them so thick they kind of clogged up the air, and altogether he shed seventeen suits. And, then, there he was, slim and handsome, and dressed the <u>gaudiest</u> and prettiest you

---

4. **bridle.** Harness on a horse's head to guide him by
5. **astraddle.** With a leg on either side of the horse

Words
For
Everyday
Use

pat (pat) *adj.,* exactly suited to the occasion
gau • dy (gôd´y) *adj.,* showy, flashy, tawdry

ever saw, and he lit into that horse with his whip and made him fairly hum—and finally skipped off, and made his bow and danced off to the dressing room, and everybody just a-howling with pleasure and astonishment.

Then the ringmaster he see how he had been fooled, and he *was* the sickest ringmaster you ever see, I reckon. Why, it was one of his own men! He had got up that joke all out of his own head, and never let on to nobody. Well, I felt sheepish enough to be took in so, but I wouldn't 'a' been in that ringmaster's place, not for a thousand dollars. I don't know; there may be bullier circuses than what that one was, but I never struck them yet. Anyways, it was plenty good enough for *me*; and wherever I run across it, it can have all of *my* custom every time.

Well, that night we had *our* show; but there warn't only about twelve people there—just enough to pay expenses. And they laughed all the time, and that made the duke mad; and everybody left, anyway, before the show was over, but one boy which was asleep. So the duke said these Arkansaw lunkheads couldn't come up to Shakespeare; what they wanted was low comedy—and maybe something ruther worse than low comedy, he reckoned. He said he could size their style. So next morning he got some big sheets of wrapping paper and some black paint, and drawed off some handbills, and stuck them up all over the village. The bills said:

◄ What happens on the first night of the Shakespeare show? According to the duke, why does the show fail? What does he decide the people in the town must want?

AT THE COURT HOUSE!
FOR 3 NIGHTS ONLY!
The World-Renowned Tragedians
DAVID GARRICK THE YOUNGER!
AND
EDMUND KEAN THE ELDER!
Of the London and Continental Theatres,
In their Thrilling Tragedy of
THE KING'S CAMELEOPARD,
OR
THE ROYAL NONESUCH ! ! !
Admission 50 cents.

Then at the bottom was the biggest line of all, which said:

LADIES AND CHILDREN NOT ADMITTED.

◄ What line in the sign does the duke believe will attract people?

"There," says he, "if that line don't fetch them, I don't know Arkansaw!"

CHAPTER 23

The Orneriness of Kings

Well, all day him and the king was hard at it, rigging up a stage and a curtain and a row of candles for footlights; and that night the house was jam full of men in no time. When the place couldn't hold no more, the duke he quit tending door and went around the back way and come onto the stage and stood up before the curtain and made a little speech, and praised up this tragedy, and said it was the most thrillingest one that ever was; and so he went on a-bragging about the tragedy, and about Edmund Kean the Elder, which was to play the main principal part in it; and at last when he'd got everybody's expectations up high enough, he rolled up the curtain, and the next minute the king come a-prancing out on all fours, naked; and he was painted all over, ring-streaked and striped, all sorts of colors, as splendid as a rainbow. And—but never mind the rest of his outfit; it was just wild, but it was awful funny. The people most killed themselves laughing; and when the king got done capering and capered off behind the scenes, they roared and clapped and stormed and haw-hawed till he come back and done it over again, and after that they made him do it another time. Well, it would make a cow laugh to see the shines that old idiot cut.

> ▶ What happens in the "tragedy" set up by the king and the duke?

Then the duke he lets the curtain down, and bows to the people, and says the great tragedy will be performed only two nights more, on accounts of <u>pressing</u> London engagements, where the seats is all sold already for it in Drury Lane; and then he makes them another bow, and says if he has succeeded in pleasing them and instructing them, he will be deeply obleeged if they will mention it to their friends and get them to come and see it.

Twenty people sings out:

"What, is it over? Is that all?"

The duke says yes. Then there was a fine time. Everybody sings out, "Sold!"[1] and rose up mad, and was a-going for that stage and them tragedians. But a big, fine-looking man jumps up on a bench and shouts:

---

1. **Sold.** Fooled; cheated

Words For Everyday Use

press • ing (pres´iŋ) *adj.*, urgent

"Hold on! Just a word, gentlemen." They stopped to listen. "We are sold—mighty badly sold. But we don't want to be the laughingstock of this whole town, I reckon, and never hear the last of this thing as long as we live. No. What we want is to go out of here quiet, and talk this show up, and sell the rest of the town! Then we'll all be in the same boat. Ain't that sensible?" ("You bet it is!—the jedge is right!" everybody sings out.) "All right, then—not a word about any sell. Go along home, and advise everybody to come and see the tragedy."

◄ Why do people advise their friends to go see the tragedy, even though they feel that they were cheated?

Next day you couldn't hear nothing around that town but how splendid that show was. House was jammed again that night, and we sold this crowd the same way. When me and the king and the duke got home to the raft we all had a supper; and by and by, about midnight, they made Jim and me back her out and float her down the middle of the river, and fetch her in and hide her about two mile below town.

The third night the house was crammed again—and they warn't newcomers this time, but people that was at the show the other two nights. I stood by the duke at the door, and I see that every man that went in had his pockets bulging, or something muffled up under his coat—and I see it warn't no perfumery, neither, not by a long sight. I smelt sickly eggs by the barrel, and rotten cabbages, and such things; and if I know the signs of a dead cat being around, and I bet I do, there was sixty-four of them went in. I shoved in there for a minute, but it was too various for me; I couldn't stand it. Well, when the place couldn't hold no more people the duke he give a fellow a quarter and told him to tend door for him a minute, and then he started around for the stage door, I after him; but the minute we turned the corner and was in the dark he says:

◄ What items are people bringing into the theater, under their jackets?

"Walk fast now till you get away from the houses, and then shin for the raft like the dickens was after you!"

I done it, and he done the same. We struck the raft at the same time, and in less than two seconds we was gliding downstream, all dark and still, and edging towards the middle of the river, nobody saying a word. I reckoned the poor king was in for a gaudy time of it with the audience, but nothing of the sort; pretty soon he crawls out from under the wigwam, and says:

◄ What does the duke tell Huck to do as soon as the house is full? Where has the king been?

"Well, how'd the old thing pan out this time, duke?" He hadn't been uptown at all.

We never showed a light till we was about ten mile below the village. Then we lit up and had a supper, and the king and the duke fairly laughed their bones loose over the way they'd served them people. The duke says:

"Greenhorns,[2] flatheads! *I* knew the first house would keep mum and let the rest of the town get roped in; and I knew they'd lay for us the third night, and consider it was their turn now. Well, it is their turn, and I'd give something to know how much they'd take for it. I would just like to know how they're putting in their opportunity. They can turn it into a picnic if they want to—they brought plenty <u>provisions</u>."

Them rapscallions took in four hundred and sixty-five dollars in that three nights. I never see money hauled in by the wagon-load like that before. By and by, when they was asleep and snoring, Jim says:

"Don't it s'prise you de way dem kings carries on, Huck?"

"No," I says, "it don't."

"Why don't it, Huck?"

"Well, it don't, because it's in the breed. I reckon they're all alike,"

"But, Huck, dese kings o' ourn is rapscallions; dat's jist what dey is; dey's reglar rapscallions."

"Well, that's what I'm a-saying; all kings is mostly rapscallions, as fur as I can make out."

"Is dat so?"

"You read about them once—you'll see. Look at Henry the Eight; this 'n 's a Sunday school superintendent to him. And look at Charles Second, and Louis Fourteen, and Louis Fifteen, and James Second, and Edward Second, and Richard Third, and forty more; besides all them Saxon heptarchies[3] that used to rip around so in old times and raise Cain. My, you ought to seen old Henry the Eight when he was in bloom. He was a blossom. He used to marry a new wife every day, and chop off her head next morning. And he would do it just as <u>indifferent</u> as if he was ordering up eggs. 'Fetch up Nell Gwynn,' he says. They fetch her up. Next morning, 'Chop off her head!' And they chop it off. 'Fetch up Jane Shore,' he says; and up she comes. Next morning, 'Chop off her head'—and they chop it off. 'Ring up Fair Rosamun.'[4] Fair Rosamun answers the bell. Next morning, 'Chop off her head.' And he made every one of them tell him a tale every

▶ How much money have the king and duke swindled from the people of the town?

▶ According to Huck, why is the behavior of the king and the duke not surprising? What is his opinion of kings?

---

2. **Greenhorns.** Inexperienced persons, easily deceived

3. **heptarchies.** Kingdoms of Anglo-Saxon England before the ninth century

4. **Nell Gwynn . . . Rosamun.** While Henry VIII did have two of his wives beheaded, none of these women were his wives, but rather mistresses of other kings of England.

Words For Everyday Use

pro • vi • sions (prō vizh´əns) *n.*, stock of food supplies

in • dif • fer • ent (in dif´ rent) *adj.*, uncaring, unconcerned

night; and he kept that up till he had hogged a thousand and one tales that way, and then he put them all in a book, and called it Domesday Book[5]—which was a good name and stated the case. You don't know kings, Jim, but I know them; and this old rip of ourn is one of the cleanest I've struck in history. Well, Henry he takes a notion he wants to get up some trouble with this country. How does he go at it—give notice?—give the country a show? No. All of a sudden he heaves all the tea in Boston Harbor overboard, and whacks out a declaration of independence, and dares them to come on. That was his style—he never give anybody a chance. He had suspicions of his father, the Duke of Wellington. Well, what did he do? Ask him to show up? No—drownded him in a butt of mamsey, like a cat.[6] S'pose people left money laying around where he was—what did he do? He collared it. S'pose he contracted to do a thing, and you paid him, and didn't set down there and see that he done it—what did he do? He always done the other thing. S'pose he opened his mouth—what then? If he didn't shut it up powerful quick he'd lose a lie every time. That's the kind of a bug Henry was; and if we'd 'a' had him along 'stead of our kings he'd 'a' fooled that town a heap worse than ourn done. I don't say that ourn is lambs, because they ain't, when you come right down to the cold facts; but they ain't nothing to that old ram, anyway. All I say is, kings is kings, and you got to make allowances. Take them all around, they're a mighty ornery lot. It's the way they're raised."

"But dis one do smell so like de nation, Huck."

"Well, they all do, Jim. *We* can't help the way a king smells; history don't tell no way."

"Now de duke, he's a tolerble likely man in some ways."

"Yes, a duke's different. But not very different. This one's a middling[7] hard lot for a duke. When he's drunk there ain't no near-sighted man could tell him from a king."

"Well, anyways, I doan' <u>hanker</u> for no mo' un um, Huck. Dese is all I kin stan'."

---

5. **tell him a tale . . . Domesday Book.** Huck confuses the history of Henry VIII with the *Thousand and One Nights*. The Domesday Book was a census taken by William the Conqueror.

6. **the tea in Boston Harbor . . . like a cat.** More wild combinations of people and events

7. **middling.** Fairly, moderately

Words
For
Everyday
Use

han • ker (han´ ker) *vi.*, yearn, long

▶ How do Huck and Jim feel about continuing to have the kings on the raft with them? Why doesn't Huck tell Jim that he doesn't believe the kings are really kings?

▶ What is Jim doing when Huck awakens? According to Huck, what is bothering Jim? What is Huck beginning to realize?

"It's the way I feel, too, Jim. But we've got them on our hands, and we got to remember what they are, and <u>make allowances</u>. Sometimes I wish we could hear of a country that's out of kings."

What was the use to tell Jim these warn't real kings and dukes? It wouldn't 'a' done no good; and, besides, it was just as I said: you couldn't tell them from the real kind.

I went to sleep, and Jim didn't call me when it was my turn. He often done that. When I waked up just at daybreak he was sitting there with his head down betwixt his knees, moaning and mourning to himself. I didn't take notice nor let on. I knowed what it was about. He was thinking about his wife and his children, away up yonder, and he was low and homesick; because he hadn't ever been away from home before in his life; and I do believe he cared just as much for his people as white folks does for their'n. It don't seem natural, but I reckon it's so. He was often moaning and mourning that way nights, when he judged I was asleep, and saying, "Po' little 'Lizabeth! po' little Johnny! it's mighty hard; I spec' I ain't ever gwyne to see you no mo', no mo'!" He was a mighty good nigger, Jim was.

But this time I somehow got to talking to him about his wife and young ones; and by and by he says:

"What makes me feel so bad dis time 'uz bekase I hear sumpn over yonder on de bank like a whack, er a slam, while ago, en it mine me er de time I treat my little 'Lizabeth so ornery. She warn't on'y 'bout fo' year ole, en she tuck de sk'yarlet fever,[8] en had a powful rough spell; but she got well, en one day she was a-stannin' aroun', en I says to her, I says:

"'Shet de do'.'

"She never done it; jis' stood dah, kiner smilin' up at me. It make me mad; en I says agin, mighty loud, I says:

"'Doan' you hear me? Shet de do'!'

"She jis stood de same way, kiner smilin' up. I was abilin'! I says:

"'I lay I make you mine!'

"En wid dat I fetch' her a slap side de head dat sont her

---

8. **sk'yarlet fever.** Scarlet fever; contagious disease, especially of children, marked by high fever, sore throat, and red rash

Words For Everyday Use

make a • low • ance (māk e lou´ans) *vt.*, take circumstances into consideration

a-sprawlin'. Den I went into de yuther room, en 'uz gone 'bout ten minutes; en when I come back dah was dat do' a-stannin' open yit, en dat chile stannin' mos' right in it, a-lookin' down and mournin', en de tears runnin' down. My, but I wuz mad! I was a-gwyne for de chile, but jis' den—it was a do' dat open innerds—jis' den, 'long come de wind en slam it to, behine de chile, ker-blam!—en my lan', de chile never move'! My breff mos' hop outer me; en I feel so—so— I doan' know how I feel. I crope out, all a-tremblin', en crope aroun' en open de do' easy en slow, en poke my head in behine de chile, sof' en still, en all uv a sudden I says pow! jis' as loud as I could yell. She never budge! Oh, Huck, I bust out a-cryin' en grab her up in my arms, en say, 'Oh, de po' little thing! De Lord God Amighty fogive po' ole Jim, kaze he never gwyne to fogive hisself as long's he live!' Oh, she was plumb deef en dumb, Huck, plumb deef en dumb—en I'd ben a-treat'n her so!"

◄ Why is Jim angry with himself when he remembers his daughter? What did he not understand about his daughter's condition when he punished her for not shutting the door?

Responding to the Selection

"It's lovely to live on a raft," Huck observes. What makes it lovely, in his opinion?

Reviewing the Selection

Recalling and Interpreting

1. **R:** With what do Huck and Jim fill their time as they travel on their raft before they encounter the king and the duke?

2. **I:** Do Huck and Jim seem content? Why do you think Huck says "we would watch the lonesomeness of the river." What does he mean?

3. **R:** Why does Huck cross over to land when they find a canoe? When he sees two running men, what does he assume? When they beg Huck to save them, what does he do?

4. **I:** Why doesn't Huck want them to jump into the canoe immediately? Why is it not in Huck's character to question the men about who they are or what they are trying to escape before he helps them?

5. **R:** From whom are the two men escaping? Why? How do they present themselves to Huck and Jim?

6. **I:** What kind of things do the self-styled duke and king do to make a living? Why do you think they decide to call themselves a duke and a king? How would you describe the duke and the king? Why does Huck decide not to question their stories, even though he doesn't believe them? In what way might challenging these men put Jim at risk?

7. **R:** With whom does the character Boggs have a quarrel? What comes of it?

8. **I:** What are some of the ways the townspeople react to Boggs's death? Is anyone outraged? Is their attempt to lynch Col. Sherburn done in the name of justice or to feed their appetite for more violence?

Synthesizing

9. Despite their lack of shame, in what ways are the duke and the king clever and knowledgeable about human nature? Why do their scams succeed so well?

10. At the end of chapter 23, Jim reveals some of his feelings toward his daughter. Why is he feeling guilt? What does his guilt reveal about Jim as a person and a father? What does Huck learn about Jim in listening to his story? What important thing does Huck recognize? In what way is Jim different from many of the other adults in Huck's life?

Understanding Literature (QUESTIONS FOR DISCUSSION)

1. Description. A **description** portrays a character, an object, or a scene. Descriptions make use of sensory details—words and phrases that describe how things look, sound, smell, taste, or feel. What sensory details are used to create the description at the beginning of chapter 19?

2. Character, Characterization and Satire. A **character** is a person who figures in the action of a literary work. **Characterization** is the use of literary techniques to create a character. Writers use three major techniques to create characters: direct description, portrayal of characters' behavior, and representations of characters' internal states. What do you learn about the attitudes, beliefs, and personal qualities of the duke and the king from their words and actions? **Satire** is humorous writing or speech intended to point out errors, falsehoods, or failings. In what way is the characterization of the duke and the king satiric? Consider their claims about their lineage, their acting, and the faulty historical and literary allusions they make.

CHAPTER 24

The King Turns Parson

Next day, towards night, we laid up under a little willow towhead out in the middle, where there was a village on each side of the river, and the duke and the king begun to lay out a plan for working them towns. Jim he spoke to the duke, and said he hoped it wouldn't take but a few hours, because it got mighty heavy and tiresome to him when he had to lay all day in the wigwam tied with the rope. You see, when we left him all alone we had to tie him, because if anybody happened on to him all by himself and not tied it wouldn't look much like he was a runaway nigger, you know. So the duke said it *was* kind of hard to have to lay roped all day, and he'd cipher out some way to get around it.

> ▶ What plans do the king and the duke make? What is Jim's concern as he listens to them discuss their plans?

He was uncommon bright, the duke was, and he soon struck it. He dressed Jim up in King Lear's outfit—it was a long curtain-calico gown, and a white horsehair wig and whiskers; and then he took his theater paint and painted Jim's face and hands and ears and neck all over a dead, dull, solid blue, like a man that's been drownded nine days. Blamed if he warn't the horriblest looking outrage I ever see. Then the duke took and wrote out a sign on a shingle so:

Sick Arab—but harmless when not out of his head.

And he nailed that shingle to a lath, and stood the lath up four or five foot in front of the wigwam. Jim was satisfied. He said it was a sight better than lying tied a couple of years every day, and trembling all over every time there was a sound. The duke told him to make himself free and easy, and if anybody ever come meddling around, he must hop out of the wigwam, and carry on a little, and fetch a howl or two like a wild beast, and he reckoned they would light out and leave him alone. Which was sound enough judgment; but you take the average man, and he wouldn't wait for him to howl. Why, he didn't only look like he was dead, he looked considerable more than that.

> ▶ What does the duke tell Jim to do if anyone comes "meddling around"?

These rapscallions wanted to try the Nonesuch again, because there was so much money in it, but they judged it wouldn't be safe, because maybe the news might 'a' worked along down by this time. They couldn't hit no project that suited exactly; so at last the duke said he reckoned he'd lay off and work his brains an hour or two and see if he couldn't put up something on the Arkansaw village; and the king he allowed he would drop over to t'other village without any

> ▶ What do the king and the duke want to try again? Why do they think it might be too dangerous?

plan, but just trust in Providence to lead him the profitable way—meaning the devil, I reckon. We had all bought store clothes where we stopped last; and now the king put his'n on, and he told me to put mine on. I done it, of course. The king's duds was all black, and he did look real swell and starchy. I never knowed how clothes could change a body before. Why, before, he looked like the orneriest old rip that ever was; but now, when he'd take off his new white beaver[1] and make a bow and do a smile, he looked that grand and good and <u>pious</u> that you'd say he had walked right out of the ark, and maybe was old Leviticus[2] himself. Jim cleaned up the canoe, and I got my paddle ready. There was a big steamboat laying at the shore away up under the point, about three mile above the town—been there a couple of hours, taking on freight. Says the king:

"Seein' how I'm dressed, I reckon maybe I better arrive down from St. Louis or Cincinnati, or some other big place. Go for the steamboat, Huckleberry; we'll come down to the village on her."

◄ How do they plan to get to the next village?

I didn't have to be ordered twice to go and take a steamboat ride. I fetched the shore a half a mile above the village, and then went scooting along the bluff bank in the easy water. Pretty soon we come to a nice innocent looking young country jake[3] setting on a log swabbing the sweat off of his face, for it was powerful warm weather; and he had a couple of big carpetbags by him.

"Run her nose in shore," says the king. I done it. "Wher' you bound for, young man?"

"For the steamboat; going to Orleans."

"Git aboard," says the king. "Hold on a minute, my servant 'll he'p you with them bags. Jump out and he'p the gentleman, Adolphus"—meaning me, I see.

I done so, and then we all three started on again. The young chap was mighty thankful; said it was tough work toting his baggage such weather. He asked the king where he was going, and the king told him he'd come down the river and landed at the other village this morning, and now he

---

1. **beaver.** High silk hat
2. **Leviticus.** Huck confuses this book of the Old Testament with the character Noah.
3. **jake.** Unsophisticated country boy

Words For Everyday Use   pi • ous (pī´əs) *adj.*, having or showing religious devotion

► For whom does the young country boy mistake the king?

was going up a few mile to see an old friend on a farm up there. The young fellow says:

"When I first see you I says to myself, 'It's Mr. Wilks, sure, and he come mighty near getting here in time.' But then I says again, 'No, I reckon it ain't him, or else he wouldn't be paddling up the river.' You ain't him, are you?"

"No, my name's Blodgett—Elexander Blodgett—*Reverend* Elexander Blodgett, I s'pose I must say, as I'm one o' the Lord's poor servants. But still I'm jist as able to be sorry for Mr. Wilks for not arriving in time, all the same, if he's missed anything by it—which I hope he hasn't."

► What information about Mr. Wilks does the king manage to get? What has Mr. Wilks missed?

"Well, he don't miss any property by it, because he'll get that all right; but he's missed seeing his brother Peter die— which he mayn't mind, nobody can tell as to that—but his brother would 'a' give anything in this world to see him before he died; never talked about nothing else all these three weeks; hadn't seen him since they was boys together— and hadn't ever seen his brother William at all—that's the deef and dumb one—William ain't more than thirty or thirty-five. Peter and George were the only ones that come out here; George was the married brother; him and his wife both died last year. Harvey and William's the only ones that's left now; and, as I was saying, they haven't got here in time."

"Did anybody send 'em word?"

"Oh, yes; a month or two ago, when Peter was first took; because Peter said then that he sorter felt like he warn't going to get well this time. You see, he was pretty old, and George's g'yirls was too young to be much company for him, except Mary Jane, the red-headed one; and so he was kinder lonesome after George and his wife died, and didn't seem to care much to live. He most desperately wanted to see Harvey—and William, too, for that matter—because he was one of them kind that can't bear to make a will. He left a let-

► What did the dying brother leave behind for Mr. Wilks? Where does Mr. Wilks live?

ter behind for Harvey, and said he'd told in it where his money was hid, and how he wanted the rest of the property divided up so George's g'yirls would be all right—for George didn't leave nothing. And that letter was all they could get him to put a pen to."

"Why do you reckon Harvey don't come? Wher' does he live?"

"Oh, he lives in England—Sheffield—preaches there—hasn't ever been in this country. He hasn't had any too much time—and besides he mightn't 'a' got the letter at all, you know."

"Too bad, too bad he couldn't a lived to see his brothers, poor soul. You going to Orleans, you say?"

"Yes, but that ain't only a part of it. I'm going in a ship, next Wednesday, for Ryo Janeero, where my uncle lives."

"It's a pretty long journey. But it'll be lovely; wisht I was a-going. Is Mary Jane the oldest? How old is the others?"

"Mary Jane's nineteen, Susan's fifteen, and Joanna's about fourteen—that's the one that gives herself to good works and has a harelip."[3]

"Poor things! to be left alone in the cold world so."

"Well, they could be worse off. Old Peter had friends, and they ain't going to let them come to no harm. There's Hobson, the Babtis' preacher; and Deacon Lot Hovey, and Ben Rucker, and Abner Shackleford, and Levi Bell, the lawyer; and Dr. Robinson, and their wives, and the widow Bartley, and—well, there's a lot of them; but these are the ones that Peter was thickest with, and used to write about sometimes, when he wrote home; so Harvey 'll know where to look for friends when he gets here."

Well, the old man went on asking questions till he just fairly emptied that young fellow. Blamed if he didn't inquire about everybody and everything in that blessed town, and all about the Wilkses; and about Peter's business—which was a tanner; and about George's—which was a carpenter; and about Harvey's—which was a dissentering[4] minister; and so on, and so on. Then he says:

"What did you want to walk all the way up to the steamboat for?"

"Because she's a big Orleans boat, and I was afeard she mightn't stop there. When they're deep they won't stop for a <u>hail</u>. A Cincinnati boat will, but this is a St. Louis one."

"Was Peter Wilks well off?"

"Oh, yes, pretty well off. He had houses and land, and it's reckoned he left three or four thousand in cash hid up som'ers."

"When did you say he died?"

"I didn't say, but it was last night."

"Funeral tomorrow, likely?"

"Yes, 'bout the middle of the day."

◄ *What question does the king ask about Peter Wilks? Why might this information interest him?*

---

3. **harelip.** Cleft palate, a birth defect that affects one's speech
4. **dissentering.** Dissenting; English Protestant who is not a member of the Anglican Church

| Words For Everyday Use | **hail** (hāl) *n.*, signal summoning something or someone |

"Well, it's all terrible sad; but we've all got to go, one time or another. So what we want to do is to be prepared; then we're all right."

"Yes, sir, it's the best way. Ma used to always say that."

When we struck the boat she was about done loading, and pretty soon she got off. The king never said nothing about going aboard, so I lost my ride, after all. When the boat was gone the king made me paddle up another mile to a lonesome place, and then he got ashore and says:

"Now hustle back, right off, and fetch the duke up here, and the new carpetbags. And if he's gone over to t'other side, go over there and git him. And tell him to git himself up regardless. Shove along, now."

▶ What does Huck suspect the king is "up to"? Why do you think the king is trying to talk like an Englishman?

I see what *he* was up to; but I never said nothing, of course. When I got back with the duke we hid the canoe, and then they set down on a log, and the king told him everything, just like the young fellow had said it—every last word of it. And all the time he was a-doing it he tried to talk like an Englishman; and he done it pretty well, too, for a slouch. I can't imitate him, and so I ain't a-going to try to; but he really done it pretty good. Then he says:

"How are you on the deef and dumb, Bilgewater?"

The duke said, leave him alone for that; said he had played a deef and dumb person on the histrionic boards. So then they waited for a steamboat.

About the middle of the afternoon a couple of little boats come along, but they didn't come from high enough up the river; but at last there was a big one, and they hailed her. She sent out her yawl,[5] and we went aboard, and she was from Cincinnati; and when they found we only wanted to go four or five mile they was booming mad, and gave us a cussing, and said they wouldn't land us. But the king was ca'm. He says:

"If gentlemen kin afford to pay a dollar a mile apiece to be took on and put off in a yawl, a steamboat kin afford to carry 'em, can't it?"

So they softened down and said it was all right; and when we got to the village they yawled us ashore. About two dozen men flocked down when they see the yawl a-coming, and when the king says:

▶ What does the king want to know when he gets off the steamboat? Whom is he pretending to be?

"Kin any of you gentlemen tell me wher' Mr. Peter Wilks lives?" they give a glance at one another, and nodded their heads, as much as to say, "What 'd I tell you?" Then one of them says, kind of soft and gentle:

---

5. **yawl.** Small rowboat carried by a larger vessel to pull closer to shore than the larger boat can go

"I'm sorry, sir, but the best we can do is to tell you where he *did* live yesterday evening."

Sudden as winking the ornery old cretur went all to smash, and fell up against the man, and put his chin on his shoulder, and cried down his back, and says:

"Alas, alas, our poor brother—gone, and we never got to see him; oh, it's too, *too* hard!"

Then he turns around, blubbering, and makes a lot of idiotic signs to the duke on his hands, and blamed if *he* didn't drop a carpetbag and bust out a-crying. If they warn't the beatenest lot, them two frauds, that ever I struck.

Well, the men gathered around and sympathized with them, and said all sorts of kind things to them, and carried their carpetbags up the hill for them, and let them lean on them and cry, and told the king all about his brother's last moments, and the king he told it all over again on his hands to the duke, and both of them took on about that dead tanner like they'd lost the twelve disciples.[6] Well, if ever I struck anything like it, I'm a nigger. It was enough to make a body ashamed of the human race.

◄ *How do people treat the king? Of what does the king's behavior make Huck ashamed?*

---

6. **twelve disciples.** Original followers of Jesus

All Full of Tears and Flapdoodle

► How do the townspeople react to the appearance of "the Wilks brothers"? Does anyone seem to suspect that they aren't who they claim to be?

The news was all over town in two minutes, and you could see the people tearing down on the run from every which way, some of them putting on their coats as they come. Pretty soon we was in the middle of a crowd, and the noise of the tramping was like a soldier march. The windows and dooryards was full; and every minute somebody would say, over a fence:

"Is it them?"

And somebody trotting along with the gang would answer back and say:

"You bet it is."

When we got to the house the street in front of it was packed, and the three girls was standing in the door. Mary Jane *was* red-headed, but that don't make no difference, she was most awful beautiful, and her face and her eyes was all lit up like glory, she was so glad her uncles was come. The king he spread his arms, and Mary Jane she jumped for them, and the harelip jumped for the duke, and there they had it! Everybody most, leastways women, cried for joy to see them meet again at last and have such good times.

Then the king he hunched the duke private—I see him do it—and then he looked around and see the coffin, over in the corner on two chairs; so then him and the duke, with a hand across each other's shoulder, and t'other hand to their eyes, walked slow and solemn over there, everybody dropping back to give them room, and all the talk and noise stopping, people saying "Sh!" and all the men taking their hats off and drooping their heads, so you could 'a' heard a pin fall. And when they got there they bent over and looked in the coffin, and took one sight, and then they bust out a-crying so you could 'a' heard them to Orleans, most; and then they put their arms around each other's necks, and hung their chins over each other's shoulders; and then for three minutes, or maybe four, I never see two men leak the way they done. And, mind you, everybody was doing the same; and the place was that damp I never see anything like it. Then one of them got on one side of the coffin, and t'other on t'other side, and they kneeled down and rested their foreheads on the coffin, and let on to pray all to themselves. Well, when it come to that it worked the crowd like you never see anything like it, and everybody broke down and went to sobbing

► How do the king and duke behave when they approach the coffin? What effect does their behavior have on the rest of the room? How does Huck feel about the scene?

right out loud—the poor girls, too; and every woman, nearly, went up to the girls, without saying a word, and kissed them, solemn, on the forehead, and then put their hand on their head, and looked up towards the sky, with the tears running down, and then busted out and went off sobbing and swabbing, and give the next woman a show. I never see anything so disgusting.

Well, by and by the king he gets up and comes forward a little, and works himself up and slobbers out a speech, all full of tears and flapdoodle[1] about its being a sore trial for him and his poor brother to lose the diseased,[2] and to miss seeing diseased alive after the long journey of four thousand mile, but it's a trial that's sweetened and <u>sanctified</u> to us by this dear sympathy and these holy tears, and so he thanks them out of his heart and out of his brother's heart, because out of their mouths they can't, words being too weak and cold, and all that kind of rot and slush, till it was just sickening; and then he blubbers out a pious goody-goody Amen, and turns himself loose and goes to crying fit to bust.

And the minute the words were out of his mouth somebody over in the crowd struck up the doxolojer,[3] and everybody joined in with all their might, and it just warmed you up and made you feel as good as church letting out. Music *is* a good thing; and after all that soul-butter and hogwash I never see it freshen up things so, and sound so honest and bully.

Then the king begins to work his jaw again, and says how him and his nieces would be glad if a few of the main principal friends of the family would take supper here with them this evening, and help set up with the ashes of the diseased; and says if his poor brother laying yonder could speak he knows who he would name, for they was names that was very dear to him, and mentioned often in his letters; and so he will name the same, to wit, as follows, viz.:[4]—Rev. Mr. Hobson, and Deacon Lot Hovey, and Mr. Ben Rucker, and Abner Shackleford, and Levi Bell, and Dr. Robinson, and their wives, and the widow Bartley.

---

1. **flapdoodle.** Colloquial word meaning "nonsense"
2. **diseased.** Deceased; dead
3. **doxolojer.** Doxology; hymn of praise
4. **viz.** That is, namely

Words
For
Everyday
Use

sanc • ti • fied (saŋk´tə fīd) *adj.,* made holy

Rev. Hobson and Dr. Robinson was down to the end of the town a-hunting together—that is, I mean the doctor was shipping a sick man to t'other world, and the preacher was pinting[5] him right. Lawyer Bell was away up to Louisville on business. But the rest was on hand, and so they all come and shook hands with the king and thanked him and talked to him; and then they shook hands with the duke and didn't say nothing, but just kept a-smiling and bobbing their heads like a passel[6] of sapheads whilst he made all sorts of signs with his hands and said "Goo-goo—goo-goo-goo" all the time, like a baby that can't talk.

▶ Where did the king get his information about the townspeople?

So the king he blattered along, and managed to inquire about pretty much every body and dog in town, by his name, and mentioned all sorts of little things that happened one time or another in the town, or to George's family, or to Peter. And he always let on that Peter wrote him the things; but that was a lie: he got every blessed one of them out of that young flathead that we canoed up to the steamboat.

Then Mary Jane she fetched the letter her father left behind, and the king he read it out loud and cried over it. It give the dwelling-house and three thousand dollars, gold, to the girls; and it give the tanyard (which was doing a good business), along with some other houses and land (worth about seven thousand), and three thousand dollars in gold to Harvey and William, and told where the six thousand cash was hid down cellar. So these two frauds said they'd go and fetch it up, and have everything square and aboveboard; and told me to come with a candle. We shut the cellar door behind us, and when they found the bag they spilt it out on the floor, and it was a lovely sight, all them yaller-boys.[7] My, the way the king's eyes did shine! He slaps the duke on the shoulder and says:

▶ What did Peter leave to Harvey and William?

"Oh, *this* ain't bully nor noth'n! Oh, no, I reckon not! Why, Biljy, it beats the Nonesuch, don't it?"

The duke allowed it did. They pawed the yaller-boys, and sifted them through their fingers and let them jingle down on the floor; and the king says:

"It ain't no use talkin'; bein' brothers to a rich dead man and representatives of furrin heirs that's got left is the line for you and me, Bilge. Thish yer comes of trust'n to Providence. It's the best way, in the long run. I've tried 'em all, and ther' ain't no better way."

---

5. **pinting.** Pointing
6. **passel.** Large group
7. **yaller-boys.** Gold coins

Most everybody would 'a' been satisfied with the pile, and took it on trust; but no, they must count it. So they counts it, and it comes out four hundred and fifteen dollars short. Says the king:

"Dern him, I wonder what he done with that four hundred and fifteen dollars?"

They worried over that awhile, and <u>ransacked</u> all around for it. Then the duke says:

"Well, he was a pretty sick man, and likely he made a mistake—I reckon that's the way of it. The best way's to let it go, and keep still about it. We can spare it."

"Oh, shucks, yes, we can spare it. I don't k'yer noth'n 'bout that—it's the count I'm thinkin' about. We want to be awful square and open and aboveboard here, you know. We want to lug this h'yer money upstairs and count it before everybody—then ther' ain't noth'n suspicious. But when the dead man says ther's six thous'n dollars, you know, we don't want to—"

"Hold on," says the duke. "Le's make up the <u>deffisit</u>," and he begun to haul out yaller-boys out of his pocket.

"It's a most amaz'n' good idea, duke—you have got a rattlin' clever head on you," says the king. "Blest if the old Nonesuch ain't a heppin' us out agin," and he begun to haul out yaller-jackets and stack them up.

It most busted them, but they made up the six thousand clean and clear.

"Say," says the duke, "I got another idea. Le's go upstairs and count this money, and then take and give it to the girls."

"Good land, duke, lemme hug you! It's the most dazzling idea 'at ever a man struck. You have cert'nly got the most astonishin' head I ever see. Oh, this is the boss dodge, ther' ain't no mistake 'bout it. Let 'em fetch along their suspicions now if they want to—this 'll lay 'em out."

When we got upstairs everybody gethered around the table, and the king he counted it and stacked it up, three hundred dollars in a pile—twenty elegant little piles. Everybody looked hungry at it, and licked their chops. Then they raked it into the bag again, and I see the king begin to swell himself up for another speech. He says:

◀ *What do the king and the duke plan to discourage suspicion?*

Words
For
Everyday
Use

ran • sack (ran´sak) *vi.*, search thoroughly

def • i • cit (def´ə sit) *n.*, shortage, deficiency

CHAPTER 25   **169**

"Friends all, my poor brother that lays yonder has done generous by them that's left behind in the vale of sorrers.[8] He has done generous by these yer poor little lambs that he loved and sheltered, and that's left fatherless and motherless. Yes, and we that knowed him knows that he would a done *more* generous by 'em if he hadn't ben afeard o' woundin' his dear William and me. Now, *wouldn't* he? Ther' ain't no question 'bout it in *my* mind. Well, then, what kind o' brothers would it be that 'd stand in his way at sech a time? And what kind o' uncles would it be that'd rob—yes, *rob*—sech poor sweet lambs as these 'at he loved so at sech a time? If I know William—and I *think* I do—he—well, I'll jest ask him." He turns around and begins to make a lot of signs to the duke with his hands, and the duke he looks at him stupid and leather-headed awhile; then all of a sudden he seems to catch his meaning, and jumps for the king, goo-gooing with all his might for joy, and hugs him about fifteen times before he lets up. Then the king says, "I knowed it; I reckon *that*'ll convince anybody the way he feels about it. Here, Mary Jane, Susan, Joanner, take the money—take it *all*. It's the gift of him that lays yonder, cold but joyful."

Mary Jane she went for him, Susan and the harelip went for the duke, and then such another hugging and kissing I never see yet. And everybody crowded up with the tears in their eyes, and most shook the hands off of them frauds, saying all the time:

"You *dear* good souls!—how lovely!—how *could* you!"

Well, then, pretty soon all hands got to talking about the diseased again, and how good he was, and what a loss he was, and all that; and before long a big iron-jawed man worked himself in there from outside, and stood a-listening and looking, and not saying anything; and nobody saying anything to him either, because the king was talking and they was all busy listening. The king was saying—in the middle of something he'd started in on—

"—they bein' partickler friends o' the diseased. That's why they're invited here this evenin'; but tomorrow we want all to come—everybody; for he respected everybody, he liked everybody, and so it's fitten that his funeral <u>orgies</u> sh'd be public."

---

8. **vale of sorrers.** Vale of sorrows; conventional way of referring to life on earth as opposed to heaven

Words For Everyday Use

or • gy (ôr´gē) *n.*, wild merrymaking

And so he went a-mooning on and on, liking to hear himself talk, and every little while he fetched in his funeral orgies again, till the duke he couldn't stand it no more; so he writes on a little scrap of paper, "*Obsequies*, you old fool," and folds it up, and goes to goo-gooing and reaching it over people's heads to him. The king he reads it and puts it in his pocket, and says:

"Poor William, afflicted as he is, his heart's aluz right. Asks me to invite everybody to come to the funeral—wants me to make 'em all welcome. But he needn't 'a' worried—it was jest what I was at."

Then he weaves along again, perfectly ca'm, and goes to dropping in his funeral orgies again every now and then, just like he done before. And when he done it the third time he says:

"I say orgies, not because it's the common term, because it ain't—obsequies bein' the common term—but because orgies is the right term. Obsequies ain't used in England no more now—it's gone out. We say orgies now in England. Orgies is better, because it means the thing you're after more exact. It's a word that's made up out'n the Greek *orgo*, outside, open, abroad; and the Hebrew *Jeesum*, to plant, cover up; hence inter. So, you see, funeral orgies is an open er public funeral."

He was the worst I ever struck. Well, the iron-jawed man he laughed right in his face. Everybody was shocked. Everybody says, "Why, *doctor!*" and Abner Shackleford says:

"Why, Robinson, hain't you heard the news? This is Harvey Wilks."

The king he smiled eager, and shoved out his flapper, and says:

"*Is* it my poor brother's dear good friend and physician? I—"

"Keep your hands off me!" says the doctor. "*You* talk like an Englishman, *don't* you? It's the worst imitation I ever heard. *You* Peter Wilks's brother! You're a fraud, that's what you are!"

Well, how they all took on! They crowded around the doctor and tried to quiet him down, and tried to explain to him and tell him how Harvey 'd showed in forty ways that he was Harvey, and knowed everybody by name, and the names of

◄ What shocking accusation does the doctor make? What do the townspeople say in support of the king? Why does the doctor believe Harvey to be a fraud?

Words For Everyday Use

ob • se • quies (äb´si kwēs) *n.*, funeral rites or ceremonies

the very dogs, and begged and *begged* him not to hurt Harvey's feelings and the poor girls' feelings, and all that. But it warn't no use; he stormed right along, and said any man that pretended to be an Englishman and couldn't imitate the <u>lingo</u> no better than what he did was a fraud and a liar. The poor girls was hanging to the king and crying; and all of a sudden the doctor ups and turns on them. He says:

"I was your father's friend, and I'm your friend; and I warn you as a friend, and an honest one that wants to protect you and keep you out of harm and trouble, to turn your backs on that <u>scoundrel</u> and have nothing to do with him, the ignorant tramp, with his idiotic Greek and Hebrew, as he calls it. He is the thinnest kind of an impostor—has come here with a lot of empty names and facts which he picked up somewheres, and you take them for *proofs,* and are helped to fool yourselves by these foolish friends here, who ought to know better. Mary Jane Wilks, you know me for your friend, and for your unselfish friend, too. Now listen to me; turn this pitiful rascal out—I beg you to do it. Will you?"

Mary Jane straightened herself up, and my, but she was handsome! She says:

► *What is Mary Jane's response to the doctor's accusations?*

"Here is my answer." She hove up the bag of money and put it in the king's hands, and says, "Take this six thousand dollars, and invest for me and my sisters anyway you want to, and don't give us no receipt for it."

Then she put her arm around the king on one side, and Susan and the harelip done the same on the other. Everybody clapped their hands and stomped on the floor like a perfect storm, whilst the king held up his head and smiled proud. The doctor says:

► *What warning does the doctor give the girls?*

"All right; I wash *my* hands of the matter. But I warn you all that a time's coming when you're going to feel sick whenever you think of this day." And away he went.

"All right, doctor," says the king, kinder mocking him; "we'll try and get 'em to send for you"; which made them all laugh, and they said it was a prime good hit.

Words For Everyday Use	**lin • go** (liŋ´gō) *n.,* jargon; special vocabulary that is unfamiliar
	scoun • drel (skoun´drəl) *n.,* wicked, mean, or immoral person

CHAPTER 26

I Steal the King's Plunder

Well, when they was all gone the king he asks Mary Jane how they was off for spare rooms, and she said she had one spare room, which would do for Uncle William, and she'd give her own room to Uncle Harvey, which was a little bigger, and she would turn into the room with her sisters and sleep on a cot; and up garret was a little cubby, with a pallet[1] in it. The king said the cubby would do for his valley[2]—meaning me.

So Mary Jane took us up, and she showed them their rooms, which was plain but nice. She said she'd have her frocks[3] and a lot of other traps took out of her room if they was in Uncle Harvey's way, but he said they warn't. The frocks was hung along the wall, and before them was a curtain made out of calico that hung down to the floor. There was an old hair trunk[4] in one corner, and a guitar-box in another, and all sorts of little knickknacks and jimcracks around, like girls brisken up a room with. The king said it was all the more homely and more pleasanter for these fixings, and so don't disturb them. The duke's room was pretty small, but plenty good enough, and so was my cubby.

That night they had a big supper, and all them men and women was there, and I stood behind the king and the duke's chairs and waited on them, and the niggers waited on the rest. Mary Jane she set at the head of the table, with Susan alongside of her, and said how bad the biscuits was, and how mean the preserves was, and how ornery and tough the fried chicken was—and all that kind of rot, the way women always do for to force out compliments; and the people all knowed everything was tiptop, and said so—said "How *do* you get biscuits to brown so nice?" and "Where, for the land's sake, *did* you get these amaz'n pickles?" and all that kind of humbug[5] talky-talk, just the way people always does at a supper.

And when it was all done me and the harelip had supper in the kitchen off of the leavings, whilst the others was helping the niggers clean up the things. The harelip she got to pumping me about England, and blest if I didn't think the ice was getting mighty thin sometimes. She says:

---

1. **garret . . . pallet.** Attic room with a bed made up on the floor
2. **valley.** Valet; man's personal servant
3. **frocks.** Dresses
4. **hair trunk.** Trunk covered with horsehair
5. **humbug.** Sham; said to deceive

"Did you ever see the king?"

"Who? William Fourth? Well, I bet I have—he goes to our church." I knowed he was dead years ago, but I never let on. So when I says he goes to our church, she says:

"What—regular?"

"Yes—regular. His pew's right over opposite ourn—on t'other side the pulpit."

"I thought he lived in London?"

"Well, he does. Where *would* he live?"

"But I thought *you* lived in Sheffield?"

I see I was up a stump. I had to let on to get choked with a chicken bone, so as to get time to think how to get down again. Then I says:

"I mean he goes to our church regular when he's in Sheffield. That's only in the summer time, when he comes there to take the sea baths."

"Why, how you talk—Sheffield ain't on the sea."

"Well, who said it was?"

"Why, you did."

"I *didn't* nuther."

"You did!"

"I didn't."

"You did."

"I never said nothing of the kind."

"Well, what *did* you say, then?"

"Said he come to take the sea *baths*—that's what I said."

"Well, then, how's he going to take the sea baths if it ain't on the sea?"

"Looky here," I says; "did you ever see any Congress water?"[6]

"Yes."

"Well, did you have to go to Congress to get it?"

"Why, no."

"Well, neither does William Fourth have to go to the sea to get a sea bath."

"How does he get it, then?"

"Gets it the way people down here gets Congress water—in barrels. There in the palace at Sheffield they've got furnaces, and he wants his water hot. They can't bile that amount of water away off there at the sea. They haven't got no conveniences for it."

"Oh, I see, now. You might 'a' said that in the first place and saved time."

When she said that I see I was out of the woods again, and so I was comfortable and glad. Next, she says:

What blunders es Huck make in alking about life in England?

---

6. **Congress water.** Mineral water from Congress Spring, Saratoga, New York

"Do you go to church, too?"

"Yes—regular."

"Where do you set?"

"Why, in our pew."

"*Whose* pew?"

"Why, *ourn*—your Uncle Harvey's."

"His'n? What does *he* want with a pew?"

"Wants it to set in. What did you *reckon* he wanted with it?"

"Why, I thought he'd be in the pulpit."

Rot him, I forgot he was a preacher. I see I was up a stump again, so I played another chicken bone and got another think. Then I says:

"Blame it, do you suppose there ain't but one preacher to a church?"

"Why, what do they want with more?"

"What!—to preach before a king? I never did see such a girl as you. They don't have no less than seventeen."

"Seventeen! My land! Why, I wouldn't set out such a string as that, not if I *never* got to glory. It must take 'em a week."

"Shucks, they don't all of 'em preach the same day—only one of 'em."

"Well, then, what does the rest of 'em do?"

"Oh, nothing much. Loll around, pass the plate—and one thing or another. But mainly they don't do nothing."

"Well, then, what are they *for*?"

"Why, they're for *style*. Don't you know nothing?"

"Well, I don't want to know no such foolishness as that. How is servants treated in England? Do they treat 'em better 'n we treat our niggers?"

"*No!* A servant ain't nobody there. They treat them worse than dogs."

"Don't they give 'em holidays, the way we do, Christmas and New Year's week, and Fourth of July?"

"Oh, just listen! A body could tell *you* hain't ever been to England by that. Why, Hare-l—why, Joanna, they never see a holiday from year's end to year's end; never go to the circus, nor theater, nor nigger shows, nor nowheres."

"Nor church?"

"Nor church."

"But *you* always went to church."

◀ What does Huck forget when he talks about going to church in England with "Uncle Harvey"? What does he say to try to cover his mistake?

Words
For
Everyday
Use

loll (läl) *vi.,* lean or lounge about in a relaxed manner

Well, I was gone up again. I forgot I was the old man's servant. But next minute I whirled in on a kind of an explanation how a valley was different from a common servant and *had* to go to church whether he wanted to or not, and set with the family, on account of its being the law. But I didn't do it pretty good, and when I got done I see she warn't satisfied. She says:

"Honest injun, now, hain't you been telling me a lot of lies?"

"Honest injun," says I.

"None of it at all?"

"None of it at all. Not a lie in it," says I.

"Lay your hand on this book and say it."

I see it warn't nothing but a dictionary, so I laid my hand on it and said it. So then she looked a little better satisfied, and says:

"Well, then, I'll believe some of it; but I hope to gracious if I'll believe the rest."

"What is it you won't believe, Joe?" says Mary Jane, stepping in with Susan behind her. "It ain't right nor kind for you to talk so to him, and him a stranger and so far from his people. How would you like to be treated so?"

"That's always your way, Maim—always sailing in to help somebody before they're hurt. I hain't done nothing to him. He's told some stretchers, I reckon, and I said I wouldn't swallow it all; and that's every bit and grain I did say. I reckon he can stand a little thing like that, can't he?"

"I don't care whether 'twas little or whether 'twas big; he's here in our house and a stranger, and it wasn't good of you to say it. If you was in his place it would make you feel ashamed; and so you oughtn't to say a thing to another person that will make *them* feel ashamed."

"Why, Maim, he said—"

"It don't make no difference what he said—that ain't the thing. The thing is for you to treat him kind, and not be saying things to make him remember he ain't in his own country and amongst his own folks."

I says to myself, this is a girl that I'm letting that old reptile rob her of her money!

Then Susan she waltzed in; and if you'll believe me, she did give Harelip hark from the tomb![7]

Says I to myself, and this is *another* one that I'm letting him rob her of her money!

Then Mary Jane she took another inning, and went in sweet and lovely again—which was her way; but when she

► What does Joanna suspect Huck has been doing? What does she force him to do?

► About what does Mary Jane scold her sister? Why does Huck feel slightly ashamed?

---

7. **hark from the tomb.** A shocking experience

got done there warn't hardly anything left o' poor Harelip. So she hollered.

"All right, then," says the other girls; "you just ask his pardon."

She done it, too; and she done it beautiful. She done it so beautiful it was good to hear; and I wished I could tell her a thousand lies, so she could do it again.

I says to myself, this is *another* one that I'm letting him rob her of her money. And when she got through they all jest laid theirselves out to make me feel at home and know I was amongst friends. I felt so ornery and lowdown and mean that I says to myself, my mind's made up; I'll hive that money for them or bust.

So then I lit out—for bed, I said, meaning some time or another. When I got by myself I went to thinking the thing over. I says to myself, shall I go to that doctor, private, and blow on these frauds? No—that won't do. He might tell who told him; then the king and the duke would make it warm for me. Shall I go, private, and tell Mary Jane? No—I dasn't do it. Her face would give them a hint, sure; they've got the money, and they'd slide right out and get away with it. If she was to fetch in help I'd get mixed up in the business before it was done with, I judge. No; there ain't no good way but one. I got to steal that money, somehow; and I got to steal it some way that they won't suspicion that I done it. They've got a good thing here, and they ain't a-going to leave till they've played this family and this town for all they're worth, so I'll find a chance time enough. I'll steal it and hide it; and by and by, when I'm away down the river, I'll write a letter and tell Mary Jane where it's hid. But I better hive it tonight if I can, because the doctor maybe hasn't let up as much as he lets on he has; he might scare them out of here yet.

So, thinks I, I'll go and search them rooms. Upstairs the hall was dark, but I found the duke's room, and started to paw around it with my hands; but I recollected it wouldn't be much like the king to let anybody else take care of that money but his own self; so then I went to his room and begun to paw around there. But I see I couldn't do nothing without a candle, and I dasn't light one, of course. So I judged I'd got to do the other thing—lay for them and eavesdrop. About that time I hears their footsteps coming, and was going to skip under the bed; I reached for it, but it wasn't where I thought it would be; but I touched the curtain that hid Mary Jane's frocks, so I jumped in behind that and snuggled in amongst the gowns, and stood there perfectly still.

◄ *What questions does Huck ask himself? What does he decide he must do?*

◄ *Where is Huck hiding when the king and the duke enter the room?*

They come in and shut the door; and the first thing the duke done was to get down and look under the bed. Then I was glad I hadn't found the bed when I wanted it. And yet, you know, it's kind of natural to hide under the bed when you are up to anything private. They sets down then, and the king says:

"Well, what is it? And cut it middlin' short, because it's better for us to be down there a-whoopin' up the mournin' than up here givin' 'em a chance to talk us over."

"Well, this is it, Capet. I ain't easy; I ain't comfortable. That doctor lays on my mind. I wanted to know your plans. I've got a notion, and I think it's a sound one."

"What is it, duke?"

"That we better glide out of this before three in the morning, and clip it down the river with what we've got. Specially, seeing we got it so easy—*given* back to us, flung at our heads, as you may say, when of course we allowed to have to steal it back. I'm for knocking off and lighting out."

That made me feel pretty bad. About an hour or two ago it would 'a' been a little different, but now it made me feel bad and disappointed. The king rips out and says:

"What! And not sell out the rest o' the property? March off like a passel of fools and leave eight or nine thous'n' dollars' worth o' property layin' around jest sufferin' to be scooped in?—and all good, <u>salable</u> stuff, too."

The duke he grumbled; said the bag of gold was enough, and he didn't want to go no deeper—didn't want to rob a lot of orphans of *everything* they had.

"Why, how you talk!" says the king. "We sha'n't rob 'em of nothing at all but jest this money. The people that *buys* the property is the suff'rers; because as soon 's it's found out 'at we didn't own it—which won't be long after we've slid—the sale won't be <u>valid</u>, and it'll all go back to the estate. These yer orphans 'll git their house back ag'in, and that's enough for *them*; they're young and <u>spry</u>, and k'n easy earn a livin'. *They* ain't a-goin to suffer. Why, jest think—there's thous'n's and thous'n's that ain't nigh so well off. Bless you, *they* ain't got noth'n' to complain of."

Well, the king he talked him blind; so at last he give in, and said all right, but said he believed it was blamed foolishness to stay, and that doctor hanging over them. But the king says:

► Why is the duke feeling uncomfortable? What does he want to do? Why does the king object to his plan?

► Why is the duke against selling the estate? What does the king say to justify selling it?

Words For Everyday Use	
sal • a • ble (sāl´ə bəl) *adj.*, that can be sold; marketable	
val • id (val id) *adj.*, legal, legitimate	
spry (sprī) *adj.*, active, nimble, lively	

"Cuss the doctor! What do we k'yer for *him*? Hain't we got all the fools in town on our side? And ain't that a big enough majority in any town?"

So they got ready to go downstairs again. The duke says:

"I don't think we put that money in a good place."

That cheered me up. I'd begun to think I warn't going to get a hint of no kind to help me. The king says:

"Why?"

"Because Mary Jane 'll be in mourning from this out; and first you know the nigger that does up the rooms will get an order to box these duds up and put 'em away; and do you reckon a nigger can run across money and not borrow some of it?"

"Your head's level ag'in, duke," says the king; and he comes a-fumbling under the curtain two or three foot from where I was. I stuck tight to the wall and kept mighty still, though <u>quivery</u>; and I wondered what them fellows would say to me if they catched me; and I tried to think what I'd better do if they did catch me. But the king he got the bag before I could think more than about a half a thought, and he never suspicioned I was around. They took and shoved the bag through a rip in the straw tick that was under the feather-bed, and crammed it in a foot or two amongst the straw and said it was all right now, because a nigger only makes up the feather-bed, and don't turn over the straw tick only about twice a year, and so it warn't in no danger of getting stole now.

But I knowed better. I had it out of there before they was halfway downstairs. I groped along up to my cubby, and hid it there till I could get a chance to do better. I judged I better hide it outside of the house somewheres, because if they missed it they would give the house a good ransacking: I knowed that very well. Then I turned in, with my clothes all on; but I couldn't 'a' gone to sleep if I'd 'a' wanted to, I was in such a sweat to get through with the business. By and by I heard the king and the duke come up; so I rolled off my pallet and laid with my chin at the top of my ladder, and waited to see if anything was going to happen. But nothing did.

So I held on till all the late sounds had quit and the early ones hadn't begun yet; and then I slipped down the ladder.

◄ *Where does Huck take the money?*

Words For Everyday Use

quiv • er • y (kwiv´ər ē) *adj.,* shaky, trembling

CHAPTER 27

Dead Peter Has His Gold

I crept to their doors and listened; they was snoring. So I tiptoed along, and got downstairs all right. There warn't a sound anywheres. I peeped through a crack of the dining room door, and see the men that was watching the corpse all sound asleep on their chairs. The door was open into the parlor, where the corpse was laying, and there was a candle in both rooms. I passed along, and the parlor door was open; but I see there warn't nobody in there but the remainders[1] of Peter; so I shoved on by; but the front door was locked, and the key wasn't there. Just then I heard somebody coming down the stairs, back behind me. I run in the parlor and took a swift look around, and the only place I see to hide the bag was in the coffin. The lid was shoved along about a foot, showing the dead man's face down in there, with a wet cloth over it, and his shroud on. I tucked the moneybag in under the lid, just down beyond where his hands was crossed, which made me creep, they was so cold, and then I run back across the room and in behind the door.

The person coming was Mary Jane. She went to the coffin, very soft, and kneeled down and looked in; then she put up her handkerchief, and I see she begun to cry, though I couldn't hear her, and her back was to me. I slid out, and as I passed the dining room I thought I'd make sure them watchers hadn't seen me; so I looked through the crack, and everything was all right. They hadn't stirred.

I slipped up to bed, feeling ruther blue, on accounts of the thing playing out that way after I had took so much trouble and run so much resk about it. Says I, if it could stay where it is, all right; because when we get down the river a hundred mile or two I could write back to Mary Jane, and she could dig him up again and get it; but that ain't the thing that's going to happen; the thing that's going to happen is, the money'll be found when they come to screw on the lid. Then the king'll get it again, and it'll be a long day before he gives anybody another chance to smouch it from him. Of course I *wanted* to slide down and get it out of there, but I dasn't try it. Every minute it was getting earlier now, and pretty soon some of them watchers would begin to stir, and I might get catched—catched with six thousand dollars in my hands

When Huck hears someone coming down the stairs, where does he hide the money?

When does Huck believe the money will be found? Why doesn't he go back to the coffin and get it?

---

1. **remainders.** Remains; body of the deceased

that nobody hadn't hired me to take care of. I don't wish to be mixed up in no such business as that, I says to myself.

When I got downstairs in the morning the parlor was shut up, and the watchers was gone. There warn't nobody around but the family and the widow Bartley and our tribe. I watched their faces to see if anything had been happening, but I couldn't tell.

Towards the middle of the day the undertaker come with his man, and they set the coffin in the middle of the room on a couple of chairs, and then set all our chairs in rows, and borrowed more from the neighbors till the hall and the parlor and the dining room was full. I see the coffin lid was the way it was before, but I dasn't go to look in under it, with folks around.

Then the people begun to flock in, and the beats[2] and the girls took seats in the front row at the head of the coffin, and for a half an hour the people filed around slow, in single rank, and looked down at the dead man's face a minute, and some dropped in a tear, and it was all very still and solemn, only the girls and the beats holding handkerchiefs to their eyes and keeping their heads bent, and sobbing a little. There warn't no other sound but the scraping of the feet on the floor and blowing noses—because people always blows them more at a funeral than they do at other places except church.

When the place was packed full the undertaker he slid around in his black gloves with his softy soothering ways, putting on the last touches, and getting people and things all ship-shape and comfortable, and making no more sound than a cat. He never spoke; he moved people around, he squeezed in late ones, he opened up passageways, and done it with nods, and signs with his hands. Then he took his place over against the wall. He was the softest, glidingest, stealthiest man I ever see; and there warn't no more smile to him than there is to a ham.

They had borrowed a melodeum[3]—a sick one; and when everything was ready a young woman set down and worked it, and it was pretty skreeky and colicky,[4] and everybody joined in and sung, and Peter was the only one that had a good thing, according to my notion. Then the Reverend Hobson opened up, slow and solemn, and begun to talk; and straight off the most outrageous row busted out in the cellar a body ever heard; it was only one dog, but he made a most powerful racket, and he kept it up right along; the parson he

---

2. **beats.** Deadbeats, cheats; i.e., the duke and the king
3. **melodeum.** Melodeon, a small reed organ
4. **colicky.** Making sounds indicating intense abdominal pain

had to stand there, over the coffin, and wait—you couldn't hear yourself think. It was right down awkward, and nobody didn't seem to know what to do. But pretty soon they see that long-legged undertaker make a sign to the preacher as much as to say, "Don't you worry—just depend on me." Then he stooped down and begun to glide along the wall, just his shoulders showing over the people's heads. So he glided along, and the powwow and racket getting more and more outrageous all the time; and at last, when he had gone around two sides of the room, he disappears down cellar. Then in about two seconds we heard a whack, and the dog he finished up with a most amazing howl or two, and then everything was dead still, and the parson begun his solemn talk where he left off. In a minute or two here comes this undertaker's back and shoulders gliding along the wall again; and so he glided and glided around three sides of the room, and then rose up, and shaded his mouth with his hands, and stretched his neck out towards the preacher, over the people's heads, and says, in a kind of a coarse whisper, "*He had a rat!*" Then he drooped down and glided along the wall again to his place. You could see it was a great satisfaction to the people, because naturally they wanted to know. A little thing like that don't cost nothing, and it's just the little things that makes a man to be looked up to and liked. There warn't no more popular man in town than what that undertaker was.

Well, the funeral sermon was very good, but pison[5] long and tiresome; and then the king he shoved in and got off some of his usual rubbage, and at last the job was through, and the undertaker begun to sneak up on the coffin with his screwdriver. I was in a sweat then, and watched him pretty keen. But he never meddled at all; just slid the lid along as soft as mush, and screwed it down tight and fast. So there I was! I didn't know whether the money was in there or not. So, says I, s'pose somebody has hogged that bag on the sly?— now how do *I* know whether to write to Mary Jane or not? S'pose she dug him up and didn't find nothing, what would she think of me? Blame it, I says, I might get hunted up and jailed; I'd better lay low and keep dark, and not write at all; the thing's awful mixed now; trying to better it, I've worsened it a hundred times, and I wish to goodness I'd just let it alone, dad fetch the whole business!

They buried him, and we come back home, and I went to watching faces again—I couldn't help it, and I couldn't rest easy. But nothing come of it; the faces didn't tell me nothing.

The king he visited around in the evening, and sweetened

▶ Why does Huck feel he's made the situation worse by trying to hide the money from the duke and the king?

---

5. **pison.** Poisonously

everybody up, and made himself ever so friendly; and he give out the idea that his congregation over in England would be in a sweat about him, so he must hurry and settle up the <u>estate</u> right away and leave for home. He was very sorry he was so pushed, and so was everybody; they wished he could stay longer, but they said they could see it couldn't be done. And he said of course him and William would take the girls home with them; and that pleased everybody too, because then the girls would be well fixed and amongst their own relations; and it pleased the girls, too—tickled them so they clean forgot they ever had a trouble in the world; and told him to sell out as quick as he wanted to, they would be ready. Them poor things was that glad and happy it made my heart ache to see them getting fooled and lied to so, but I didn't see no safe way for me to chip in and change the general tune.

Well, blamed if the king didn't bill the house and the niggers and all the property for auction straight off—sale two days after the funeral; but anybody could buy private beforehand if they wanted to.

So the next day after the funeral, along about noontime, the girls' joy got the first jolt. A couple of nigger-traders come along, and the king sold them the niggers reasonable, for three-day drafts[6] as they called it, and away they went, the two sons up the river to Memphis, and their mother down the river to Orleans. I thought them poor girls and them niggers would break their hearts for grief; they cried around each other, and took on so it most made me down sick to see it. The girls said they hadn't ever dreamed of seeing the family separated or sold away from the town. I can't ever get it out of my memory, the sight of them poor miserable girls and niggers hanging around each other's necks and crying; and I reckon I couldn't 'a' stood it all, but would 'a' had to bust out and tell on our gang if I hadn't knowed the sale warn't no account and the niggers would be back home in a week or two.

The thing made a big stir in the town, too, and a good many come out flatfooted and said it was <u>scandalous</u> to separate the mother and the children that way. It injured the frauds some; but the old fool he bulled right along, spite of all the duke

◄ Where do the girls believe they will be living when the estate is sold? When does the king sell the estate?

◄ How does Huck feel when he watches the selling of the slaves? What is the only thing that keeps him from turning in the king and the duke? Why does this sale create scandal in the town?

---

6. **three-day drafts.** Written orders instructing a bank to pay out cash after three days

Words For Everyday Use

es • tate (e stāt´) *n.*, property left by the dead
scan • da • lous (skan´də ləs) *adj.*, shocking, shameful

could say or do, and I tell you the duke was powerful uneasy.

Next day was auction day. About broad day in the morning the king and the duke come up in the garret and woke me up, and I see by their look that there was trouble. The king says:

"Was you in my room night before last?"

"No, your majesty"—which was the way I always called him when nobody but our gang warn't around.

"Was you in there yisterday er last night?"

"No, your majesty."

"Honor bright, now—no lies."

"Honor bright, your majesty, I'm telling you the truth. I hain't been a-near your room since Miss Mary Jane took you and the duke and showed it to you."

The duke says:

"Have you seen anybody else go in there?"

"No, your grace, not as I remember, I believe."

"Stop and think."

I studied awhile and see my chance; then I says:

"Well, I see the niggers go in there several times."

Both of them gave a little jump, and looked like they hadn't ever expected it, and then like they had. Then the duke says:

"What, *all* of them?"

"No—leastways, not all at once—that is, I don't think I ever see them all come out at once but just one time."

"Hello! When was that?"

"It was the day we had the funeral. In the morning. It warn't early, because I overslept. I was just starting down the ladder, and I see them."

"Well, go on, *go* on! What did they do? How'd they act?"

"They didn't do nothing. And they didn't act anyway much, as fur as I see. They tiptoed away; so I seen, easy enough, that they'd shoved in there to do up your majesty's room, or something, s'posing you was up; and found you warn't up, and so they was hoping to slide out of the way of trouble without waking you up, if they hadn't already waked you up."

"Great guns, *this* is a go!" says the king; and both of them looked pretty sick and tolerable silly. They stood there a-thinking and scratching their heads a minute, and the duke he bust into a kind of a little <u>raspy</u> chuckle, and says:

▶ Why are the king and the duke questioning Huck? What have they likely discovered? What does Huck try to make them believe?

Words
For
Everyday
Use

ras • py (ras pē) *adj.*, rough-sounding

"It does beat all how neat the niggers played their hand. They let on to be *sorry* they was going out of this region! And I believed they *was* sorry, and so did you, and so did everybody. Don't ever tell me any more that a nigger ain't got any histrionic talent. Why, the way they played that thing it would fool *anybody*. In my opinion, there's a fortune in 'em. If I had <u>capital</u> and a theater, I wouldn't want a better layout than that—and here we've gone and sold 'em for a song. Yes, and ain't privileged[7] to sing the song yet. Say, where is that song—that draft?"

"In the bank for to be collected. Where *would* it be?"

"Well, *that's* all right then, thank goodness."

Says I, kind of timid-like:

"Is something gone wrong?"

The king whirls on me and rips out:

"None o' your business! You keep your head shet, and mind y'r own affairs—if you got any. Long as you're in this town don't you forgit *that*—you hear?" Then he says to the duke, "We got to jest swaller it and say noth'n': mum's the word for *us*."

As they was starting down the ladder the duke he chuckles again, and says:

"Quick sales *and* small profits! It's a good business—yes."

The king snarls around on him and says:

"I was trying to do for the best in sellin' 'em out so quick. If the profits has turned out to be none, lackin' considable, and none to carry, is it my fault any more'n it's yourn?"

◀ Why does the duke blame the king for the disappearance of the money?

"Well, *they'd* be in this house yet and we *wouldn't* if I could 'a' got my advice listened to."

The king sassed back as much as was safe for him, and then swapped around and lit into *me* again. He give me down the banks for not coming and *telling* him I see the niggers come out of his room acting that way—said any fool would 'a' *knowed* something was up. And then waltzed in and cussed *himself* awhile, and said it all come of him not laying late and taking his natural rest that morning, and he'd be blamed if he'd ever do it again. So they went off a-jawing; and I felt dreadful glad I'd worked it all off onto the niggers, and yet hadn't done the niggers no harm by it.

◀ About what does Huck feel glad?

---

7. **privileged.** Having the right to do something

Words For Everyday Use

cap • i • tal (kap′ət l) *n.*, wealth, money

CHAPTER 28

Overreaching Don't Pay

By and by it was getting-up time. So I come down the ladder and started for downstairs; but as I come to the girls' room the door was open, and I see Mary Jane setting by her old hair trunk, which was open and she'd been packing things in it—getting ready to go to England. But she had stopped now with a folded gown in her lap, and had her face in her hands, crying. I felt awful bad to see it; of course anybody would. I went in there and says:

"Miss Mary Jane, you can't a-bear to see people in trouble, and *I* can't—most always. Tell me about it."

So she done it. And it was the niggers—I just expected it. She said the beautiful trip to England was most about spoiled for her; she didn't know *how* she was ever going to be happy there, knowing the mother and the children warn't ever going to see each other no more—and then busted out bitterer than ever, and flung up her hands, and says:

"Oh, dear, dear, to think they ain't *ever* going to see each other any more!"

"But they *will*—and inside of two weeks—and I *know* it!" says I.

Laws, it was out before I could think! And before I could budge she throws her arms around my neck and told me to say it *again*, say it *again*, say it *again*!

I see I had spoke too sudden and said too much, and was in a close place. I asked her to let me think a minute; and she set there, very impatient and excited and handsome, but looking kind of happy and eased-up, like a person that's had a tooth pulled out. So I went to studying it out. I says to myself, I reckon a body that ups and tells the truth when he is in a tight place is taking considerable many resks, though I ain't had no experience, and can't say for certain; but it looks so to me, anyway; and yet here's a case where I'm blest if it don't look to me like the truth is better and actly *safer* than a lie. I must lay it by in my mind, and think it over some time or other, it's so kind of strange and unregular. I never see nothing like it. Well, I says to myself at last, I'm a-going to chance it; I'll up and tell the truth this time, though it does seem most like setting down on a kag of powder[1] and touching it off just to see where you'll go to. Then I says:

▶ *Why is Mary Jane upset? What does Huck say accidentally, trying to make her feel better?*

---

1. **kag of powder.** Keg, or barrel, of gunpowder

"Miss Mary Jane, is there any place out of town a little ways where you could go and stay three or four days?"

"Yes; Mr. Lothrop's. Why?"

"Never mind why yet. If I'll tell you how I know the niggers will see each other again inside of two weeks—here in this house—and *prove* how I know it—will you go to Mr. Lothrop's and stay four days?"

"Four days!" she says; "I'll stay a year!"

"All right," I says, "I don't want nothing more out of *you* than just your word—I druther have it than another man's kiss-the-Bible." She smiled and reddened up very sweet, and I says, "If you don't mind it, I'll shut the door—and bolt it."

Then I come back and set down again, and says:

"Don't you holler. Just set still and take it like a man. I got to tell the truth, and you want to brace up, Miss Mary, because it's a bad kind, and going to be hard to take, but there ain't no help for it. These uncles of yourn ain't no uncles at all; they're a couple of frauds—regular deadbeats. There, now we're over the worst of it, you can stand the rest middling easy."

◀ What does Huck finally tell Mary Jane?

It jolted her up like everything, of course; but I was over the shoal water[2] now, so I went right along, her eyes a-blazing higher and higher all the time, and told her every blame thing, from where we first struck that young fool going up to the steamboat, clear through to where she flung herself on to the king's breast at the front door and he kissed her sixteen or seventeen times—and then up she jumps, with her face afire like sunset, and says:

"The brute! Come, don't waste a minute—not a *second*— we'll have them tarred and feathered, and flung in the river!"

Says I:

"Cert'nly. But do you mean *before* you go to Mr. Lothrop's, or—"

"Oh," she says, "what am I *thinking* about!" she says, and set right down again. "Don't mind what I said—please don't—you *won't*, now, *will* you?" Laying her silky hand on mine in that kind of a way that I said I would die first. "I never thought, I was so stirred up," she says; "now go on, and I won't do so anymore. You tell me what to do, and whatever you say I'll do it."

"Well," I says, "it's a rough gang, them two frauds, and I'm

---

2. **shoal water.** Shallow, and therefore dangerous, water

Words For Everyday Use   **brute** (bro͞ot) *n.*, stupid, cruel, savage person

▶ Why is Huck afraid for the king and duke to know that he gave them away?

fixed so I got to travel with them awhile longer, whether I want to or not—I druther not tell you why; and if you was to blow on them this town would get me out of their claws, and I'd be all right; but there'd be another person that you don't know about who'd be in big trouble. Well, we got to save *him*, hain't we? Of course. Well, then, we won't blow on them."

Saying them words put a good idea in my head. I see how maybe I could get me and Jim rid of the frauds; get them jailed here, and then leave. But I didn't want to run the raft in the daytime without anybody aboard to answer questions but me; so I didn't want the plan to begin working till pretty late tonight. I says:

"Miss Mary Jane, I'll tell you what we'll do, and you won't have to stay at Mr. Lothrop's so long, nuther. How fur is it?"

"A little short of four miles—right out in the country, back here."

▶ What does Huck instruct Mary to do?

"Well, that'll answer.[3] Now you go along out there, and lay low till nine or half-past tonight, and then get them to fetch you home again—tell them you've thought of something. If you get here before eleven put a candle in this window, and if I don't turn up wait *till* eleven, and *then* if I don't turn up it means I'm gone, and out of the way, and safe. Then you come out and spread the news around, and get these beats jailed."

"Good," she says, "I'll do it."

"And if it just happens so that I don't get away, but get took up along with them, you must up and say I told you the whole thing beforehand, and you must stand by me all you can."

"Stand by you! indeed I will. They sha'n't touch a hair of your head!" she says, and I see her nostrils spread and her eyes snap when she said it, too.

"If I get away I sha'n't be here," I says, "to prove these rapscallions ain't your uncles, and I couldn't do it if I *was* here. I could swear they was beats and bummers, that's all, though that's worth something. Well, there's others can do that better than what I can, and they're people that ain't going to be doubted as quick as I'd be. I'll tell you how to find them. Gimme a pencil and a piece of paper. There—'*Royal Nonesuch, Bricksville.*' Put it away, and don't lose it. When the court wants to find out something about these two, let them send up to Bricksville and say they've got the men that played the Royal Nonesuch, and ask for some witnesses—why, you'll have that entire town down here before you can hardly wink, Miss Mary. And they'll come a-biling, too."

▶ Why does Huck give Mary information about the Royal Nonesuch? In what way will this information help her?

I judged we had got everything fixed about right now. So I says:

---

3. **answer.** Be suitable to the situation

"Just let the auction go right along, and don't worry. Nobody don't have to pay for the things they buy till a whole day after the auction on accounts of the short notice, and they ain't going out of this till they get that money; and the way we've fixed it the sale ain't going to count, and they ain't going to *get* no money. It's just like the way it was with the niggers—it warn't no sale, and the niggers will be back before long. Why, they can't collect the money for the *niggers* yet—they're in the worst kind of a fix, Miss Mary."

"Well," she says, "I'll run down to breakfast now, and then I'll start straight for Mr. Lothrop's."

"'Deed, *that* ain't the ticket, Miss Mary Jane," I says, "by no manner of means; go *before* breakfast."

"Why?"

"What did you reckon I wanted you to go at all for, Miss Mary?"

"Well, I never thought—and come to think, I don't know. What was it?"

"Why, it's because you ain't one of these leather-face people. I don't want no better book than what your face is. A body can set down and read it off like coarse print. Do you reckon you can go and face your uncles when they come to kiss you good-morning, and never—"

◄ Why does Huck want Mary Jane to leave for Mr. Lothrop's before breakfast?

"There, there, don't! Yes, I'll go before breakfast—I'll be glad to. And leave my sisters with them?"

"Yes; never mind about them. They've got to stand it yet awhile. They might suspicion something if all of you was to go. I don't want you to see them, nor your sisters, nor nobody in this town; if a neighbor was to ask how is your uncles this morning your face would tell something. No, you go right along, Miss Mary Jane, and I'll fix it with all of them. I'll tell Miss Susan to give your love to your uncles and say you've went away for a few hours for to get a little rest and change, or to see a friend, and you'll be back tonight or early in the morning."

"Gone to see a friend is all right, but I won't have my love given to them."

"Well, then, it sha'n't be." It was well enough to tell *her* so—no harm in it. It was only a little thing to do, and no trouble; and it's the little things that smooths people's roads the most, down here below; it would make Mary Jane comfortable, and it wouldn't cost nothing. Then I says: "There's one more thing—that bag of money."

"Well, they've got that; and it makes me feel pretty silly to think *how* they got it."

"No, you're out, there. They hain't got it."

"Why, who's got it?"

"I wish I knowed, but I don't. I *had* it, because I stole it from them; and I stole it to give to you; and I know where I hid it, but I'm afraid it ain't there no more. I'm awful sorry, Miss Mary Jane, I'm just as sorry as I can be; but I done the best I could; I did honest. I come nigh getting caught, and I had to shove it into the first place I come to, and run—and it warn't a good place."

"Oh, stop blaming yourself—it's too bad to do it, and I won't allow it—you couldn't help it; it wasn't your fault. Where did you hide it?"

▶ Why does Huck write Mary Jane a letter telling her where the money is? How does he feel as he writes the letter?

I didn't want to set her to thinking about her troubles again; and I couldn't seem to get my mouth to tell her what would make her see that corpse laying in the coffin with that bag of money on his stomach. So for a minute I didn't say nothing; then I says:

"I'd ruther not *tell* you where I put it, Miss Mary Jane, if you don't mind letting me off; but I'll write it for you on a piece of paper, and you can read it along the road to Mr. Lothrop's, if you want to. Do you reckon that'll do?"

"Oh, yes."

So I wrote: "I put it in the coffin. It was in there when you was crying there, away in the night. I was behind the door, and I was mighty sorry for you, Miss Mary Jane."

It made my eyes water a little to remember her crying there all by herself in the night, and them devils laying there right under her own roof, shaming her and robbing her; and when I folded it up and give it to her I see the water come into her eyes, too; and she shook me by the hand, hard, and says:

"*Good-bye.* I'm going to do everything just as you've told me; and if I don't ever see you again, I sha'n't ever forget you, and I'll think of you a many and a many a time, and I'll *pray* for you, too!"—and she was gone.

▶ What does Huck feel for Mary Jane?

Pray for me! I reckoned if she knowed me she'd take a job that was more nearer her size. But I bet she done it, just the same—she was just that kind. She had the grit to pray for Judas[4] if she took the notion—there warn't no back-down to her, I judge. You may say what you want to, but in my opinion she had more sand[5] in her than any girl I ever see; in my opinion she was just full of sand. It sounds like flattery, but it ain't no flattery. And when it comes to beauty—and goodness, too—she lays over them all. I hain't ever seen her since

4. **Judas.** Betrayer of Jesus
5. **sand.** Grit, courage

that time that I see her go out of that door; no, I hain't ever seen her since, but I reckon I've thought of her a many and a many a million times, and of her saying she would pray for me; and if ever I'd 'a' thought it would do any good for me to pray for her, blamed if I wouldn't 'a' done it or bust.

Well, Mary Jane she lit out the back way, I reckon; because nobody see her go. When I struck Susan and the harelip, I says:

"What's the name of them people over on t'other side of the river that you all goes to see sometimes?"

They says:

"There's several; but it's the Proctors, mainly."

"That's the name," I says; "I most forgot it. Well, Miss Mary Jane she told me to tell you she's gone over there in a dreadful hurry—one of them's sick."

"Which one?"

"I don't know; leastways, I kinder forget; but I thinks it's—"

"Sakes alive, I hope it ain't *Hanner?*"

"I'm sorry to say it," I says, "but Hanner's the very one."

"My goodness, and she so well only last week! Is she took bad?"

"It ain't no name for it. They set up with her all night, Miss Mary Jane said, and they don't think she'll last many hours."

◀ What story does Huck tell Mary Jane's sisters to explain where she is?

"Only think of that, now! What's the matter with her?"

I couldn't think of anything reasonable, right off that way, so I says:

"Mumps."

"Mumps your granny! They don't set up with people that's got the mumps."

"They don't, don't they? You better bet they do with *these* mumps. These mumps is different. It's a new kind, Miss Mary Jane said."

"How's it a new kind?"

"Because it's mixed up with other things."

"What other things?"

"Well, measles, and whooping-cough, and erysiplas, and consumption, and yaller janders,[6] and brain-fever, and I don't know what all."

"My land! And they call it the *mumps?*"

"That's what Miss Mary Jane said."

"Well, what in the nation do they call it the *mumps* for?"

"Why, because it *is* the mumps. That's what it starts with."

---

6. **erysiplas . . . consumption . . . yaller janders.** Erysipelas, a skin disorder; tuberculosis, a lung disease; and jaundice, a liver disease

"Well, ther' ain't no sense in it. A body might stump his toe, and take pison, and fall down the well, and break his neck, and bust his brains out, and somebody come along and ask what killed him, and some numskull up and say, 'Why, he stumped his *toe*.' Would ther' be any sense in that? *No*. And ther' ain't no sense in *this*, nuther. Is it ketching?"

"Is it *ketching*? Why, how you talk. Is a *harrow* catching—in the dark? If you don't hitch on to one tooth, you're bound to on another, ain't you? And you can't get away with that tooth without fetching the whole harrow along, can you? Well, these kind of mumps is a kind of a harrow, as you may say—and it ain't no slouch of a harrow, nuther, you come to get it hitched on good."

"Well, it's awful, *I* think," says the harelip. "I'll go to Uncle Harvey and—"

"Oh, yes," I says, "I *would*. Of *course* I would. I wouldn't lose no time."

"Well, why wouldn't you?"

"Just look at it a minute, and maybe you can see. Hain't your uncles obleeged to get along home to England as fast as they can? And do you reckon they'd be mean enough to go off and leave you to go all that journey by yourselves? *You* know they'll wait for you. So fur, so good. Your uncle Harvey's a preacher, ain't he? Very well, then; is a *preacher* going to deceive a steamboat clerk? is he going to deceive a *ship clerk?*—so as to get them to let Miss Mary Jane go aboard? Now *you* know he ain't. What *will* he do, then? Why, he'll say, 'It's a great pity, but my church matters has got to get along the best way they can; for my niece has been exposed to the dreadful pluribus-unum[7] mumps, and so it's my bounden duty to set down here and wait the three months it takes to show on her if she's got it.' But never mind, if you think it's best to tell your uncle Harvey—"

"Shucks, and stay fooling around here when we could all be having good times in England whilst we was waiting to find out whether Mary Jane's got it or not? Why, you talk like a muggins."

"Well, anyway, maybe you'd better tell some of the neighbors."

"Listen at that, now. You do beat all for natural stupidness. Can't you *see* that *they'd* go and tell? Ther' ain't no way but just to not tell anybody at *all*."

▶ *What does Huck say to convince the young women not to mention the mumps to "Uncle Harvey" or the neighbors?*

---

7. **pluribus-unum.** From the United States motto *E pluribus unum*, "out of many, one"

"Well, maybe you're right—yes, I judge you *are* right."

"But I reckon we ought to tell Uncle Harvey she's gone out awhile, anyway, so he won't be uneasy about her?"

"Yes, Miss Mary Jane she wanted you to do that. She says, 'Tell them to give Uncle Harvey and William my love and a kiss, and say I've run over the river to see Mr.'—Mr.—what *is* the name of that rich family your uncle Peter used to think so much of?—I mean the one that—"

"Why, you must mean the Apthorps, ain't it?"

"Of course; bother them kind of names, a body can't ever seem to remember them, half the time, somehow. Yes, she said, say she has run over for to ask the Apthorps to be sure and come to the auction and buy this house, because she allowed her uncle Peter would ruther they had it than anybody else; and she's going to stick to them till they say they'll come, and then, if she ain't too tired, she's coming home; and if she is, she'll be home in the morning anyway. She said, don't say nothing about the Proctors, but only about the Apthorps—which 'll be perfectly true, because she *is* going there to speak about their buying the house; I know it, because she told me so herself."

"All right," they said, and cleared out to lay for their uncles, and give them the love and the kisses, and tell them the message.

Everything was all right now. The girls wouldn't say nothing because they wanted to go to England; and the king and the duke would ruther Mary Jane was off working for the auction than around in reach of Doctor Robinson. I felt very good; I judged I had done it pretty neat—I reckoned Tom Sawyer couldn't 'a' done it no neater himself. Of course he would 'a' throwed more style into it, but I can't do that very handy, not being brung up to it.

◄ *Why does Huck feel good about himself?*

Well, they held the auction in the public square, along towards the end of the afternoon, and it strung along, and strung along, and the old man he was on hand and looking his level pisonest, up there longside of the auctioneer, and chipping in a little Scripture[8] now and then, or a little goody-goody saying of some kind, and the duke he was around goo-gooing for sympathy all he knowed how, and just spreading himself generly.

But by and by the thing dragged through, and everything was sold—everything but a little old trifling lot in the graveyard. So they'd got to work *that* off—I never see such a

◄ *Why is the crowd shouting and laughing? Who has just arrived by steamboat?*

---

8. **Scripture.** Bible passages

giraftt[9] as the king was for wanting to swallow *everything*. Well, whilst they was at it a steamboat landed, and in about two minutes up comes a crowd a-whooping and yelling and laughing and carrying on, and singing out:

"*Here's* your opposition line! here's your two sets o' heirs to old Peter Wilks—and you pays your money and you takes your choice!"

---

9. **giraftt.** Giraffe

CHAPTER 29

I Light Out in the Storm

They was fetching a very nice-looking old gentleman along, and a nice-looking younger one, with his right arm in a sling. And, my souls, how the people yelled and laughed, and kept it up. But I didn't see no joke about it, and I judged it would strain the duke and the king some to see any. I reckoned they'd turn pale. But no, nary a pale did *they* turn. The duke he never let on he suspicioned what was up, but just went a goo-gooing around, happy and satisfied, like a jug that's googling out buttermilk; and as for the king, he just gazed and gazed down sorrowful on them newcomers like it give him the stomach ache in his very heart to think there could be such frauds and rascals in the world. Oh, he done it admirable. Lots of the principal people gethered around the king, to let him see they was on his side. That old gentleman that had just come looked all puzzled to death. Pretty soon he begun to speak, and I see straight off he pronounced *like* an Englishman—not the king's way, though the king's *was* pretty good for an imitation. I can't give the old gent's words, nor I can't imitate him; but he turned around to the crowd, and says, about like this:

"This is a surprise to me which I wasn't looking for; and I'll acknowledge, <u>candid</u> and <u>frank</u>, I ain't very well fixed to meet it and answer it; for my brother and me has had misfortunes; he's broke his arm, and our baggage got put off at a town above here last night in the night by a mistake. I am Peter Wilks's brother Harvey, and this is his brother William, which can't hear nor speak—and can't even make signs to amount to much, now't he's only got one hand to work them with. We are who we say we are; and in a day or two, when I get the baggage, I can prove it. But up till then I won't say nothing more, but go to the hotel and wait."

So him and the new dummy started off; and the king he laughs, and blethers out:

"Broke his arm—*very* likely, *ain't* it?—and very convenient, too, for a fraud that's got to make signs, and ain't learnt

How do the king and the duke react to the appearance of the real Wilks brothers? Do they receive support from the crowd? What does Huck notice right away when the real Harvey Wilks begins to speak?

Why did the real brothers miss the funeral?

What does the king tell the crowd? What does he want people to believe?

| Words For Everyday Use | **can • did** (kan´did) *adj.* honest and sincere; incapable of deception |
| | **frank** (fraŋk) *adj.,* blunt in expressing truth without conventional holding back |

how. Lost their baggage! That's *mighty* good!—and mighty ingenious—under the *circumstances!*

So he laughed again; and so did everybody else, except three or four, or maybe half a dozen. One of these was that doctor; another one was a sharp-looking gentleman, with a carpetbag of the old-fashioned kind made out of carpet stuff, that had just come off of the steamboat and was talking to him in a low voice, and glancing towards the king now and then and nodding their heads—it was Levi Bell, the lawyer that was gone up to Louisville; and another one was a big rough husky that come along and listened to all the old gentleman said, and was listening to the king now. And when the king got done this husky up and says:

"Say, looky here; if you are Harvey Wilks, when'd you come to this town?"

"The day before the funeral, friend," says the king.

"But what time o' day?"

"In the evenin'—'bout an hour er two before sundown."

"*How'd* you come?"

"I come down on the *Susan Powell* from Cincinnati."

"Well, then, how'd you come to be up at the Pint in the *mornin'*—in a canoe?"

"I warn't up at the Pint in the mornin'."

"It's a lie."

Several of them jumped for him and begged him not to talk that way to an old man and a preacher.

▶ *What does one person remember about the day the king arrived in town?*

"Preacher be hanged, he's a fraud and a liar. He was up at the Pint that mornin'. I live up there, don't I? Well, I was up there, and he was up there. I *see* him there. He come in a canoe, along with Tim Collins and a boy."

The doctor he up and says:

"Would you know the boy again if you was to see him, Hines?"

"I reckon I would, but I don't know. Why, yonder he is, now. I know him perfectly easy."

It was me he pointed at. The doctor says:

"Neighbors, I don't know whether the new couple is frauds or not; but if *these* two ain't frauds, I am an idiot, that's all. I think it's our duty to see that they don't get away from here till we've looked into this thing. Come along, Hines; come along, the rest of you. We'll take these fellows to the tavern

Words For Everyday Use	**in • gen • ious** (in jēn´yəs) *adj.*, clever, inventive

and <u>affront</u> them with t'other couple, and I reckon we'll find out *something* before we get through."

It was nuts for the crowd, though maybe not for the king's friends; so we all started. It was about sundown. The doctor he led me along by the hand, and was plenty kind enough, but he never let *go* my hand.

We all got in a big room in the hotel, and lit up some candles, and fetched in the new couple. First, the doctor says:

"I don't wish to be too hard on these two men, but *I* think they're frauds, and they may have complices[1] that we don't know nothing about. If they have, won't the complices get away with that bag of gold Peter Wilks left? It ain't unlikely. If these men ain't frauds, they won't object to sending for that money and letting us keep it till they prove they're all right—ain't that so?"

◄ What suggestion does the doctor offer?

Everybody agreed to that. So I judged they had our gang in a pretty tight place right at the outstart. But the king he only looked sorrowful, and says:

"Gentlemen, I wish the money was there, for I ain't got no <u>disposition</u> to throw anything in the way of a fair, open, out-and-out investigation o' this misable business; but, alas, the money ain't there; you k'n send and see, if you want to."

"Where is it, then?"

"Well, when my niece give it to me to keep for her I took and hid it inside o' the straw tick o' my bed, not wishin' to bank it for the few days we'd be here, and considerin' the bed a safe place, we not bein' used to niggers, and suppos'n' 'em honest, like servants in England. The niggers stole it the very next mornin' after I had went downstairs; and when I sold 'em I hadn't missed the money yit, so they got clean away with it. My servant here k'n tell you 'bout it, gentlemen."

◄ What does the king explain to the crowd? Do people believe him?

The doctor and several said "Shucks!" and I see nobody didn't altogether believe him. One man asked me if I see the niggers steal it. I said no, but I see them sneaking out of the room and hustling away, and I never thought nothing, only I reckoned they was afraid they had waked up my master and was trying to get away before he made trouble with them. That was all they asked me. Then the doctor whirls on me and says:

"Are *you* English, too?"

---

1. **complices.** Accomplices; partners in crime

Words For Everyday Use	**af • front** (ə front´) *vt.,* confront; bring face to face with
	dis • po • si • tion (dis´pə zish´ən) *n.,* tendency

I says yes; and him and some others laughed, and said, "Stuff!"

Well, then they sailed in on the general investigation, and there we had it, up and down, hour in, hour out, and nobody never said a word about supper, nor ever seemed to think about it—and so they kept it up, and kept it up; and it *was* the worst mixed-up thing you ever see. They made the king tell his yarn, and they made the old gentleman tell his'n; and anybody but a lot of <u>prejudiced</u> chuckleheads would 'a' *seen* that the old gentleman was spinning truth and t'other one lies. And by and by they had me up to tell what I knowed. The king he give me a left-handed look out of the corner of his eye, and so I knowed enough to talk on the right side. I begun to tell about Sheffield, and how we lived there, and all about the English Wilkses, and so on; but I didn't get pretty fur till the doctor begun to laugh; and Levi Bell, the lawyer, says:

"Set down, my boy; I wouldn't strain myself if I was you. I reckon you ain't used to lying, it don't seem to come handy; what you want is practice."

I didn't care nothing for the compliment, but I was glad to be let off, anyway.

The doctor he turns and says:

"If you'd been in town at first, Levi Bell—" The king broke in and reached out his hand, and says:

"Why, is this my poor dead brother's old friend that he's wrote so often about?"

The lawyer and him shook hands, and the lawyer smiled and looked pleased, and they talked right along awhile, and then got to one side and talked low; and at last the lawyer speaks up and says:

"That'll fix it. I'll take the order and send it, along with your brother's, and then they'll know it's all right."

So they got some paper and a pen, and the king he set down and twisted his head to one side, and chawed his tongue, and scrawled off something; and then they give the pen to the duke—and then for the first time the duke looked sick. But he took the pen and wrote. So then the lawyer turns to the new old gentleman and says:

"You and your brother please write a line or two and sign your names."

▶ *Why does the lawyer tell Huck to stop talking?*

Words For Everyday Use

prej • u • diced (prej´ o͞o dist) *adj.,* biased; having made a prejudgment

The old gentleman wrote, but nobody couldn't read it. The lawyer looked powerful astonished, and says:

"Well, it beats *me*"—and snaked a lot of old letters out of his pocket, and examined them, and then examined the old man's writing, and then them again; and then says: "These old letters is from Harvey Wilks; and here's *these* two hand-writings, and anybody can see *they* didn't write them" (the king and the duke looked sold and foolish, I tell you, to see how the lawyer had took them in), "and here's *this* old gentleman's handwriting, and anybody can tell, easy enough, *he* didn't write them—fact is, the scratches he makes ain't properly *writing* at all. Now, here's some letters from—"

The new old gentleman says:

"If you please, let me explain. Nobody can read my hand but my brother there—so he copies for me. It's *his* hand you've got there, not mine."

"*Well!*" says the lawyer, "this *is* a state of things. I've got some of William's letters, too; so if you'll get him to write a line or so we can com—"

"He *can't* write with his left hand," says the old gentleman. "If he could use his right hand, you would see that he wrote his own letters and mine too. Look at both, please—they're by the same hand."

The lawyer done it, and says:

"I believe it's so—and if it ain't so, there's a heap stronger resemblance than I'd noticed before, anyway. Well, well, well! I thought we was right on the track of a slution, but it's gone to grass, partly. But anyway, one thing is proved—*these* two ain't either of 'em Wilkses"—and he wagged his head towards the king and the duke.

Well, what do you think? That muleheaded old fool wouldn't give in *then!* Indeed he wouldn't. Said it warn't no fair test. Said his brother William was the cussedest joker in the world, and hadn't *tried* to write—*he* see William was going to play one of his jokes the minute he put the pen to paper. And so he warmed up and went warbling right along till he was actuly beginning to believe what he was saying *himself,* but pretty soon the new gentleman broke in, and says:

"I've thought of something. Is there anybody here that helped to lay out my br—helped to lay out the late Peter Wilks for burying?"

"Yes," says somebody, "me and Ab Turner done it. We're both here."

Then the old man turns towards the king, and says:

"Peraps this gentleman can tell me what was tattooed on his breast?"

◄ What trap does the lawyer set for the frauds?

◄ What does the lawyer feel he has proven? What is the king's response?

◄ What question does the real Wilks ask the king?

Blamed if the king didn't have to brace up mighty quick, or he'd 'a' squshed down like a bluff bank that the river has cut under, it took him so sudden; and, mind you, it was a thing that was calculated to make most *anybody* sqush to get fetched such a solid one as that without any notice, because how was *he* going to know what was tattooed on the man? He whitened a little; he couldn't help it; and it was mighty still in there, and everybody bending a little forwards and gazing at him. Says I to myself, *Now* he'll throw up the sponge— there ain't no more use. Well, did he? A body can't hardly believe it, but he didn't. I reckon he thought he'd keep the thing up till he tired them people out, so they'd thin out, and him and the duke could break loose and get away. Anyway, he set there, and pretty soon he begun to smile, and says:

▶ What is the king's answer to the gentleman's question? Is he correct?

"Mf! It's a *very* tough question, *ain't* it! *Yes,* sir, I k'n tell you what's tattooed on his breast. It's jest a small, thin, blue arrow—that's what it is; and if you don't look clost, you can't see it. *Now* what do you say—hey?"

Well, I never see anything like that old blister for clean out-and-out cheek.

The new old gentleman turns brisk towards Ab Turner and his pard, and his eye lights up like he judged he'd got the king *this* time, and says:

"There—you've heard what he said! Was there any such mark on Peter Wilks's breast?"

Both of them spoke up and says:

"We didn't see no such mark."

"Good!" says the old gentleman. "Now, what you *did* see on his breast was a small dim P, and a B (which is an initial he dropped when he was young), and a W, with dashes between them, so: P—B—W"—and he marked them that way on a piece of paper. "Come, ain't that what you saw?"

Both of them spoke up again, and says:

"No, we *didn't*. We never seen any marks at all."

Well, everybody was in a state of mind now, and they sings out:

"The whole *bilin'* of 'm 's frauds! Le's duck 'em! le's drown 'em! le's ride 'em on a rail!" and everybody was whooping at once, and there was a rattling powwow. But the lawyer he jumps on the table and yells, and says:

▶ Why does the crowd suddenly decide that all four men are frauds? What does the lawyer decide they must do?

"Gentlemen—gentle*men!* Hear me just a word—just a *single* word—if you *please!* There's one way yet—let's go and dig up the corpse and look."

That took them.

"Hooray!" they all shouted, and was starting right off; but the lawyer and the doctor sung out:

"Hold on, hold on! Collar all these four men and the boy, and fetch *them* along, too!"

"We'll do it!" they all shouted; "and if we don't find them marks we'll lynch the whole gang!"

I *was* scared, now, I tell you. But there warn't no getting away, you know. They gripped us all, and marched us right along, straight for the graveyard, which was a mile and a half down the river, and the whole town at our heels, for we made noise enough, and it was only nine in the evening.

As we went by our house I wished I hadn't sent Mary Jane out of town; because now if I could tip her the wink she'd light out and save me, and blow on our deadbeats.

Well, we swarmed along down the river road, just carrying on like wildcats; and to make it more scary the sky was darking up, and the lightning beginning to wink and flitter, and the wind to shiver amongst the leaves. This was the most awful trouble and most dangersome I ever was in; and I was kinder stunned; everything was going so different from what I had allowed for; stead of being fixed so I could take my own time if I wanted to, and see all the fun, and have Mary Jane at my back to save me and set me free when the close-fit come, here was nothing in the world betwixt me and sudden death but just them tattoo marks. If they didn't find them—

◄ *Why does Huck wish for Mary Jane? In what way could she help him?*

I couldn't bear to think about it; and yet, somehow, I couldn't think about nothing else. It got darker and darker, and it was a beautiful time to give the crowd the slip; but that big husky had me by the wrist—Hines—and a body might as well try to give Goliar[2] the slip. He dragged me right along, he was so excited, and I had to run to keep up.

When they got there they swarmed into the graveyard and washed over it like an overflow. And when they got to the grave they found they had about a hundred times as many shovels as they wanted, but nobody hadn't thought to fetch a lantern. But they sailed into digging anyway by the flicker of the lightning, and sent a man to the nearest house, a half a mile off, to borrow one.

So they dug and dug like everything; and it got awful dark, and the rain started, and the wind swished and swushed along, and the lightning come brisker and brisker, and the thunder boomed; but them people never took no notice of it, they was so full of this business; and one minute you could see everything and every face in that big crowd, and the shovelfuls of dirt sailing up out of the grave, and the next second the dark wiped it all out, and you couldn't see nothing at all.

---

2. **Goliar.** Goliath, Old Testament giant

At last they got out the coffin and begun to unscrew the lid, and then such another crowding and shouldering and shoving as there was, to scrouge in and get a sight, you never see; and in the dark, that way, it was awful. Hines he hurt my wrist dreadful pulling and tugging so, and I reckon he clean forgot I was in the world, he was so excited and panting.

All of a sudden the lightning let go a perfect sluice[3] of white glare, and somebody sings out:

"By the living jingo, here's the bag of gold on his breast!"

► What do the people find in the coffin with Peter? What does Huck do as soon as his wrist is freed?

Hines let out a whoop, like everybody else, and dropped my wrist and give a big surge to bust his way in and get a look, and the way I lit out and shinned for the road in the dark there ain't nobody can tell.

I had the road all to myself, and I fairly flew—leastways, I had it all to myself except the solid dark, and the now-and-then glares, and the buzzing of the rain, and the thrashing of the wind, and the splitting of the thunder; and sure as you are born I did clip it along!

When I struck the town I see there warn't nobody out in the storm, so I never hunted for no back streets, but humped it straight through the main one; and when I begun to get towards our house I aimed my eye and set it. No light there; the house all dark—which made me feel sorry and disappointed, I didn't know why. But at last, just as I was sailing by, *flash* comes the light in Mary Jane's window! and my heart swelled up sudden, like to bust; and the same second the house and all was behind me in the dark, and wasn't ever going to be before me no more in this world. She was the best girl I ever see, and had the most sand.

The minute I was far enough above the town to see I could make the towhead, I begun to look sharp for a boat to borrow, and the first time the lightning showed me one that wasn't chained I snatched it and shoved. It was a canoe, and warn't fastened with nothing but a rope. The towhead was a rattling big distance off, away out there in the middle of the river, but I didn't lose no time; and when I struck the raft at last I was so fagged I would 'a' just laid down to blow and gasp if I could afforded it. But I didn't. As I sprung aboard I sung out:

► What does Huck do to get to the raft?

"Out with you, Jim, and set her loose! Glory be to goodness, we're shut of them!"

Jim lit out, and was a-coming for me with both arms spread, he was so full of joy; but when I glimpsed him in the lightning my heart shot up in my mouth and I went overboard backwards; for I forgot he was old King Lear and a drownded A-rab all in one, and it most scared the livers and

---

3. **sluice.** Rush, as a rush of water through a channel

lights[4] out of me. But Jim fished me out, and was going to hug me and bless me, and so on, he was so glad I was back and we was shut of the king and the duke, but I says:

"Not now; have it for breakfast, have it for breakfast! Cut loose and let her slide!"

So in two seconds away we went a-sliding down the river, and it *did* seem so good to be free again and all by ourselves on the big river, and nobody to bother us. I had to skip around a bit, and jump up and crack my heels a few times— I couldn't help it; but about the third crack I noticed a sound that I knowed mighty well, and held my breath and listened and waited; and sure enough, when the next flash busted out over the water, here they come!—and just a-laying to their oars and making their skiff hum! It was the king and the duke.

So I wilted right down on to the planks then, and give up; and it was all I could do to keep from crying.

◄ *Where are the king and the duke? How does Huck feel when he sees them?*

---

4. **livers and lights.** Liver and lungs

CHAPTER 30

The Gold Saves the Thieves

When they got aboard the king went for me, and shook me by the collar, and says:

"Tryin' to give us the slip, was ye, you pup! Tired of our company, hey?"

I says:

"No, your majesty, we warn't—please don't, your majesty!"

"Quick, then, and tell us what was your idea, or I'll shake the insides out o' you!"

"Honest, I'll tell you everything just as it happened, your majesty. The man that had a-holt of me was very good to me, and kept saying he had a boy about as big as me that died last year, and he was sorry to see a boy in such a dangerous fix; and when they was all took by surprise by finding the gold, and made a rush for the coffin, he lets go of me and whispers, 'Heel it now, or they'll hang ye, sure!' and I lit out. It didn't seem no good for *me* to stay—I couldn't do nothing, and I didn't want to be hung if I could get away. So I never stopped running till I found the canoe; and when I got here I told Jim to hurry, or they'd catch me and hang me yet, and said I was afeard you and the duke wasn't alive now, and I was awful sorry, and so was Jim, and was awful glad when we see you coming; you may ask Jim if I didn't."

Jim said it was so; and the king told him to shut up, and said, "Oh, yes, it's mighty likely!" and shook me up again, and said he reckoned he'd drownd me. But the duke says:

"Leggo the boy, you old idiot! Would *you* 'a' done any different? Did you inquire around for *him* when you got loose? I don't remember it."

So the king let go of me, and begun to cuss that town and everybody in it. But the duke says:

"You better a blame' sight give *yourself* a good cussing, for you're the one that's entitled to it most. You hain't done a thing from the start that had any sense in it, except coming out so cool and cheeky with that imaginary blue-arrow mark. That *was* bright—it was right down bully; and it was the thing that saved us. For if it hadn't been for that they'd 'a' jailed us till them Englishmen's baggage come—and then—

▶ *What excuse does Huck give for having run off without the king and the duke?*

▶ *According to the duke, what is the only thing the king has done right?*

the penitentiary, you bet! But that trick took 'em to the graveyard, and the gold done us a still bigger kindness; for if the excited fools hadn't let go all holts and made that rush to get a look we'd 'a' slept in our cravats[1] tonight—cravats warranted to *wear,* too—longer than *we'd* need 'em."

They was still a minute—thinking; then the king says, kind of absent-minded like:

"Mf! And we reckoned the *niggers* stole it!"

That made me squirm!

"Yes," says the duke, kinder slow and deliberate and sarcastic, "*we* did."

After about a half a minute the king drawls out:

"Leastways, *I* did."

The duke says, the same way:

"On the contrary, *I* did."

The king kind of ruffles up, and says:

"Looky here, Bilgewater, what'r you referrin' to?"

The duke says, pretty brisk:

"When it comes to that, maybe you'll let me ask, what was you referring to?"

"Shucks!" says the king, very sarcastic; "but I don't know—maybe you was asleep, and didn't know what you was about."

The duke bristles up now, and says:

"Oh, let *up* on this cussed nonsense; do you take me for a blame' fool? Don't you reckon *I* know who hid that money in that coffin?"

◄ *Of what does the king accuse the duke?*

"*Yes,* sir! I know you *do* know, because you done it yourself!"

"It's a lie!"—and the duke went for him. The king sings out:

"Take y'r hands off!—leggo my throat!—I take it all back!"

The duke says:

"Well, you just own up, first, that you *did* hide that money there, intending to give me the slip one of these days, and come back and dig it up, and have it all to yourself."

"Wait jest a minute, duke—answer me this one question, honest and fair; if you didn't put the money there, say it, and I'll b'lieve you, and take back everything I said."

"You old scoundrel, I didn't, and you know I didn't. There, now!"

---

1. **slept in our cravats.** Died in hangman's nooses

Words For Everyday Use	**pen • i • ten • tia • ry** (pen´i ten´ shə rē) *n.,* state or federal prison for those convicted of serious crimes	**war • ran • ted** (wôr´ənt əd) *adj.,* guaranteed **bris • tle** (bris´əl) *vi.,* become tense with resentment

"Well, then, I b'lieve you. But answer me only jest this one more—now *don't* git mad; didn't you have it in your *mind* to hook the money and hide it?"

The duke never said nothing for a little bit; then he says:

"Well, I don't care if I *did*, I didn't *do* it, anyway. But you not only had it in mind to do it, but you *done* it."

"I wisht I never die if I done it, duke, and that's honest. I won't say I warn't goin' to do it, because I *was*, but you—I mean somebody—got in ahead o' me."

"It's a lie! You done it, and you got to *say* you done it, or —"

The king began to gurgle, and then he gasps out:

"'Nough!—I *own up!*"

I was very glad to hear him say that; it made me feel much more easier than what I was feeling before. So the duke took his hands off and says:

"If you ever deny it again I'll drown you. It's *well* for you to set there and blubber like a baby—it's fitten for you, after the way you've acted. I never see such an old ostrich for wanting to gobble everything—and I a-trusting you all the time, like you was my own father. You ought to been ashamed of yourself to stand by and hear it saddled on to a lot of poor niggers, and you never say a word for 'em. It makes me feel ridiculous to think I was soft enough to *believe* that rubbage. Cuss you, I can see now why you was so anxious to make up the deffisit—you wanted to get what money I'd got out of the 'Nonesuch' and one thing or another, and scoop it *all!*"

The king says, timid, and still a-snuffling:

"Why, duke, it was you that said make up the deffisit; it warn't me."

"Dry up! I don't want to hear no more *out* of you!" says the duke. "And *now* you see what you *got* by it. They've got all their own money back, and all of *ourn* but a shekel[2] or two besides. G'long to bed, and don't you deffersit *me* no more deffersits, long 's *you* live!"

So the king sneaked into the wigwam and took to his bottle for comfort, and before long the duke tackled *his* bottle; and so in about a half an hour they was as thick as thieves again, and the tighter they got the lovinger they got, and went off a-snoring in each other's arms. They both got powerful mellow, but I noticed the king didn't get mellow enough to forget to remember to not deny about hiding the moneybag again. That made me feel easy and satisfied. Of course when they got to snoring we had a long gabble, and I told Jim everything.

▶ How does the duke get the king to say he hid the money? What does the duke claim he will do if the king ever denies doing it again?

▶ What have the king and the duke lost?

▶ What does Huck do when the king and the duke are asleep?

---

2. **shekel.** Small coin

Responding to the Selection

Of all the characters Huck has encountered, what makes the duke and king the most outrageous? Explain what you think of people who will do anything to make a dollar.

Reviewing the Selection

Recalling and Interpreting

1. **R:** What story do the travelers on the raft hear from the innocent young man they encounter? How does this information change their plans?

2. **I:** How have the duke and king taken over the river trip? Why do you think Huck and Jim lose control of the situation?

3: **R:** What do the duke and king intend to do about the inheritance left by Peter Wilks?

4: **I:** Does anyone question the two men when they turn up to claim the inheritance? Is anything about them suspicious? What does Huck think of their plans?

5. **R:** Why does Huck decide to take the money the duke and king have stolen? What does he plan to do with it? What happens to prevent him?

6. **I:** What inspires Huck to risk telling the truth to Mary Jane? What qualities about her impress him?

7: **R:** At what point do the townspeople begin to doubt the king and duke's claims? What increases their suspicions? How do they decide to resolve the question of the identity of the genuine relatives? When do the duke and king finally give up?

8: **I:** In what ways does the greed of the duke and king get them into trouble even before the arrival of the other claimants? What could they have done differently that might have allowed them to pull off their scam? Why do you think it takes so long for them to give up and run?

Synthesizing

9. In what ways are the duke and king using Huck and Jim? At what point does Huck realize how dangerous they are to him and to Jim? Had the townspeople caught the duke and king and Huck with them, do you think they would have spared Huck or considered him just as guilty? What might have saved Huck?

10. "I wilted right down on to the planks then, and give up; and it was all I could do to keep from crying." This is what Huck says when the king and duke reappear just as Jim and Huck are about to get away without them. Why has Huck stayed with the king and the duke for so long?

Understanding Literature (QUESTIONS FOR DISCUSSION)

Suspense. Suspense is a feeling of expectation, anxiousness, or curiosity created by questions raised in the mind of a reader. Find some examples of suspense in chapters 24–30. What events cause you to feel anxious for Huck? Do you think he is ever in genuine danger? What do you think the duke and king would have done to him had they learned that he was the one to hide the gold? Do you ever feel any anxiety for the duke and king? Why, or why not?

CHAPTER 31

You Can't Pray a Lie

We dasn't stop again at any town for days and days; kept right along down the river. We was down south in the warm weather now, and a mighty long ways from home. We begun to come to trees with Spanish moss[1] on them, hanging down from the limbs like long, gray beards. It was the first I ever see it growing, and it made the woods look solemn and dismal. So now the frauds reckoned they was out of danger, and they begun to work the villages again.

First they done a lecture on temperance; but they didn't make enough for them both to get drunk on. Then in another village they started a dancing school; but they didn't know no more how to dance than a kangaroo does; so the first prance they made the general public jumped in and pranced them out of town. Another time they tried to go at yellocution;[2] but they didn't yellocute long till the audience got up and give them a solid good cussing, and made them skip out. They tackled missionarying, and mesmerizing, and doctoring, and telling fortunes, and a little of everything; but they couldn't seem to have no luck. So at last they got just about dead broke, and laid around the raft as she floated along, thinking and thinking, and never saying nothing, by the half a day at a time, and dreadful blue and desperate.

And at last they took a change and begun to lay their heads together in the wigwam and talk low and confidential two or three hours at a time. Jim and me got uneasy. We didn't like the look of it. We judged they was studying up some kind of worse deviltry than ever. We turned it over and over, and at last we made up our minds they was going to break into somebody's house or store, or was going into the counterfeit-money business, or something. So then we was pretty scared, and made up an agreement that we wouldn't have nothing in the world to do with such actions, and if we ever got the least show we would give them the cold shake and clear out and leave them behind. Well, early one morning we hid the raft in a good, safe place about two mile below a little bit of a shabby village named Pikesville, and the king he went ashore and told us all to stay hid whilst he went up to town and smelt around to see if anybody had got any wind of the "Royal Nonesuch" there yet. ("House to rob, you *mean*," says

◄ *When they are sure that they are out of trouble, what do the king and the duke do to try to get money? Are they successful?*

◄ *What do Jim and Huck believe the king and the duke might be planning?*

---

1. **Spanish moss.** Rootless plant of the pineapple family that grows in long graceful strands along the branches of trees in the southeastern states
2. **Yellocution.** Elocution; art of public speaking

► *What do Jim and Huck intend to do as soon as the duke and the king are away?*

I to myself; "and when you get through robbing it you'll come back here and wonder what has become of me and Jim and the raft—and you'll have to take it out in wondering.") And he said if he warn't back by midday the duke and me would know it was all right, and we was to come along.

So we stayed where we was. The duke he fretted and sweated around, and was in a mighty sour way. He scolded us for everything, and we couldn't seem to do nothing right; he found fault with every little thing. Something was a-brewing, sure. I was good and glad when midday come and no king; we could have a change, anyway—and maybe a chance for *the* chance on top of it. So me and the duke went up to the village, and hunted around there for the king, and by and by we found him in the back room of a little low dog-gery,[3] very tight,[4] and a lot of loafers bullyragging him for sport, and he a-cussing and a-threatening with all his might, and so tight he couldn't walk, and couldn't do nothing to

► *When does Huck get the chance to leave?*

them. The duke he begun to abuse him for an old fool, and the king begun to sass back, and the minute they was fairly at it I lit out and shook the reefs[5] out of my hind legs, and spun down the river road like a deer, for I see our chance; and I made up my mind that it would be a long day before they ever see me and Jim again. I got down there all out of breath but loaded up with joy, and sung out:

"Set her loose, Jim! we're all right now!"

But there warn't no answer, and nobody come out of the wigwam. Jim was gone! I set up a shout—and then another—and then another one; and run this way and that in the woods, whooping and screeching; but it warn't no use—old Jim was gone. Then I set down and cried; I couldn't help it. But I couldn't set still long. Pretty soon I went out on the road, trying to think what I better do, and I run across a boy walking, and asked him if he'd seen a strange nigger dressed so and so, and he says:

"Yes."

"Whereabouts?" says I.

► *What has happened to Jim?*

"Down to Silas Phelps's place, two mile below here. He's a runaway nigger, and they've got him. Was you looking for him?"

"You bet I ain't! I run across him in the woods about an hour or two ago, and he said if I hollered he'd cut my livers out—and told me to lay down and stay where I was; and I done it. Been there ever since; afeard to come out."

"Well," he says, "you needn't be afeard no more, becuz

---

3. **doggery.** Saloon
4. **tight.** Drunk
5. **shook the reefs.** Unfolded the sails, i.e., got ready to run

they've got him. He run off f'm down South, som'ers."

"It's a good job they got him."

"Well, I *reckon!* There's two hunderd dollars reward on him. It's like picking up money out'n the road."

"Yes, it is—and *I* could 'a' had it if I'd been big enough; I see him *first.* Who nailed him?"

"It was an old fellow—a stranger—and he sold out his chance in him for forty dollars, becuz he's got to go up the river and can't wait. Think o' that, now! You bet *I'd* wait, if it was seven year."

"That's me, every time," says I. "But maybe his chance ain't worth no more than that, if he'll sell it so cheap. Maybe there's something ain't straight about it."

"But it *is*, though—straight as a string. I see the handbill myself. It tells all about him, to a dot—paints him like a picture, and tells the plantation he's frum, below Newr*leans.* No-sirree-*bob*, they ain't no trouble 'bout *that* speculation, you bet you. Say, gimme a chaw tobacker, won't ye?"

I didn't have none, so he left. I went to the raft, and set down in the wigwam to think. But I couldn't come to nothing. I thought till I wore my head sore, but I couldn't see no way out of the trouble. After all this long journey, and after all we'd done for them scoundrels, here it was all come to nothing, everything all busted up and ruined, because they could have the heart to serve Jim such a trick as that, and make him a slave again all his life, and amongst strangers, too, for forty dirty dollars.

◄ Who does Huck believe turned Jim in?

Once I said to myself it would be a thousand times better for Jim to be a slave at home where his family was, as long as he'd *got* to be a slave, and so I'd better write a letter to Tom Sawyer and tell him to tell Miss Watson where he was. But I soon give up that notion for two things: she'd be mad and disgusted at his rascality and ungratefulness for leaving her, and so she'd sell him straight down the river again; and if she didn't, everybody naturally despises an ungrateful nigger, and they'd make Jim feel it all the time, and so he'd feel ornery and disgraced. And then think of *me!* It would get all around that Huck Finn helped a nigger to get his freedom; and if I was ever to see anybody from that town again I'd be ready to get down and lick his boots for shame. That's just the way: a person does a low down thing, and then he don't want to take no consequences of it. Thinks as long as he can hide, it ain't no disgrace. That was my fix exactly. The more I studied about this the more my conscience went to grinding me, and the more wicked and low down and ornery I got to feeling. And at last, when it hit me all of a sudden that

◄ Why does Huck consider writing to Tom Sawyer? Why does he change his mind?

selfish reasons

here was the plain hand of Providence slapping me in the face and letting me know my wickedness was being watched all the time from up there in heaven, whilst I was stealing a poor old woman's nigger that hadn't ever done me no harm, and now was showing me there's One that's always on the lookout, and ain't a-going to allow no such miserable doings to go only just so fur and no further, I most dropped in my tracks I was so scared. Well, I tried the best I could to kinder soften it up somehow for myself by saying I was brung up wicked, and so I warn't so much to blame; but something inside of me kept saying, "There was the Sunday school, you could 'a' gone to it; and if you'd 'a' done it they'd 'a' learnt you there that people that acts as I'd been acting about that nigger goes to everlasting fire."

▶ For what does Huck blame himself?

It made me shiver. And I about made up my mind to pray, and see if I couldn't try to quit being the kind of a boy I was and be better. So I kneeled down. But the words wouldn't come. Why wouldn't they? It warn't no use to try and hide it from Him. Nor from *me*, neither. I knowed very well why they wouldn't come. It was because my heart warn't right; it was because I warn't square; it was because I was playing double. I was letting *on* to give up sin, but away inside of me I was holding on to the biggest one of all. I was trying to make my mouth *say* I would do the right thing and the clean thing, and go and write to that nigger's owner and tell where he was; but deep down in me I knowed it was a lie, and He knowed it. You can't pray a lie—I found that out.

▶ Why does Huck believe he can't pray?

So I was full of trouble, full as I could be; and didn't know what to do. At last I had an idea; and I says, I'll go and write the letter—and *then* see if I can pray. Why, it was astonishing, the way I felt as light as a feather right straight off, and my troubles all gone. So I got a piece of paper and a pencil, all glad and excited, and set down and wrote:

> Miss Watson, your runaway nigger Jim is down here two mile below Pikesville, and Mr. Phelps has got him and he will give him up for the reward if you send.
>
> HUCK FINN

I felt good and all washed clean of sin for the first time I had ever felt so in my life, and I knowed I could pray now. But I didn't do it straight off, but laid the paper down and set there thinking—thinking how good it was all this happened so, and how near I come to being lost and going to hell. And went on thinking. And got to thinking over our trip down the river; and I see Jim before me all the time: in the day and in the nighttime, sometimes moonlight, sometimes storms,

▶ What thoughts prevent Huck from feeling completely satisfied with himself?

and we a-floating along, talking and singing and laughing. But somehow I couldn't seem to strike no places to harden me against him, but only the other kind. I'd see him standing my watch on top of his'n, 'stead of calling me, so I could go on sleeping; and see him how glad he was when I come back out of the fog; and when I come to him again in the swamp, up there where the feud was; and such-like times; and would always call me honey, and pet me and do everything he could think of for me, and how good he always was; and at last I struck the time I saved him by telling the men we had smallpox aboard, and he was so grateful, and said I was the best friend old Jim ever had in the world, and the *only* one he's got now; and then I happened to look around and see that paper.

It was a close place. I took it up, and held it in my hand. I was a-trembling, because I'd got to decide, forever, betwixt two things, and I knowed it. I studied a minute, sort of holding my breath, and then says to myself:

"All right, then, I'll *go* to hell"—and tore it up.

It was awful thoughts and awful words, but they was said. And I let them stay said; and never thought no more about reforming. I shoved the whole thing out of my head, and said I would take up wickedness again, which was in my line, being brung up to it, and the other warn't. And for a starter I would go to work and steal Jim out of slavery again; and if I could think up anything worse, I would do that, too; because as long as I was in, and in for good, I might as well go the whole hog.

Then I set to thinking over how to get at it, and turned over some considerable many ways in my mind; and at last fixed up a plan that suited me. So then I took the bearings of a woody island that was down the river a piece, and as soon as it was fairly dark I crept out with my raft and went for it, and hid it there, and then turned in. I slept the night through, and got up before it was light, and had my breakfast, and put on my store clothes, and tied up some others and one thing or another in a bundle, and took the canoe and cleared for shore. I landed below where I judged was Phelps's place, and hid my bundle in the woods, and then filled up the canoe with water, and loaded rocks into her and sunk her where I could find her again when I wanted her, about a quarter of a mile below a little steam sawmill that was on the bank.

Then I struck up the road, and when I passed the mill I see a sign on it, "Phelps's Sawmill," and when I come to the farmhouses, two or three hundred yards further along, I kept

◄ In what way is Huck going to take up "wickedness" again? What does Huck decide he must do?

my eyes peeled, but didn't see nobody around, though it was good daylight now. But I didn't mind, because I didn't want to see nobody just yet—I only wanted to get the lay of the land. According to my plan, I was going to turn up there from the village, not from below. So I just took a look, and shoved along, straight for town. Well, the very first man I see when I got there was the duke. He was sticking up a bill for the "Royal Nonesuch"—three-night performance—like that other time. *They* had the cheek, them frauds! I was right on him before I could <u>shirk</u>. He looked astonished, and says:

▶ Whom does Huck see when he gets to Phelps's Sawmill? What is he doing?

"Hel-*lo!* Where'd *you* come from?" Then he says, kind of glad and eager, "Where's the raft?—got her in a good place?"

I says:

"Why, that's just what I was going to ask your grace."

Then he didn't look so joyful, and says:

"What was your idea for asking *me?*" he says.

"Well," I says, "when I see the king in that doggery yesterday I says to myself, we can't get him home for hours, till he's soberer; so I went a-loafing around town to put in the time and wait. A man up and offered me ten cents to help him pull a skiff over the river and back to fetch a sheep, and so I went along; but when we was dragging him to the boat, and the man left me a-holt of the rope and went behind him to shove him along, he was too strong for me and jerked loose and run, and we after him. We didn't have no dog, and so we had to chase him all over the country till we tired him out. We never got him till dark; then we fetched him over, and I started down for the raft. When I got there and see it was gone, I says to myself, 'They've got into trouble and had to leave; and they've took my nigger, which is the only nigger I've got in the world, and now I'm in a strange country, and ain't got no property no more, nor nothing, and no way to make my living'; so I set down and cried. I slept in the woods all night. But what *did* become of the raft, then?—and Jim—poor Jim!"

▶ What does Huck ask the duke? What is the duke's explanation of what happened?

"Blamed if *I* know—that is, what's become of the raft. That old fool had made a trade and got forty dollars, and when we found him in the doggery the loafers had matched half-dollars with him and got every cent but what he'd spent for whisky; and when I got him home late last night and found the raft gone, we said, 'That little rascal has stole our raft and shook

Words For Everyday Use	**shirk** (shurk) *vi.,* avoid work or duty

us, and run off down the river.'"

"I wouldn't shake my *nigger*, would I?—the only nigger I had in the world, and the only property."

"We never thought of that. Fact is, I reckon we'd come to consider him *our* nigger; yes, we did consider him so—goodness knows we had trouble enough for him. So when we see the raft was gone and we flat broke, there warn't anything for it but to try the 'Royal Nonesuch' another shake. And I've pegged along ever since, dry as a powder-horn. Where's that ten cents? Give it here."

I had considerable money, so I give him ten cents, but begged him to spend it for something to eat, and give me some, because it was all the money I had, and I hadn't had nothing to eat since yesterday. He never said nothing. The next minute he whirls on me and says:

"Do you reckon that nigger would blow[6] on us? We'd skin him if he done that!"

"How can he blow? Hain't he run off?"

"No! That old fool sold him, and never divided with me, and the money's gone."

◄ Why is the duke angry with the king? What has the king done?

"*Sold* him?" I says, and begun to cry; "why, he was *my* nigger, and that was my money. Where is he?—I want my nigger."

"Well, you can't *get* your nigger, that's all—so dry up your blubbering. Looky here—do you think *you'd* venture to blow on us? Blamed if I think I'd trust you. Why, if you *was* to blow on us—"

He stopped, but I never see the duke look so ugly out of his eyes before. I went on a-whimpering, and says:

"I don't want to blow on nobody; and I ain't got no time to blow, nohow. I got to turn out and find my nigger."

He looked kinder bothered, and stood there with his bills fluttering on his arm, thinking, and wrinkling up his forehead. At last he says:

"I'll tell you something. We got to be here three days. If you'll promise you won't blow, and won't let the nigger blow, I'll tell you where to find him."

◄ What deal does the duke try to make with Huck? According to the duke, where is Jim? Is he telling the truth?

So I promised, and he says:

"A farmer by the name of Silas Ph——" and then he stopped. You see, he started to tell me the truth; but when he stopped that way, and begun to study and think again, I reckoned he was changing his mind. And so he was. He wouldn't trust me; he wanted to make sure of having me out of the way the whole three days. So pretty soon he says:

---

6. **blow.** Inform on, reveal the truth about

"The man that bought him is named Abram Foster— Abram G. Foster—and he lives forty mile back here in the country, on the road to Lafayette."

"All right," I says, "I can walk it in three days. And I'll start this very afternoon."

"No you won't, you'll start *now;* and don't you lose any time about it, neither, nor do any gabbling by the way. Just keep a tight tongue in your head and move right along, and then you won't get into trouble with *us,* d'ye hear?"

That was the order I wanted, and that was the one I played for. I wanted to be left free to work my plans.

"So clear out," he says; "and you can tell Mr. Foster whatever you want to. Maybe you can get him to believe that Jim *is* your nigger—some idiots don't require documents—leastways I've heard there's such down south here. And when you tell him the handbill and the reward's <u>bogus</u>, maybe he'll believe you when you explain to him what the idea was for getting 'em out. Go 'long now, and tell him anything you want to; but mind you don't work your jaw any *between* here and there."

So I left, and struck for the back country. I didn't look around, but I kinder felt like he was watching me. But I knowed I could tire him out at that. I went straight out in the country as much as a mile before I stopped; then I doubled back through the woods towards Phelps's. I reckoned I better start in on my plan straight off without fooling around, because I wanted to stop Jim's mouth till these fellows could get away. I didn't want no trouble with their kind. I'd seen all I wanted to of them, and wanted to get entirely shut of them.

▶ *Why does Huck want the duke and the king to get away?*

CHAPTER 32

I Have a New Name

When I got there it was all still and Sunday-like, and hot and sunshiny; the hands was gone to the fields; and there was them kind of faint <u>dronings</u> of bugs and flies in the air that makes it seem so lonesome and like everybody's dead and gone; and if a breeze fans along and quivers the leaves it makes you feel mournful, because you feel like it's spirits whispering—spirits that's been dead ever so many years—and you always think they're talking about *you*. As a general thing it makes a body wish *he* was dead, too, and done with it all.

Phelps's was one of these little one-horse[1] cotton <u>plantations</u>, and they all look alike. A rail fence round a two-acre yard; a stile made out of logs sawed off and upended in steps, like barrels of a different length, to climb over the fence with, and for the women to stand on when they are going to jump on to a horse; some sickly grass-patches in the big yard, but mostly it was bare and smooth, like an old hat with the nap rubbed off; big double log house for the white folks— hewed logs, with the chinks stopped up with mud or mortar, and these mudstripes been whitewashed some time or another; round-log kitchen, with a big broad, open but roofed passage joining it to the house; log smokehouse back of the kitchen; three little log nigger-cabins in a row t'other side the smokehouse; one little hut all by itself away down against the back fence, and some outbuildings down a piece the other side; ash-hopper[2] and big kettle to bile soap in by the little hut; bench by the kitchen door, with bucket of water and a gourd; hound asleep there in the sun; more hounds asleep round about; about three shade trees away off in a corner; some currant bushes and gooseberry bushes in one place by the fence; outside of the fence a garden and a watermelon patch; then the cotton fields begins, and after the fields the woods.

I went around and clumb over the back stile by the ash-hopper, and started for the kitchen. When I got a little ways I heard the

◀ *How does the breeze through the leaves make Huck feel? What does it sound like to him?*

---

1. **one-horse.** Small
2. **ash-hopper.** Container for lye for making soap

dim hum of a spinning wheel[3] wailing along up and sinking along down again; and then I knowed for certain I wished I was dead—for that *is* the lonesomest sound in the whole world.

▶ Does Huck have a plan? What does Huck notice about "Providence"?

I went right along, not fixing up any particular plan, but just trusting to Providence to put the right words in my mouth when the time come; for I'd noticed that Providence always did put the right words in my mouth if I left it alone.

When I got halfway, first one hound and then another got up and went for me, and of course I stopped and faced them, and kept still. And such another powwow as they made! In a quarter of a minute I was a kind of a <u>hub</u> of a wheel, as you may say—spokes made out of dogs—circle of fifteen of them packed together around me, with their necks and noses stretched up towards me, a-barking and howling; and more a-coming; you could see them sailing over fences and around corners from everywheres.

A nigger woman come tearing out of the kitchen with a rolling pin in her hand, singing out, "Begone! *you* Tige! you Spot! begone sah!" and she fetched first one and then another of them a clip and sent them howling, and then the rest followed; and the next second half of them come back, wagging their tails around me, and making friends with me. There ain't no harm in a hound, nohow.

And behind the woman comes a little nigger girl and two little nigger boys without anything on but tow-linen shirts, and they hung on to their mother's gown, and peeped out from behind her at me, bashful, the way they always do. And here comes the white woman running from the house, about forty-five or fifty year old, bareheaded, and her spinning-stick in her hand; and behind her comes her little white children, acting the same way the little niggers was going. She was smiling all over so she could hardly stand—and says:

"It's *you*, at last!—*ain't* it?"

I out with a "Yes'm" before I thought.

▶ What strange reception does Huck get from the woman who lives on the plantation? Who does she think he is?

She grabbed me and hugged me tight; and then gripped me by both hands and shook and shook; and the tears come in her eyes, and run down over; and she couldn't seem to hug and shake enough, and kept saying, "You don't look as much like your mother as I reckoned you would; but law sakes, I don't care for that, I'm *so* glad to see you! Dear, dear,

---

3. **spinning wheel.** Device for spinning wool into thread

Words
For
Everyday
Use   **hub** (hub) *n.*, center part of a wheel

it does seem like I could eat you up! Children, it's your cousin Tom!—tell him howdy."

But they ducked their heads, and put their fingers in their mouths, and hid behind her. So she run on:

"Lize, hurry up and get him a hot breakfast right away—or did you get your breakfast on the boat?"

I said I had got it on the boat. So then she started for the house, leading me by the hand, and the children tagging after. When we got there she set me down in a split-bottomed chair, and set herself down on a little low stool in front of me, holding both of my hands, and says:

"Now I can have a *good* look at you; and, laws-a-me, I've been hungry for it a many and a many a time, all these long years, and it's come at last! We been expecting you a couple of days and more. What kep' you?—boat get aground?"

"Yes'm—she—"

"Don't say yes'm—say Aunt Sally. Where'd she get aground?"

I didn't rightly know what to say, because I didn't know whether the boat would be coming up the river or down. But I go a good deal on <u>instinct</u>; and my instinct said she would be coming up—from down towards Orleans. That didn't help me much, though; for I didn't know the names of bars down that way. I see I'd got to invent a bar, or forget the name of the one we got aground on—or—Now I struck an idea, and fetched it out:

"It warn't the grounding—that didn't keep us back but a little. We blowed out a cylinder-head."

"Good gracious! anybody hurt?"

"No'm. Killed a nigger."

"Well, it's lucky; because sometimes people do get hurt. Two years ago last Christmas your uncle Silas was coming up from Newrleans on the old *Lally Rook*, and she blowed out a cylinder-head and crippled a man. And I think he died afterwards. He was a Baptist. Your uncle Silas knowed a family in Baton Rouge that knowed his people very well. Yes, I remember now, he *did* die. Mortification[4] set in, and they had to <u>amputate</u> him. But it didn't save him. Yes, it was mortification—that was it. He turned blue all over, and died in the hope of a glorious <u>resurrection</u>. They say he was a sight to look at. Your uncle's been up to the town every day to fetch

---

4. **Mortification.** Gangrene; death of live tissue

Words For Everyday Use	in • stinct (inˊstiŋkt) *n.*, natural, unlearned response
	am • pu • tate (amˊpyoo tāt́) *vt.*, remove a limb surgically
	res • ur • rec • tion (rezˊə rekˊshən) *n.*, rise from the dead

you. And he's gone again, not more'n an hour ago; he'll be back any minute now. You must a met him on the road, didn't you?—oldish man, with a—"

"No, I didn't see nobody, Aunt Sally. The boat landed just at daylight, and I left my baggage on the wharf-boat and went looking around the town and out a piece in the country, to put in the time and not get here too soon; and so I come down the back way."

"Who'd you give the baggage to?"

"Nobody."

"Why, child, it'll be stole!"

"Not where *I* hid it I reckon it won't," I says.

"How'd you get your breakfast so early on the boat?"

It was kinder thin ice, but I says:

"The captain see me standing around, and told me I better have something to eat before I went ashore; so he took me in the texas to the officers' lunch, and give me all I wanted."

▶ Why does Huck have his mind on the children? In what way does he think they might help him?

I was getting so uneasy I couldn't listen good. I had my mind on the children all the time; I wanted to get them out to one side and pump them a little, and find out who I was. But I couldn't get no show, Mrs. Phelps kept it up and run on so. Pretty soon she made the cold chills streak all down my back, because she says:

"But here we're a-running on this way, and you hain't told me a word about Sis, nor any of them. Now I'll rest my words a little, and you start up yourn; just tell me *everything*—tell me all about 'm all every one of 'm; and how they are, and what they're doing, and what they told you to tell me; and every last thing you can think of."

▶ Why is Huck about to give up and tell the woman the truth? What prevents him from doing so?

Well, I see I was up a stump—and up it good. Providence had stood by me this fur all right, but I was hard and tight aground now. I see it warn't a bit of use to try to go ahead—I'd got to throw up my hand. So I says to myself, here's another place where I got to resk the truth. I opened my mouth to begin; but she grabbed me and hustled me in behind the bed, and says:

"Here he comes! Stick your head down lower—there, that'll do; you can't be seen now. Don't you let on you're here. I'll play a joke on him. Children, don't you say a word."

I see I was in a fix now. But it warn't no use to worry; there warn't nothing to do but just hold still, and try and be ready to stand from under when the lightning struck.

I had just one little glimpse of the old gentleman when he come in; then the bed hid him. Mrs. Phelps she jumps for him, and says:

"Has he come?"

"No," says her husband.

"Good-*ness* gracious!" she says, "what in the warld *can* have become of him?"

"I can't imagine," says the old gentleman; "and I must say it makes me dreadful uneasy."

"Uneasy!" she says; "I'm ready to go <u>distracted</u>! He *must* 'a' come; and you've missed him along the road. I *know* it's so—something *tells* me so."

"Why, Sally, I *couldn't* miss him along the road—*you* know that."

"But oh, dear, dear, what *will* Sis say! He must 'a' come! You must 'a' missed him. He—"

"Oh, don't distress me any more'n I'm already distressed. I don't know what in the world to make of it. I'm at my wit's end, and I don't mind acknowledging 't I'm right down scared. But there's no hope that he's come; for he *couldn't* come and me miss him. Sally, it's terrible—just terrible—something's happened to the boat, sure!"

"Why, Silas! Look yonder!—up the road!—ain't that somebody coming?"

He sprung to the window at the head of the bed, and that give Mrs. Phelps the chance she wanted. She stooped down quick at the foot of the bed and give me a pull, and out I come; and when he turned back from the window there she stood, a-beaming and a-smiling like a house afire, and I standing pretty <u>meek</u> and sweaty alongside. The old gentleman stared, and says:

"Why, who's that?"

"Who do you reckon 'tis?"

"I hain't no idea. Who *is* it?"

"It's *Tom Sawyer*!"

By jings, I most slumped through the floor! But there warn't no time to swap knives; the old man grabbed me by the hand and shook, and kept on shaking; and all the time how the woman did dance around and laugh and cry; and then how they both did fire off questions about Sid, and Mary, and the rest of the tribe.

But if they was joyful, it warn't nothing to what I was; for it was like being born again, I was so glad to find out who I was. Well, they froze to me for two hours; and at last, when my chin was so tired it couldn't hardly go any more, I had

Searching for identity

◀ *Who does it turn out "Cousin Tom" is? Why is Huck relieved?*

Words For Everyday Use	**dis • tract • ed** (di strakt´əd) *adj.*, afflicted by mental distress
	meek (mēk) *adj.*, spiritless

told them more about my family—I mean the Sawyer family—than ever happened to any six Sawyer families. And I explained all about how we blowed out a cylinder-head at the mouth of White River, and it took us three days to fix it. Which was all right, and worked first-rate; because *they* didn't know but what it would take three days to fix it. If I'd 'a' called it 'a' bolthead it would 'a' done just as well.

Now I was feeling pretty comfortable all down one side, and pretty uncomfortable all up the other. Being Tom Sawyer was easy and comfortable, and it stayed easy and comfortable till by and by I hear a steamboat coughing along down the river. Then I says to myself, s'pose Tom Sawyer comes down on that boat? And s'pose he steps in here any minute, and sings out my name before I can throw him a wink to keep quiet?

Well, I couldn't *have* it that way; it wouldn't do at all. I must go up the road and waylay[5] him. So I told the folks I reckoned I would go up to the town and fetch down my baggage. The old gentleman was for going along with me, but I said no, I could drive the horse myself, and I druther he wouldn't take no trouble about me.

▶ How does Huck feel about his new role? What is his one concern?

---

5. **waylay.** Lie in wait for

CHAPTER 33

The Pitiful Ending of Royalty

So I started for town in the wagon, and when I was half-way I see a wagon coming, and sure enough it was Tom Sawyer, and I stopped and waited till he come along. I says "Hold on!" and it stopped alongside, and his mouth opened up like a trunk, and stayed so; and he swallowed two or three times like a person that's got a dry throat, and then says:

"I hain't ever done you no harm. You know that. So, then, what you want to come back and ha'nt[1] *me* for?"

I says:

"I hain't come back—I hain't been *gone*."

When he heard my voice it righted him up some, but he warn't quite satisfied yet. He says:

"Don't you play nothing on me, because I wouldn't on you. Honest injun, you ain't a ghost?"

"Honest injun, I ain't," I says.

"Well—I—I—well, that ought to settle it, of course; but I can't somehow seem to understand it no way. Looky here, warn't you ever murdered *at all*?"

"No. I warn't ever murdered at all—I played it on them. You come in here and feel of me if you don't believe me."

So he done it; and it satisfied him; and he was that glad to see me again he didn't know what to do. And he wanted to know all about it right off, because it was a grand adventure, and mysterious, and so it hit him where he lived. But I said, leave it alone till by and by; and told his driver to wait, and we drove off a little piece, and I told him the kind of a fix I was in, and what did he reckon we better do? He said, let him alone a minute, and don't disturb him. So he thought and thought, and pretty soon he says:

"It's all right; I've got it. Take my trunk in your wagon, and let on it's your'n; and you turn back and fool along slow, so as to get to the house about the time you ought to; and I'll go towards town a piece, and take a fresh start, and get there a quarter or a half an hour after you; and you needn't let on to know me at first."

I says:

"All right; but wait a minute. There's one more thing—a thing that *nobody* don't know but me. And that is, there's a nigger here that I'm a-trying to steal out of slavery, and his

◄ Why is Tom so shocked to see Huck? As far as he knew, what had happened to Huck?

◄ What is Tom's plan? What does Huck tell Tom?

---

1. **ha'nt.** Haunt

name is *Jim*—old Miss Watson's Jim."

He says:

" What! Why, Jim is—"

He stopped and went to studying. I says:

"*I* know what you'll say. You'll say it's dirty, lowdown business; but what if it is? *I'm* low down; and I'm a-going to steal him, and I want you keep <u>mum</u> and not let on. Will you?"

His eye lit up, and he says:

"I'll *help* you steal him!"

Well, I let go all holts then, like I was shot. It was the most astonishing speech I ever heard—and I'm bound to say Tom Sawyer fell considerable in my estimation. Only I couldn't believe it. Tom Sawyer a *nigger-stealer!*

"Oh, shucks!" I says; "you're joking."

"I ain't joking, either."

"Well, then," I says, "joking or no joking, if you hear anything said about a runaway nigger, don't forget to remember that *you* don't know nothing about him, and *I* don't know nothing about him."

Then we took the trunk and put it in my wagon, and he drove off his way and I drove mine. But of course I forgot all about driving slow on accounts of being glad and full of thinking; so I got home a heap too quick for that length of a trip. The old gentleman was at the door, and he says:

"Why, this is wonderful! Whoever would 'a' thought it was in that mare to do it? I wish we'd 'a' timed her. And she hain't sweated a hair—not a hair. It's wonderful. Why, I wouldn't take a hundred dollars for that horse now—I wouldn't, honest; and yet I'd 'a' sold her for fifteen before, and thought 'twas all she was worth."

That's all he said. He was the innocentest, best old soul I ever see. But it warn't surprising; because he warn't only just a farmer, he was a preacher, too, and had a little one-horse log church down back of the plantation, which he built it himself at his own expense, for a church and schoolhouse, and never charged nothing for his preaching, and it was worth it, too. There was plenty other farmer-preachers like that, and done the same way, down South.

In about half an hour Tom's wagon drove up to the front stile, and Aunt Sally she see it through the window, because it was only about fifty yards, and says:

▶ *What does Tom say that shocks Huck?*

Confidence

Words
For
Everyday
Use

mum (mum) *adj.*, silent

"Why, there's somebody come! I wonder who 'tis? Why, I do believe it's a stranger. Jimmy" (that's one of the children), "run and tell Lize to put on another plate for dinner."

Everybody made a rush for the front door, because, of course, a stranger don't come *every* year, and so he lays over the yaller-fever, for interest, when he does come. Tom was over the stile and starting for the house; the wagon was spinning up the road for the village, and we was all bunched in the front door. Tom had his store clothes on, and an audience—and that was always nuts for Tom Sawyer. In them circumstances it warn't no trouble to him to throw in an amount of style that was suitable. He warn't a boy to meeky along up that yard like a sheep; no, he come ca'm and important, like the ram. When he got a-front of us he lifts his hat ever so gracious and dainty, like it was the lid of a box that had butterflies asleep in it and he didn't want to disturb them, and says:

"Mr. Archibald Nichols, I presume?"

"No, my boy," says the old gentleman, "I'm sorry to say 't your driver has deceived you; Nichols's place is down a matter of three mile more. Come in, come in."

Tom he took a look back over his shoulder, and says, "Too late—he's out of sight."

"Yes, he's gone, my son, and you must come in and eat your dinner with us; and then we'll hitch up and take you down to Nichols's."

"Oh, I *can't* make you so much trouble; I couldn't think of it. I'll walk—I don't mind the distance."

"But we won't *let* you walk—it wouldn't be Southern hospitality to do it. Come right in."

"Oh, do," says Aunt Sally; "it ain't a bit of trouble to us, not a bit in the world. You *must* stay. It's a long, dusty three mile, and we *can't* let you walk. And, besides, I've already told 'em to put on another plate when I see you coming; so you mustn't disappoint us. Come right in and make yourself at home."

So Tom he thanked them very hearty and handsome, and let himself be persuaded, and come in; and when he was in he said he was a stranger from Hicksville, Ohio, and his name was William Thompson—and he made another bow.

Well, he run on, and on, and on, making up stuff about

How does the family react to the arrival of Tom, "a stranger" to them? For whom does Tom claim to be looking?

What does the family invite Tom to do?

Words For Everyday Use

hos • pi • tal • i • ty (häs´pi tal´ə tē) *n.*, act of welcoming guests

Hicksville and everybody in it he could invent, and I getting a little nervous, and wondering how this was going to help me out of my scrape; and at last, still talking along, he reached over and kissed Aunt Sally right on the mouth, and then settled back again in his chair comfortable, and was going on talking; but she jumped up and wiped it off with the back of her hand, and says:

"You owdacious[2] puppy!"

He looked kind of hurt, and says:

"I'm surprised at you, m'am."

▶ What does Tom do to offend Aunt Sally?

"You're s'rp—Why, what do you reckon _I_ am? I've a good notion to take and—Say, what do you mean by kissing me?"

He looked kind of humble, and says:

"I didn't mean nothing, m'am. I didn't mean no harm. I—I—thought you'd like it."

"Why, you born fool!" She took up the spinning stick, and it looked like it was all she could do to keep from giving him a crack with it. "What made you think I'd like it?"

"Well, I don't know. Only, they—they—told me you would."

"_They_ told you I would. Whoever told you's _another_ lunatic. I never heard the beat of it. Who's _they_?"

"Why, everybody. They all said so, m'am."

It was all she could do to hold in; and her eyes snapped, and her fingers worked like she wanted to scratch him; and she says:

"Who's 'everybody'? Out with their names, or ther'll be an idiot short."

He got up and looked distressed, and fumbled his hat, and says:

"I'm sorry, and I warn't expecting it. They told me to. They all told me to. They all said, kiss her; and said she'd like it. They all said it—every one of them. But I'm sorry, m'am, and I won't do it no more—I won't, honest."

"You won't, won't you? Well, I sh'd _reckon_ you won't!"

"No'm, I'm honest about it; I won't ever do it again—till you ask me."

"Till I ask you! Well, I never see the beat of it in my born days! I lay you'll be the Methusalem-numskull[3] of creation

---

2. **owdacious.** Audacious; overly bold, daring
3. **Methuselam-numskull.** Stupid person as old as Methuselah, an Old Testament man who lived 969 years

Words For Everyday Use

hum • ble (hum´b'l) _adj._, modest, not proud
lu • na • tic (lōōn´ə tik) _n._, insane person

before ever *I* ask you—or the likes of you."

"Well," he says, "it does surprise me so. I can't make it out, somehow. They said you would, and I thought you would. But—" He stopped and looked around slow, like he wished he could run across a friendly eye somewheres, and fetched up on the old gentleman's, and says, "Didn't you think she'd like me to kiss her, sir?"

"Why, no; I—I—well, no, I b'lieve I didn't."

Then he looks on around the same way to me, and says:

"Tom, didn't you think Aunt Sally 'd open out her arms and say, 'Sid Sawyer—'"

"My land!" she says, breaking in and jumping for him, "you <u>impudent</u> young rascal, to fool a body so —" and was going to hug him, but he <u>fended</u> her off, and says:

"No, not till you've asked me first."

So she didn't lose no time, but asked him; and hugged him and kissed him over and over again, and then turned him over to the old man, and he took what was left. And after they got a little quiet again she says:

"Why, dear me, I never see such a surprise. We warn't looking for *you* at all, but only Tom. Sis never wrote to me about anybody coming but him."

"It's because it warn't *intended* for any of us to come but Tom," he says; "but I begged and begged, and at the last minute she let me come, too; so, coming down the river, me and Tom thought it would be a first-rate surprise for him to come here to the house first, and for me to by and by tag along and drop in, and let on to be a stranger. But it was a mistake, Aunt Sally. This ain't no healthy place for a stranger to come."

"No—not impudent whelps,[4] Sid. You ought to had your jaws boxed;[5] I hain't been so put out since I don't know when. But I don't care, I don't mind the <u>terms</u>—I'd be willing to stand a thousand such jokes to have you here. Well, to think of that performance! I don't deny it, I was most <u>putrified</u> with astonishment when you give me that smack."

We had dinner out in that broad open passage betwixt the house and the kitchen; and there was things enough on that

◄ *When does Aunt Sally forgive Tom? Whom does he tell her he is?*

---

4. **whelps.** Puppies
5. **boxed.** Struck on both sides with the fists

Words For Everyday Use	**im • pu • dent** (im´pyoo dənt) *adj.*, disrespectful, impertinent
	fend (fend) *vt.*, repel, resist
	terms (tʉrms) *n.*, conditions of a contract
	pu • tre • fied (pyoo´trə fīd) *adj.*, decayed, rotten

table for seven families—and all hot, too; none of your flabby, tough meat that's laid in a cupboard in a damp cellar all night and tastes like a hunk of old cold <u>cannibal</u> in the morning. Uncle Silas he asked a pretty long blessing over it, but it was worth it; and it didn't cool it a bit, neither, the way I've seen them kind of interruptions do lots of times.

There was a considerable good deal of talk all the afternoon, and me and Tom was on the lookout all the time; but it warn't no use, they didn't happen to say nothing about any runaway nigger, and we was afraid to try to work up to it. But at supper, at night, one of the little boys says:

"Pa, mayn't Tom and Sid and me go to the show?"

"No," says the old man, "I reckon there ain't going to be any; and you couldn't go if there was; because the runaway nigger told Burton and me all about that scandalous show, and Burton said he would tell the people; so I reckon they've drove the owdacious loafers out of town before this time."

So there it was!—but *I* couldn't help it. Tom and me was to sleep in the same room and bed; so, being tired, we bid goodnight and went up to bed right after supper, and clumb out of the window and down the lightning rod, and shoved for the town; for I didn't believe anybody was going to give the king and the duke a hint, and so if I didn't hurry up and give them one they'd get into trouble sure.

On the road Tom he told me all about how it was reckoned I was murdered, and how Pap disappeared pretty soon, and didn't come back no more, and what a stir there was when Jim run away; and I told Tom all about our "Royal Nonesuch" rapscallions, and as much of the raft voyage as I had time to; and as we struck into the town and up through the middle of it—here comes a raging rush of people with torches, and an awful whooping and yelling, and banging tin pans and blowing horns; and we jumped to one side to let them go by; and as they went by I see they had the king and the duke astraddle of a rail—that is, I knowed it *was* the king and the duke, though they was all over tar and feathers, and didn't look like nothing in the world that was human—just looked like a couple of monstrous big soldier-plumes.[6] Well, it made me sick to see it; and I was sorry for

▶ To what show are the children referring? Why does Huck want to sneak over to the show?

▶ What are people doing to the king and the duke? How does Huck feel as he watches the "poor pitiful rascals"? What does he observe about human beings?

---

5. **soldier-plumes.** Feathers on a military hat

Words For Everyday Use	**can • ni • bal** (kan´ə bəl) *n.*, member of a species, especially human beings, that eats others of its kind

them poor pitiful rascals, it seemed like I couldn't ever feel any hardness against them any more in the world. It was a dreadful thing to see. Human beings *can* be awful cruel to one another.

We see we was too late—couldn't do no good. We asked some <u>stragglers</u> about it, and they said everybody went to the show looking very innocent; and laid low and kept dark till the poor old king was in the middle of his <u>cavortings</u> on the stage; then somebody give a signal, and the house rose up and went for them.

So we poked along back home, and I warn't feeling so <u>brash</u> as I was before, but kind of ornery, and humble, and to blame, somehow—though *I* hadn't done nothing. But that's always the way; it don't make no difference whether you do right or wrong, a person's conscience ain't got no sense, and just goes for him *anyway*. If I had a yaller dog that didn't know no more than a person's conscience does I would pison him. It takes up more room than all the rest of a person's insides, and yet ain't no good, nohow. Tom Sawyer he says the same.

◄ *What is Huck's opinion of a person's "conscience"?*

Words For Everyday Use

strag • gler (strag′lər) *n.*, one who wanders away from the group

ca • vor • ting (kə vort′iŋ) *n.*, prancing, leaping about

brash (brash) *adj.*, bold

Responding to the Selection

Describe your feelings toward the king and the duke when you learn that the king has betrayed Jim for forty dollars. How does Huck feel? Do you understand why Huck has trouble deciding what he should do about Jim? Have you ever had to decide against popular opinion in favor of what you believed to be right?

Reviewing the Selection

Recalling and Interpreting

1. **R:** When the king goes ashore and doesn't return, what makes Huck think "something is a-brewing"? He also thinks maybe it is "a chance for *the* chance." What chance does Huck have in mind? What is actually happening while the others wait for the king to return?

2. **I:** Why do you think Huck has such a difficult time getting rid of the king and the duke? Have the king and the duke helped Jim and Huck at all, or was their presence on the raft completely unnecessary?

3. **R:** After Huck finds out that Jim has been captured, he has a crisis of conscience as he tries to decide what to do. What does he think is the right thing to do? Why? Does he decide to do what he believes is the right thing?

4. **I:** What forces are at work in Huck as he struggles to decide what to do about Jim? Is the choice he makes really the "wicked" choice, as he says?

5. **R:** What eventually happens to the duke and king?

6. **I:** Why do you think Huck wants to warn the king and the duke? What does Huck's sympathy for them reveal about his character?

7. **R:** As Huck spins a story for Aunt Sally, what does he tell her happened to the boat he was supposedly traveling on? What is her reaction? How does Huck answer her when she asks if anyone was hurt?

8. **I:** How do you feel about Huck's response to the question about who was hurt on the boat? Why do you think he said this? Why is Aunt Sally not shocked? Do you think Huck's response reflects how he really feels, or is he playing a part?

Synthesizing

9. When Huck watches the king and duke being punished, he says "It was a dreadful thing to see. Human beings *can* be awful cruel to one another." What other incidents of human cruelty in this section leave Huck baffled and confused? Why are such things beyond his understanding?

10. Why does Huck believe that Tom should not want to help rescue Jim? Why does he believe Tom should feel differently?

Understanding Literature (QUESTIONS FOR DISCUSSION)

1. **Character.** A **character** is a person who figures in the action of a literary work. A **one-dimensional character**, or **flat character** is one who exhibits a single dominant quality. A **three-dimensional, full,** or **rounded character** is one who exhibits the complexity of traits associated with actual human beings. Would you call the king and the duke one-dimensional or three-dimensional? To formulate your response, think about the following questions: Do the king and the duke ever feel any remorse for their actions? What traits do they exhibit? How do they compare with characters like Huck and Jim, who are three-dimensional? Explain your response.

2. **Irony.** **Irony** is the difference between appearance and reality. A type of irony is **dramatic irony,** in which something is known by the reader or audience but unknown to the character. How is Huck's crisis of conscience and the decision he makes about Jim an example of dramatic irony? Consider how he describes his decision to help Jim: "a low-down thing," "wicked," and "a disgrace." What about his statement, "All right, then, I'll *go* to hell"? How do you think Twain intended the reader to regard Huck's decisions? What does the reader know that Huck does not know? Does Huck's belief that his actions and his decision to follow his heart are wrong make his decision braver? more noble? Explain.

CHAPTER 34

We Cheer Up Jim

We stopped talking, and got to thinking. By and by Tom says:

"Looky here, Huck, what fools we are to not think of it before! I bet I know where Jim is."

"No! Where?"

"In that hut down by the ash-hopper. Why, looky here. When we was at dinner, didn't you see a nigger man go in there with some vittles?"[1]

"Yes."

"What did you think the vittles was for?"

"For a dog."

"So 'd I. Well, it wasn't for a dog."

"Why?"

"Because part of it was watermelon."

"So it was—I noticed it. Well, it does beat all that I never thought about a dog not eating watermelon. It shows how a body can see and don't see at the same time."

"Well, the nigger unlocked the padlock when he went in, and he locked it again when he came out. He fetched uncle a key about the time we got up from table—same key, I bet. Watermelon shows man, lock shows prisoner; and it ain't likely there's two prisoners on such a little plantation, and where the people's all so kind and good. Jim's the prisoner. All right—I'm glad we found it out detective fashion; I wouldn't give shucks for any other way. Now you work your mind, and study out a plan to steal Jim, and I will study out one, too; and we'll take the one we like the best."

What a head for just a boy to have! If I had Tom Sawyer's head I wouldn't trade it off to be a duke, nor mate of a steamboat, nor clown in a circus, nor nothing I can think of. I went to thinking out a plan, but only just to be doing something; I knowed very well where the right plan was going to come from. Pretty soon Tom says:

"Ready?"

"Yes," I says.

"All right—bring it out."

"My plan is this," I says. "We can easy find out if it's Jim in there. Then get up my canoe tomorrow night, and fetch my raft over from the island. Then the first dark night that

---

1. **vittles.** Victuals; food

► Where does Tom believe Jim is?

► What does Tom say that he and Huck should do in trying to find the best way to steal Jim? How does Huck feel about Tom's mind?

comes steal the key out of the old man's britches after he goes to bed, and shove off down the river on the raft with Jim, hiding daytimes and running nights, the way me and Jim used to do before. Wouldn't that plan work?"

"*Work*? Why, cert'nly it would work, like rats a-fighting. But it's too blame' simple; there ain't nothing to it. What's the good of a plan that ain't no more trouble than that? It's as mild as goose-milk. Why, Huck, it wouldn't make no more talk than breaking into a soap factory."

◄ Why does Tom dislike Huck's plan? Why is Tom's plan better? Is Huck surprised that he likes Tom's plan more than his own?

I never said nothing, because I warn't expecting nothing different; but I knowed mighty well that whenever he got *his* plan ready it wouldn't have none of them objections to it.

And it didn't. He told me what it was, and I see in a minute it was worth fifteen of mine for style, and would make Jim just as free a man as mine would, and maybe get us all killed besides. So I was satisfied, and said we would waltz in on it. I needn't tell what it was here, because I knowed it wouldn't stay the way it was. I knowed he would be changing it around every which way as we went along, and heaving in new bullinesses wherever he got a chance. And that is what he done.

Well, one thing was dead sure, and that was that Tom Sawyer was in earnest, and was actly going to help steal that nigger out of slavery. That was the thing that was too many for me. Here was a boy that was respectable and well brung up; and had a character to lose; and folks at home that had characters; and he was bright and not leather-headed; and knowing and not ignorant; and not mean, but kind; and yet here he was, without any more pride, or rightness, or feeling, than to stoop to this business, and make himself a shame, and his family a shame, before everybody. I *couldn't* understand it no way at all. It was outrageous, and I knowed I ought to just up and tell him so; and so be his true friend, and let him quit the thing right where he was and save himself. And I *did* start to tell him; but he shut me up, and says:

◄ Why is Huck concerned about his friend? What is Tom's response to Huck's concern?

"Don't you reckon I know what I'm about? Don't I gen'rly know what I'm about?"

"Yes."

"Didn't I *say* I was going to help steal the nigger?"

"Yes."

"*Well*, then."

That's all he said, and that's all I said. It warn't no use to say any more; because when he said he'd do a thing, he always done it. But *I* couldn't make out how he was willing to go into this thing; so I just let it go, and never bothered no more about it. If he was bound to have it so, *I* couldn't help it.

When we got home the house was all dark and still; so we went on down to the hut by the ash-hopper for to examine it.

We went through the yard so as to see what the hounds would do. They knowed us, and didn't make no more noise than country dogs is always doing when anything comes by in the night. When we got to the cabin we took a look at the front and the two sides; and on the side I warn't acquainted with—which was the north side—we found a square window hole, up tolerable high, with just one stout board nailed across it. I says:

"Here's the ticket. This hole's big enough for Jim to get through if we wrench off the board."

Tom says:

"It's as simple as tit-tat-toe, three-in-a-row, and as easy as playing hooky. I should *hope* we can find a way that's a little more complicated than that, Huck Finn."

"Well, then," I says, "how'll it do to saw him out, the way I done before I was murdered that time?"

"That's more *like*," he says. "It's real mysterious, and troublesome, and good," he says; "but I bet we can find a way that's twice as long. There ain't no hurry; le's keep on looking around."

Betwixt the hut and the fence, on the back side, was a lean-to that joined the hut at the eaves, and was made out of plank. It was as long as the hut, but narrow—only about six foot wide. The door to it was at the south end, and was padlocked. Tom he went to the soap kettle and searched around, and fetched back the iron thing they lift the lid with; so he took it and prized out one of the staples. The chain fell down, and we opened the door and went in, and shut it, and struck a match, and see the shed was only built against a cabin and hadn't no connection with it; and there warn't no floor to the shed, nor nothing in it but some old rusty played-out hoes and spades and picks and a crippled plow. The match went out, and so did we, and shoved in the staple again, and the door was locked as good as ever. Tom was joyful. He says;

▶ Why is Tom joyful? What does he decide they'll have to do to get Jim out?

"Now we're all right. We'll *dig* him out. It'll take about a week!"

Then we started for the house, and I went in the back door—you only have to pull a buckskin latchstring,[2] they don't fasten the doors—but that warn't romantical enough for Tom Sawyer; no way would do him but he must climb up the lightning rod.[3] But after he got up halfway about three times, and missed fire and fell every time, and the last time most busted his brains out, he thought he'd got to give it up; but after he was rested he allowed he would give her one

---

2. **buckskin latchstring.** String made out of deerhide that lifted a bar, thus opening a door

3. **lightning rod.** Metal stick fastened high on a building and grounded below; it attracts lightning bolts and conducts the electricity away from the structure.

more turn for luck, and this time he made the trip.

In the morning we was up at break of day, and down to the nigger cabins to pet the dogs and make friends with the nigger that fed Jim—if it *was* Jim that was being fed. The niggers was just getting through breakfast and starting for the fields; and Jim's nigger was piling up a tin pan with bread and meat and things; and whilst the others was leaving, the key come from the house.

This nigger had a good-natured, chuckleheaded face, and his wool[4] was all tied up in little bunches with thread. That was to keep witches off. He said the witches was pestering him awful these nights, and making him see all kinds of strange things, and hear all kinds of strange words and noises, and he didn't believe he was ever witched so long before in his life. He got so worked up, and got to running on so about his troubles, he forgot all about what he'd been a-going to do. So Tom says:

"What's the vittles for? Going to feed the dogs?"

The nigger kind of smiled around graduly over his face, like when you heave a brickbat in a mud puddle, and he says:

"Yes, Mars Sid, *a* dog. Cur'us dog, too. Does you want to go en look at 'im?"

"Yes."

I hunched Tom, and whispers:

"You going, right here in the daybreak? *That* warn't the plan."

"No, it warn't; but it's the plan *now*."

So, drat him, we went along, but I didn't like it much. When we got in we couldn't hardly see anything, it was so dark; but Jim was there, sure enough, and could see us; and he sings out:

"Why, *Huck!* En good *lan'!* ain' dat Misto Tom?"

I just knowed how it would be; I just expected it. *I* didn't know nothing to do; and if I had I couldn't 'a' done it, because that nigger busted in and says:

"Why, de gracious sakes! do he know you genlmen?"

We could see pretty well now. Tom he looked at the nigger, steady and kind of wondering, and says:

"Does *who* know us?"

"Why, dis-yer runaway nigger."

"I don't reckon he does; but what put that into your head?"

"What *put* it dar? Didn' he jis' dis minute sing out like he knowed you?"

Tom says, in a puzzled-up kind of way:

"Well, that's mighty curious. *Who* sung out? *When* did he sing out? *What* did he sing out?" And turns to me, perfectly ca'm, and says, "Did *you* hear anybody sing out?"

◀ What does Tom do that isn't part of the plan? What does Jim do when he sees them? In what way might this disturb their plan?

◀ What do Huck and Tom say to the man who hears Jim call them by name?

---

4. **wool.** Hair

Of course there warn't nothing to be said but the one thing; so I says:

"No; *I* ain't heard nobody say nothing."

Then he turns to Jim, and looks him over like he never see him before, and says:

"Did you sing out?"

"No, sah," says Jim; " *I* hain't said nothing, sah."

"Not a word?"

"No, sah, I hain't said a word."

"Did you ever see us before?"

"No, sah; not as *I* knows on."

So Tom turns to the nigger, which was looking wild and <u>distressed</u>, and says, kind of <u>severe</u>:

"What do you reckon's the matter with you, anyway? What made you think somebody sung out?"

"Oh, it's de dad-blame' witches, sah, en I wisht I was dead, I do. Dey's awluz at it, sah, en dey do mos' kill me, dey sk'yers me so. Please to don't tell nobody 'bout it sah, er ole Mars Silas he'll scole me; 'kase he say dey *ain't* no witches. I jis' wish to goodness he was heah now—den what would he say! I jis' bet he couldn' fine no way to git aroun' it *dis* time. But it's awluz jis' so; people dat's *sot*,[5] stays sot; dey won't look into noth'n' en fine it out f'r deyselves, en when *you* fine it out en tell um 'bout it, dey doan' b'lieve you."

Tom give him a dime, and said we wouldn't tell nobody; and told him to buy some more thread to tie up his wool with; and then looks at Jim, and says:

"I wonder if Uncle Silas is going to hang this nigger. If I was to catch a nigger that was ungrateful enough to run away, *I* wouldn't give him up, I'd hang him." And whilst the nigger stepped to the door to look at the dime and bite it to see if it was good, he whispers to Jim and says:

"Don't ever let on to know us. And if you hear any digging going on nights, it's us; we're going to set you free."

Jim only had time to grab us by the hand and squeeze it; then the nigger come back, and we said we'd come again some time if the nigger wanted us to; and he said he would, more particular if it was dark, because the witches went for him mostly in the dark, and it was good to have folks around then.

---

5. **sot.** Set

Words For Everyday Use	**dis • tressed** (dis strest´) *adj.*, anxious, troubled
	se • vere (sə vir´) *adj.*, harsh, strict

CHAPTER 35

Dark, Deep-laid Plans

It would be most an hour yet till breakfast, so we left and struck down into the woods; because Tom said we got to have *some* light to see how to dig by, and a lantern makes too much, and might get us into trouble; what we must have was a lot of them rotten chunks that's called fox fire,[1] and just makes a soft kind of a glow when you lay them in a dark place. We fetched an armful and hid it in the weeds, and set down to rest, and Tom says, kind of dissatisfied:

◀ What do Huck and Tom gather so that they can see as they dig?

"Blame it, this whole thing is just as easy and awkward as it can be. And so it makes it so rotten difficult to get up a difficult plan. There ain't no watchman to be drugged—now there *ought* to be a watchman. There ain't even a dog to give a sleeping-mixture to. And there's Jim chained by one leg, with a ten-foot chain, to the leg of his bed: why, all you got to do is to lift up the bedstead and slip off the chain. And Uncle Silas he trusts everybody; sends the key to the punkin-headed nigger, and don't send nobody to watch the nigger. Jim could 'a' got out of that window-hole before this, only there wouldn't be no use trying to travel with a ten-foot chain on his leg. Why, drat it, Huck, it's the stupidest arrangement I ever see. You got to invent *all* the difficulties. Well, we can't help it; we got to do the best we can with the materials we've got. Anyhow, there's one thing—there's more honor in getting him out through a lot of difficulties and dangers, where there warn't one of them <u>furnished</u> to you by the people who it was their duty to furnish them, and you had to <u>contrive</u> them all out of your own head. Now look at just that one thing of the lantern. When you come down to the cold facts, we simply got to *let on* that a lantern's resky. Why, we could work with a torchlight procession if we wanted to, I believe. Now, whilst I think of it, we got to hunt up something to make a saw out of the first chance we get."

◀ What does Tom call the "stupidest arrangement I ever see"? What does he have to invent? In what does he believe there is more honor?

"What do we want of a saw?"

"What do we *want* of a saw? Hain't we got to saw the leg of Jim's bed off, so as to get the chain loose?"

---

1. **fox fire.** Phosphorescent glow given off by rotting wood

Words For Everyday Use	**fur • nish** (fu̇r´nish) *vt.*, provide, supply **con • trive** (kən trīv´) *vt.*, think up, devise

▶ Why does Tom object to Huck's plan to lift the bed and slip off the chain? What does Tom feel they need to do? From where does he get his ideas?

"Why, you just said a body could lift up the bedstead and slip the chain off."

"Well, if that ain't just like you, Huck Finn. You *can* get up the infant-schooliest ways of going at a thing. Why, hain't you ever read any books at all?—Baron Trenck, nor Casanova, nor Benvenuto Chelleeny, nor Henri IV,[2] nor none of them heroes? Who ever heard of getting a prisoner loose in such an old-maidy way as that? No; the way all the best <u>authorities</u> does is to saw the bed-leg in two, and leave it just so, and swallow the sawdust, so it can't be found, and put some dirt and grease around the sawed place so the very keenest seneskal[3] can't see no sign of it's being sawed, and thinks the bed-leg is perfectly sound. Then, the night you're ready, fetch the leg a kick, down she goes; slip off your chain, and there you are. Nothing to do but hitch your rope ladder to the battlements, shin down it, break your leg in the moat—because a rope ladder is nineteen foot too short, you know—and there's your horses and your trusty vassles,[4] and they scoop you up and fling you across a saddle, and away you go to your native Langudoc, or Navarre, or wherever it is. It's gaudy, Huck. I wish there was a moat to this cabin. If we get time, the night of the escape, we'll dig one."

I says:

"What do we want of a moat when we're going to snake him out from under the cabin?"

But he never heard me. He had forgot me and everything else. He had his chin in his hand, thinking. Pretty soon he sighs and shakes his head; then sighs again, and says:

"No, it wouldn't do—there ain't necessity enough for it."

"For what?" I says.

"Why, to saw Jim's leg off," he says.

"Good land!" I says; "why, there ain't *no* necessity for it. And what would you want to saw his leg off for, anyway?"

"Well, some of the best authorities has done it. They couldn't get the chain off, so they just cut their hand off and shoved. And a leg would be better still. But we got to let that go. There ain't necessity enough in this case; and, besides, Jim's a nigger, and wouldn't understand the reasons for it,

▶ What wild idea does Tom consider, but regretfully reject because there isn't "necessity enough"? What does he decide they need to make for Jim? Does Huck agree?

---

2. **Baron Trenck . . . Henry IV.** Four historical figures who made famous escapes; Chelleeny is Cellini

3. **seneskal.** Seneschal; the powerful steward or administrator of a medieval lord

4. **battlements . . . moat . . . vassles.** Notched walls of a castle; flooded pit surrounding a castle; and servants of a medieval lord

| Words For Everyday Use | **au • thor • i • ty** (ə thôr′ə tē) *n.*, reliable source of information |

and how it's the custom in Europe; so we'll let it go. But there's one thing—he can have a rope ladder; we can tear up our sheets and make him a rope ladder easy enough. And we can send it to him in a pie; it's mostly done that way. And I've et worse pies."

"Why, Tom Sawyer, how you talk," I says; "Jim ain't got no use for a rope ladder."

"He *has* got use for it. How *you* talk, you better say; you don't know nothing about it. He's *got* to have a rope ladder; they all do."

"What in the nation can he *do* with it?"

"*Do* with it? He can hide it in his bed, can't he?" That's what they all do; and *he's* got to, too. Huck, you don't ever seem to want to do anything that's regular; you want to be starting something fresh all the time. S'pose he *don't* do nothing with it? ain't it there in his bed, for a clue, after he's gone? and don't you reckon they'll want clues? Of course they will. And you wouldn't leave them any? That would be a *pretty* howdy-do, *wouldn't* it! I never heard of such a thing."

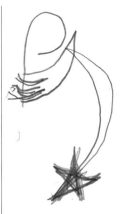

◀ *Does Tom seem to be most interested in saving Jim or having an adventure?*

"Well," I says, "if it's in the regulations, and he's got to have it, all right, let him have it; because I don't wish to go back on no regulations; but there's one thing, Tom Sawyer—if we go to tearing up our sheets to make Jim a rope ladder, we're going to get into trouble with Aunt Sally, just as sure as you're born. Now, the way I look at it, a hickry-bark ladder don't cost nothing, and don't waste nothing, and is just as good to load up a pie with, and hide in a straw tick, as any rag ladder you can start; and as for Jim, he ain't had no experience, and so he don't care what kind of a —"

"Oh, shucks, Huck Finn, if I was as ignorant as you I'd keep still—that's what *I'd* do. Who ever heard of a state prisoner escaping by a hickry-bark ladder? Why, it's perfectly ridiculous."

"Well, all right, Tom, fix it your own way; but if you'll take my advice, you'll let me borrow a sheet off of the clothesline."

He said that would do. And that gave him another idea, and he says:

"Borrow a shirt, too."

"What do we want of a shirt, Tom?"

"Want it for Jim to keep a journal on."

"Journal your granny—*Jim* can't write."

"S'pose he *can't* write—he can make marks on the shirt, can't he, if we make him a pen out of an old pewter spoon or a piece of an old iron barrel-hoop?"

"Why, Tom, we can pull a feather out of a goose and make him a better one; and quicker, too."

"*Prisoners* don't have geese running around the donjon-keep[5] to pull pens out of, you muggins. They *always* make

◀ *Why does Tom feel they need to borrow a shirt? Why does Huck find this idea ridiculous?*

5. **donjon-keep.** Locked dungeon

their pens out of the hardest, toughest, troublesomest piece of old brass candlestick or something like that they can get their hands on; and it takes them weeks and weeks and months and months to file it out, too, because they've got to do it by rubbing it on the wall. *They* wouldn't use a goose-quill if they had it. It ain't regular."

"Well, then, what'll we make him the ink out of?"

"Many makes it out of iron-rust and tears; but that's the common sort and women; the best authorities uses their own blood. Jim can do that; and when he wants to send any little common ordinary mysterious message to let the world know where he's captivated, he can write it on the bottom of a tin plate with a fork and throw it out of the window. The Iron Mask[6] always done that, and it's a blame' good way, too."

"Jim ain't got no tin plates. They feed him in a pan."

"That ain't nothing; we can get him some."

"Can't nobody *read* his plates."

"That ain't got anything to *do* with it, Huck Finn. All *he's* got to do is to write on the plate and throw it out. You don't *have* to be able to read it. Why, half the time you can't read anything a prisoner writes on a tin plate, or anywhere else."

"Well, then, what's the sense in wasting the plates?"

"Why, blame it all, it ain't the *prisoner's* plates."

"But it's *somebody's* plates, ain't it?"

"Well, spos'n it is? What does the *prisoners* care whose—"

He broke off there, because we heard the breakfast-horn blowing. So we cleared out for the house.

► According to Tom, why is it acceptable for them to steal right now?

Along during the morning I borrowed a sheet and a white shirt off of the clothesline; and I found an old sack and put them in it, and we went down and got the fox fire, and put that in too. I called it borrowing, because that was what Pap always called it; but Tom said it warn't borrowing, it was stealing. He said we was representing prisoners; and prisoners don't care how they get a thing so they get it, and nobody don't blame them for it, either. It ain't no crime in a prisoner to steal the thing he needs to get away with, Tom said; it's his right; and so, as long as we was representing a prisoner, we had a perfect right to steal anything on this place we had the least use for to get ourselves out of prison with. He said if we warn't prisoners it would be a very different thing, and nobody but a mean, ornery person would steal when he warn't a prisoner. So we allowed we would steal everything there was that come handy. And yet he made a mighty fuss, one day, after that, when I stole a watermelon out of the nigger patch and eat it; and he made me go and give the niggers a dime without

► Why does Tom scold Huck for stealing a watermelon? Why, according to Tom, is stealing something like that not acceptable? What are the only things acceptable to steal?

6. **The Iron Mask.** Refers to a mysterious masked prisoner, a character in *The Man in the Iron Mask*, a novel by Alexander Dumas

telling them what it was for. Tom said that what he meant was, we could steal anything we *needed*. Well, I says, I needed the watermelon. But he said I didn't need it to get out of prison with; there's where the difference was. He said if I'd 'a' wanted it to hide a knife in, and smuggle it to Jim to kill the seneskal with, it would 'a' been all right. So I let it go at that, though I couldn't see no advantage in my representing a prisoner if I got to set down and chaw over a lot of gold-leaf <u>distinctions</u> like that every time I see a chance to hog a watermelon.

Well, as I was saying, we waited that morning till everybody was settled down to business, and nobody in sight around the yard; then Tom he carried the sack into the lean-to whilst I stood off a piece to keep watch. By and by he come out, and we went and set down on the woodpile to talk. He says:

"Everything's all right now except tools; and that's easy fixed."

"Tools?" I says.

"Yes."

"Tools for what?"

"Why, to dig with. We ain't a-going to *gnaw* him out, are we?"

"Ain't them old crippled picks and things in there good enough to dig a nigger out with?" I says.

He turns on me, looking pitying enough to make a body cry, and says:

"Huck Finn, did you *ever* hear of a prisoner having picks and shovels, and all the modern conveniences in his wardrobe to dig himself out with? Now I want to ask you— if you got any reasonableness in you at all—what kind of a show would *that* give him to be a hero? Why, they might as well lend him the key and done with it. Picks and shovels— why, they wouldn't furnish 'em to a king."

"Well, then," I says, "if we don't want the picks and shovels, what do we want?"

"A couple of case knives."[7]

"To dig the foundations out from under that cabin with?"

"Yes."

"Confound it, it's foolish, Tom."

"It don't make no difference how foolish it is, it's the *right* way—and it's the regular way. And there ain't no *other* way, that ever *I* heard of, and I've read all the books that gives any information about these things. They always dig out with a

◄ *Why won't Tom allow them to use picks and shovels? What does he insist they use for digging?*

---

7. **case knives.** Long kitchen knives

case knife—and not through dirt, mind you; generly it's through solid rock. And it takes them weeks and weeks and weeks, and for ever and ever. Why, look at one of them prisoners in the bottom dungeon of the Castle Deef,[8] in the harbor of Marseilles, that dug himself out that way; how long was *he* at it, you reckon?"

"I don't know."

"Well, guess."

"I don't know. A month and a half."

"*Thirty-seven year*—and he come out in China. *That's* the kind. I wish the bottom of *this* fortress was solid rock."

"*Jim* don't know nobody in China."

"What's *that* got to do with it? Neither did that other fellow. But you're always a-wandering off on a side issue. Why can't you stick to the main point?"

"All right—*I* don't care where he comes out, so he *comes* out; and Jim don't, either, I reckon. But there's one thing, anyway—Jim's too old to be dug out with a case knife. He won't last."

"Yes he will *last*, too. You don't reckon it's going to take thirty-seven years to dig out through a *dirt* foundation, do you?"

"How long will it take, Tom?"

"Well, we can't resk being as long as we ought to, because it mayn't take very long for Uncle Silas to hear from down there by New Orleans. He'll hear Jim ain't from there. Then his next move will be to advertise Jim, or something like that. So we can't resk being as long digging him out as we ought to. By rights I reckon we ought to be a couple of years; but we can't. Things being so uncertain, what I recommend is this: that we really dig right in, as quick as we can; and after that, we can *let on*, to ourselves, that we was at it thirty-seven years. Then we can snatch him out and rush him away the first time there's an alarm. Yes, I reckon that'll be the best way."

"Now, there's *sense* in that," I says. "Letting on don't cost nothing; letting on ain't no trouble; and if it's any object, I don't mind letting on we was at it a hundred and fifty year. It wouldn't strain me none, after I got my hand in. So I'll mosey along now, and smouch a couple of case knives."

"Smouch three," he says; "we want one to make a saw out of."

"Tom, if it ain't unregular and irreligious to sejest it," I says, "there's an old rusty saw-blade around yonder sticking under the weather boarding behind the smokehouse."

He looked kind of weary and discouraged-like, and says:

"It ain't no use to try to learn you nothing, Huck. Run along and smouch the knives—three of them." So I done it.

▶ *Why, according to Tom, can't they take as long as he feels they should to free Jim? What will they have to do instead?*

---

8. **Chateau d'If.** Prison that held the hero of *The Count of Monte Cristo*

CHAPTER 36

Trying to Help Jim

As soon as we reckoned everybody was asleep that night we went down the lightning rod, and shut ourselves up in the lean-to, and got out our pile of fox fire, and went to work. We cleared everything out of the way, about four or five foot along the middle of the bottom log. Tom said we was right behind Jim's bed now, and we'd dig in under it, and when we got through there couldn't nobody in the cabin ever know there was any hole there, because Jim's counterpin[1] hung down most to the ground, and you'd have to raise it up and look under to see the hole. So we dug and dug with the case knives till most midnight; and then we was dog-tired, and our hands was blistered, and yet you couldn't see we'd done anything hardly. At last I says:

"This ain't no thirty-seven year job; this is a thirty-eight year job, Tom Sawyer."

He never said nothing. But he sighed, and pretty soon he stopped digging, and then for a good little while I knowed that he was thinking. Then he says:

"It ain't no use, Huck, it ain't a-going to work. If we was prisoners it would, because then we'd have as many years as we wanted, and no hurry; and we wouldn't get but a few minutes to dig, every day, while they was changing watches, and so our hands wouldn't get blistered, and we could keep it up right along, year in and year out, and do it right, and the way it ought to be done. But *we* can't fool along; we got to rush; we ain't got no time to spare. If we was to put in another night this way we'd have to knock off for a week to let our hands get well—couldn't touch a case knife with them sooner."

"Well, then, what we going to do, Tom?"

"I'll tell you. It ain't right, and it ain't moral, and I wouldn't like it to get out; but there ain't only just the one way: we got to dig him out with the picks, and let on it's case knives."

"Now you're talking!" I says; "your head gets leveler and leveler all the time, Tom Sawyer," I says. "Picks is the thing, moral or no moral; and as for me, I don't care shucks for the morality of it, nohow. When I start in to steal a nigger, or a watermelon, or a Sunday school book, I ain't no ways

◄ *What do Huck and Tom realize about the case knives? Why don't they have the time most prisoners would have? What does Tom decide that they can do?*

---

1. **counterpin.** Counterpane; bedspread

particular how it's done so it's done. What I want is my nigger; or what I want is my watermelon; or what I want is my Sunday school book; and if a pick's the handiest thing, that's the thing I'm a-going to dig that nigger or that watermelon or that Sunday school book out with; and I don't give a dead rat what the authorities thinks about it nuther."

"Well," he says, "there's excuse for picks and letting-on in a case like this; if it warn't so, I wouldn't approve of it, nor I wouldn't stand by and see the rules broke—because right is right, and wrong is wrong, and a body ain't got no business doing wrong when he ain't ignorant and knows better. It might answer for you to dig Jim out with a pick, without any letting on, because you don't know no better; but it wouldn't for me, because I do know better. Gimme a case knife."

He had his own by him, but I handed him mine. He flung it down, and says:

"Gimme a *case knife*."

I didn't know just what to do—but then I thought. I scratched around amongst the old tools, and got a pickaxe and give it to him, and he took it and went to work, and never said a word.

He was always just that particular. Full of <u>principle</u>.

So then I got a shovel, and then we picked and shoveled, turn about, and made the fur fly. We stuck to it about a half an hour, which was as long as we could stand up; but we had a good deal of a hole to show for it. When I got up stairs I looked out at the window and see Tom doing his level best with the lightning rod, but he couldn't come it, his hands was so sore. At last he says:

"It ain't no use, it can't be done. What you reckon I better do? Can't you think of no way?"

"Yes," I says, "but I reckon it ain't regular. Come up the stairs, and let on it's a lightning rod."

So he done it.

Next day Tom stole a pewter spoon and a brass candlestick in the house, for to make some pens for Jim out of, and six tallow candles; and I hung around the nigger cabins and laid for a chance, and stole three tin plates. Tom says it wasn't enough; but I said nobody wouldn't ever see the plates that Jim throwed out, because they'd fall in the dog-fennel and jimpson weeds under the window-hole—then we could tote

► What does Huck suggest Tom do instead of actually climbing a lightning rod?

Still pretending

Words For Everyday Use

prin • ci • ple (prin´sə pəl) *n.*, rule of right conduct

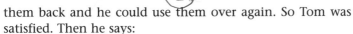

them back and he could use them over again. So Tom was satisfied. Then he says:

"Now, the thing to study out is, how to get the things to Jim."

"Take them in through the hole," I says, "when we get it done."

He only just looked <u>scornful</u>, and said something about nobody ever heard of such an idiotic idea, and then he went to studying. By and by he said he had ciphered out two or three ways, but there warn't no need to decide on any of them yet. Said we'd got to post Jim first.

That night we went down the lightning rod a little after ten, and took one of the candles along, and listened under the window-hole, and heard Jim snoring; so we pitched it in, and it didn't wake him. Then we whirled in with the pick and shovel, and in about two hours and a half the job was done. We crept in under Jim's bed and into the cabin, and pawed around and found the candle and lit it, and stood over Jim awhile, and found him looking hearty and healthy, and then we woke him up gentle and gradual. He was so glad to see us he most cried; and called us honey, and all the pet names he could think of; and was for having us hunt up a cold chisel to cut the chain off of his leg with right away, and clearing out without losing any time. But Tom he showed him how unregular it would be, and set down and told him all about our plans, and how we could <u>alter</u> them in a minute any time there was an alarm; and not to be the least afraid, because we would see he got away, sure. So Jim he said it was all right, and we set there and talked over old times awhile, and then Tom asked a lot of questions, and when Jim told him Uncle Silas come in every day or two to pray with him, and Aunt Sally come in to see if he was comfortable and had plenty to eat, and both of them was kind as they could be, Tom says:

"*Now* I know how to fix it. We'll send you some things by them."

I said, "Don't do nothing of the kind; it's one of the most jackass ideas I ever struck"; but he never paid no attention to me; went right on. It was his way when he'd got his plans set.

So he told Jim how we'd have to smuggle in the rope-ladder pie and other large things by Nat, the nigger that fed him, and

◄ When does Tom "pay no attention" to Huck? How does Tom intend to smuggle items into Jim's room? What is Jim's attitude toward these plans?

Words
For
Everyday
Use

scorn • ful (skôrn´fəl) *adj.*, contemptuous, disdainful
al • ter (ôl´tər) *vt.*, change

he must be on the lookout, and not be surprised, and not let Nat see him open them; and we would put small things in uncle's coatpockets and he must steal them out; and we would tie things to aunt's apron strings or put them in her apron pocket, if we got a chance; and told him what they would be and what they was for. And told him how to keep a journal on the shirt with his blood, and all that. He told him everything. Jim he couldn't see no sense in the most of it, but he allowed we was white folks and knowed better than him; so he was satisfied, and said he would do it all just as Tom said.

Jim had plenty corncob pipes and tobacco; so we had a right down good sociable time; then we crawled out through the hole, and so home to bed, with hands that looked like they'd been chawed. Tom was in high spirits. He said it was the best fun he ever had in his life, and the most intellectural;[2] and said if he only could see his way to it we would keep it up all the rest of our lives and leave Jim to our children to get out; for he believed Jim would come to like it better and better the more he got used to it. He said that in that way it could be strung out to as much as eighty year, and would be the best time on record. And he said it would make us all <u>celebrated</u> that had a hand in it.

▶ *How does Tom get the piece of candlestick in to Jim?*

In the morning we went out to the woodpile and chopped up the brass candlestick into handy sizes, and Tom put them and the pewter spoon in his pocket. Then we went to the nigger cabins, and while I got Nat's notice off, Tom shoved a piece of candlestick into the middle of a cornpone that was in Jim's pan, and we went along with Nat to see how it would work, and it just worked noble; when Jim bit into it it most mashed all his teeth out; and there warn't ever anything could 'a' worked better. Tom said so himself. Jim he never let on but what it was only just a piece of rock or something like that that's always getting into bread, you know; but after that he never bit into nothing but what he jabbed his fork into it in three or four places first.

And whilst we was a-standing there in the dimmish light, here comes a couple of the hounds bulging in from under Jim's bed; and they kept on piling in till there was eleven of them, and there warn't hardly room in there to get your

---

2. **intellectural.** Intellectual; appealing to the mind

Words For Everyday Use

cel • e • brat • ed (sel´ə brāt id) *adj.,* famous

breath. By jings, we forgot to fasten that lean-to door! The nigger Nat he only just hollered "Witches" once, and <u>keeled</u> over onto the floor amongst the dogs, and begun to groan like he was dying. Tom jerked the door open and flung out a slab of Jim's meat, and the dogs went for it, and in two seconds he was out himself and back again and shut the door, and I knowed he'd fixed the other door too. Then he went to work on the nigger, coaxing him and petting him, and asking him if he'd been imagining he saw something again. He raised up, and blinked his eyes around, and says:

"Mars Sid, you'll say I's a fool, but if I didn't b'lieve I see most a million dogs, er devils, er some'n, I wisht I may die right heah in dese tracks. I did, mos' sholy. Mars Sid, I felt um—I felt um, sah; dey was all over me. Dad fetch it, I jis' wisht I could git my han's on one er dem witches jis' wunst— on'y jis' wunst—it's all *I*'d ast. But mos'ly I wisht dey'd lemme 'lone, I does."

Tom says:

"Well, I tell you what *I* think. What makes them come here just at this runaway nigger's breakfast time? It's because they're hungry; that's the reason. You make them a witch pie; that's the thing for you to do."

"But my lan', Mars Sid, how's I gwyne to make 'm a witch pie? I doan' know how to make it. I hain't ever hearn er sich a thing b'fo'."

"Well, then, I'll have to make it myself."

"Will you do it, honey? will you? I'll wusshup de groun' und' yo' foot, I will!"

"All right, I'll do it, seeing it's you, and you've been good to us and showed us the runaway nigger. But you got to be mighty careful. When we come around, you turn your back; and then whatever we've put in the pan, don't you let on you see it at all. And don't you look when Jim unloads the pan—something might happen, I don't know what. And above all, don't you handle the witch-things."

"Hannel 'm, Mars Sid? What *is* you a-talkin' 'bout? I wouldn' lay de weight er my finger on um, not f'r ten hund'd thous'n billion dollars, I wouldn't."

Words
For
Everyday
Use

keel (kēl) *vi.*, fall

CHAPTER 37

Jim Gets His Witch Pie

That was all fixed. So then we went away and went to the rubbage pile in the back yard, where they keep the old boots, and rags, and pieces of bottles, and wore-out tin things, and all such truck, and scratched around and found an old tin washpan, and stopped up the holes as well as we could, to bake the pie in, and took it down cellar and stole it full of flour and started for breakfast, and found a couple of shingle-nails that Tom said would be handy for a prisoner to scrabble his name and sorrows on the dungeon walls with, and dropped one of them in Aunt Sally's apron pocket which was hanging on a chair, and t'other we stuck in the band of Uncle Silas's hat, which was on the bureau, because we heard the children say their pa and ma was going to the runaway nigger's house this morning, and then went to breakfast, and Tom dropped the pewter spoon in Uncle Silas's coat pocket, and Aunt Sally wasn't come yet, so we had to wait a little while.

▶ Why is Aunt Sally cross? Why does Huck's "heart fall" and Tom turn "kinder blue around the gills"?

And when she come she was hot and red and cross, and couldn't hardly wait for the blessing; and then she went to sluicing out coffee with one hand and cracking the handiest child's head with her thimble with the other, and says:

"I've hunted high and I've hunted low, and it does beat all what has become of your other shirt."

My heart fell down amongst my lungs and livers and things, and a hard piece of corn crust started down my throat after it and got met on the road with a cough, and was shot across the table, and took one of the children in the eye and curled him up like a fishing worm, and let a cry out of him the size of a war whoop, and Tom he turned kinder blue around the gills,[1] and it all amounted to a considerable state of things for about a quarter of a minute or as much as that, and I would 'a' sold out for half price if there was a bidder. But after that we was all right again—it was the sudden surprise of it that knocked us so kind of cold. Uncle Silas he says:

"It's most uncommon curious, I can't understand it. I know perfectly well I took it off, because—"

"Because you hain't got but one on. Just listen at the man! *I* know you took it off, and know it by a better way than your wool-gethering[2] memory, too, because it was on the clo's line

---

1. **turned kinder blue around the gills.** Looked sick or uncomfortable
2. **Wool-gethering.** Wool-gathering; absent-minded

yesterday—I see it there myself. But it's gone, that's the long and the short of it, and you'll just have to change to a red flann'l one till I can get time to make a new one. And it'll be the third I've made in two years. It just keeps a body on the jump to keep you in shirts; and whatever you do manage to *do* with 'm all is more'n *I* can make out. A body'd think you *would* learn to take some sort of care of 'em at your time of life."

"I know it, Sally, and I do try all I can. But it oughtn't to be altogether my fault, because, you know, I don't see them nor have nothing to do with them except when they're on me; and I don't believe I've ever lost one of them *off* of me."

"Well, it ain't *your* fault if you haven't, Silas; you'd 'a' done it if you could, I reckon. And the shirt ain't all that's gone, nuther. Ther's a spoon gone; and *that* ain't all. There was ten, and now ther's only nine. The calf got the shirt, I reckon, but the calf never took the spoon, *that's* certain."

"Why, what else is gone, Sally?"

"Ther's six *candles* gone—that's what. The rats could 'a' got the candles, and I reckon they did; I wonder they don't walk off with the whole place, the way you're always going to stop their holes and don't do it; and if they warn't fools they'd sleep in your hair, Silas—*you'd* never find it out; but you can't lay the *spoon* on the rats, and that I know."

"Well, Sally, I'm in fault, and I acknowledge it; I've been <u>remiss</u>; but I won't let tomorrow go by without stopping up them holes."

"Oh, I wouldn't hurry; next year 'll do. Matilda Angelina Araminta *Phelps!*"

Whack comes the thimble, and the child snatches her claws out of the sugar bowl without fooling around any. Just then the nigger woman steps on to the passage, and says:

"Missus, dey's a sheet gone."

"A sheet gone! Well, for the land's sake!"

"I'll stop up them holes today," says Uncle Silas, looking sorrowful.

"Oh, do shet up!—s'pose the rats took the sheet? Where's it gone, Lize?"

"Clah to goodness I hain't no notion, Miss' Sally. She wuz on de clo'sline yistiddy, but she done gone: she ain' dah no mo' now."

Words For Everyday Use

re • miss (ri mis´) *adj.*, careless, neglectful

▶ Besides the shirt, what other items are missing from the Phelps home?

"I reckon the world *is* coming to an end. I *never* see the beat of it in all my born days. A shirt, and a sheet, and a spoon, and six can—"

"Missus," comes a young yaller wench, "dey's a brass cannelstick miss'n."

"Cler out from here, you hussy, er I'll take a skillet to ye!"

Well, she was just a-biling. I begun to lay for a chance; I reckoned I would sneak out and go for the woods till the weather <u>moderated</u>. She kept a-raging right along, running her <u>insurrection</u> all by herself, and everybody else mighty meek and quiet; and at last Uncle Silas, looking kind of foolish, fishes up that spoon out of his pocket. She stopped, with her mouth open and her hands up; and as for me, I wished I was in Jeruslem or somewheres. But not long, because she says:

"It's *just* as I expected. So you had it in your pocket all the time; and like as not you've got the other things there, too. How'd it get there?"

"I reely don't know, Sally," he says, kind of apologizing, "or you know I would tell. I was a-studying over my text in Acts Seventeen[3] before breakfast, and I reckon I put it in there, not noticing, meaning to put my Testament in, and it must be so, because my Testament ain't in; but I'll go and see; and if the Testament is where I had it, I'll know I didn't put it in, and that will show that I laid the Testament down and took up the spoon, and—"

"Oh, for the land's sake! Give a body a rest! Go 'long now, the whole kit and biling of ye; and don't come nigh me again till I've got back my peace of mind."

I'd 'a' heard her if she'd 'a' said it to herself, let alone speaking it out; and I'd 'a' got up and obeyed her if I'd 'a' been dead. As we was passing through the setting room the old man he took up his hat, and the shingle-nail fell out on the floor, and he just merely picked it up and laid it on the mantel shelf, and never said nothing, and went out. Tom see him do it, and remembered about the spoon, and says:

▶ In what way does Mr. Phelps do Huck and Tom a "good turn" with the spoon? What will they do to pay him back?

"Well, it ain't no use to send things by *him* no more, he ain't reliable." Then he says: "But he done us a good turn with the spoon, anyway, without knowing it, and so we'll go and do him one without *him* knowing it—stop up his rat holes."

---

3. **Acts Seventeen.** Book and chapter of the New Testament

Words For Everyday Use	**mod • er • ate** (mäd´ər āt) *vi.*, become calm **in • su • rec • tion** (in´sə rek´shən) *n.*, rebellion, revolt

There was a noble good lot of them down cellar, and it took us a whole hour, but we done the job tight and good and shipshape. Then we heard steps on the stairs, and blowed out our light and hid; and here comes the old man, with a candle in one hand and a bundle of stuff in t'other, looking as absent-minded as year before last. He went a-mooning around, first to one rat hole and then another, till he'd been to them all. Then he stood about five minutes, picking tallow-drip[4] off of his candle and thinking. Then he turns off slow and dreamy towards the stairs, saying:

"Well, for the life of me I can't remember when I done it. I could show her now that I warn't to blame on account of the rats. But never mind—let it go. I reckon it wouldn't do no good."

And so he went on a-mumbling upstairs, and then we left. He was a mighty nice old man. And always is.

Tom was a good deal bothered about what to do for a spoon, but he said we'd got to have it; so he took a think. When he had ciphered it out he told me how we was to do; then we went and waited around the spoon basket till we see Aunt Sally coming, and then Tom went to counting the spoons and laying them out to one side, and I slid one of them up my sleeve, and Tom says:

"Why, Aunt Sally, there ain't but nine spoons *yet*."

She says:

"Go 'long to your play, and don't bother me. I know better, I counted 'm myself."

"Well, I've counted them twice, Aunty, and I can't make but nine."

She looked out of all patience, but of course she come to count—anybody would.

"I declare to gracious ther' *ain't* but nine!" she says. "Why, what in the world—plague *take* the things, I'll count 'm again."

So I slipped back the one I had, and when she got done counting, she says:

"Hang the troublesome rubbage, ther's *ten* now!" and she looked huffy and bothered both. But Tom says:

◄ *What trick are Huck and Tom playing on Aunt Sally? How does Aunt Sally react to the trick?*

---

4. **tallow-drip.** Candle wax

"Why, Aunty, *I* don't think there's ten."

"You numskull, didn't you see me count 'm?"

"I know, but—"

"Well, I'll count 'm again."

So I smouched one, and they come out nine, same as the other time. Well, she *was* in a tearing way—just a-trembling all over, she was so mad. But she counted and counted till she got that <u>addled</u> she'd start to count in the *basket* for a spoon sometimes; and so, three times they come out right, and three times they come out wrong. Then she grabbed up the basket and slammed it across the house and knocked the cat galley-west;[5] and she said cle'r out and let her have some peace, and if we come bothering around her again betwixt that and dinner she'd skin us. So we had the odd spoon, and dropped it in her apron pocket whilst she was a-giving us our sailing orders, and Jim got it all right, along with her shingle-nail, before noon. We was very well satisfied with this business, and Tom allowed it was worth twice the trouble it took, because he said now she couldn't ever count them spoons twice alike again to save her life; and wouldn't believe she'd counted them right if she did, and said that after she'd about counted her head off for the next three days he judged she'd give it up and offer to kill anybody that wanted her to ever count them any more.

So we put the sheet back on the line that night, and stole one out of her closet; and kept on putting it back and stealing it again for a couple of days till she didn't know how many sheets she had any more, and she didn't care, and warn't a-going to bullyrag the rest of her soul out about it, and wouldn't count them again not to save her life; she druther die first.

So we was all right now, as to the shirt and the sheet and the spoon and the candles, by the help of the calf and the rats and the mixed-up counting; and as to the candlestick, it warn't no consequence, it would blow over by and by.

But that pie was a job; we had no end of trouble with that pie. We fixed it up away down in the woods, and cooked it there; and we got it done at last, and very satisfactory, too; but not all in one day; and we had to use up three wash pans

▶ *What happens to Huck and Tom as they try to cook their pie? Why is the pie hollow? What are they planning to do with it?*

---

5. **galley-west.** Into confusion or inaction

Words
For
Everyday
Use

ad • dled (ad´´ld) *adj.,* confused, muddled

full of flour before we got through, and we got burnt pretty much all over, in places, and eyes put out with the smoke; because, you see, we didn't want nothing but a crust, and we couldn't prop it up right, and she would always cave in. But of course we thought of the right way at last—which was to cook the ladder, too, in the pie. So then we laid in with Jim the second night, and tore up the sheet all in little strings and twisted them together, and long before daylight we had a lovely rope that you could 'a' hung a person with. We let on it took nine months to make it.

And in the forenoon we took it down to the woods, but it wouldn't go into the pie. Being made of a whole sheet, that way, there was rope enough for forty pies if we'd 'a' wanted them, and plenty left over for soup, or sausage, or anything you choose. We could 'a' had a whole dinner.

But we didn't need it. All we needed was just enough for the pie, and so we throwed the rest away. We didn't cook none of the pies in the wash pan—afraid the solder[6] would melt; but Uncle Silas he had a noble brass warming pan which he thought considerable of, because it belonged to one of his ancestors with a long wooden handle that come over from England with William the Conqueror[7] in the *Mayflower* or one of them early ships and was hid away up garret with a lot of other old pots and things that was valuable, not on account of being any account, because they warn't, but on account of them being relicts,[8] you know, and we snaked her out, private, and took her down there, but she failed on the first pies, because we didn't know how, but she come up smiling on the last one. We took and lined her with dough, and set her in the coals, and loaded her up with rag rope, and put on a dough roof, and shut down the lid, and put hot embers on top, and stood off five foot, with the long handle, cool and comfortable, and in fifteen minutes she turned out a pie that was a satisfaction to look at. But the person that et it would want to fetch a couple of kags of toothpicks along, for if that rope ladder wouldn't cramp him down to business I don't know nothing what I'm talking about, and lay him in enough stomach ache to last him till next time, too.

Nat didn't look when we put the witch pie in Jim's pan; and we put the three tin plates in the bottom of the pan

◄ *What does Jim do as soon as he gets the pie?*

---

6. **solder.** Soft metal melted and used to join metal parts
7. **William the Conqueror . . . *Mayflower*.** William invaded Britain in 1066. The pilgrims sailed to America on the *Mayflower* in 1620.
8. **relicts.** Relics; objects that have survived from the past

under the vittles; and so Jim got everything all right, and as soon as he was by himself he busted into the pie and hid the rope ladder inside of his straw tick, and scratched some marks on a tin plate and throwed it out of the window-hole.

CHAPTER 38

"Here a Captive Heart Busted"

Making them pens was a distressid tough job, and so was the saw; and Jim allowed the <u>inscription</u> was going to be the toughest of all. That's the one which the prisoner has to scrabble on the wall. But he had to have it; Tom said he'd got to; there warn't no case of a state prisoner not scrabbling his <u>inscription</u> to leave behind, and his coat of arms.

◀ What does Tom believe Jim must have? What does Jim say in protest?

"Look at Lady Jane Grey," he says; "look at Gilford Dudley; look at old Northumberland![1] Why, Huck, s'pose it *is* considerble trouble?—what you going to do?—how you going to get around it? Jim's got to do his inscription and coat of arms.[2] They all do."

Jim says:

"Why, Mars Tom, I hain't got no coat o' arm; I hain't got nuffn but dish yer ole shirt, en you knows I got to keep de journal on dat."

"Oh, you don't understand, Jim; a coat of arms is very different."

"Well," I says, "Jim's right, anyway, when he says he ain't got no coat of arms, because he hain't."

"I reckon *I* knowed that," Tom says, "but you bet he'll have one before he goes out of this—because he's going out *right*, and there ain't going to be no flaws in his record."

So whilst me and Jim filed away at the pens on a brickbat apiece, Jim a-making his'n out of the brass and I making mine out of the spoon, Tom set to work to think out the coat of arms. By and by he said he'd struck so many good ones he didn't hardly know which to take, but there was one which he reckoned he'd decide on. He says:

"On the scutcheon we'll have a bend *or* in the dexter base, a saltire *murrey* in the fess, with a dog, couchant, for common charge, and under his foot a chain embattled, for slavery, with a chevron *vert* in a chief engrailed, and three invected

---

1. **Lady Jane Grey . . . Northumberland.** Queen of England who, with her husband and father-in-law, was imprisoned and executed
2. **coat of arms.** Symbols and figures signifying a person, family, or institution

Words
For
Everyday
Use

in • scrip • tion (in skrip´shen) *n.*, something written, marked, or carved into some surface

lines on a field *azure*, with the nombril points rampant on a dancette indented; crest, a runaway nigger, *sable*, with his bundle over his shoulder on a bar sinister; and a couple of gules for supporters, which is you and me; motto, *Maggiore fretta, minore atto.*[3] Got it out of a book—means the more haste the less speed."

"Geewhillikins," I says, "but what does the rest of it mean?"

"We ain't got no time to bother over that," he says; "we got to dig in like all git-out."

"Well, anyway," I says, "what's *some* of it? What's a fess?"

"A fess—a fess is—*you* don't need to know what a fess is. I'll show him how to make it when he gets to it."

"Shucks, Tom," I says, "I think you might tell a person. What's a bar sinister?"

"Oh, I don't know. But he's got to have it. All the nobility does."

That was just his way. If it didn't suit him to explain a thing to you, he wouldn't do it. You might pump at him a week, it wouldn't make no difference.

He'd got all that coat of arms business fixed, so now he started in to finish up the rest of that part of the work, which was to plan out a mournful inscription—said Jim got to have one, like they all done. He made up a lot, and wrote them out on a paper, and read them off, so:

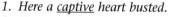

> ► What does Tom practice writing? How do his own words affect him?

1. *Here a <u>captive</u> heart busted.*
2. *Here a poor prisoner, forsook by the world and friends, <u>fretted</u> his sorrowful life.*
3. *Here a lonely heart broke, and a worn spirit went to its rest, after thirty-seven years of solitary captivity.*
4. *Here, homeless and friendless, after thirty-seven years of bitter captivity, <u>perished</u> a noble stranger, natural son of Louis XIV.*

Tom's voice trembled whilst he was reading them, and he most broke down. When he got done he couldn't no way make up his mind which one for Jim to scrabble on to the

---

3. **scutcheon . . . *atto.*** Tom uses the devices and language of medieval heraldry, the art of coats of arms.

Words For Everyday Use	**cap • tive** (kap´tiv) *adj.*, imprisoned
	fret (fret) *vt.*, worry over
	per • ish (per´ish) *vi.*, die a violent or untimely death

wall, they was all so good; but at last he allowed he would let him scrabble them all on. Jim said it would take him a year to scrabble such a lot of truck on to the logs with a nail, and he didn't know how to make letters, besides; but Tom said he would block them out for him, and then he wouldn't have nothing to do but just follow the lines. Then pretty soon he says:

"Come to think, the logs ain't a-going to do; they don't have log walls in a dungeon: we got to dig the inscriptions into a rock. We'll fetch a rock."

◄ According to Tom, where must the inscriptions be written?

Jim said the rock was worse than the logs; he said it would take him such a pison long time to dig them into a rock he wouldn't ever get out. But Tom said he would let me help him do it. Then he took a look to see how me and Jim was getting along with the pens. It was most pesky <u>tedious</u> hard work and slow, and didn't give my hands no show to get well of the sores, and we didn't seem to make no <u>headway</u>, hardly; so Tom says:

"I know how to fix it. We got to have a rock for the coat of arms and mournful inscriptions, and we can kill two birds with that same rock. There's a gaudy big grindstone[4] down at the mill, and we'll smouch it, and carve the things on it, and file out the pens and the saw on it, too."

◄ Why do they want the grindstone?

It warn't no slouch of an idea; and it warn't no slouch of a grindstone nuther; but we allowed we'd tackle it. It warn't quite midnight yet, so we cleared out for the mill, leaving Jim at work. We smouched the grindstone, and set out to roll her home, but it was a most nation tough job. Sometimes, do what we could, we couldn't keep her from falling over, and she come mighty near mashing us every time. Tom said she was going to get one of us, sure, before we got through. We got her half way; and then we was plumb played out, and most drownded with sweat. We see it warn't no use; we got to go and fetch Jim. So he raised up his bed and slid the chain off of the bed-leg, and wrapt it round and round his neck, and we crawled out through our hole and down there, and Jim and me laid into that grindstone and walked her along like nothing; and Tom <u>superintended</u>. He could out-superintend any boy I ever see. He knowed how to do everything.

---

4. **grindstone.** Revolving stone wheel used to sharpen blades and polish metal

Words For Everyday Use	ted • i • ous (tē´dē əs) *adj.*, tiresome, boring
	head • way (hed´wā´) *n.*, progress
	su • per • in • tend (sū´pər in tend´) *vi.*, direct, manage

Our hole was pretty big, but it warn't big enough to get the grindstone through; but Jim he took the pick and soon made it big enough. Then Tom marked out them things on it with the nail, and set Jim to work on them, with the nail for a chisel and an iron bolt from the rubbage in the lean-to for a hammer, and told him to work till the rest of his candle quit on him, and then he could go to bed, and hide the grindstone under his straw tick and sleep on it. Then we helped him fix his chain back on the bed-leg, and was ready for bed ourselves. But Tom thought of something, and says:

"You got any spiders in here, Jim?"

"No, sah, thanks to goodness I hain't, Mars Tom."

"All right, we'll get you some."

"But bless you, honey, I doan' *want* none. I's afeard un um. I jis' 's soon have rattlesnakes aroun'."

Tom thought a minute or two, and says:

"It's a good idea. And I reckon it's been done. It *must* 'a' been done; it stands to reason. Yes, it's a prime good idea. Where could you keep it?"

"Keep what, Mars Tom?"

"Why, a rattlesnake."

"De goodness gracious alive, Mars Tom! Why, if dey was a rattlesnake to come in heah I'd take en bust right out thoo dat log wall, I would, wid my head."

"Why, Jim, you wouldn't be afraid of it after a little. You could tame it."

"*Tame* it!"

"Yes—easy enough. Every animal is grateful for kindness and petting, and they wouldn't *think* of hurting a person that pets them. Any book will tell you that. You try—that's all I ask; just try for two or three days. Why, you can get him so in a little while that he'll love you; and sleep with you; and won't stay away from you a minute; and will let you wrap him round your neck and put his head in your mouth."

"*Please*, Mars Tom—*doan'* talk so! I can't *stan'* it! He'd *let* me shove his head in my mouf—fer a favor, hain't it? I lay he'd wait a pow'ful long time 'fo' I *ast* him. En mo' en dat, I doan' *want* him to sleep wid me."

"Jim, don't act so foolish. A prisoner's *got* to have some kind of a dumb pet, and if a rattlesnake hain't ever been tried, why, there's more glory to be gained in your being the first to ever try it than any other way you could ever think of to save your life."

"Why, Mars Tom, I doan' *want* no sich glory. Snake take 'n' bite Jim's chin off, den *whah* is de glory? No, sah, I doan' want no sich doin's."

► Why does Tom want Jim to have a rattlesnake? What is Jim's reaction to the idea?

"Blame it, can't you *try*? I only *want* you to try—you needn't keep it up if it don't work."

"But de trouble all *done* ef de snake bite me while I's a-tryin' him. Mars Tom, I's willin' to tackle mos' anything 'at ain't onreasonable, but ef you en Huck fetches a rattlesnake in heah for me to tame, I's gwyne to *leave*, dat's *shore*."

"Well, then, let it go, let it go, if you're so bullheaded about it. We can get you some garter snakes, and you can tie some buttons on their tails, and let on they're rattlesnakes, and I reckon that'll have to do."

"I k'n stan' dem, Mars Tom, but blame' 'f I couldn' get along widout um, I tell you dat. I never knowed b'fo' 'twas so much bother and trouble to be a prisoner."

"Well, it *always* is when it's done right. You got any rats around here?"

"No, sah, I hain't seed none."

"Well, we'll get you some rats."

"Why, Mars Tom, I doan' *want* no rats. Dey's de dad-blamedest creturs to 'sturb a body, en rustle roun' over 'im, en bite his feet, when he's tryin' to sleep, I ever see. No, sah, gimme g'yarter-snakes, 'f I's got to have 'm, but doan' gimme no rats; I hain' got no use f'r um, skasely."

◄ *According to Tom, why must Jim have rats? Is Jim agreeable to this idea?*

"But, Jim, you got to have 'em—they all do. So don't make no more fuss about it. Prisoners ain't ever without rats. There ain't no instance of it. And they train them, and pet them, and learn them tricks, and they get to be as sociable as flies. But you got to play music to them. You got anything to play music on?"

"I ain' got nuffn but a coase comb en a piece o' paper, en a juice-harp; but I reck'n dey wouldn' take no stock in a juice-harp."

"Yes they would. *They* don't care what kind of music 'tis. A jew's-harp's plenty good enough for a rat. All animals like music—in a prison they <u>dote on</u> it. Specially, painful music; and you can't get no other kind out of a jew's-harp. It always interests them; they come out to see what's the matter with you. Yes, you're all right; you're fixed very well. You want to set on your bed nights before you go to sleep, and early in the mornings, and play your jew's-harp; play 'The Last Link is Broken'—that's the thing that'll scoop a rat quicker 'n

Words For Everyday Use   **dote on** (dōt´ än) *vt.*, feel foolishly fond of

anything else; and when you've played about two minutes you'll see all the rats, and the snakes, and spiders, and things begin to feel worried about you, and come. And they'll just fairly <u>swarm</u> over you, and have a noble good time."

"Yes, *dey* will, I reck'n, Mars Tom, but what kine er time is *Jim* havin'? Blest if I kin see de pint. But I'll do it ef I got to. I reck'n I better keep de animals satisfied, en not have no trouble in de house."

Tom waited to think it over, and see if there wasn't nothing else; and pretty soon he says:

"Oh, there's one thing I forgot. Could you raise a flower here, do you reckon?"

"I doan know but maybe I could, Mars Tom; but it's tolable dark in heah, en I ain' got no use f'r no flower, nohow, en she'd be a pow'ful sight o' trouble."

"Well, you try it, anyway. Some other prisoners has done it."

"One er dem big cat-tail-lookin' mullen-stalks would grow in heah, Mars Tom, I reck'n, but she wouldn't be wuth half de trouble she'd coss."

"Don't you believe it. We'll fetch you a little one and you plant it in the corner over there, and raise it. And don't call it mullen, call it Pitchiola—that's its right name when it's in a prison. And you want to water it with your tears."

"Why, I got plenty spring water, Mars Tom."

"You don't *want* spring water; you want to water it with your tears. It's the way they always do."

"Why, Mars Tom, I lay I kin raise one er dem mullen-stalks twyste wid spring water whiles another man's a *start'n* one wid tears."

"That ain't the idea. You *got* to do it with tears."

"She'll die on my han's, Mars Tom, she sholy will; kase I doan' skasely ever cry."

▶ *What will Jim do with an onion?*

So Tom was stumped. But he studied it over, and then said Jim would have to worry along the best he could with an onion. He promised he would go to the nigger cabins and drop one, private, in Jim's coffee pot, in the morning. Jim said he would "jis' 's soon have tobacker in his coffee"; and found so much fault with it, and with the work and bother of raising the mullen, and jew's-harping the rats, and petting and flattering up the snakes and spiders and things, on top

| Words For Everyday Use | **swarm** (swôrm) *vt.*, crowd around |

of all the other work he had to do on pens, and inscriptions, and journals, and things, which made it more trouble and worry and responsibility to be a prisoner than anything he ever undertook, that Tom most lost all patience with him; and said he was just loadened down with more gaudier chances than a prisoner ever had in the world to make a name for himself, and yet he didn't know enough to appreciate them, and they was just about wasted on him. So Jim he was sorry, and said he wouldn't behave so no more, and then me and Tom shoved for bed.

◄ Why does Tom lose patience with Jim?

CHAPTER 39

Tom Writes Nonnamous Letters

► *Where do Tom and Huck keep the rats they capture? What do the children do?*

In the morning we went up to the village and bought a wire rat trap and fetched it down, and unstopped the best rat hole, and in about an hour we had fifteen of the bulliest kind of ones; and then we took it and put it in a safe place under Aunt Sally's bed. But while we was gone for spiders little Thomas Franklin Benjamin Jefferson Elexander Phelps found it there, and opened the door of it to see if the rats would come out, and they did; and Aunt Sally she come in, and when we got back she was a-standing on top of the bed raising Cain, and the rats was doing what they could to keep off the dull times for her. So she took and dusted us both with the hickry,[1] and we was as much as two hours catching another fifteen or sixteen, drat that meddlesome cub,[2] and they warn't the <u>likeliest</u>, nuther, because the first haul was the pick of the flock. I never see a likelier lot of rats than what that first haul was.

We got a splendid stock of sorted spiders, and bugs, and frogs, and caterpillars, and one thing or another; and we like to got a hornet's nest, but we didn't. The family was at home. We didn't give it right up, but stayed with them as long as we could; because we allowed we'd tire them out or they'd got to tire us out, and they done it. Then we got allycumpain[3] and rubbed on the places, and was pretty near all right again, but couldn't set down convenient. And so we went for the snakes, and grabbed a couple of dozen garters and house-snakes, and put them in a bag, and put it in our room, and by that time it was supper time, and a rattling good honest day's work: and hungry?—oh, no, I reckon not! And there warn't a blessed snake up there when we went back—we didn't half tie the sack, and they worked out somehow, and left. But it didn't matter much, because they was still on the <u>premises</u> somewheres. So we judged we could get some of them again. No, there warn't no real <u>scarcity</u> of snakes about

► *What happens to the snakes Huck and Tom capture?*

---

1. **dusted us both with the hickry.** Struck both of us with a hickory tree branch
2. **meddlesome cub.** Interfering little boy
3. **allycumpain.** Elecampane; medicinal herb

Words For Everyday Use	
lik • li • est (līk´lē ist) *adj.*, best, most promising
prem • is • es (prem´is is) *n.*, property
scar • ci • ty (sker´sə tē) *n.*, inadequate supply

the house for a considerable spell. You'd see them dripping from the rafters and places every now and then; and they generly landed in your plate, or down the back of your neck, and most of the time where you didn't want them. Well, they was handsome and striped, and there warn't no harm in a million of them; but that never made no difference to Aunt Sally; she <u>despised</u> snakes, be the breed what they might, and she couldn't stand them no way you could fix it; and every time one of them flopped down on her, it didn't make no difference what she was doing, she would just lay that work down and light out. I never see such a woman. And you could hear her whoop to Jericho. You couldn't get her to take a-holt of one of them with the tongs. And if she turned over and found one in bed she would scramble out and lift a howl that you would think the house was afire. She disturbed the old man so that he said he could most wish there hadn't ever been no snakes created. Why, after every last snake had been gone clear out of the house for as much as a week Aunt Sally warn't over it yet; she warn't near over it; when she was setting thinking about something you could touch her on the back of her neck with a feather and she would jump right out of her stockings. It was very curious. But Tom said all women was just so. He said they was made that way for some reason or other.

We got a licking every time one of our snakes come in her way, and she allowed these lickings warn't nothing to what she would do if we ever loaded up the place again with them. I didn't mind the lickings, because they didn't amount to nothing; but I minded the trouble we had to lay in another lot. But we got them laid in, and all the other things; and you never see a cabin as <u>blithesome</u> as Jim's was when they'd all swarm out for music and go for him. Jim didn't like the spiders, and the spiders didn't like Jim; and so they'd lay for him, and make it mighty warm for him. And he said that between the rats and the snakes and the grindstone there warn't no room in bed for him, skasely; and when there was, a body couldn't sleep, it was so lively, and it was always lively, he said, because *they* never all slept at one time, but took turn about, so when the snakes was asleep the rats was on deck, and when the rats turned in the snakes come on watch, so he always had one gang under him, in his way, and

◀ *Why does Jim have trouble sleeping in his cabin? What is in the cabin besides Jim?*

Words For Everyday Use

de • spise (di spīz´) *vt.*, hate
blithe • some (blīth´səm) *adj.*, cheerful

t'other gang having a circus over him, and if he got up to hunt a new place the spiders would take a chance at him as he crossed over. He said if he ever got out this time he wouldn't ever be a prisoner again, not for a salary.

Well, by the end of three weeks everything was in pretty good shape. The shirt was sent in early, in a pie, and every time a rat bit Jim he would get up and write a line in his journal whilst the ink was fresh; the pens was made, the inscriptions and so on was all carved on the grindstone; the bed-leg was sawed in two, and we had et up the sawdust, and it give us a most amazing stomachache. We reckoned we was all going to die, but didn't. It was the most undigestible sawdust I ever see; and Tom said the same. But as I was saying, we'd got all the work done now, at last; and we was all pretty much fagged out, too, but mainly Jim. The old man had wrote a couple of times to the plantation below Orleans to come and get their runaway nigger, but hadn't got no answer, because there warn't no such plantation; so he allowed he would advertise Jim in the St. Louis and New Orleans papers; and when he mentioned the St. Louis ones it give me the cold shivers, and I see we hadn't no time to lose. So Tom said, now for the nonnamous[4] letters.

"What's them?" I says.

"Warnings to the people that something is up. Sometimes it's done one way, sometimes another. But there's always somebody spying around that gives notice to the governor of the castle. When Louis XVI was going to light out of the Tooleries[5] a servant-girl done it. It's a very good way, and so is the nonnamous letters. We'll use them both. And it's usual for the prisoner's mother to change clothes with him, and she stays in, and he slides out in her clothes. We'll do that, too."

"But looky here, Tom, what do we want to *warn* anybody for that something's up? Let them find it out for themselves—it's their lookout."

"Yes, I know; but you can't depend on them. It's the way they've acted from the very start—left us to do *everything*. They're so confiding and mullet-headed[6] they don't take notice of nothing at all. So if we don't *give* them notice there won't be nobody nor nothing to interfere with us, and so after all our hard work and trouble this escape 'll go off perfectly flat; won't amount to nothing—won't be nothing *to* it."

> ▶ Why is Phelps unable to get a response from the plantation below New Orleans? What lie did the king tell him?

> ▶ According to Tom, what is a usual way for a prisoner to escape? Why does Tom wish to warn people about the escape? Why will the whole escape be ruined for him if he doesn't experience some type of resistance?

---

4. **nonnamous.** Anonymous; unsigned
5. **Tooleries.** Tuileries Palace in Paris
6. **confiding and mullet-headed.** Trusting and stupid

"Well, as for me, Tom, that's the way I'd like."

"Shucks!" he says, and looked disgusted. So I says:

"But I ain't going to make no complaint. Any way that suits you suits me. What you going to do about the servant-girl?"

"You'll be her. You slide in, in the middle of the night, and hook that yaller girl's frock."

"Why, Tom, that'll make trouble next morning; because, of course, she prob'bly hain't got any but that one."

"I know; but you don't want it but fifteen minutes, to carry the nonnamous letter and shove it under the front door."

"All right, then, I'll do it; but I could carry it just as handy in my own togs."[7]

"You wouldn't look like a servant-girl *then*, would you?"

"No, but there won't be nobody to see what I look like, *anyway*."

"That ain't got nothing to do with it. The thing for us to do is just to do our *duty*, and not worry about whether any-body *sees* us do it or not. Hain't you got no principle at all?"

"All right, I ain't saying nothing; I'm the servant-girl. Who's Jim's mother?"

"I'm his mother. I'll hook a gown from Aunt Sally."

"Well, then, you'll have to stay in the cabin when me and Jim leaves."

"Not much. I'll stuff Jim's clothes full of straw and lay it on his bed to represent his mother in disguise, and Jim'll take Aunt Sally's gown off of me and wear it, and we'll all <u>evade</u> together. When a prisoner of style escapes it's called an eva-sion. It's always called so when a king escapes, f'rinstance. And the same with a king's son; it don't make no difference whether he's a natural one or an unnatural one."

So Tom he wrote the nonnamous letter, and I smouched the yaller wench's frock that night, and put it on, and shoved it under the front door, the way Tom told me to. It said:

Beware. Trouble is brewing. Keep a sharp lookout.

UNKNOWN FRIEND.

Next night we stuck a picture, which Tom drawed in blood, of a skull and crossbones on the front door; and next

◄ What message do the boys leave for the family to find? How do the mes-sages affect the family?

---

7. **togs.** Clothes

Words For Everyday Use   **evade** (ē vād´) *vi.*, get away

night another one of a coffin on the back door. I never see a family in such a sweat. They couldn't 'a' been worse scared if the place had 'a' been full of ghosts laying for them behind everything and under the beds and shivering through the air. If a door banged, Aunt Sally she jumped and said "ouch!" if anything fell, she jumped and said "ouch!" if you happened to touch her, when she warn't noticing, she done the same; she couldn't face noway and be satisfied, because she allowed there was something behind her every time—so she was always a-whirling around sudden, and saying "ouch," and before she'd got two-thirds around she'd whirl back again, and say it again; and she was afraid to go to bed, but she dasn't set up. So the thing was working very well, Tom said; he said he never see a thing work more satisfactory. He said it showed it was done right.

So he said, now for the grand bulge! So the very next morning at the streak of dawn we got another letter ready, and was wondering what we better do with it, because we heard them say at supper they was going to have a nigger on watch at both doors all night. Tom he went down the lightning rod to spy around; and the nigger at the back door was asleep, and he stuck it in the back of his neck and come back. This letter said:

▶ Of what does the letter inform people?

Don't <u>betray</u> me, I wish to be your friend. There is a desprate gang of cutthroats[8] from over in the Indian Territory[9] going to steal your runaway nigger tonight, and they have been trying to scare you so as you will stay in the house and not bother them. I am one of the gang, but have got relliggion and wish to quit it and lead an honest life again, and will betray the helish design. They will sneak down from northards, along the fence, at midnight exact, with a false key, and go in the nigger's cabin to get him. I am to be off a piece and blow a tin horn if I see any danger; but stead of that I will BA like a sheep soon as they get in and not blow at all; then whilst they are getting his chains loose, you slip there and lock them in, and can kill them at your leasure. Don't do anything but just the way I am telling you; if you do they will suspicion something and raise whoop-jamboreehoo. I do not wish any reward but to know I have done the right thing. UNKNOWN FRIEND

---

8. **cutthroats.** Murderers
9. **Indian Territory.** Land set aside for Native Americans who were forced from their lands. Outlaws took refuge there.

Words
For
Everyday
Use

be • tray (bē trā´) *vt.*, turn in, reveal

CHAPTER **40**

A Mixed-up and Splendid Rescue

We was feeling pretty good after breakfast, and took my canoe and went over the river a-fishing, with a lunch, and had a good time, and took a look at the raft and found her all right, and got home late to supper, and found them in such a sweat and worry they didn't know which end they was standing on, and made us go right off to bed the minute we was done supper, and wouldn't tell us what the trouble was, and never let on a word about the new letter, but didn't need to, because we knowed as much about it as anybody did, and as soon as we was half upstairs and her back was turned we slid for the cellar cubboard and loaded up a good lunch and took it up to our room and went to bed, and got up about half past eleven, and Tom put on Aunt Sally's dress that he stole and was going to start with the lunch, but says:

"Where's the butter?"

"I laid out a hunk of it," I says, "on a piece of a cornpone."

"Well, you *left* it laid out, then—it ain't here."

"We can get along without it," I says.

"We can get along *with* it, too," he says; "just you slide down cellar and fetch it. And then mosey right down the lightning rod and come along. I'll go and stuff the straw into Jim's clothes to represent his mother in disguise, and be ready to *ba* like a sheep and shove soon as you get there."

◀ What is Huck told to do? What is Tom going to do?

So out he went, and down cellar went I. The hunk of butter, big as a person's fist, was where I had left it, so I took up the slab of cornpone with it on, and blowed out my light, and started upstairs very stealthy, and got up to the main floor all right, but here comes Aunt Sally with a candle, and I clapped the truck in my hat, and clapped my hat on my head, and the next second she see me; and she says:

◀ Where does Huck hide the butter when Aunt Sally enters the basement?

"You been down cellar?"

"Yes'm."

"What you been doing down there?"

"Noth'n."

"*Noth'n!*"

"No'm."

"Well, then, what possessed you to go down there this time of night?"

"I don't know 'm."

"You don't *know*? Don't answer me that way. Tom, I want to know what you been *doing* down there."

"I hain't been doing a single thing, Aunt Sally, I hope to gracious if I have."

I reckoned she'd let me go now, and as a generl thing she would; but I s'pose there was so many strange things going on she was just in a sweat about every little thing that warn't yardstick straight; so she says, very decided:

"You just march into that setting-room and stay there till I come. You been up to something you no business to, and I lay I'll find out what it is before *I'm* done with you."

So she went away as I opened the door and walked into the setting-room. My, but there was a crowd there! Fifteen farmers, and every one of them had a gun. I was most powerful sick, and slunk to a chair and set down. They was setting around, some of them talking a little, in a low voice, and all of them <u>fidgety</u> and uneasy, but trying to look like they warn't; but I knowed they was, because they was always taking off their hats, and putting them on, and scratching their heads, and changing their seats, and fumbling with their buttons. I warn't easy myself, but I didn't take my hat off, all the same.

I did wish Aunt Sally would come, and get done with me, and lick me, if she wanted to, and let me get away and tell Tom how we'd overdone this thing, and what a thundering hornet's nest we'd got ourselves into, so we could stop fooling around straight off, and clear out with Jim before these rips got out of patience and come for us.

At last she come and begun to ask me questions, but I *couldn't* answer them straight, I didn't know which end of me was up; because these men was in such a fidget now that some was wanting to start right *now* and lay for them <u>desperadoes</u>, and saying it warn't but a few minutes to midnight; and others was trying to get them to hold on and wait for the sheep-signal; and here was Aunty pegging away at the questions, and me a-shaking all over and ready to sink down in my tracks I was that scared; and the place getting hotter and hotter, and the butter beginning to melt and run down my neck and behind my ears; and pretty soon, when one of them says, "*I'm* for going and getting in the cabin *first* and right *now*, and catching them when they come," I most dropped; and a streak of butter come a-trickling down my forehead, and Aunt Sally she see it, and turns white as a

▶ What does Aunt Sally order Huck to do when she catches him in the cellar? When Huck enters the sitting room, what does he see? Why does he feel "powerful sick"?

▶ For what does Huck wish? What does he want to do?

▶ What suggestion by one of the farmers makes Huck very nervous? What does Aunt Sally think when she sees warm butter dripping from under Huck's hat? When she discovers the truth, where does she send Huck?

Words For Everyday Use	**fidg • e • ty** (fij´it ē) *adj.*, nervous, squirming
	des • per • a • do (des´pər ä dō) *n.*, outlaw, reckless criminal

sheet, and says:

"For the land's sake, what *is* the matter with the child? He's got the brain-fever as shore as you're born, and they're oozing out!"

And everybody runs to see, and she snatches off my hat, and out comes the bread and what was left of the butter, and she grabbed me, and hugged me, and says:

"Oh, what a turn you did give me! and how glad and grateful I am it ain't no worse; for luck's against us, and it never rains but it pours, and when I see that truck I thought we'd lost you, for I knowed by the color and all it was just like your brains would be if—Dear, dear, whyd'nt you tell me that was what you'd been down there for, *I* wouldn't 'a' cared. Now cler out to bed, and don't lemme see no more of you till morning!"

I was upstairs in a second, and down the lightning rod in another one, and shinning through the dark for the lean-to. I couldn't hardly get my words out, I was so anxious; but I told Tom as quick as I could we must jump for it now, and not a minute to lose—the house full of men, yonder, with guns!

His eyes just blazed; and he says:

"No!—is that so? *Ain't* it bully! Why, Huck, if it was to do over again, I bet I could fetch two hundred! If we could put it off till—"

"Hurry! *Hurry!*" I says. "Where's Jim?"

"Right at your elbow; if you reach out your arm you can touch him. He's dressed, and everything's ready. Now we'll slide out and give the sheep-signal."

But then we heard the tramp of men coming to the door, and heard them begin to fumble with the padlock, and heard a man say:

"I told you we'd be too soon; they haven't come—the door is locked. Here, I'll lock some of you into the cabin, and you lay for 'em in the dark and kill 'em when they come; and the rest scatter around a piece, and listen if you can hear 'em coming."

So in they come, but couldn't see us in the dark, and most trod on us whilst we was hustling to get under the bed. But we got under all right, and out through the hole, swift but soft—Jim first, me next, and Tom last, which was according to Tom's orders. Now we was in the lean-to, and heard trampings close by outside. So we crept to the door, and Tom stopped us there and put his eye to the crack, but couldn't make out nothing, it was so dark; and whispered and said he would listen for the steps to get further, and when he nudged

◄ When Huck tells Tom about the armed men in the house, what is Tom's response?

◄ Why do the men enter the cabin? What are they planning to do?

us Jim must glide out first, and him last. So he set his ear to the crack and listened, and listened, and listened, and the steps a-scraping around out there all the time; and at last he nudged us, and we slid out, and stooped down, not breathing, and not making the least noise, and slipped <u>stealthy</u> towards the fence in Injun file,[1] and got to it all right, and me and Jim over it; but Tom's britches catched fast on a splinter on the top rail, and then he hear the steps coming, so he had to pull loose, which snapped the splinter and made a noise; and as he dropped in our tracks and started somebody sings out:

"Who's that? Answer, or I'll shoot!"

But we didn't answer; we just <u>unfurled</u> our heels and shoved. Then there was a rush, and a *bang, bang, bang!* and the bullets fairly whizzed around us! We heard them sing out:

"Here they are! They've broke for the river! After 'em, boys, and turn loose the dogs!"

So here they come, <u>full tilt</u>. We could hear them because they wore boots and yelled, but we didn't wear no boots and didn't yell. We was in the path to the mill; and when they got pretty close on to us we dodged into the bush and let them go by, and then dropped in behind them. They'd had all the dogs shut up, so they wouldn't scare off the robbers; but by this time somebody had let them loose, and here they come, making powwow enough for a million; but they was our dogs; so we stopped in our tracks till they catched up; and when they see it warn't nobody but us, and no excitement to offer them, they only just said howdy, and tore right ahead towards the shouting and clattering; and then we upsteam again, and whizzed along after them till we was nearly to the mill, and then struck up through the bush to where my canoe was tied, and hopped in and pulled for dear life towards the middle of the river, but didn't make no more noise than we was obleeged to.[2] Then we struck out, easy and comfortable, for the island where my raft was; and we could hear them yelling and barking at each other all up and down the bank, till we was so far away the sounds got dim and died out. And when we stepped on to the raft I says:

▶ *Where do the boys run? What does Huck say to Jim as soon as they are all safe? Why is Tom the "gladdest of all" after the escape attempt?*

---

1. **Injun file.** Single file
2. **obleeged to.** Obliged to; forced to

<table>
<tr><td rowspan="3">Words
For
Everyday
Use</td><td>**stealth • y** (stəl´thē) *adj.,* secret, sly</td></tr>
<tr><td>**un • furl** (un furl´) *vt.,* let loose</td></tr>
<tr><td>**full tilt** (fool´tilt´) *adv.,* at full speed</td></tr>
</table>

"*Now*, old Jim, you're a free man *again*, and I bet you won't ever be a slave no more."

"En a mighty good job it wuz, too, Huck. It 'uz planned beautiful, en it 'uz done beautiful; en dey ain't *nobody* kin git up a plan dat's mo' mixed-up en splendid den what dat one wuz."

We was all glad as we could be, but Tom was the gladdest of all because he had a bullet in the calf of his leg.

When me and Jim heard that we didn't feel so brash as what we did before. It was hurting him considerable, and bleeding; so we laid him in the wigwam and tore up one of the duke's shirts for to bandage him, but he says:

"Gimme the rags; I can do it myself. Don't stop now; don't fool around here, and the evasion booming along so handsome; man the sweeps, and set her loose! Boys, we done it elegant!—'deed we did. I wish we'd 'a' had the handling of Louis XVI, there wouldn't 'a' been no 'Son of Saint Louis, ascend to heaven!' wrote down in *his* biography; no, sir, we'd a whooped him over the *border*—that's what we'd a done with *him*—and done it just as slick as nothing at all, too. Man the sweeps—man the sweeps!"

But me and Jim was consulting—and thinking. And after we'd thought a minute, I says:

"Say it, Jim."

So he says:

"Well, den, dis is de way it look to me, Huck. Ef it wuz *him* dat 'uz bein' sot free, en one er de boys wuz to git shot, would he say, 'Go on en save me, nemmine 'bout a doctor f'r to save dis one?' Is dat like Mars Tom Sawyer? Would he say dat? You *bet* he wouldn't! *Well*, den, is *Jim* gywne to say it? No, sah—I doan' budge a step out'n dis place 'dout a *doctor*, not if it's forty year!"

◄ Why does Jim want to get a doctor for Tom, despite the fact that it might jeopardize his escape? How does Tom feel about getting a doctor?

I knowed he was white inside, and I reckoned he'd say what he did say—so it was all right now, and I told Tom I was a-going for a doctor. He raised considerable row about it, but me and Jim stuck to it and wouldn't budge; so he was for crawling out and setting the raft loose himself; but we wouldn't let him. Then he give us a piece of his mind, but it didn't do no good.

So when he sees me getting the canoe ready, he says:

"Well, then, if you're bound to go, I'll tell you the way to do when you get to the village. Shut the door and blindfold the doctor tight and fast, and make him swear to be silent as the grave, and put a purse full of gold in his hand, and then take and lead him all around the back alleys and everywheres in the dark, and then fetch him here in the canoe, in a

◄ What special instructions does Tom give Huck before he leaves to find a doctor?

roundabout way amongst the islands, and search him and take his chalk away from him, and don't give it back to him till you get him back to the village, or else he will chalk this raft so he can find it again. It's the way they all do."

So I said I would, and left, and Jim was to hide in the woods when he see the doctor coming till he was gone again.

"Must 'a' Been Sperits"

The doctor was an old man; a very nice, kind-looking old man when I got him up. I told him me and my brother was over on Spanish Island hunting yesterday afternoon, and camped on a piece of a raft we found, and about midnight he must 'a' kicked his gun in his dreams, for it went off and shot him in the leg, and we wanted him to go over there and fix it and not say nothing about it, nor let anybody know, because we wanted to come home this evening and surprise the folks.

"Who is your folks?" he says.

"The Phelpses, down yonder."

"Oh," he says. And after a minute, he says:

"How'd you say he got shot?"

"He had a dream," I says, "and it shot him."

"<u>Singular</u> dream," he says.

So he lit up his lantern, and got his saddlebags, and we started. But when he sees the canoe he didn't like the look of her—said she was big enough for one, but didn't look pretty safe for two. I says:

"Oh, you needn't be afeard, sir, she carried the three of us easy enough."

"What three?"

"Why, me and Sid, and—and—and *the guns;* that's what I mean."

"Oh," he says.

But he put his foot on the gunnel[1] and rocked her, and shook his head, and said he reckoned he'd look around for a bigger one. But they was all locked and chained; so he took my canoe, and said for me to wait till he come back, or I could hunt around further, or maybe I better go down home and get them ready for the surprise if I wanted to. But I said I didn't; so I told him just how to find the raft, and then he started.

I struck an idea pretty soon. I says to myself, spos'n he

How does Huck explain Tom's injury to the doctor?

Why does the doctor go by himself to the raft?

---

1. **gunnel.** Gunwhale; upper edge of the side of a boat

Words For Everyday Use

sing • u • lar (siŋ gyə lər) *adj.*, extraordinary, remarkable

can't fix that leg just in three shakes of a sheep's tail, as the saying is? spos'n it takes him three or four days? What are we going to do?—lay around there till he lets the cat out of the bag? No, sir; I know what *I'll* do. I'll wait, and when he comes back if he says he's got to go any more I'll get down there, too, if I swim; and we'll take and tie him, and keep him, and shove out down the river; and when Tom's done with him we'll give him what it's worth, or all we got, and then let him get ashore.

So then I crept into a lumber pile to get some sleep; and next time I waked up the sun was away up over my head! I shot out and went for the doctor's house, but they told me he'd gone away in the night some time or other, and warn't back yet. Well, thinks I, that looks powerful bad for Tom, and I'll dig out for the island right off. So away I shoved, and turned the corner, and nearly rammed my head into Uncle Silas's stomach! He says:

"Why, *Tom!* Where you been all this time, you rascal?"

"*I* hain't been nowheres," I says, "only just hunting for the runaway nigger—me and Sid."

"Why, where ever did you go?" he says. "Your aunt's been mighty uneasy."

"She needn't," I says, "because we was all right. We followed the men and the dogs, but they outrun us, and we lost them; but we thought we heard them on the water, so we got a canoe and took out after them and crossed over, but couldn't find nothing of them; so we cruised along up-shore till we got kind of tired and beat out; and tied up the canoe and went to sleep, and never waked up till about an hour ago; then we paddled over here to hear the news, and Sid's at the post office to see what he can hear, and I'm a-branching out to get something to eat for us, and then we're going home."

So then we went to the post office to get "Sid"; but just as I suspicioned, he warn't there; so the old man he got a letter out of the office, and we waited awhile longer, but Sid didn't come; so the old man said, come along, let Sid foot it home, or canoe it, when he got done fooling around—but we would ride. I couldn't get him to let me stay and wait for Sid; and he said there warn't no use in it, and I must come along, and let Aunt Sally see we was all right.

When we got home Aunt Sally was that glad to see me she laughed and cried both, and hugged me, and give me one of them lickings of hern that don't amount to shucks, and said she'd serve Sid the same when he come.

And the place was plum full of farmers and farmers' wives, to dinner; and such another clack a body never heard. Old

▶ *Why does Mr. Phelps force Huck to go home?*

Mrs. Hotchkiss was the worst; her tongue was a-going all the time. She says:

"Well, Sister Phelps, I've ransacked that-air cabin over, an' I b'lieve the nigger was crazy. I says to Sister Damrell—didn't I, Sister Damrell?—s'I, he's crazy, s'I—them's the very words I said. You all hearn me: he's crazy, s'I; everything shows it, s'I. Look at that-air grindstone, s'I; want to tell *me't* any cretur 't's in his right mind 's a-goin' to scrabble all them crazy things onto a grindstone, s'I? Here sich 'n' sich a person busted his heart; 'n' here so 'n' so pegged along for thirty-seven year, 'n' all that—natcherl son o' Louis somebody, 'n' sich everlast'n rubbage. He's plumb crazy, s'I; it's what I says in the fust place, it's what I says in the middle, 'n' it's what I says last 'n' all the time—the nigger's crazy—crazy 's Nebokoodneezer,[2] s'I."

◀ What are people saying about Jim? Why are they saying this?

"An' look at that-air ladder made out'n rags, Sister Hotchkiss," says old Mrs. Damrell; "what in the name o' goodness *could* he ever want of—"

"The very words I was a-sayin' no longer ago th'n this minute to Sister Utterback, 'n' she'll tell you so herself. Sh-she, look at that-air rag ladder, sh-she; 'n' s'I, yes, *look* at it, s'I—what *could* he a-wanted of it? s'I. Sh-she, Sister Hotchkiss, sh-she—"

"But how in the nation'd they ever *git* that grindstone in there, *anyway*? 'n' who dug that-air *hole*? 'n' who—"

"My very *words*, Brer Penrod! I was a-sayin'—pass that-air sasser o' m'lasses, won't ye?—I was a-sayin' to Sister Dunlap, jist this minute, how *did* they git that grindstone in there, s'I. Without *help* mind you—'thout *help*! *That's* wher 'tis. Don't tell *me*, s'I; there *wuz* help, s'I; 'n' ther' wuz a *plenty* help, too, s'I; ther's ben a *dozen* a-helpin' that nigger, 'n' I lay I'd skin every last nigger on this place but *I'd* find out who done it, s'I; 'n' moreover, s'I—"

"A *dozen* says you!—*forty* couldn't 'a' done everything that's been done. Look at them case knife saws and things, how tedious they've been made; look at that bed-leg sawed off with 'm, a week's work for six men; look at that nigger made out'n straw on the bed; and look at—"

◀ What do the people say about the work that was done in Jim's cabin? How many people do they believe are responsible?

"You may *well* say it, Brer Hightower! It's jist as I was a-sayin' to Brer Phelps, his own self. S'e, what do *you* think of it, Sister Hotchkiss, s'e? Think o' what, Brer Phelps, s'I? Think o' that bed-leg sawed off that a way, s'e? *Think* of it, s'I. I lay it never sawed *itself* off, s'I—somebody sawed it, s'I; that's my opinion, take it or leave it, it mayn't be no 'count,

---

2. **Nebokoodneezer.** Nebuchadnazzar; king of ancient Babylon who became insane

s'I, but sich as 'tis, it's my opinion, s'I, 'n' if anybody k'n start a better one, s'I, let him *do* it, s'I, that's all. I says to Sister Dunlap, s'I—"

"Why, dog my cats, they must a ben 'a' houseful o' niggers in there every night for four weeks to 'a' done all that work, Sister Phelps. Look at that shirt—every last inch of it kivered over with secret African writ'n done with blood! Must 'a' ben a raft uv 'm at it right along, all the time, amost. Why, I'd give two dollars to have it read to me; 'n' as for the niggers that wrote it, I 'low I'd take 'n' lash 'm t'll—"

"People to *help* him, Brother Marples! Well, I reckon you'd *think* so if you'd 'a' been in this house for a while back. Why, they've stole everything they could lay their hands on—and we a-watching all the time, mind you. They stole that shirt right off o' the line! And as for that sheet they made the rag ladder out of, ther' ain't no telling how many times they *didn't* steal that; and flour, and candles, and candlesticks, and spoons, and the old warming pan, and most a thousand things that I disremember now, and my new calico dress; and me and Silas and my Sid and Tom on the constant watch day *and* night, as I was a-telling you, and not a one of us could catch hide nor hair nor sight nor sound of them; and here at the last minute, lo and behold you, they slides right in under our noses and fools us, and not only fools *us* but the Injun Territory robbers too, and actuly gets *away* with that nigger safe and sound, and that with sixteen men and twenty-two dogs right on their very heels at that very time! I tell you, it just bangs anything I ever *heard* of. Why, *sperits* couldn't 'a' done better and been no smarter. And I reckon they must 'a' *'been* sperits—because, *you* know our dogs, and ther' ain't no better; well, them dogs never even got on the *track* of 'm once! You explain *that* to me if you can!—*any* of you!"

"Well, it does beat—"

"Laws alive, I never—"

"So help me, I wouldn't 'a' be—"

"House-thieves as well as—"

"Goodnessgracioussakes, I'd 'a' ben afeard to live in sich a—"

"'Fraid to *live*!—why, I was that scared I dasn't hardly go to bed, or get up, or lay down, or *set* down, Sister Ridgeway. Why, they'd steal the very—why, goodness sakes, you can guess what kind of a <u>fluster</u> *I* was in by the time midnight

▶ *How is Huck feeling as he listens to Aunt Sally tell about the thievery?*

Words For Everyday Use

flus • ter (flus´tər) *n.,* state of confusion

come last night. I hope to gracious if I warn't afraid they'd steal some o' the family! I was just to that pass I didn't have no reasoning <u>faculties</u> no more. It looks foolish enough *now*, in the daytime; but I says to myself, there's my two poor boys asleep, 'way upstairs in that lonesome room, and I declare to goodness I was that uneasy 't I crep' up there and locked 'em in! I *did*. And anybody would. Because, you know, when you get scared that way, and it keeps running on, and getting worse and worse all the time, and your wits gets to addling, and you get to doing all sorts o' wild things, and by and by you think to yourself, spos'n *I* was a boy, and was away up there, and the door ain't locked, and you—" She stopped, looking kind of wondering, and then she turned her head around slow, and when her eye lit on me—I got up and took a walk.

Says I to myself, I can explain better how we come to not be in that room this morning if I go out to one side and study over it a little. So I done it. But I dasn't go fur, or she'd 'a' sent for me. And when it was late in the day the people all went, and then I come in and told her the noise and shooting waked up me and "Sid," and the door was locked, and we wanted to see the fun, so we went down the lightning rod, and both of us got hurt a little, and we didn't never want to try *that* no more. And then I went on and told her all what I told Uncle Silas before; and then she said she'd forgive us, and maybe it was all right enough anyway, and about what a body might expect of boys, for all boys was a pretty harum-scarum[3] lot as fur as she could see; and so, as long as no harm hadn't come of it, she judged she better put in her time being grateful we was alive and well and she had us still, stead of fretting over what was past and done. So then she kissed me, and patted me on the head, and dropped into a kind of a brown study;[4] and pretty soon jumps up, and says:

"Why, lawsamercy, it's most night, and Sid not come yet! What *has* become of that boy?"

I see my chance; so I skips up and says:

"I'll run right up to town and get him," I says.

> ◄ What story does Huck tell Aunt Sally about where he and Tom were last night?

---

3. **harum-scarum.** Reckless, wild
4. **brown study.** Condition of being deep in thought

Words For Everyday Use	**fac • ul • ty** (fak´əl tē) *n.*, any power of the mind

▶ Why is Aunt Sally uneasy when Uncle Silas returns? Why does Huck feel "mean" when Aunt Sally tucks him into bed?

"No you won't," she says. "You'll stay right wher' you are; *one's* enough to be lost at a time. If he ain't here to supper, your uncle' ll go."

Well, he warn't there to supper; so right after supper uncle went.

He come back about ten a little bit uneasy; hadn't run across Tom's track. Aunt Sally was a good *deal* uneasy; but Uncle Silas he said there warn't no occasion to be—boys will be boys, he said, and you'll see this one turn up in the morning all sound and right. So she had to be satisfied. But she said she'd set up for him awhile anyway, and keep a light burning so he could see it.

And then when I went up to bed she come up with me and fetched her candle, and tucked me in, and mothered me so good I felt mean, and like I couldn't look her in the face; and she set down on the bed and talked with me a long time, and said what a splendid boy Sid was, and didn't seem to want to ever stop talking about him; and kept asking me every now and then if I reckoned he could 'a' got lost, or hurt, or maybe drownded, and might be laying at this minute somewheres suffering or dead, and she not by him to help him, and so the tears would drip down silent, and I would tell her that Sid was all right, and would be home in the morning, sure; and she would squeeze my hand, or maybe kiss me, and tell me to say it again, and keep on saying it, because it done her good, and she was in so much trouble. And when she was going away she looked down in my eyes so steady and gentle, and says:

"The door ain't going to be locked, Tom, and there's the window and the rod; but you'll be good, *won't* you? And you won't go? For *my* sake."

Laws knows I *wanted* to go bad enough to see about Tom, and was all intending to go; but after that I wouldn't 'a' went, not for kingdoms.

▶ Why is Huck restless? What is the only thing he can think to do for Aunt Sally?

But she was on my mind and Tom was on my mind, so I slept very restless. And twice I went down the rod away in the night, and slipped around front, and see her setting there by her candle in the window with her eyes towards the road and the tears in them; and I wished I could do something for her, but I couldn't, only to swear that I wouldn't never do nothing to grieve her any more. And the third time I waked up at dawn, and slid down, and she was there yet, and her candle was most out, and her old gray head was resting on her hand, and she was asleep.

CHAPTER **42**

Why They Didn't Hang Jim

The old man was uptown again before breakfast, but couldn't get no track of Tom; and both of them set at the table thinking, and not saying nothing, and looking mournful, and their coffee getting cold, and not eating anything. And by and by the old man says:

"Did I give you the letter?"

"What letter?"

"The one I got yesterday out of the post office."

"No, you didn't give me no letter."

"Well, I must 'a' forgot it."

So he rummaged his pockets, and then went off somewheres where he had laid it down, and fetched it, and give it to her. She says:

"Why, it's from St. Petersburg—it's from Sis."

I allowed another walk would do me good; but I couldn't stir. But before she could break it open she dropped it and run—for she see something. And so did I. It was Tom Sawyer on a mattress; and that old doctor; and Jim, in *her* calico dress, with his hands tied behind him; and a lot of people. I hid the letter behind the first thing that come handy, and rushed. She flung herself at Tom, crying, and says:

"Oh, he's dead, he's dead, I know he's dead!"

And Tom he turned his head a little, and muttered something or other, which showed he warn't in his right mind; then she flung up her hands, and says:

"He's alive, thank God! And that's enough!" and she snatched a kiss of him, and flew for the house to get the bed ready, and scattering orders right and left at the niggers and everybody else, as fast as her tongue could go, every jump of the way.

I followed the men to see what they was going to do with Jim; and the old doctor and Uncle Silas followed after Tom into the house. The men was very huffy, and some of them wanted to hang Jim for an example to all the other niggers around there, so they wouldn't be trying to run away like Jim done, and making such a raft of trouble, and keeping a whole family scared most to death for days and nights. But the others said, don't do it, it wouldn't answer at all; he ain't our nigger, and his owner would turn up and make us pay for him, sure. So that cooled them down a little, because the people that's always the most anxious for to hang a nigger

◀ What does Aunt Sally see that causes her to drop the letter and run?

that hain't done just right is always the very ones that ain't the most anxious to pay for him when they've got their satisfaction out of him.

They cussed Jim considerble, though, and give him a cuff or two side the head once in a while, but Jim never said nothing, and he never let on to know me, and they took him to the same cabin, and put his own clothes on him, and chained him again, and not to no bed-leg this time, but to a big staple drove into the bottom log, and chained his hands, too, and both legs, and said he warn't to have nothing but bread and water to eat after this till his owner come, or he was sold at auction because he didn't come in a certain length of time, and filled up our hole, and said a couple of farmers with guns must stand watch around about the cabin every night, and a bulldog tied to the door in the daytime; and about this time they was through with the job and was <u>tapering</u> off with a kind of generl good-bye cussing, and then the old doctor comes and takes a look, and says:

"Don't be no rougher on him than you're obleeged to, because he ain't a bad nigger. When I got to where I found the boy I see I couldn't cut the bullet out without some help, and he warn't in no condition for me to leave to go and get help; and he got a little worse and a little worse, and after a long time he went out of his head, and wouldn't let me come a-nigh him any more, and said if I chalked his raft he'd kill me, and no end of wild foolishness like that, and I see I couldn't do anything at all with him; so I says, I got to have *help* somehow; and the minute I says it out crawls this nigger from somewheres and says he'll help, and he done it, too, and done it very well. Of course I judged he must be a runaway nigger, and there I *was!* and there I had to stick right straight along all the rest of the day and all night. It was a fix, I tell you! I had a couple of patients with the chills, and of course I'd of liked to run up to town and see them, but I dasn't, because the nigger might get away, and then I'd be to blame; and yet never a skiff come close enough for me to hail. So there I had to stick plumb until daylight this morning; and I never see a nigger that was a better nuss[1] or faithfuler, and yet he was risking his freedom to do it, and was all

▶ How do people treat Jim?

▶ Why does the doctor stand up for Jim?

---

1. **nuss.** Nurse

Words For Everyday Use

ta • per off (tā′pər ôf) *vi.*, gradually stop

tired out, too, and I see plain enough he'd been worked main hard lately. I liked the nigger for that; I tell you, gentlemen, a nigger like that is worth a thousand dollars—and kind treatment, too. I had everything I needed, and the boy was doing as well there as he would 'a' done at home—better, maybe, because it was so quiet; but there I *was*, with both of 'm on my hands, and there I had to stick till about dawn this morning; then some men in a skiff come by, and as good luck would have it the nigger was setting by the pallet with his head propped on his knees sound asleep; so I motioned them in quiet, and they slipped up on him and grabbed him and tied him before he knowed what he was about, and we never had no trouble. And the boy being in a kind of a flighty sleep, too, we muffled the oars and hitched the raft on, and towed her over very nice and quiet, and the nigger never made the least row nor said a word from the start. He ain't no bad nigger, gentlemen; that's what I think about him."

Somebody says:

"Well, it sounds very good, doctor, I'm obleeged to say."

Then the others softened up a little, too, and I was mighty thankful to that old doctor for doing Jim that good turn; and I was glad it was according to my judgment of him, too; because I thought he had a good heart in him and was a good man the first time I see him. Then they all agreed that Jim had acted very well, and was deserving to have some notice took of it, and reward. So every one of them promised, right out and hearty, that they wouldn't cuss him no more.

◀ How do people react to the doctor's defense of Jim?

Then they come out and locked him up. I hoped they was going to say he could have one or two of the chains took off, because they was rotten heavy, or could have meat and greens with his bread and water; but they didn't think of it, and I reckoned it warn't best for me to mix in, but I judged I'd get the doctor's yarn to Aunt Sally somehow or other as soon as I'd got through the breakers that was laying just ahead of me—explanations, I mean, of how I forgot to mention about Sid being shot when I was telling how him and me put in that dratted night paddling around hunting the runaway nigger.

But I had plenty time. Aunt Sally she stuck to the sickroom all day and all night, and every time I see Uncle Silas mooning around I dodged him.

Next morning I heard Tom was a good deal better, and they said Aunt Sally was gone to get a nap. So I slips to the sickroom, and if I found him awake I reckoned we could put up a yarn for the family that would wash. But he was sleeping, and sleeping very peaceful, too; and pale, not fire-faced the way he was when he come. So I set down and laid for him to

◀ Why is Huck anxious for Tom to awaken? What does Aunt Sally say about Tom's condition?

wake. In about half an hour Aunt Sally comes gliding in, and there I was, up a stump again! She motioned me to be still, and set down by me, and begun to whisper, and said we could all be joyful now, because all the symptoms was first-rate, and he'd been sleeping like that for ever so long, and looking better and peacefuler all the time, and ten to one he'd wake up in his right mind.

So we set there watching, and by and by he stirs a bit, and opened his eyes very natural, and takes a look, and says:

"Hello!—why, I'm at *home!* How's that? Where's the raft?"

"It's all right," I says.

"And *Jim?*"

"The same," I says, but couldn't say it pretty brash. But he never noticed, but says:

"Good! Splendid! *Now* we're all right and safe! Did you tell Aunty?"

I was going to say yes; but she chipped in and says: "About what, Sid?"

"Why, about the way the whole thing was done."

"What whole thing?"

"Why, *the* whole thing. There ain't but one; how we set the runaway nigger free—me and Tom."

"Good land! Set the run—What *is* the child talking about! Dear, dear, out of his head again!"

"*No*, I ain't out of my *head*, I know all what I'm talking about. We did set him free—me and Tom. We laid out to do it, and we *done* it. And we done it elegant, too." He'd got a start, and she never checked him up, just set and stared and stared, and let him clip along, and I see it warn't no use for *me* to put in. "Why, Aunty, it cost us a power of work—weeks of it—hours and hours, every night, whilst you was all asleep. And we had to steal candles, and the sheet, and the shirt, and your dress, and spoons, and tin plates, and case knives, and the warming pan, and the grindstone, and flour, and just no end of things, and you can't think what work it was to make the saws, and pens, and inscriptions, and one thing or another, and you can't think *half* the fun it was. And we had to make up the pictures of coffins and things, and nonnamous letters from the robbers, and get up and down the lightning rod, and dig the hole into the cabin, and made the rope ladder and send it in cooked up in a pie, and send in spoons and things to work with in your apron pocket—"

"Mercy sakes!"

"—and load up the cabin with rats and snakes and so on, for company for Jim; and then you kept Tom here so long with the butter in his hat that you come near spiling the

▶ What does Tom reveal to Aunt Sally?

whole business, because the men come before we was out of the cabin, and we had to rush, and they heard us and let drive at us, and I got my share, and we dodged out of the path and let them go by, and when the dogs come they warn't interested in us, but went for the most noise, and we got our canoe, and made for the raft, and was all safe, and Jim was a free man, and we done it all by ourselves, and *wasn't* it bully, Aunty!"

"Well, I never heard the likes of it in all my born days! So it was *you*, you little rapscallions, that's been making all this trouble, and turned everybody's wits clean inside out and scared us all most to death. I've as good a notion as ever I had in my life to take it out o' you[2] this very minute. To think, here I've been, night after night, a—*you* just get well once, you young scamp, and I lay I'll tan the Old Harry[3] out o' both o' ye!"

But Tom, he *was* so proud and joyful, he just *couldn't* hold in, and his tongue just *went* it—she a-chipping in, and spitting fire all along, and both of them going it at once, like a cat convention; and she says:

"*Well*, you get all the enjoyment you can out of it *now*, for mind I tell you if I catch you meddling with him again—"

"Meddling with *who?*" Tom says, dropping his smile and looking surprised.

"With *who?* Why, the runaway nigger, of course. Who'd you reckon?"

Tom looks at me very grave, and says:

"Tom, didn't you just tell me he was all right? Hasn't he got away?"

"*Him?*" says Aunt Sally; "the runaway nigger? 'Deed he hasn't. They've got him back, safe and sound, and he's in that cabin again, on bread and water, and loaded down with chains, till he's claimed or sold!"

Tom rose square up in bed, with his eye hot, and his nostrils opening and shutting like gills, and sings out to me:

"They hain't no *right* to shut him up! *Shove!*—and don't you lose a minute. Turn him loose! he ain't no slave; he's as free as any cretur that walks this earth!"

"What *does* the child mean?"

"I mean every word I say, Aunt Sally, and if somebody don't go, *I'll* go. I've knowed him all his life, and so has Tom, there. Old Miss Watson died two months ago, and she was ashamed she ever was going to sell him down the river, and *said* so; and she set him free in her will."

---

2. **take it out o' you.** Whip you
3. **Old Harry.** The devil

◄ How does Tom feel about all he and Huck have done? How does Aunt Sally react to Tom's information?

◄ According to Tom, why do people have no right to imprison Jim? What did Miss Watson do in her will? Why did she do this? Why did Tom want to set Jim free, when he knew he was already free?

"Then what on earth did *you* want to set him free for, seeing he was already free?"

"Well, that *is* a question, I must say; and *just* like women! Why, I wanted the *adventure* of it; and I'd 'a' waded neck-deep in blood to—goodness alive, *Aunt Polly!*"

If she warn't standing right there, just inside the door, looking as sweet and contented as an angel half full of pie, I wish I may never!

Aunt Sally jumped for her, and most hugged the head off of her, and cried over her, and I found a good enough place for me under the bed, for it was getting pretty <u>sultry</u> for *us*, seemed to me. And I peeped out, and in a little while Tom's Aunt Polly shook herself loose and stood there looking across at Tom over her spectacles—kind of grinding him into the earth, you know. And then she says:

"Yes, you *better* turn y'r head away—I would if I was you, Tom."

"Oh, deary me!" says Aunt Sally; "*Is* he changed so? Why, that ain't *Tom*, it's Sid; Tom's—Tom's—why, where is Tom? He was here a minute ago."

"You mean where's Huck *Finn*—that's what you mean! I reckon I hain't raised such a scamp as my Tom all these years not to know him when I *see* him. That *would* be a pretty howdy-do. Come out from under that bed, Huck Finn."

So I done it. But not feeling brash.

Aunt Sally she was one of the mixed-upest-looking persons I ever see—except one, and that was Uncle Silas, when he come in and they told it all to him. It kind of made him drunk, as you may say, and he didn't know nothing at all the rest of the day, and preached a prayer-meeting sermon that night that gave him a rattling ruputation,[4] because the oldest man in the world couldn't 'a' understood it. So Tom's Aunt Polly, she told all about who I was, and what; and I had to up and tell how I was in such a tight place that when Mrs. Phelps took me for Tom Sawyer—she chipped in and says, "Oh, go on and call me Aunt Sally, I'm used to it now, and 'tain't no need to change"—that when Aunt Sally took me for Tom Sawyer I had to stand it—there warn't no other way, and I knowed he wouldn't mind, because it would be nuts

▶ *Who finally exposes the true identities of Huck and Tom?*

---

4. **rattling ruputation.** Splendid fame

Words
For
Everyday
Use

sul • try (sul′trē) *adj.*, hot

for him, being a mystery, and he'd make an adventure out of it, and be perfectly satisfied. And so it turned out, and he let on to be Sid, and made things as soft as he could for me.

And his Aunt Polly she said Tom was right about old Miss Watson setting Jim free in her will; and so, sure enough, Tom Sawyer had gone and took all that trouble and bother to set a free nigger free! and I couldn't ever understand before, until that minute and that talk, how he *could* help a body set a nigger free with his bringing-up.

Well, Aunt Polly she said that when Aunt Sally wrote to her that Tom and *Sid* had come all right and safe, she says to herself:

◀ *Why did Aunt Polly feel that she should come out to the Phelps farm?*

"Look at that, now! I might have expected it, letting him go off that way without anybody to watch him. So now I got to go and trapse⁵ all the way down the river, eleven hundred mile, and find out what that creetur's up to *this* time, as long as I couldn't seem to get any answer out of you about it."

"Why, I never heard nothing from you," says Aunt Sally.

"Well, I wonder! Why, I wrote you twice to ask you what you could mean by Sid being here."

"Well, I never got 'em, Sis."

Aunt Polly she turns around slow and severe, and says:

"You, Tom!"

"Well—*what*?" he says, kind of pettish.

"Don't you what *me*, you impudent thing—hand out them letters."

"What letters?"

"*Them* letters. I be bound, if I have to take a-holt of you I'll—"

◀ *Why did Tom hide the letters written by Aunt Polly?*

"They're in the trunk. There, now. And they're just the same as they was when I got them out of the office. I hain't looked into them, I hain't touched them. But I knowed they'd make trouble, and I thought if you warn't in no hurry, I'd—"

"Well, you *do* need skinning, there ain't no mistake about it. And I wrote another one to tell you I was coming; and I s'pose he—"

"No, it come yesterday; I hain't read it yet, but *it's* all right, I've got that one."

I wanted to offer to bet two dollars she hadn't, but I reckoned maybe it was just as safe to not to. So I never said nothing.

---

5. **trapse.** Traipse; travel

Nothing More to Write

The first time I catched Tom private I asked him what was his idea, time of the evasion?—what it was he'd planned to do if the evasion worked all right and he managed to set a nigger free that was already free before? And he said, what he had planned in his head from the start, if we got Jim out all safe, was for us to run him down the river on the raft, and have adventures plumb to the mouth of the river, and then tell him about his being free, and take him back up home on a steamboat, in style, and pay him for his lost time, and write word ahead and get out all the niggers around, and have them waltz him into town with a torchlight procession and a brass band, and then he would be a hero, and so would we. But I reckoned it was about as well the way it was.

We had Jim out of the chains in no time, and when Aunt Polly and Uncle Silas and Aunt Sally found out how good he helped the doctor nurse Tom, they made a heap of fuss over him, and fixed him up prime, and give him all he wanted to eat, and a good time, and nothing to do. And we had him up to the sick room, and had a high talk; and Tom give Jim forty dollars for being prisoner for us so patient, and doing it up so good, and Jim was pleased most to death, and busted out, and says:

"*Dah*, now, Huck, what I tell you?—what I tell you up dah on Jackson Islan'? I *tole* you I got a hairy breas', en what's de sign un it; en I *tole* you I ben rich wunst, en gwineter to be rich *agin*; en it's come true; en heah she is! *Dah*, now! doan' talk to *me*—signs is *signs*, mine I tell you; en I knowed jis' 's well 'at I 'uz gwineter be rich ag'in as I's a-stannin' heah dis minute!"

And then Tom he talked along and talked along, and says, le's all three slide out of here one of these nights and get an outfit, and go for howling adventures amongst the Injuns, over in the Territory, for a couple of weeks or two; and I says, all right, that suits me, but I ain't got no money for to buy the outfit, and I reckon I couldn't get none from home, because it's likely Pap's been back before now, and got it all away from Judge Thatcher and drunk it up.

"No, he hain't," Tom says; "it's all there yet—six thousand dollars and more; and your pap hain't ever been back since. Hadn't when I come away, anyhow."

Jim says, kind of solemn:

Margin questions:

► What had been Tom's plan all along, as he was arranging to free Jim?

► How do people treat Jim on hearing that he is free? What does Jim say to Huck?

► What does Huck believe has happened to his money? What does Tom tell him?

"He ain't a-comin' back no mo', Huck."

I says:

"Why, Jim?"

"Nemmine why, Huck—but he ain't comin' back no mo."

But I kept at him; so at last he says:

"Doan' you 'member de house dat was float'n down de river, en dey wuz a man in dah, kivered up, en I went in en unkivered him and didn' let you come in? Well, den, you kin git yo' money when you wants it, kase dat wuz him."

◄ How does Jim know for sure that Pap is dead?

Tom's most well now, and got his bullet around his neck on a watch-guard for a watch, and is always seeing what time it is, and so there ain't nothing more to write about, and I am rotten glad of it, because if I'd 'a' knowed what a trouble it was to make a book I wouldn't 'a' tackled it, and ain't a-going to no more. But I reckon I got to light out for the Territory ahead of the rest, because Aunt Sally she's going to adopt me and sivilize me, and I can't stand it. I been there before.

◄ What does Huck say about making a book? Why does Huck feel he has to leave town? What is Aunt Sally trying to do to him?

Responding to the Selection

What was your reaction when you found out that the ordeals Tom put everyone through to arrange Jim's escape weren't necessary? Can you understand why he did it? What might you have said to him if you were there when all was revealed?

Reviewing the Selection

Recalling and Interpreting

1. **R:** Where is Jim imprisoned? For what are the people who are holding him waiting?

2. **I:** Do you think Jim is ready to give up hope at this point? How does he react when he sees the boys? When Tom tries to persuade the slave that Jim hadn't called their names, what does Jim do? Is it surprising that Jim goes along with Tom in his lie? Do you think the Jim you met at the beginning of the book would have done the same thing? How has Jim changed?

3. **R:** When Huck outlines his plan for Jim's escape, Tom observes, "Well, if that ain't just like you, Huck Finn. You *can* get up the infant-schooliest ways of going at a thing." What does Tom say is wrong with Huck's idea? How does Tom's plan differ?

4. **I:** Why does Tom favor such a complicated and risky method of escape? Why doesn't Huck argue against it more strenuously?

5. **R:** What experience causes Tom to admit his plans are somewhat unrealistic? Does he abandon his plans altogether? How does he reconcile himself to the fact that they can't dig an escape tunnel with knives?

6. **I:** Huck says Tom is "always just that particular. Full of principle." What effect do his "principles" have on those around him, including his aunt, uncle, and Jim? Does Tom seem to be aware of the suffering he is causing anyone else?

7. **R:** What final touch does Tom add to the escape plan? What reaction do his warnings provoke? What does Tom say when Huck tells him the house is full of men with guns?

8. **I:** Has Tom achieved what he set out to do with his escape plan? In what way does Tom's escape plan differ from Huck's escape plan in the beginning of the book? When Huck planned his escape, what was his primary goal? What is Tom's primary goal in this escape?

Synthesizing

9. What does Jim's willingness to sacrifice his own safety for Tom's well-being say about Jim's character? What does Tom's unwillingness to sacrifice the adventure to see a doctor, even when he is seriously hurt, say about Tom's character?

10. At the beginning of the story, Huck was concerned about attempts to civilize him. Has this happened to him? What negative aspects of being "civilized," or following the rules of society, has Huck managed to avoid? What positive aspects of being "civilized" have helped Huck?

Understanding Literature (QUESTIONS FOR DISCUSSION)

1. **Irony. Irony** is the difference between appearance and reality. Types of irony include **dramatic irony**, in which something is known to the reader but unknown to the characters, and **irony of situation**, in which an event occurs that violates the expectation of the characters or the reader. What is the irony in Tom's escape plan for Jim? In the same way, how might you say that that the entire voyage down the river is ironic? In what way is the escape of Huck from his father and Jim from slavery similarly ironic to Tom's elaborate release of Jim from his imprisonment? Was the voyage necessary for Jim or for Huck? In what ways was it necessary for their growth as characters?

2. **Character.** A **character** is a person who figures in the action of a literary work. Describe the character of Jim and his relationship with Huck throughout the novel. When he learned earlier in the novel that Pap was the dead man in the floating house, why did he keep this information from Huck? Compare his concern for Huck to Pap's relationship with Huck. In what way is Jim the most honest, caring adult Huck has encountered?

Plot Analysis of *Adventures of Huckleberry Finn*

The following diagram, known as Freytag's Pyramid, illustrates the main plot of *Adventures of Huckleberry Finn*. For definitions and more information on the parts of a plot illustrated below, see the Handbook of Literary Terms.

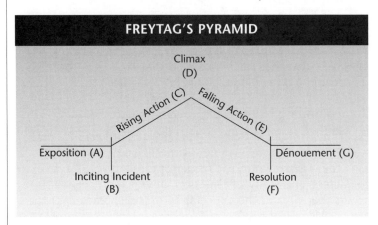

Exposition (A)

The reader meets Huckleberry Finn, the narrator, who describes what has happened to him since he and his friend, Tom Sawyer, discovered a treasure that allotted $6,000 to each boy. Huck, who had been living a vagabond existence, has been taken in by the well-meaning Widow Douglas who is attempting to "civilize" him. In spite of the comforts of his new life, he yearns for his old freedom.

Inciting Incident (B)

Huck's father, an abusive drunkard, returns and tries to claim Huck's money for himself. When it appears that his efforts in the courts will fail, he takes Huck and holds him prisoner in a cabin. When Huck decides he cannot tolerate his father's abuse anymore, he plans his escape by faking his own death. He flees to nearby Jackson's Island.

Rising Action (C)

On Jackson's Island, Huck discovers Jim, a slave who has run away after hearing that his owner meant to sell him "down the river." The two stay together on the island until Huck ventures ashore, disguised as a girl, and learns that a reward has been offered for Jim, and that a search party is coming to Jackson's

Island. He and Jim set off on a raft down the river, intending to go to Cairo where, at a junction in the river, they can catch a steamboat heading north to a "free" state. Inadvertently, they drift past Cairo and travel into the Deep South.

Climax (D)

Among the characters they meet along the way, Huck and Jim encounter two scoundrels who make their living as swindlers. Passing themselves off as a duke and a king, they travel with Huck and Jim. When their schemes to make money fail, the men betray Jim for forty dollars. Jim is taken prisoner and held by a preacher-farmer until he can be claimed. Huck, doubting that he is doing the right thing, nonetheless determines to help Jim escape. He goes to the farm where the farmer's wife is revealed to be Tom Sawyer's Aunt Sally, who is expecting a visit from Tom. She mistakes Huck for Tom. Tom arrives, and poses as his brother, Sid. Tom says he will help with Jim's escape.

Falling Action (E)

Tom devises an elaborate escape plot to get Jim out of the cabin where he is imprisoned. He and Huck begin to carry it out, wreaking havoc on the household.

Resolution (F)

The boys and Jim manage to escape from the cabin, but Tom, who has roused the fear of the neighborhood with anonymous letters, is shot in the leg. Jim refuses to travel because Tom needs medical attention. Huck summons a doctor for Tom, who remains in hiding while Huck returns to the house.

Dénouement (G)

The doctor returns with both Tom and Jim. Tom reveals that he has known all along that Jim is a free man, freed by his owner soon after he ran away. Jim then tells Huck that a dead man they discovered earlier on the river was Huck's father. With Jim finally free, Huck makes plans to escape before anyone else tries to civilize him.

Creative Writing Activities

Creative Writing Activity A: Creating Characters

Mark Twain based his characters on people he knew as a boy and drew adventures from his own childhood experiences. Think about the people you know: friends, relatives, neighbors, teachers. Is there someone you know who would make a memorable character in a story? Think about what makes this person unique and memorable. Is it something he or she does or believes or is it some experience the person has had? Write a description of this person, including details of what he or she looks like, and what he or she likes, believes, and does. Now try to create a character based on this person, giving him or her a new name. Remember that as a fiction writer, you have the freedom to change reality to suit a story. Write a description of your character and see how it differs from the original.

Creative Writing Activity B: Writing a Sequel

Readers often wonder when they finish a story, "What happens next?" Imagine that twenty or forty years have gone by since the end of *Huckleberry Finn* and you have a chance to visit Huck, Tom, and Jim. What do you discover has happened to each of them? Where are they living and how? Write an account of your visits with each.

Creative Writing Activity C: Adventure Stories

Using a narrator who speaks in the first person is often an effective way to recount adventures, because the reader can closely share the narrator's feelings. As Huck and Jim travel down the river, Huck gives the reader a vivid impression of the adventures he and Jim have, describing his thoughts, fears, and reactions. Imagine yourself in an adventurous situation and write a narration of it, using the first person. Whether you base your story on an experience you've actually had, or you draw it entirely from your own imagination, include your feelings and reactions as the adventure unfolds.

Creative Writing Activity D: Diary

Adventures of Huckleberry Finn is told from Huck's perspective, but imagine that you are one of the characters in the story who encounters Huck, such as Mary Jane, Aunt Sally, the duke, the king, or Jim. Write a few diary entries describing your experiences with Huck and your impressions of him and what happens when you are with him.

Creative Writing Activity E: Personal Manifesto

A manifesto is a public declaration of views, intentions, and motives. One of the most moving parts of this novel occurs when Huck wrestles with his conscience over what to do about Jim. Huck's impulse is to help Jim gain his freedom, in spite of the fact that the society of his time makes him believe his instincts are sinful. He decides, nonetheless, to help Jim. What does this tell you about Huck's beliefs and about what is important to him? Think about your own beliefs and values. If you had been in Huck's situation, what would you have done? What have you done in your own life because of personal conviction even if it has gone against popular attitudes or beliefs? Write a personal manifesto, expressing your values and beliefs about how you should live your life.

Critical Writing Activities

Critical Writing Activity A: The Theme of *Huckleberry Finn*

At the beginning of the novel, Mark Twain includes a notice stating, "Persons attempting to find a motive in this narrative will be prosecuted; persons attempting to find a moral in it will be banished; persons attempting to find a plot in it will be shot." The author does not, however, forbid people to speculate on the theme, or central idea of the story. What do you think is the theme of this book? Is it freedom, adventure, friendship, or something else? State your theme, and then find supporting evidence from the story. Use specific examples to show how the author develops this theme.

Critical Writing Activity B: Comparison and Contrast of Huck Finn's Time and Contemporary Times

Adventures of Huckleberry Finn has sparked considerable criticism ever since it was written, partly because some readers have felt it is racist in its portrayal of black Americans. What, however, are the differences between the time in which this story is set and our own time? What was the attitude toward slavery and slaves in Twain's time? Did everyone share the view that slavery was acceptable and slaves were only property? Do all the characters in this book accept that view? Do you think the author condones slavery? How has our society and its laws changed since then? If Jim were living today, how would his life be different? What challenges and problems would he face? Consider Huck and his abusive father. How might his life be different if he were living now? Would there be more or fewer protections for people like Huck and Jim in our world? Write an essay comparing and contrasting the world we live in with the world of Huck and Jim.

Critical Writing Activity C: Huck Finn as Protagonist

A protagonist is the central figure in a literary work. Mark Twain said Huck Finn was based on a boy he knew in his youth who was envied by all the other boys for his freedom and independence. What makes Huck a good protagonist? Do you envy him? Do you admire him? What do you like about him? Do you care what happens to him? Why?

Write an essay describing Huck as a protagonist in which you decide whether he is effective and admirable. As you work, consider some of these questions: What has made Huck the way he is? Does he have a system of values that he follows? What qualities does he show as he escapes from his father and befriends Jim? as they travel down the river? How do others, including Jim, Tom Sawyer, the duke and king, and Huck's father, view him? Are their views accurate? In what ways does he change in the course of the story? Use examples from the story to support your views.

Projects

Project A: Newspaper

Create a newspaper that relates some of the events that take place in *Adventures of Huckleberry Finn*. Choose one of the settings in which major action takes place; you might set your paper in Huck's hometown, in the area of the Grangerford plantation, in Peter Wilks's hometown, or in the area of the Phelps's farm. Divide your newspaper into sections including news stories, social or feature news, and editorials. Retell the events that happened in this setting in your newspaper, using the details provided in the story or adding others from your imagination. You may want to add other features, such as letters to the editor, a gossip column, horoscopes, or an advice column. After you have written the articles, find photos or draw pictures or cartoons to accompany them. Lay out the paper in columns, and create catchy headlines for the stories and features. You may want to design your newspaper using a computer page layout program.

Project B: Popular Interests of Huck Finn's Time

The schemes of the duke and the king demonstrate the

popularity of the pseudosciences hawked by traveling entrepreneurs who made extravagant claims for their powers. Hypnotism, phrenology, and miracle cures that the duke and king promote, are among these. Research these pseudosciences and what they were purported to do. Is there validity to any of them? See if you can find examples of any advertisements of the time that sellers created to lure the public. Then create your own amazing product, complete with a descriptive poster that you think would catch the attention of the public in Huck Finn's time or today.

Project C: Plan an Adventure

As they travel down the river, Huck tells Jim that they are having adventures. Plan your own adventure. Where would you go? Why? Visit a travel agent, the library, or the Internet to find more information about your destination and plan an itinerary. How long would your trip take? What kind of clothes or equipment would you require? How much would it cost? Would you travel alone, with a companion, or with a group? What goals would you have? What dangers might you face? What obstacles to your goal might you encounter? What skills do you have or would you need to have to help you in your adventure?

Project D: Social Activism

In Huck and Jim's time, many activists worked to abolish slavery. Research the Abolitionist movement in the United States. What kinds of activities did these people undertake to outlaw slavery and to help slaves? Then look at our society, and decide what problem exists today that you might like to help change. How would you like to change it? What do you think you could do? Could you adopt any ideas or strategies used by the Abolitionists that would be useful in your plans? Write a description of the problem and a proposed plan of action to change it.

Project E: Chart the Raft Trip

Research the route Huck and Jim followed in their travels down the Mississippi River. Create a map, trying to pinpoint where you think major events took place. Include the surrounding states, noting which states were free and which allowed slavery. See if you can find photos of these places as they look now and, if possible, as they existed in Huck's time. How have they changed? How has transportation on the river changed? How has the river itself changed? Would it be possible to recreate their trip now?

Glossary

Pronunciation Key

Vowel Sounds

a	hat	ō	go	ʉ	burn
ā	play	ô	paw, born	ə	extra
ä	star	o͞o	book, put		under
e	then	o͞o	blue, stew		civil
ē	me	oi	boy		honor
i	sit	ou	wow		bogus
ī	my	u	up		

Consonant Sounds

b	but	l	lip	t	sit
ch	watch	m	money	th	with
d	do	n	on	v	valley
f	fudge	ŋ	song, sink	w	work
g	go	p	pop	y	yell
h	hot	r	rod	z	pleasure
j	jump	s	see		
k	brick	sh	she		

a • breast (ə brest´) *adv.*, side by side with

ac • know • ledge (ak näl´ij) *vt.*, recognize the claims of

ac • quit (ə kwit´) *vt.*, clear of guilt

ad • dled (ad´´ld) *adj.*, confused, muddled

af • front (ə front´) *vt.*, confront; bring face to face with

ag • gra • vate (ag´rə vāt´) *vt.*, annoy

airs (erz) *n.*, affected, superior manners

a • loft (ə lôft´) *adv.*, far above the ground

al • low (ə lou´) *vt.*, give as one's opinion

al • ter (ôl´tər) *vt.*, change

am • pu • tate (am´pyo͞o tāt´) *vt.*, remove a limb surgically

ar • is • toc • ra • cy (ar´i stä´krə sē) *n.*, privileged ruling class; nobility

au • thor • i • ty (ə thôr´ə tē) *n.*, reliable source of information

bel • low (bel´ō) *vi.*, roar

ben • e • fac • tor (ben ə fak´tər) *n.*, person who gives help, especially financial help

be • tray (bē trā´) *vt.*, turn in, reveal

be • twixt (bē twikst´) *adv.*, between

blithe • some (blīth´səm) *adj.*, cheerful

bluff (bluf) *n.*, steep bank or cliff

bo • gus (bō´gəs) *adj.*, not genuine, untrue

bow (bou) *n.*, front end of a boat

brash (brash) *adj.*, bold

bray (brā) *vi.*, make a loud, harsh cry like a donkey

bris • tle (bris´əl) *vi.*, become tense with resentment

brute (bro͞ot) *n.*, stupid, cruel, savage person

can • did (kan´did) *adj.*, honest and sincere; incapable of deception

can • ni • bal (kan´ə bəl) *n.*, member of a species, especially human beings, that eats others of its kind

ca • per (kā´pər) *vi.*, skip or jump about

cap • i • tal (kap´ət 'l) *n.*, wealth, money

cap • tive (kap´tiv) *adj.*, imprisoned

ca • reened (kə rēnd´) *adj.*, tilted

car • cass (kär´kəs) *n.*, dead body, especially of an animal that has been slaughtered

ca • vort (kə vôrt´) *vi.*, prance about, frolic

ca • vor • ting (kə vort´iŋ) *n.*, prancing, leaping about

cel • e • brat • ed (sel´ə brāt id) *adj.*, famous

chink (chiŋk) *n.*, gap, narrow opening

clap • board (klab´ərd) *n.*, long, narrow board with one edge thicker than the other, used as siding on a building

com • mence (kə mens´) *vi.*, begin

con • se • quence (kän´si kwens´) *n.*, importance

con • sec • u • tive (kən sek´yo͞o tiv) *adj.*, continuous, one after the other

con • trite (kən trīt´) *adj.*, remorseful, sorry, penitent

con • trive (kən trīv´) *vt.*, think up, devise

coun • ter • feit (kount´ər fit´) *adj.*, imitation, fake

crock • er • y (kräk´ər ē) *adj.*, made of baked clay

dan • dy (dan´dē) *n.*, man who pays too much attention to his clothes and appearance

dea • con (dē´kən) *n.*, officer of the church who helps the minister with duties not related to worship

def • i • cit (def´ə sit) *n.*, shortage, deficiency

de • grad • ed (dē grād´id) *adj.*, brought down in disgrace

de • lib • er • ate (di lib´ə rit) *adj.*, unhurried and methodical

des • per • a • do (des´pər ä dō) *n.*, outlaw, reckless criminal

de • spise (di spīz´) *vt.*, hate

dis • mal (diz´məl) *adj.*, causing gloom or misery; depressing

dis • po • si • tion (dis´pə zish´ən) *n.*, frame of mind, temperament

dis • si • pate (dis´ə pāt) *vt.*, break up

di • stinc • tion (di stiŋk´shən) *n.*, quality that makes one thing different from another similar thing

dis • tract • ed (di strakt´əd) *adj.*, afflicted by mental distress

dis • tressed (dis strest´) *adj.*, anxious, troubled

dodge (däj) *n.*, trick or strategy of evasion

dote on (dōt´ än) *vt.*, feel foolishly fond of

drear (drir) *adj.*, gloomy

dron • ing (drōn´iŋ) *n.*, continuous humming sound

en • core (än´kôr´) *n.*, demand for further performance, shown by continued applause by the audience

en • dure (en do͞or´) *vt.*, hold up under, bear

es • tate (e stāt´) *n.*, condition; property left by the dead

evade (ē vād´) *vi.*, get away

ex • iled (eks´īld) *adj.*, cast out of one's birthplace

fac • ul • ty (fak´əl tē) *n.*, any power of the mind

fel • on (fel´ən) *n.*, criminal

fend (fend) *vt.*, repel, resist

feud (fyo͞od) *n.*, longlasting quarrel, sometimes between two families

fidg • e • ty (fij´it ē) *adj.*, nervous, squirming

flus • ter (flus´tər) *n.*, state of confusion

for • lorn (fôr lôrn´) *adj.*, wretched; without hope

frank (fraŋk) *adj.*, blunt in expressing truth without conventional holding back

fraud (frôd) *n.*, person who deceives

fret (fret) *vt.*, worry over

full tilt (fool´tilt´) *adv.*, at full speed

fur • nish (fʉr´nish) *vt.*, provide, supply

gape (gāp) *vi.*, stare, gawk

gau • dy (gôd´y) *adj.*, showy, flashy, tawdry

ge • nie (jē´nē) *n.*, magic spirit believed to take human form and serve the person who calls it

gump • tion (gump´shən) *n.*, enterprise, common sense

hail (hāl) *n.*, signal summoning something or someone

han • ker (haŋ´ker) *vi.*, yearn, long

haugh • ty (hôt´ē) *adj.*, proud

head • way (hed´wā´) *n.*, progress

his • tri • on • ic (his´trē än´ik) *adj.*, having to do with acting

hoist (hoist) *vt.*, raise

hos • pi • tal •i •ty (häs´pi tal´ə tē) *n.*, act of welcoming guests

hub (hub) *n.*, center part of a wheel

huf • fy (huf´ē) *adj.*, easily offended; touchy

hum • ble (hum´b'l) *adj.*, modest, not proud

ig • no • rant (ig´nə rənt) *adj.*, uninformed, inexperienced

im • pair (im per´) *vt.*, spoil, injure

im • per • a • tive (im per´ə tiv) *adj.*, command

im • pu • dent (im´pyo͞o dənt) *adj.*, disrespectful, impertinent in • dif • fer • ent (in dif´ər ənt) *adj.*, uncaring, unconcerned

in • fer • nal (in fur´nəl) *adj.*, hellish, inhuman

in • gen • ious (in jēn´yəs) *adj.*, clever, inventive

in • got (in´gət) *n.*, bar of gold

in • scrip • tion (in skrip´shen) *n.*, something written, marked, or carved into some surface

in • stinct (in´stinkt) *n.*, natural, unlearned response

in • su • rec • tion (in´sə rek´shən) *n.*, rebellion, revolt

in • ter • pret (in tur´prət) *vt.*, explain the meaning of

keel (kēl) *vi.*, fall

kin (kin) *n.*, relatives, family

kin • folk (kin´ fōk) *n.*, family, relatives

lank • y (laŋk´ē) *adj.*, tall and thin

light (līt) *vi.*, come to rest after traveling through the air

lik • li • est (līk´lē ist) *adj.*, best, most promising

limb (lim) *n.*, branch of a tree

lim • ber (lim´bər) *adj.*, easily bent, flexible

lin • go (liŋ´gō) *n.*, jargon; special vocabulary that one is unfamiliar with

loll (läl) *vi.*, lean or lounge about in a relaxed manner

lu • na • tic (lōōn´ə tik) *n.*, insane person

lynch (linch) *vt.*, murder by mob action without trial

make a • low • ance (māk ə lou´əns) *vt.*, take circumstances into consideration

meek (mēk) *adj.*, spiritless

mere (mir) *adj.*, nothing more than; only a

mire (mīr) *n.*, mud

mod • er • ate (mäd´ər āt) *vi.*, become calm

mon • strous (män´strəs) *adv.*, extremely

mum (mum) *adj.*, silent

muse (myōōz) *n.*, mythical spirit that inspires artists—here, actors

oath (ōth) *n.*, pledge, vow

o • bit • u • ar • y (ō bich´ōō er´ē) *n.*, published death notice

ob • se • quies (äb´si kwēs) *n.*, funeral rites or ceremonies

op • pres • sion (ə presh´ən) *n.*, tyranny, domination

or • gy (ôr´gē) *n.*, wild merrymaking

or • ner • y (ôr´nər ē) *adj.*, mean, unpleasant

out • land • ish (out´lan´dish) *adj.*, very odd, strange

pa • la • ver (pə lav´ər) *vi.*, chatter, prattle

par • lia • ment (pär´lə mənt) *n.*, lawmaking body of government

par • tic • u • lar (pər tik´yə lər) *adj.*, difficult to satisfy, choosy

pat (pat) *adj.*, exactly suited to the occasion

pen • i • ten • tia • ry (pen´i ten´ shə rē) *n.*, state or federal prison for those convicted of serious crimes

per • ish (per´ish) *vi.*, die a violent or untimely death

pi • ous (pī´əs) *adj.*, having or showing religious devotion

pine (pīn) *vi.*, waste away through grief

plan • ta • tion (plan tā´shən) *n.*, large piece of land in a tropical or semitropical climate cultivated by workers—here slaves—living on it

plun • der (plun´dər) *n.*, loot, booty

pow • wow (pou´wou´) *vi.*, hold a conference

prej • u • diced (prej´ōō dist) *adj.*, biased; having made a prejudgment

prem • is • es (prem´is is) *n.*, property

press • ing (pres´iŋ) *adj.*, urgent

prin • ci • ple (prin´sə pəl) *n.*, rule of right conduct

pro • ces • sion (prō sesh´ən) *n.*, parade or other formal movement of a group

pro • vi • sions (prō vizh´əns) *n.*, stock of food supplies

pu • tre • fied (pyōō´trə fīd) *adj.*, decayed, rotten

quar • ry (kwôr´ē) *n.*, excavation site for stones, rock

quiv • er • y (kwiv´ər ē) *adj.*, shaky, trembling

rank (rank) *adj.*, foul smelling

ran • sack (ran´sak) *vi.*, search thoroughly

ran • som (ran´səm) *vt.*, release from capture by paying a fee to the captors

rasp • y (ras´pē) *adj.*, grating, irritating; rough-sounding

realm (relm) *n.*, region

reck • on (rek´ən) *vt.*, figure, suppose

rec • ol • lec • tion (rek´ə lek´shən) *n.*, memory

re • form (ri´fôrm) *vt.*, cause or persuade a person to give up misconduct and behave better

re • miss (ri mis´) *adj.*, careless, neglectful

re • nowned (ri nound´) *adj.*, famous

res • ur • rec • tion (rez´ə rek´shən) *n.,* rise from the dead

roost • ing (rōōst´iŋ) *vi.,* resting on a perch

row (rou) *n.,* noisy quarrel

rum • mag • ing (rum´ij iŋ) *n.,* thorough search

sal • a • ble (sāl´ə bəl) *adj.,* that can be sold; marketable

sanc • ti • fied (saŋk´tə fīd) *adj.,* made holy

sar • cas • tic (sär kas´tik) *adj.,* taunting, mocking, scornful

scan • da • lous (skan´də ləs) *adj.,* shocking, shameful

scar (scär) *n.,* disfiguring mark

scar • ci • ty (sker´sə tē) *n.,* inadequate supply

scorch (skôrch) *vt.,* damage, burn

scorn • ful (skôrn´fəl) *adj.,* contemptuous, disdainful

scoun • drel (skoun´drəl) *n.,* wicked, mean, or immoral person

scoured (skour'd) *adj.,* polished

scrab • ble (skrab´əl) *vi.,* paw or scratch as in looking for something

se • cu • ri • ty (si kyōōr´ə tē) *n.,* something given as a pledge for repayment

se • vere (sə vir´) *adj.,* harsh, strict

shan • ty (shan´tē) *n.,* small, shabby dwelling; shack

shirk (shʉrk) *vi.,* avoid work or duty

sing • u • lar (siŋ gyə lər) *adj.,* extraordinary, remarkable

sit • u • a • tion (sich´ōō ā´shən) *n.,* position of employment

so • ber (sō´bər) *adj.,* not drunk

sol • emn (säl´əm) *adj.,* serious, grave, impressive

so • lil • o • quy (sə lil´ə kwē) *n.,* lines in a drama that a character speaks as if to himself or herself

spec • i • men (spes´ə mən) *n.,* sample, example

spec • u • late (spek´yōō lāt´) *vi.,* invest in a risky business

spry (sprī) *adj.,* active, nimble, lively

spunk (spuŋk) *n.,* courage

stealth • y (stəl´thē) *adj.,* secret, sly

stern (stʉrn) *n.,* rear end of a boat

stow (stō) *vt.,* store away

strag • gler (strag´lər) *n.,* one who wanders away from the group

su • blime (sə blīm´) *adj.,* noble, exalted, grand

sub • mit (sub mit´) *vi.,* give in to the power of another person

sul • try (sul´trē) *adj.,* hot

su • per • in • tend (sū´pər in tend´) *vi.,* direct, manage

swarm (swôrm) *vt.,* crowd around

ta • per off (tā´pər ôf) *vi.,* gradually stop

ted • i • ous (tē´dē əs) *adj.,* tiresome, boring

tem • per • ance (tem´pər əns) *n.,* moderation or abstinence in the drinking of alcoholic beverages

terms (tʉrms) *n.,* conditions of a contract

thick • et (thik´ət) *n.,* thick growth of shrubs or small trees

thrash (thrash) *vt.,* give a severe beating

trance (trans) *n.,* state resembling sleep during which voluntary action is lost

trib • ute (trib´yōōt) *n.,* something done in gratitude or to give honor

un • dis • posed (un dis pōzd´) *adj.,* unwilling

un • furl (un fʉrl´) *vt.,* let loose

val • id (val´id) *adj.,* legal, legitimate

vault (vôlt) *n.,* secure storage place

vict • uals (vit´'lz) *n.,* food

war • ran • ted (wôr´ənt əd) *adj.,* guaranteed

welt (welt) *n.,* ridge raised on the skin by a blow

yarn (yärn) *n.,* tale or story

yon • der (yän´dər) *adv.,* over there

Handbook of Literary Terms

Character. A **character** is a person (or sometimes an animal) who figures in the action of a literary work. A *protagonist,* or *main character,* is the central figure in a literary work. An *antagonist* is a character who is pitted against a protagonist. *Major characters* are those who play significant roles in a work. *Minor characters* are those who play lesser roles. A *one-dimensional character, flat character,* or *caricature* is one who exhibits a single dominant quality, or *character trait.* A *three-dimensional, full,* or *rounded character* is one who exhibits the complexity of traits associated with actual human beings. A *static character* is one who does not change during the course of the action. A *dynamic character* is one who does change. A *stock character* is one found again and again in different literary works. An example of a stock character is the mad scientist of nineteenth- and twentieth-century science fiction.

Characterization. Characterization is the use of literary techniques to create a character. Writers use three major techniques to create characters: direct description, portrayal of characters' behavior, and representations of characters' internal states. When using direct description, the writer, through a speaker, a narrator, or another character, simply comments on the character, telling the reader about such matters as the character's appearance, habits, dress, background, personality, motivations, and so on. In portrayal of a character's behavior, the writer presents the actions and speech of the character, allowing the reader to draw his or her own conclusions from what the character says or does. When using representations of internal states, the writer reveals directly the character's private thoughts and emotions, often by means of what is known as the internal monologue. See *character.*

Climax. See *plot.*

Conflict. A **conflict** is a struggle between two forces in a literary work. A *plot* involves the introduction, development, and eventual resolution of a conflict. One side of the *central conflict* in a story or drama is usually taken by the *main character.* That character may struggle against another character, against the forces of nature, against society or social norms, against fate, or against some element within himself or herself. A struggle that takes place between a character and some outside force is called an *external conflict.* A struggle that takes place within a character is called an *internal conflict.* See *plot.*

Dénouement. See *plot.*

Description. A **description**, one of the modes of writing, portrays a chracter, an object, or a scene. Descriptions make use of *sensory details*—words and phrases that describe how things look, sound, smell, taste, or feel.

Dialect. A **dialect** is a version of a language spoken by the people of a particular place, time, or social group. A *regional dialect* is one spoken in a particular place. A *social dialect* is one spoken by members of a particular social group or class.

Dramatic Irony. See *irony.*

Exposition. See *plot.*

External Conflict. See *conflict.*

Falling Action. See *plot.*

Inciting Incident. See *plot.*

Internal Conflict. See *conflict.*

Irony. **Irony** is a difference between appearance and reality. Types of irony include the following: *dramatic irony,* in which something is known by the reader or audience but unknown to the characters; *verbal irony,* in which a statement is made that implies its opposite; and *irony of situation,* in which an event occurs that violates the expectations of the characters, the reader, or the audience.

Irony of Situation. See *irony.*

Motif. A **motif** is any element that recurs in one or more works of literature or art. Examples of common folk tale motifs found in oral traditions throughout the world include grateful animals or the greateful dead, three wiches, the trial or quest, and the magical metamorphosis, or transformation of one thing into another.

Motivation. A **motivation** is a force that moves a character to think, feel, or behave in a certain way.

Narrator. A **narrator** is one who tells a story. The narrator in a work of fiction may be a central or minor character or simply someone who witnessed or heard about the events being related. Writers achieve a wide variety of ends by varying the characteristics of the narrator chosen for a particular work. Of primary importance is the choice of the narrator's point of view. Will the narrator be omniscient, knowing all things, including the internal workings of the minds of the characters in the story, or will the narrator be limited in his or her knowledge? Will the narrator participate in the action of the story or stand outside that action and comment on it? Will the narrator be reliable or unreliable? That is, will the reader be able to trust the narrator's statements? These are all questions that a writer must answer when developing a narrator.

One-dimensional Character. See *character.*

Plot. A **plot** is a series of events related to a central *conflict,* or struggle. A typical plot involves the introduction of a conflict, its development, and its eventual resolution. Terms used to describe elements of plot include the following:

- The **exposition,** or **introduction**, sets the tone or mood, introduces the characters and the setting, and provides necessary background information.
- The **inciting incident** is the event that introduces the central conflict.
- The **rising action**, or **complication**, develops the conflict to a high point of intensity.
- The **climax** is the high point of interest or suspense in the plot.
- The **crisis**, or **turning point**, often the same event as the climax, is the point in the plot where something decisive happens to determine the future course of events and the eventual working out of the conflict.
- The **falling action** is all of the events that follow the climax.
- The **resolution** is the point at which the central conflict is ended, or resolved.
- The **dénouement** is any material that follows the resolution and that ties up loose ends.
- The **catastrophe**, in tragedy, is the event that marks the ultimate tragic fall of the central character. Often this event is the character's death.

Plots rarely contain all these elements in precisely this order. Elements of exposition may be introduced at any time in the course of a work. A work may begin with a catastrophe and then use flashback to explain it. The exposition or dénouement or even the resolution may be missing. The inciting incident may occur before the beginning of the action actually described in the work. These are but a few of the many possible variations that plots can exhibit. See *conflict.*

Point of View. Point of view is the vantage point from which a story is told. Stories are typically writen form a *first person point of view,* in which the narrator uses words such as *I* and *we,* or from a *third-person point of view,* in which the nar-